FORGET ME NOT

Melissa Morgan

Please be aware that this book discusses themes including stillbirth, difficulty conceiving, domestic violence and cancer. There are also scenes of a sexual nature.

Forget Me Not

ISBN: 9798634350974

To all the Warrior Women and their Angels

PROLOGUE

Primrose Hill was always awake. Its gates never closed, filled with open spaces and lines of Victorian street lights bleeding orange light into the darkness. From the top, it looked over the rest of London, from the Shard piercing the sky to the London Eye, bright and robotic. It was bizarre, Lizzie thought, that she could stand somewhere so tranquil and yet be watching something so alive.

There were a few people around. Twenty-something-year-olds stretched out on the grass, not seeming to care that the ground was wet, all drinking from brightly coloured mugs as one of them performed card tricks. A runner sprinted up the left side of the hill, only to turn and jog back down it, repeatedly. And two men were arguing in German just to the side. Other than that, the hill was quiet. No one was really interested in a stroll through the park at 11 p.m.

On a Tuesday.

In October.

Lizzie shivered.

In the heat of the argument, she had rushed from the flat without a coat and now there was no longer fire running through her blood, she could feel the cold against her skin. She ran a hand up and down her arm to try and ease it.

"Lizzie, you can't have children, okay? Your body doesn't work like that!"

Charles's words rang through her head again, louder this time, and more malicious. She knew he hadn't spoken in quite that tone but still...her imagination was exaggerating everything to make it ten times worse.

It really needn't have bothered. The reality was still painful enough. Her husband had finally admitted it. He had finally said the words she had been sure he was always thinking but had never said out loud. He'd even shouted, and Charles never shouted. He was the kind of person who argued quietly with cool looks and an insane ability to remain calm.

She tightened her ponytail, the pain in her head continuing to throb along to her pulse as she stared out into the night sky. His words repeated over and over in her mind and she tried her hardest to breathe through them as more hurt coiled in her chest.

It wasn't as if she disagreed with him.

It wasn't as if she hadn't thought the same thing for the past half of a decade.

So, why was it hurting so much now that Charles had finally said it?

Her phone vibrated in her pocket.

Seven missed calls.

Two from Charles, and the last five from Bex, her best friend.

Her brow creased. Had Charles told Bex to ring her?

Something twisted in her gut. It didn't sound like something he would do, unless he was completely at a loss as to where she was.

She looked down the hill towards London.

He *should know* where she was.

Really, he should.

This was their place.

Well, it had been, until all the overtime, late hours, medical tests, and doctors' rooms had taken away most of their time. She tried to think back to the last time they had come here together. Her mind struggled to find the memory, kicking up old flashes of when they first came to London together but not able to pinpoint a more recent occasion. Running away from him as he'd stuffed snow down the back of her neck, lying on the grass in the summer, coming to see the fireworks on New Year's Eve and quickly realising just what a bad idea that was because the rest of London seemed to have had the same thought. But that had all been years ago.

Had they really become that distant?

A sigh pushed its way through her body.

She had only found out last week that he had started teaching drama to the children at his school - apparently, he had been doing it for a year - and she hadn't realised he'd been promoted to Head of English at the beginning of the school term in September either.

"Don't you sometimes wish you two had never got together?"

Patricia's voice sounded clearly through her head. As did Charles's subsequent silence. He hadn't responded to his eldest sister's question. He hadn't jumped immediately to Lizzie's defence. None of the Williams siblings had known she was hovering just outside of the living room door having heard their voices when she had come downstairs to get a glass of water. Like always, they had all been staying over on the anniversary of Charles's mother's birthday in the large seven-bedroom property his parents owned in Tring. They always tried to make it a happy occasion; singing, baking, going on long walks over the fields, making it a day to celebrate Maria Williams rather than one to mourn her death. When Charles had finally come to bed, he had pulled her into his arms, pressed his chest against her back and squeezed her tightly.

She hadn't told him what she had heard.

She hadn't told him that just seconds before she had heard his familiar tread up the stairs, tears had still been streaming down her cheeks.

And that had been three weeks ago.

The painful truth of the matter was that Patricia had a point.

Everyone had said they were too young to marry, including her when Charles had initially proposed. But she had been naïve, completely in love, and, more problematically, pregnant.

Her breath hitched, pain slashing across her chest.

She couldn't think about that. Not tonight. It hurt too much at the best of times and it gutted her at the worst.

The rain was truly soaking her now, sinking into her clothes, pressing her hair flat against her head, and making her tremble even harder. She pulled her arms across herself, boxing herself in as her head continued to swirl.

"I'm a week and a half late."

"And?"

"Well, that's a good thing."

"We both know it means nothing. A week late, two weeks late, a day late, it never happens, it never works."

"It might."

"Lizzie, you can't have children, okay? Your body doesn't work like that!"

The clock on the wall had read 10.17 p.m., the romantic dinner sitting between them had been well and truly forgotten and the blue in Charles's eyes had felt like ice. She remembered all the visual details as if they were actually important, her brain trying to focus on anything but the words he had said. It couldn't distract itself for long. Instead it focused on them, playing them in her mind and stamping them into her memory.

"Do you even own a coat?"

A surprised laugh escaped her lips, a weird sense of relief swelling in her chest as she turned just in time to catch a brief glance of her husband's face before he draped his own coat over her shoulders and pulled her into him. His arms enveloped her so tightly it felt like he was trying to block out the weather.

"Somewhere," she mumbled into his chest.

"One day, I'll follow through on my threat and staple one to you." The coat drowned her. Charles was lean but he was also extremely tall and she was nearly a foot shorter than him. If she ever borrowed anything of his to wear it ended up looking like a sack. She let go of him briefly to thread her arms through the sleeves.

When she finished, he pulled her to him again, the rain battering down on their heads as he pressed his lips to her forehead.

"I'm really sorry." She could hear the grit in his voice. "God, Lizzie, I'm so sorry. I didn't mean any of it."

"I'm really sorry too," she whispered and her chest shuddered. Burying her head deeper into his jumper, she fought back the tell-tale sting of tears.

"You were right, maybe this time -"

"It's not. I checked." A huff of shaky laughter left her lips. "Joke's on me, I guess. You were right. My body doesn't work like that."

She felt the muscles in his back lock. "Lizzie, I didn't mean that-"

"You were right."

"No, I wasn't." He moved his hands to hold her shoulders, pushing her away to look down at her. Pain littered his expression and her breath caught at the emotion in his eyes. "I wasn't right at all. I was a prick. I'd had a drink and- not that it's an excuse -" He briefly let her right shoulder go, running a hand through his hair and not seeming to notice that the rain had cemented it to his head. Normally his thick, dark blonde hair had a slight wave to it but now, it was flattened to his scalp and sticking out at such ridiculous angles it was almost comical. "I'm so sorry." He pulled her back into a hug. "If I could take it all back, I would."

A lump formed in her throat. "You were right, I can't have children."

"We can't." He corrected her. "We, Lizzie. We're a team." He hesitated. "And if you really want, we can try again. I'll look at your spreadsheet." She winced as he spoke. The *spreadsheet*. The one she had tried to show him last week to prove she had found a way for them to afford another round of IVF.

He hadn't even looked at it, instead refusing to sit down at the kitchen table and telling her she'd promised the last two times that they would stop.

She turned her head and pressed her cheek into his chest, taking comfort from the rise and fall of it as she cast her eyes down the hill.

"Please forgive me, Lizzie." His voice was laced with pain. "Please forget I ever said that."

Charles Williams. The boy who she had loved since she was fourteen. It had been so embarrassing at first, realising that her heart fluttered and her stomach twisted every time she saw her brother's best friend. And as they themselves had become closer it had become infuriating. The way he would take her hand and then quickly drop it, the long emotionally charged silences between them, the way their eyes would meet across the table and then they'd both quickly look away. The way he had become so sullen and defensive when she had dated other boys. He hadn't realised that it was all for him, to try and get him to react in some way, to see her as something other than Matt's little sister.

All she had wanted was a kiss from him, to see if the chemistry between them meant anything. So much so that at seventeen, fed up with waiting, she had kissed him herself. The boy who had made her feel like someone, someone who actually mattered.

He still did, even fifteen years later.

Even after *everything*.

"I promise I didn't mean any of what I said. I want to take it all back. Every little bit."

She closed her eyes. "I wish I could too."

She wasn't just talking about their argument. Guilt had dug its way so deep inside of her that she sometimes wished she could take it all back.

Give Charles a second chance.

A better chance.

"I wish I could take it all back."

A shiver ran through her. The rain around them stopped for just a second, suspended in mid-air as if by magic. There was a singular streetlight on top of Primrose Hill, and the rain beamed like a golden halo circulating it before it fell with even more gusto. Something twisted in Lizzie's stomach and she felt an urgent tug against her feet.

"What the hell?" Charles whispered.

Pulling away, she craned her neck to look up at him only to see he wasn't there.

Lizzie blinked and turned her head this way and that. Charles had disappeared. Where he had just stood, now she could see the emerald trees and dark night sky.

But she could still smell his cologne and feel the heat of his body as if he was right in front of her.

"Charles?"

She turned, hearing her own name repeated back to her on the wind but he was nowhere to be seen.

More shivers shot up her arms and a sense of nausea shot through her.

What the hell was happening?

She turned her head to look down the hill and felt an alarming tilt in her stomach.

Primrose Hill was melting. It was almost as if it were trying to turn itself into a Van Gogh painting, the colours merging into one another in unnatural swirls and slants, the rain looking as if it was stuck in mid-air. The London cityscape was moving upwards, blurring into the dark clouds.

"Charles!" She tried to call out again but her lips weren't working and her head was being filled with white noise.

Fear clawed at her chest, she tried to swallow it away but it didn't diminish. Maybe she was overreacting, maybe she was ill? Coming down with something? Maybe it was just her? Maybe this was just some sort of paranoid vision brought on by...stress? Worry?

She blinked rapidly trying to clear her head and the sound of brakes filled her ears followed by a familiar scream.

Her brain scrambled to figure out who had screamed or where the car had come from but as she tried to focus on the sound, she felt her body peel away from the ground.

I wish I could take it all back

The words echoed in her own head.

Everything was now pure swirls of colour. She couldn't feel her feet, she couldn't feel Charles, she couldn't even feel the rain. Nothing but colour, like someone had spilled paint over London. Maybe she was dead? She waved a hand in front of her face but the bright swirls of red, orange, green and blue had taken over her eyes.

She hadn't ever thought of death as being colourful.

Her mind cast back to Leo.

There was something quite comforting about that.

And then she landed, painfully, on a green plastic floor.

She hadn't even realised she had been falling.

The colours evaporated from her vision so quickly it was as if they had never been there. Her body began to shake. She took a few large gulps of air but she still didn't settle. Even her lips were trembling.

"Charles?" She called. The sound echoed back to her in a familiar way and her brain, slowly, registered that she recognised where she was.

Her childhood bathroom.

Green laminated tiles were beneath her - they had so many scuffs on them it sort of looked like they had been part of the aesthetic to begin with. There was a white bathtub to her right and the toilet was at her back. She sat there for a few moments, breathing heavily, trying to get her head around what she was seeing. She lifted her hand to run it through her hair and dropped something in the process.

A long white something.

A something she recognised so much from the last five years she could have drawn it with her eyes closed.

She stood up quickly, her breath catching in her throat as she stepped away from it. The sight made her stomach plunge and she almost retched over the sink.

What was she doing here?

She tried to pull her hair away from her face as it suddenly now flopped in front of her shoulders, her hair band nowhere to be seen.

A flicker of movement caught her eye and she turned her head to see herself in the mirror. Her eyes were wide, her face pale, and she had a dodgy fringe hanging down over her eyebrows. Her mouth opened in horror.

Nineteen-year-old Lizzie Cartwright was staring right back at her.

THIRTEEN YEARS LATER

CHAPTER ONE

Lizzie flicked through the television channels, not knowing quite what she was in the mood to watch. She had a bowl of ice cream balanced between her knees, a cranberry juice in her hand and was trying her hardest not to spill any more of either onto herself. She flicked through more and more channels, the screen changing from laughter, to horror, to the news, and then back again.

Television was her life. Not in an obsessive kind of way but because it was her job. She was a Production Coordinator at Lightswitch Productions and she lived and breathed television all day long. Sometimes the thought of sitting down, relaxing, and finding a good show to watch was ideal - it was what she enjoyed - and at other times, it just seemed like more work.

She picked up her bowl of vanilla ice cream and put it down on the floor before swinging her legs off the sofa. Maybe she should read a book? That was a good way of switching off from a hard day, right? She racked her brains trying to remember when she had last read a book, or bought a book for that matter...

She looked up and flinched violently, spilling cranberry juice down her arm as she saw she was being watched by a man stood in her living room doorway. He had jet black hair that stuck up in all different directions, a tanned complexion, a muscular build and the exact same green eyes as her own.

"Matt, for God's sake, knock before you come into my flat."

He grinned. "I was hoping for a scream. You're no fun to scare."

She scowled at him. "Are you here for something?"

"Milk," he shrugged and peeled himself away from the doorframe. "I forgot to get any today."

"I'm pretty sure the twenty-four-hour corner shop down the road is still open, or does it have a thing against Wednesday nights?"

"It's raining."

Lizzie rolled her eyes and tried to shove him as she passed but, at five foot three, she didn't really have the impact she wanted to against her five foot ten brother's stockier frame.

"You're a thirty-five-year-old man, Matt."

"Whose little sister conveniently lives upstairs so he can borrow milk whenever he chooses. Come on, I would do the same for you."

He followed her into the kitchen and somehow, without seeming to have stepped into her living room, he had her half-finished bowl of ice cream in his hands.

Her kitchen was one of her favourite rooms in the flat. Not because she could cook, because she really couldn't, but because it felt so homely. The walls were painted a pale purple except for the one exterior brick one, the window had small flower pots growing outside of it, making it look homely despite the view being that of brick wall approximately ten feet away, and all the furniture was wooden. It was so small that if two people sat down either side of the kitchen table no one would be able to walk from one end of the room to the other, but she liked its quirkiness and its simplicity.

She opened the fridge and pulled out the milk.

"You wouldn't let me use your shower last week when my hot water stopped working."

Her brother smiled. "Not my fault, girlfriend was using the shower."

Lizzie threw him a surprised look.

"Who are you seeing now?"

He sat down with the ice cream that he had clearly now deemed as his own and gave a shrug.

"Still Zoey."

"Ah, okay." Lizzie nodded slowly as she poured a reasonable amount of milk into a glass. "She's lasted... long."

Matt was a serial monogamist. He was always faithful, invested a lot of time into each relationship and genuinely cared about each woman he dated, but it was just a conveyor belt; one girlfriend after another, after another, after another, and it didn't seem like said belt was going to stop anytime soon. The moment a girlfriend mentioned the 'L' word or tried to get closer to him than he wanted, he swiftly ended the relationship and would move on. Lizzie sympathised with them. They all thought he was wonderful: he didn't play games, he was happy to be exclusive, would fork out lots of money on fun days out and happily spend a night in with them rather than out with his friends. What they didn't realise was that for Matt, that's all it was ever going to be. No meeting the parents, no moving in, no falling in love.

Not in this timeline anyway.

Guilt threatened to raise its head and Lizzie quickly derailed her train of thought.

"She's happy," Matt said.

Lizzie raised her eyebrows but chose not to say anything. They'd had this conversation too many times before.

She pushed the glass of milk towards him.

"So, how was -?" The sound of her work phone cut across her, shrilly ringing into the kitchen. It rung off as abruptly as it had started.

"That was weird," she said, picking it up off the side and running her finger across the keys.

"Probably a scammer. PPI or 'have you had an accident?' nonsense."

"No it was Tyrone," she said, clicking onto caller ID. Tyrone was Lightswitch Productions's Operations and Facilities Manager and, more importantly, her boss. She tried to call him back but the line beeped, telling her he was on another call already. Something in her gut turned and a tickle of worry sparked at the base of her skull.

Tyrone never called after hours.

She took a deep breath and attempted to push the worry aside – she was always being told she worried too much. If it had been urgent Tyrone wouldn't have hung up. And she was sure he would text her if he was desperate. Maybe it had even been a pocket dial?

Despite her reasoning, something uneasy stirred in her stomach and she wasn't quite sure why. She ran her thumb over the keys of the old Nokia flip phone, her heart beating unnaturally in her chest.

"Is that your work phone?"

"I like it," she said defensively, knowing full well it was years behind whatever gadget Matt probably owned. He worked in IT security and it paid well. Ridiculously well. It meant he could afford pretty much whatever he chose, and do whatever he pleased, yet he still hadn't moved out of the one-bedroom flat beneath her. He said it felt like home too much and she pretended to believe him. She knew he still felt he needed to keep an eye on her.

"Yeah, I wasn't doubting that, but does it have Snake?"

She shook her head at him, a smile tugging on her lips and Tyrone's missed call forgotten. "You're not playing on my work phone."

He pouted at her. "Spoilsport."

She nodded at the glass Matt was now finishing off. "So, was that enough milk?"

He pulled a face. "Sorry, I...errr...could I have some more to take downstairs? I actually wanted it for coffee in the morning."

Rolling her eyes, she gestured for him to pass her the glass. As she turned back to the worktop a voice carried through from the living room and she almost dropped it.

It was a deep, kind, handsome voice that still had the ability to make the fine hairs on her arms stand on end.

A beat of silence pulsed through the kitchen. It filled the room and she felt her back stiffen in anticipation.

A second passed. The voice was cut off by another but it did little to ease the tension in the room. Matt stood up, his chair making a sound like a saw and it hit Lizzie's nerves like nails on a chalkboard.

"It's just the television," she said softly, trying to disguise the fact her own heart was beating painfully hard in her chest. She kept her back to her brother, giving herself some more time to draw up a familiar mask.

"Were you watching him?"

Taking a steadying breath, she turned to look at him, resting her back against the side and hoping the sharp edge of the wood would stop her heart from doing the hopscotch.

"No, of course not, it must be the news or something."

He eyed her suspiciously, his expression telling her that he didn't believe her. Choosing to ignore him she turned back around and continued to pour the milk, hoping he would sit back down.

With a sharp grunt, he left the kitchen. It gave her a moment to place her hands on the worktop, letting her walls fall as she tried her hardest to calm her body's reaction to his voice.

It was as recognisable as it always had been to her. To both of them. Except, unlike Matt, she knew every version of that voice. The way it croaked sleepily, the way it danced when playful, the way it softened when whispered. She took a deep breath and painstakingly slowly followed Matt into the living room.

It had been nearly thirteen years since that night on Primrose Hill and she was finally back to the exact age she had been then. Thirty-two, living in the same flat in Kentish Town, working at the same job, with the same friends.

Everything exactly the same.

Just without a husband. Without 'Williams' coming after her name. Without having those blue eyes sleepily smiling at her as she got ready for work, or, crying with laughter as she failed to get their front door key to work, *again*.

Somehow she had been the given the second chance she had wished for and she had taken it without question.

Charles was on the television. It was one of his old films, his hair was short and brown, a fake scar ran down the left side of his face and he was wearing glasses like Harry Potter. Lizzie always told Matt she didn't watch anything Charles featured in. It wasn't true - she really couldn't help herself - but she actually hadn't been watching him that evening. She racked her brain. In fact, she was pretty sure she had left the television on one of those channels that solely played American sit-com repeats.

The man on the screen was now an award-winning actor who probably had no recollection of the girl he had once dated, let alone had once-upon-a-time had a life with. He was now a man she couldn't claim to know despite knowing every single thing about him. He was a stranger.

"Piece of shit," Matt snarled before aggressively slamming the 'off' button on the remote.

Lizzie winced and she noted her brother's keen eyes catch it. His jaw hardened.

"Here's your milk," she said as breezily as possible, handing him the glass.

"He's filming in England soon." Matt's eyes were back on the television despite the fact the screen was now black and lifeless. "Gracing England with his presence instead of Hollywood for a change."

Lizzie sighed. "Matt, please -"

"Apparently, it's one of these biographical films that he is already tipped to win a ton of awards for. Imagine how big his ego must be to know he's already being lined up for awards when he hasn't even fucking done anything."

Lizzie couldn't imagine Charles being egotistical at all.

But then again, she reminded herself, she didn't know him anymore.

Maybe he had become egotistical. Maybe he had become a huge diva and a pain in the arse. A weird part of her hoped he had. Her hands went to her ponytail, tightening it and running her fingers through the strands.

"You alright?" Her brother eyed her.

"Yeah, fine."

He turned away from the television, his green eyes running over her carefully and she tried to make herself look relaxed. A sliver of guilt ran through her chest as she caught the concern in his expression.

"You seeing Leo this weekend?" He said, his tone more gentle.

The tension in her shoulders eased ever so slightly. "I saw him on Sunday, working for the next few weekends as Annie's off."

"I'll go visit this weekend then. Sorry, I've been a bit shit recently." His eyes clouded and he looked away, suddenly looking so much younger than he was.

Lizzie reached across and squeezed his arm gratefully.

Matt's job meant he travelled a lot. Constantly hopping on planes to Hong Kong and Singapore. It was why he was almost constantly tanned.

Whenever Matt talked about Charles, Leo was never far behind.

Leo Cartwright, 6lbs 2oz, was born in Tring Park Hill Hospital on December 7th at 5.08 a.m.

Lizzie had hoped, had wished...she had believed that maybe part of the reason she had woken up again as a pregnant nineteen-year-old was because this time, as well as changing Charles's life, she could save someone else's too.

She had hoped that this time it wasn't going to happen.

She had done everything differently, everything exactly by the book.

And maybe that was why it had hurt so much more the second time around. Maybe that was why she had felt like her heart was being pulled out of her chest as she had gone into labour. Maybe that was why it felt so much harder than last time, because for a second, for a tiny heartbeat, she had allowed herself to think maybe she had been given a second chance at life so Leo could live his.

This time around Charles hadn't been by her side. His lips hadn't been pressed to her head, his hand hadn't been wrapped around hers and he hadn't been whispering soft reassurances in her ear.

This time, when she had given birth to their son, she had been alone.

And she'd had to deal with the fact Leo wasn't breathing by herself.

CHAPTER TWO

Lizzie slanted to the side as another runner ran past her, her feet slipping slightly on the wet stone beneath her feet and her shoulder jerked as it hit the man's tall frame. He didn't so much as mumble an apology or give a sympathetic nod. She loved that she could walk to work, and she enjoyed the fact it meant she could stroll along the side of the river, but sometimes she pictured herself falling headfirst into the brown murky water and she genuinely wondered if anyone would stop to help her.

Someone would definitely stop to film it.

Her long, dark brown hair was in its usual low ponytail, her collar pulled up against the cool morning wind and her arms crossed tightly across her chest. The sky overhead was grey and unwelcoming and yet the river path was crowded with runners, speed walkers and people out with their dogs. She passed under another bridge and then followed a set of steps, that really didn't look solid enough to bear anyone's weight, upwards.

Lightswitch Productions wasn't discreet. It stood out from the mixture of Regency and Victorian architecture of King's Cross like a sore thumb with its blacked-out, glass walls and large, metal gates that looked far more secure and important than they actually were. Lizzie had worked there for just over ten years, initially as the receptionist, before moving her way into production and up the ladder.

Now, she managed *Elevenses* - a day time television show presented by Chloe Lewis and Maxine Dale. Although technically still Tyrone's responsibility, he had decided a long time ago that leaving her to do the job was a much easier option. *Elevenses* was a fun show to work on. Chloe and Maxine liked each other - which for co-presenters was rare - and made the atmosphere on set an enjoyable one.

Her office was empty but that was normal; half of her colleagues worked on *Jack and Jill* – their breakfast show – so they would already be in the studio, and the other half worked normal hours. Nice rooms in Lightswitch Productions were hard to come by as most of the studio's money went on the exterior, however, Lizzie liked her office. The door through which she'd entered was part of a glass wall, looking out solely into a staircase that led down to the dark emerald corridor; the spine of studios. The other three walls had once been white but now looked an off grey. There was no natural light in the office, no windows whatsoever, which Lizzie didn't really mind but Hugo from accounts did so he had set up his own Lumi lights all around the office. It meant the room looked slightly alien whenever she came in, small purple orbs blinking at her in the darkness before the sensors realised she was there and the room was bathed in white light.

Grabbing a banana from the fruit bowl by the door she set to work, knowing full well her inbox would have filled overnight. She didn't know when freelancers slept but it clearly wasn't when the sky was dark. Keeping her head down, only raising it to nod as other colleagues began to filter into the office, her fingers began to run over the keys and she got to work.

The stream was endless. They ranged from the ridiculous to the extreme, from the annoying to the sweet, and Lizzie soon found herself zoned out from everything but the Arial font in her inbox. Traditionally, she would go to set at 10 a.m., check everything over and make sure the crew were okay before popping into Maxine and Chloe's trailers - they were usually in one together, chatting over cups of tea. But today, it looked like she might have to send Annie to do her rounds if she wanted a hope in hell of leaving at a semi-decent hour. Especially because Thursday was a double show day - there were no live shows on a Friday so the cast and crew would film a second episode straight after they had aired the first.

"Hello, hello," a voice broke through her concentration and she looked up to see a man sit down next to her. He stretched his hands above his head and yawned loudly. Her lips twitched into a smile at the sight of him.

Neil was the little brother she had never asked for; arrogant, funny, frustratingly good looking, and on a mission to sleep with every single woman in London. Unlike Matt, Neil didn't have girlfriends, he simply had women. Lots of them. All the time. He was skinny, tall, with a flop of white blonde hair that fell into a side fringe across his face. He had a sort of indie rock band vibe which apparently worked well for him.

She glanced at her computer screen. The digital clock showed it was ten to nine. "You're in early."

"Bound to happen once in a while, Whiskers," he said cheerily, stretching his long legs out under his chair and dragging his laptop out of his rucksack.

'Whiskers' had been the nickname he had assigned to her two years ago when he realised what little social life she had. According to him she was the equivalent of a cat lady, just without the cats.

The office was busier now. There were a lot more people at their desks, either buried in work, chatting with one another, or openly staring at the monitors hanging along the opposite wall. Someone had put on the live feed into the studio where Jack and Jill were presenting. It was one of Lightswitch Production's biggest shows, boasting the largest breakfast viewing figures ever recorded and had been running for nearly four years. Jack and Jill were siblings from Clapham, highly intelligent, witty, and brought a kind of warmth to the television that people craved and connected with first thing in the morning. Jill had been labelled as a national surrogate mother whilst Jack had hundreds of marriage proposals a week. They were the first black presenters of a morning breakfast show and were loved throughout the country.

Lizzie ran her eyes over what Neil was wearing; the exact same clothes he had been wearing the day before. He cocked an eyebrow at her.

"You checking me out?"

"No. Let me guess she lived nearby?"

"Hotel in Euston, actually. Hen-do with her friends."

"Please tell me she wasn't the hen!" Lizzie groaned.

He playfully shrugged his shoulders.

"Neil, for God's sake-".

"She wasn't. Would have been very illegal to have slept with the bride given the state she was in."

Lizzie shook her head at his smile. "Didn't want to stick around for breakfast?"

"She had a train to catch and besides, our meeting with Tyrone is this morning."

Lizzie tilted her head to the right. "What meeting?"

"About the film?"

"What film?" She almost laughed. "Are you okay? Did you get drunk with hen-do girl?"

They didn't do films. They were too small of a studio and they were slap bang in the middle of London. Film productions needed larger studios, out in the suburbs, where they could use acres and acres of land to build and destroy sets. Also, in London the papers could literally set up shop right outside. No intelligent production crew would subject their actors to that.

"Tyrone didn't ring you last night?"

Something uneasy moved in her gut. "He rang me but I didn't get to it in time. I tried to ring him back but the line was engaged." She scanned Neil's face. "I presumed it wasn't important."

"Well, we have a meeting with him at 9.30."

Lizzie gestured at her laptop. "He hasn't even sent me an email about it."

"Probably expected me to tell you."

"What if I wasn't in yet?"

Neil raised an eyebrow. "Then the apocalypse would be nigh and we would have bigger things to worry about."

She sat back in her chair, surveying Neil. "There is no way we will win a commission for a film. They'd have to be desperate to try and film it here. What's Tyrone even thinking? It'll be embarrassing us even pitching for it."

Neil licked his lips and something unreadable passed behind his eyes before he dropped his gaze. "I think they were pretty desperate."

Lizzie stared at him.

"Sorry, it's already been agreed?" Her voice rose alarmingly at the end.

"Yes. And you and I are working on it."

"We can't be working on it! We haven't even heard about it!"

"I have."

"Since when?"

He turned his head away from her and a shimmer of what looked like guilt ran across his face.

But it couldn't have been that because Neil *didn't do* guilt.

"About three weeks?"

"Three weeks! Why have I heard nothing about this? Why haven't you said anything about this?"

And why had Tyrone gone to Neil and not her? A flicker of annoyance burned in her stomach. She had been here longer, she had been working with Tyrone for years, why was she just hearing about this? And why the hell were they playing host to a film?

She ran her eyes across Neil's pale face, trying her hardest to see if there was the slightest hint that he was winding her up.

"What soundstage are we going to put them in?"

"We lost *Sport Time* in Studio 3 to Waterloo, and Studio 4 is always empty around this time of year, so it's being put in both of those. They are also making a makeshift Studio 3.5 out of the canteen's staff parking area. So, they will have three soundstages, technically."

"Even three of our studios can't be big enough for a film."

"Some of the stuff will be filmed on location."

A swell of hurt rose in her chest. "Why haven't I been told any of this? Why haven't you told me any of this?"

"I was told Tyrone was going to tell you."

"That's never stopped you before." She ran her eyes over him again. Neil loved it when he knew things before she did. He teased her endlessly, would wait till she was almost frothing at the mouth and then reveal all. He loved having the upper hand, which made his discomfort and the fact he had kept this a secret all the more confusing.

He shrugged but she could see there was something hidden in his gaze. "Well, you know now."

"I have *Elevenses*, I can't work on a film as well, especially one Tyrone didn't consider me important enough to know about."

Neil shifted in his seat. "I'm getting Hazem to look after my production. I'm sure Tyrone's sorted something out for you. Annie, probably." He still didn't meet her gaze. "So, did he mention anything to you? Even the smallest hint?"

"Oh, actually, now I come to think about it, my little lady brain totally forgot about this humongous plan he told me about."

His lips thinned. "You're not funny."

"Neil, what's going on?"

"I think it would be best coming from him."

"Tell me what's going on!" She saw a couple of their colleagues turn in their seats at her outburst and her cheeks burned. Neil gave them a cocky wave as she lowered her head and leant in closer. "Neil, please." She swallowed. "You're scaring me."

He hesitated. "The film is called *Censorship.*"

He looked at her as if expecting a big reaction but Lizzie simply stared back at him blankly. She had never heard of it.

"And?"

"It's a film about journalism in World War One, how they coped with working on the Western front and how all their work had to be censored. Already tipped for Oscars, that kind of film."

Lizzie gestured with her hands for him to continue. "And?"

Neil hesitated, clicking his tongue softly.

"For fuck's sake Neil-"

"-And Charles Williams is playing the lead."

Lizzie 14, Charles 17

Lizzie woke with a start, her head pounding and her ears drumming as if she had been sprinting.

It was Matt's eighteenth birthday. At the weekend, he was going to go out with his friends to the only pub in town that didn't check people's IDs - a necessity as his November birthday meant that all of his friends were younger than him - but tonight he had insisted Charles, Lizzie and him all watched a list of gory, scary films.

Right now, she hated him for it. She sat up slowly in the living room darkness, trying her hardest to focus her eyes on something familiar but everything looked as if it were moving or about to scuttle towards her. Voices in her head told her to check this way and that, and she felt she was breathing too loudly and too obviously. Something had woken her. A loud bang of some sort. She scrambled around under the covers, trying to find the torch Matt had given her when she had needed the toilet - he had point blank refused to let her turn on any lights.

Her hands hit the body of the boy sleeping next to her on the floor but in the sea of duvets she couldn't find anything that remotely felt like a torch. She turned her head to look behind her. She could just make out Matt's shape asleep on the sofa but it looked like there was no torch with him either.

The very distinct sound of their front door being opened shot through the living room. She threw herself to the ground and the duvet over her head, rationally trying to tell herself it was probably something very normal. Her brain wouldn't listen. Instead it conjured up visions of mass murderers in white masks or zombies with their heads cut off coming to find her. Her heart was racing so fast there was a ringing in her ears. She could feel her pulse beating in her throat.

Why had she agreed to watch those horrific movies? Had it really been worth it? Did she really love Matt that much?

Someone tapped her on the shoulder and she would have screamed if they hadn't guessed what she was about to do and clamped their hand over her mouth. Charles was next to her, trying his hardest not to laugh as he took in her angry startled expression. She turned on her side to glare at him.

Charles was her brother's best friend. Tall, skinny, with wavy dark blonde hair. He had been a constant in Lizzie's life since she was nine-years-old. In that time, he hadn't seemed to stop growing. He was a boy, but he was okay. Not as annoying as some of Matt's other friends, which was a relief as he was around their house all the flipping time. Their mum always made sure she had a spare duvet ready so that he could sleep on the sofa at the end of Matt's bed.

Lizzie actually quite liked spending time with Charles – although she would never admit that.

He lowered his hand.

"What are you doing?" She hissed.

"I was just going to tell you it's your mum. You looked like you were about to have a heart attack."

"I'm fine," she snapped.

He glanced up at the duvet she had just thrown over the two of them, one eyebrow quirked upwards, and she quickly pushed the blanket away from their heads.

"Not scared then?"

"No!"

He shrugged and then, from what seemed like nowhere, held up a bag of Doritos and a red jar.

"Want some?" He shook the bag at her.

"I thought you were asleep! It's the middle of the-" they both instantly shut their eyes, stopped talking and Charles just managed to throw the blanket up and over them as the living room door was pushed open.

"Bloody kids have caused a right mess."

Lizzie's back tensed as she heard her dad's voice. It made her bite down hard on her lip and for the briefest of moments she felt Charles's hand softly brush hers.

He knew everything there was to know about her father.

Craig Rosswool's heavy tread moved around near her head. She could smell smoke on his clothes and some sort of alcohol had been spilt over his shoes because they sounded like they were sticking to the carpet. Her mum's softer footsteps followed and there was a rustling as she leant down and began to sort out some of the mess that the three of them had made.

"Can't believe our Matt is eighteen-years-old, absolutely mental," Craig said softly.

"He's an adult."

"Such a good kid."

She could imagine they were happily looking down at her brother asleep on the sofa, their eyes full of pride and their smiles wide. It was probably an image that would fill most children of divorced parents with hope.

Not Lizzie.

She had absolutely no desire for her parents to get back together whatsoever. The idea filled her with dread. She wanted her father as far away from them as he could possibly go.

There was a short silence before arguably the most uncomfortable and embarrassing sound reached her ears. The sound of kissing. She screwed her eyes tighter together.

Her parents did this occasionally - they'd appear to be back together for a month or two and then Craig would leave. Or, worse still, he would stay for the night and pretend it had never happened the next day. She would see the heartache in her mum's expression and for the next few weeks, Matt and Lizzie would lose her as she threw herself into even more Yoga and detoxing.

Lizzie hated it.

She hated *him*.

And now Charles was listening to it all as well. Her face burned at the thought. She risked opening one eye to look at him but Charles's face gave nothing away. He was pretending to be asleep awfully well, his eyes gently shut and his expression peaceful. Something fluttered in her stomach at the sight of him but she pushed it away sharply.

"Well, that was a surprise," Jean said.

"Really? I have been wanting to do that all night."

Lizzie tried not to retch at the sound of her dad's tone. She was surprised they couldn't tell she was awake by now, her face was probably glowing in the dark. As if hearing her thoughts she felt a shoe brush the top of her head. Lizzie snapped her eyes shut.

"Who's under the blanket?"

It was thrown back and Lizzie felt the cold air like water had been poured on top of her. For a second she just lay there, exposed to the living room in her dark purple pyjamas, pleased with herself that she hadn't flinched.

There was a short silence. Lizzie felt like she could practically hear it ticking as her parents' eyes ran over them.

And then her dad laughed. It wasn't warm and loud, like the laugh of Kenneth Williams - Charles's dad - but instead, it sounded sickly and strangled.

"She still in love with the Williams kid then?"

Her muscles locked.

What?

"They're friends."

"They're sharing a blanket."

"That's because Matt is on the sofa."

"There's another sofa."

"Yes, but it's over in the corner."

"They were under a blanket together, that doesn't strike you as odd at all?"

Lizzie resisted the temptation to sneak another peek at Charles. What was he thinking about all of these comments? Was he as embarrassed as her or would he find the whole thing amusing?

"The three of them are as thick as thieves when they are together," Jean said gently. "They are friends. And Charles isn't like that -"

"All boys are like that!" Craig barked.

God, Lizzie hated him.

"Not like you to take an interest in Lizzie's love life?" Her mum said softly.

Lizzie's teeth drew blood as she slammed them into her bottom lip. Why had her mum called it a love life? If there was any way the universe could hear her right now she wanted the ground to not only swallow her up but chew her into bits too. That way she would never have to face the aftermath of this situation. At this point, she would take ghosts, murderers, zombies, anything, over being there.

Craig snorted. "Love life? A Williams boy is hardly going to be interested in Lizzie. An experiment to dip his wick into, yeah, maybe."

"She's fourteen!"

"I'm only telling the truth. She hangs around with these two like a bloody dog. He's lying next to the girl. Really, if nothing has happened then he must just hate the idea of getting poor under his nails."

"Stop it, Craig!"

"Why do you let Matt hang out with him still?"

"They are friends."

"Come off it, Jean."

"They are friends," Her mum repeated, her tone more firm.

"Fucking weird friends if you ask me. You sure he isn't on some charity mission. Make friends with the less privileged, that kind of thing. Exactly the kind of thing his mum would set up."

"Don't talk about Maria like that!"

There was a heated pause. Lizzie silently begged her mum to kick him out, to tell him to go home, to stand up for herself.

Charles's family were very wealthy. Kenneth had used to play professional rugby for Ireland and the Williams lived in one of the biggest houses in Tring. Craig had hated Charles from the moment an eleven-year-old Matt had announced he was his best friend.

Finally, Jean sighed. "Can we take this upstairs, please? You're going to wake everyone up."

Lizzie's heart sank. Her dad wouldn't be leaving then.

Craig didn't respond straight away. She felt his eyes wandering over her face, but eventually, she heard them both leave the room. Their whispers carried through the darkness as they walked up the stairs, but even when she could no longer hear them she didn't dare open her eyes.

Moments later, she felt Charles tap her on the shoulder.

Inwardly, she shrunk down even further. She didn't want his sympathy.

Trying her hardest to relax her face she tried to make her breathing deeper to fake that she was asleep, mimicking how he had looked earlier.

"Lizzie?" His voice came from somewhere extremely close to her eyebrows. His breath danced across her forehead.

After a few seconds, he sat up and pulled the blanket back up towards them.

"Lizzie?" He said again.

She pressed her eyes tighter together. Surely he would get the hint even if he knew she was awake?

Suddenly, something wet was swiped across her nose. She screeched, her eyes slammed open and she pushed herself back and away. Charles was almost doubled over with laughter, an open tub of salsa in his hand. She lifted a hand to her face.

"Did you just wipe salsa over my head?"

"You were pretending to be asleep!"

"You absolute idiot!"

She lunged forward to grab tub from him. Charles managed to dodge out of her way but the tub slipped, falling towards the sofa and landing upside down on Matt's head whilst Lizzie ended up on top of Charles. Her brother didn't move, not even shifting his head as salsa dripped down and pooled where his face met the pillow.

Despite the trouble they were going to be in Lizzie could only stare at her brother for a few seconds before she had to turn and bury her head into Charles's shoulder, unable to contain her laughter any longer. Charles's body began to shake too and she felt him throw back his head and begin to silently laugh, his whole body vibrating with it. His laugh was always like that. It took over him and although Matt mocked him for it, Lizzie found it endearing. His arm was wrapped around her so tightly it felt like he was trying to cut off her blood supply and every time they tried to stop laughing they simultaneously set each other off.

Finally, when the silent hysterics had died Charles lifted his head slightly off the floor, his eyes on Matt.

"He's going to kill us when he wakes up."

"Who said anything about us? You were the one who tipped salsa on his head."

"Because you lunged at me."

"Which I wouldn't have done had you not tried to put salsa on me."

"What do you mean tried?"

Using the arm that wasn't wrapped around her, he ran a finger up her nose and she saw the red chunky dip collect onto it. His smile tilted and he tried to wipe it across her forehead but this time, she was quicker. She grabbed his wrist and pinned it above his head.

"Don't you dare!"

"Think you can hold me down, Cartwright?"

"Absolutely." And as if to prove her point she put more force onto his arm.

The movement meant her head became almost level with Charles's and she just managed to stop herself from headbutting him in the face. He tried his hardest to push back but with all of her weight pressing down onto his arm he wasn't having much luck. Her eyes slanted to the salsa on his fingertips.

"Don't you dare!"

Quickly she swiped her free hand's fingers across his and smeared what she could across Charles's forehead before he managed to grab her arms and pull her towards him.

"You're going to pay for that."

"It suits you."

"Shut up!"

Lizzie had another smart remark ready on her lips but her knee slipped slightly beneath her and her head banged against Charles's.

"Cartwright!" He said again, his tone in mock grumble as he winced, throwing back his head in a groan that she felt vibrate beneath her.

She laughed but as her eyes met his, her words stuck in her throat.

Something twisted in her stomach and she found she couldn't respond.

It was...weird.

Her whole body seemed to be hyper-aware of Charles's proximity in a way it hadn't been before and she felt her breath stop in her chest. His eyes rounded as he noted her expression.

"I'm not really annoyed at you, idiot," he said, with a lopsided smile.

Heat rushed to her cheeks.

"Erm…"

He raised an eyebrow at her. "Cartwright? Your head okay or is my skull really that strong?"

They were so close. Eye to eye. Just a few centimetres between them and Lizzie's skin was burning as if she had been left out to bake in a desert. Her head did hurt, now she came to think of it, but she couldn't really focus on that.

A Williams boy is hardly going to be interested in Lizzie.

What on earth was she doing?

She quickly shifted off Charles, sitting up and shooting him a sheepish grin as embarrassment clung to her chest. The heavy, almost hot atmosphere that had appeared in the air around her evaporated quickly, silence replacing it instead and Lizzie hoped it was just her finding it unbearably awkward. She couldn't even look at him.

Charles broke the silence first. "Your dad's a wanker."

She laughed and felt her back relax somewhat.

"Sorry about what he said about you."

Charles shrugged. "I couldn't care less about what he said about me, I care about you."

She tried to ignore the fact that his sentence sent her heart spiralling inside her chest and the temperature in her cheeks rose a few more fractions. "That's alright. I'm used to it."

He turned to look at her. "Do you two still not talk?"

"Not really."

"It wasn't your fault he was fooling around."

"Yeah, but it was my fault he got caught."

She had been three. Craig, being a local carpenter with an untrustworthy reputation, had been without work and was meant to be looking after her. She had ended up pulling a candle onto herself in the living room and although the flame had gone out the moment it had touched her clothing, the hot wax had seeped onto her bare upper thigh and burned through the skin it found. Her screams had sent the neighbours sprinting round to see what was happening. Her dad had been upstairs with a woman who was not her mother.

It had all come out. Jean threw Craig out and they'd divorced.

He hadn't spoken to Lizzie properly since.

At first it had hurt. She would cry, begging him to talk to her when he came to pick up Matt for his weekly visits. By the time she was seven she had accepted it. Now, she simply felt numb to it all.

Well, most of the time.

Charles nudged her shoulder as he settled into his spot next to her, jolting her back to the present. There was a red line of salsa still drawn across his forehead and it made her lips lift into a smile. For someone so clever he really could be so stupid.

"You can share mine if you want?"

She blinked at him. "What?"

"Dad. You can share mine."

She laughed, feeling the weird rigid tension that had set in her torso soften. Nudging him back, she moved and settled back down in their makeshift bed. He copied her.

"Thanks, might just take you up on that in the future."

"Feel free, you know what Dad's like. Loves a stray."

"Oi!" She smacked her arm across his chest and he laughed, batting it away.

"Night, Cartwright."

"Night, Charles."

.

CHAPTER THREE

"Charles Williams!" Lizzie snapped, slamming her hands down hard on Tyrone's desk, her shoulders heaving and her face the kind of red she usually turned when she had to run for a bus.

Tyrone's office was on the top floor of Lightswitch Productions. It was minimalist, with a glass wall that allowed him to see over the rail line leading up to King's Cross Station. Unlike in films, his desk actually faced the window so he could see outside.

He ignored her, not even looking up or pausing in his work.

"Sorry, Tyrone, I did try and tell her the meeting was at 9.30." Neil threw her an annoyed look. She simply raised her eyebrows at him and not-so-subtly stood on his foot. "Real mature, Whiskers," he grunted.

"*Real mature, Whiskers,*" she mimicked. She knew she was being childish but right now, the level of panic and fear that had risen up inside her was verging on breaking point.

Charles.

Here.

In her studio.

"Would you two give it a rest?" Tyrone sighed, stretched his neck to the side before closing his laptop and looking up at the two of them. He was in his late fifties with short, grey hair and a dark beard that didn't really match his appearance. Despite being one of the most senior members of staff he never dressed in suits, instead opting to wear black t-shirts and dark jeans as if he were still part of the lighting crew – his old team. A denim jacket was slung over the back of his chair and, usually, Lizzie really respected him. He had been her boss for six out of the ten years she had worked there.

"Our meeting wasn't scheduled 'til 9.30, Lizzie, it's now 9.10."

"I didn't even know there was a meeting."

Tyrone raised an eyebrow. "Didn't Neil tell you?"

"Yes, but only because-"

"Exactly. Now, would the pair of you sit down." He gestured at the white, plastic seats opposite him.

Neil took a seat but Lizzie remained upright.

"Whiskers, sit," Neil said quietly to her elbow.

"I'm not a dog."

"Debatable." He dodged as her elbow suddenly came very near his nose.

"Tyrone, you know you can't do this. He is on my Banned List."

Tyrone clasped his hands together, not appearing to be the slightest bit bothered about the fact Lizzie was still standing or what she was saying.

"Banned Lists aren't the law, they are suggested-"

"To help employees and make them feel safe in their working environment. Gee, I don't know what I was thinking about taking them seriously."

Tyrone's mouth thinned at her sarcasm.

Banned Lists had been introduced by their original CEO Rachel Gottardo. She wanted to create a production studio where, if talent or freelance crew made her staff feel uncomfortable, it didn't take a newspaper scandal for them to be forbidden from the premises. Every member of staff was allowed to state a couple of people they didn't want to ever work with. Banned Lists had always been taken seriously, often with the person on said list never being allowed to work in the building full stop, let alone on the same production. It had been a really forward thinking move of Lightswitch Productions, one which only now was being adopted by other places too. It had made Lizzie proud to work there.

It had also made her feel safe.

"I am well aware of the importance of Banned Lists."

She raised an eyebrow. "Really?"

"Lizzie," Neil said darkly, turning his head to fully glare up at her.

"This is a film production. This is the start of a brilliant turning point for Lightswitch Productions. I had to make a decision as to what was most important."

Even Neil flinched. The fire that had been running through Lizzie's body diminished as quickly as if it had been a candle blown out on a birthday cake. She stared into the eyes of her boss and her muscles slackened at the steel in his eyes.

He meant it. He *really* meant it

She slumped into the seat opposite Tyrone.

"Right then."

"Please try to understand this is a huge deal for us. This could be the gateway to-"

"No one else is going to film a film production here. It's a stupid idea."

"You never know, it may show the world our studios are capable of much more than soap operas, game shows and daytime television."

Lizzie's lips thinned. She was proud to work here. They may not work on what people called 'high-end' television productions but their shows were watched by millions and people loved them. They were cup-of-tea television; warm, comforting, interesting and needed.

She folded her arms across her chest.

Tyrone flicked his gaze towards Neil and then back again. "Why is Charles Williams on your Banned List?"

Lizzie's jaw tensed. "I don't need to explain it to you."

"No. You don't. But I'd like you to, to get a better understanding. As far as I am aware Charles Williams is extremely amicable."

She narrowed her eyes at him. "So was Ted Bundy."

Neil spluttered, forcing a laugh back down his throat as both Lizzie and Tyrone looked at him. He covered his mouth and sat back.

She turned her attention back to Tyrone. "I'm not working on it. Neil can manage the film production, I will manage *Elevenses*."

"It's a big project I need you both on it."

"What about Jonathan?"

"He's not as good as you."

Lizzie refused to feel the slightest bit pleased by his compliment.

"And Neil had a good point-"

Neil cut across him with a groan.

"Did he now?" Lizzie said, turning her head to glare at him. "And what was that point exactly?"

Neil put his head in his hands. "Tyrone, you've just fed me to the lions."

"Look, Lizzie, you put Charles Williams on your Banned List when you first joined here. When you were twenty-one. Neil suggested that maybe you put someone down because you felt you had to so as to come across as more experienced than you were."

There was a brief, stony silence. Neil cradled his head, peeking at her through the gaps in his fingers.

"Thanks for that!" She snapped, glowering at him.

"It makes sense-"

"No, it doesn't-"

Tyrone interrupted them. "Then, to repeat, why is he on your Banned List? If you tell me I will guarantee you don't have to work on this production." He flattened his hands on the table. "Even though it would be really good for your career and your involvement would show your dedication to making Lightswitch Productions a real studio to be reckoned with."

Her mouth fell open.

"I think my ten years of loyalty has already done that for me, don't you?"

"Why is Charles-?"

"I don't need to explain it to you."

"I want to make sure you feel comfortable-"

"No, you don't, otherwise you wouldn't have done this without even consulting me."

"Lizzie, try to understand-"

"I do understand!" Lizzie shouted. She stood up, the chair screeching loudly against the floor as she shoved it back. Tyrone's eyes met hers and she saw right through the fake concern to the wall up behind them. He wasn't going to budge. "The film comes first, the money comes first, I get it."

He looked as if he was about to defend himself but, after a pause, he simply shrugged. "Well, yes."

"But I won't be working on this film. You're going to have to ask one of the other Coordinators."

"That isn't going to happen, Lizzie."

"I can't work with Charles."

Something prickled along the edge of her face and she saw Neil shift in his seat, suddenly relaxing back as if he were observing her.

"If you can't explain to me why then I will not be removing you from this production. We will start preparing as of next week- "

"He's rude!" Lizzie felt the words explode from her lips before she could stop them. She could hear the desperation in her voice and her hands fisted at her sides in frustration.

"Rude?"

"Rude, arrogant, inappropriate to female members of staff, he smokes-"

"He smokes?"

"Yes, inside! He refuses to follow regulations." She clung onto what felt like a life raft, even if she was a little surprised it was the smoking thing that had caught Tyrone's attention. "He doesn't care if people are asthmatic or trying to quit. Just smokes where he likes."

Tyrone leant back in his chair. "Well, that could have changed."

"He doesn't smoke," Neil said helpfully, pointing at his phone. Lizzie turned her glare around him to slowly. What was he doing? Neil just smiled in return. "Says here his mother is a nurse so he's never touched a cigarette in his life."

"She's a midwife," Lizzie corrected before feeling her stomach tilt, her life raft punctured as a delighted expression crossed Neil's face.

"Oh, is she now?" He said. "Huh, the article doesn't mention that."

Lizzie sent him another glare and quickly turned her attention back towards Tyrone... only to find his expression mirrored Neil's. Her life raft had officially hit the bottom of the ocean.

"Could Charles Williams be on your Banned List for possibly the same reason Bex joked Idris Elba should be on hers?"

"No!" Lizzie said, slightly too indignantly. "Of course not! I don't fancy Charles!" She felt her cheeks burn hotly and out of the corner of her eye she saw Neil's smile continue to creep upwards. Why had he looked up the smoking thing? Why had he tried to prove her wrong?

"You sure?"

"Of course I am sure, this isn't a joke!"

"What did Bex say? If we could avoid working with Idris as she may be arrested if he is ever in the same vicinity as him?" Tyrone's smile widened with every word.

"That's not what this is!"

"You seem very hot and bothered about someone you don't fancy," Neil added, his voice dripping with insincere concern.

Tyrone snorted with laughter.

Lizzie stared between the both of them, her heart banging against her chest as she felt any power she had over the situation slipping away from her. Their laughs made her skull prickle uncomfortably and anger swirled in her stomach.

"Why are we even doing a film? Why did we bid for it? We are a television studios."

"The BBC lend their studios out to film productions all the time." Lizzie gestured widely. "We are not the BBC!"

"This film was due to start filming half a year ago. First, the director got pinched by another film, then SuttonXWorks, where they were meant to be filming had the whole gender pay issue exposed - blown way out of proportion my friend in their procurement team tells me - and so the new director, Susannah, made a fuss and refused to work there." Lizzie wasn't sure if Tyrone was trying to calm her down or wind her up. Even Neil was no longer looking as comfortable as he had been. Anyone in the industry knew the pay gap issue with SuttonXWorks had been grossly covered up, even by the media. "And then finally, Lewis Turner, one of the main actors, popped his clogs-"

"He died of cancer, Tyrone," Neil said, shifting in his seat. He had finally stopped smiling and instead his mouth was set in a thin line.

"We had to jump in. There's nowhere left for them to film so last minute, and they have to do it now or they lose Charles to the next production he's signed on for."

"Was that little speech meant to make me think you're doing this out of the goodness of your heart?"

Tyrone ignored her. "I will send you the details on the project," he said, a smile still on his face. "But first, we should discuss-"

She turned and walked out of the office, not caring to listen to another word he said. He called after her and she deliberately slammed the door loudly behind her. She'd never walked out of a meeting with her boss before, she had never been one for breaking rules, but this felt like one of those moments where she had to leave otherwise she might just kill him. Endorphins fired through her at the same time as a nauseating worry began to eat at her brief show of bravery.

This couldn't be happening, this *could not* be happening. She would have to talk to someone else, someone above Tyrone and just explain that...explain what?

If they asked Tyrone he would just reiterate what had just happened.

And at the end of the day, she would have absolutely no chance in persuading anyone Charles was a rude man. If they met him for ten bloody seconds they would know that wasn't true. Once again, part of her hoped he might have turned selfish and arrogant.

It felt like there was a heavy stone weighing down on her stomach. She'd had so much trust in her boss over the years. Especially when she had started. She'd worked hard because he worked hard. She had stayed late because she always saw him doing so. She tried to make sure she was the last of the *Elevenses* production team to go home, because she knew that was what he had once done. Yet now, and more so in recent years, that rose-coloured image of him was beginning to crumble. The closer she got to actually knowing him, the more she saw a different man entirely.

A hand gripped her elbow.

"Whiskers-"

Her mind had been so busy she hadn't even heard Neil follow her.

"Don't even try to apologise!" Lizzie yanked her arm away from him, stumbling back and hitting the wall.

"Wasn't going to," Neil said coolly. He looked less entertained than he had in Tyrone's office but there was still something smug about him. His eyes flicked to where she had hit the wall. "You okay?"

"I don't think we have anything more to say to one another."

"You should be thanking me."

If it was possible to choke on nothing Lizzie would have. "Excuse me?"

"You should be thanking me that I provided Tyrone with that theory as to why Charles Williams was on your Banned List and not the real one."

"The real one?" She arched her eyebrows. "You are such a prick."

Neil smiled sardonically. "You slept with him, didn't you?"

"Excuse me?"

"Look at the facts, when you joined here you were twenty-one-"

"Stop thinking my age has anything-"

"Charles Williams was still in drama school."

The air around them stilled and for a second, Lizzie felt a cold shadow move through her.

Shit.

"He may have never made it, he may have decided to change careers, but for some reason, you still felt it necessary to put him on your Banned List."

Shit. Shit.

How had she never thought of that? She had been so relieved to see in this lifetime that the Banned List system still existed that she had simply put his name down straight away. She had never even thought about timings or age. She had never doubted he would succeed.

Lizzie's brain flapped to try and come up with an excuse, a reason, an explanation of some sort, but she couldn't grasp anything that sounded reasonable. And she definitely wasn't doing it fast enough as Neil's smug smirk was growing.

"Secondly, you called him Charles in there."

"So?"

"Bit personal for a celebrity you don't know."

"It's just a name!"

"And you know his mum's a midwife."

"I must have heard it somewhere."

"You slept with him and you know it."

She jabbed her finger directly into the centre of his chest. "I did not sleep with him," Lizzie hissed darkly, her eyes daring him to try and challenge her again. "You're the King of one night stands, tell me, do you regularly ask what their mother does for a living? Is that before or after you get their name?"

He leant closer to her. "Then tell me the real reason he's on your list."

"I don't need to tell you."

"I bet you've told Bex."

She rolled her eyes. Bex was her closest friend. In this life and the last. They had known each other for years, starting at Lightswitch Productions at roughly the same time. Bex and Neil, however, did not get on well. It made making birthday arrangements particularly tricky. "I haven't actually but I'd tell her before I told you."

Something hard settled behind his eyes. "Then I am just going to have to find out then, aren't I?"

"Instead, why don't you spend your time being my friend and helping me fight Tyrone on this?"

"No point. It's already done and dusted. Tyrone's signed the paperwork."

She shook her head at him, hoping every centimetre of

disappointment she felt towards him was plastered across her face.

He didn't seem to notice.

"I have two people on my Banned List, Neil. Just the two. Why did he have to go and muck around with mine? Why didn't you warn me? You're meant to be my friend."

"I didn't think it was that big of a deal." He narrowed his eyes at her. "Why would I when, as a friend, you haven't told me why Charles is on your Banned List?" He took a step forward. "And you know I'll find out."

"Why? Why are you so bothered?" She hissed.

He smiled. "Because you've just made this a challenge, Whiskers."

CHAPTER FOUR

"AMY!" Charles half shouted, half laughed as his niece threw herself on top of him, her red hair looking as if it had never been brushed and the freckles across her nose so bright that they could have been penned on. She burst into laughter as she threw her arms around his neck and buried her head under his chin.

"I've missed you!" She stage whispered.

He managed to pull his arms out from under the duvet and wrap them around her, taking a deep inhale of her hair which oddly smelt of cinnamon and flour.

"I've missed you too, little one."

And he had. He hadn't seen Amy in over a year and his stomach twisted guiltily as he could feel that she was at least half a foot taller than when he had taken her into London to see *Mamma Mia*. It had been a late birthday present as he had been away for her birthday. Again.

Charles was in his old childhood bedroom and it looked exactly like it had when he had left it. The walls were a soft blue, the paint cracking slightly at the edges and parts had faded due to the sunlight. Across one wall hung an artistic print of The Globe Theatre against a stormy London sky. Opposite that was a huge window that looked out onto the garden and then onto the forest. Growing up, the forest had been part and parcel of the Williams' garden. They had played in it nearly every day, even when the rain had been pelting down. They had so rarely come across another person that when they did, they simply stared at them as if they were aliens. There had been four of them after all, nothing to fear when they'd been part of a team.

Photo frames were scattered across the top of his old chest of drawers and he noticed they shone slightly as if they had been recently cleaned. Photos of the Williams family were towards the front and other photos had been pushed to the back, some covered strategically with banners or leaflets. He knew which photos his mum would have decided to cover for him. Even the thought of them still in his room made something unpleasant turn in his chest.

I should get rid of those. It's been over a decade.

He turned his head away and buried his nose into Amy's hair, rocking her back and forth. She giggled loudly, the sound reverberated around his skull and he winced.

How much had he had to drink last night?

"Amy, off him."

Charles glanced to the side and saw his older brother standing in the doorway, his brown hair already looked neatly combed, his face freshly shaved and he was dressed in a navy shirt and suit trousers.

"How are you like that already?" He asked in surprise, gesturing at his brother's appearance. He shouldn't have been that surprised; Daniel was neat. It was a part of his framework. The day he appeared to be a mess would be a day to worry.

Even when Daniel had had a very good reason for appearing messy, he hadn't been. For most people, if their wife had died it would be a good enough excuse not to get dressed, to have a couple of days or even weeks without showering, and to reappear with a large beard and dirty nails, but five years ago, when Daniel had lost Helen, he had managed to still look as if he was dressed for a formal occasion every day after. Except around Christmas. Then Amy forced him to wear awful Christmas jumpers. He was completely wrapped around his little girl's finger.

Charles felt Amy slip under the covers next to him, her head resting on his shoulder and he felt his chest expand slightly at her tenderness. He didn't deserve it. He had been a rubbish uncle recently.

Actually, he was a pretty rubbish uncle in general.

Daniel ignored his question and his blue-grey eyes flicked down to his daughter.

"Why don't I ever get this kind of attention in the morning?"

"Dad!" Amy groaned theatrically. She turned her head up to Charles. "He is sooooo embarrassing."

"Trust me, I know," Charles said, squeezing her side. "I've had thirty-five years of it."

She wrinkled her nose. "I'm going to give him another ten and then I'm out."

"Oh, is that so?" Daniel raised an eyebrow at his daughter.

She giggled and buried her head further into Charles's shoulder.

Daniel shook his head at the both of them and held out a coffee towards Charles. He sat up, careful not to dislodge Amy, and took it gratefully. Taking a sip, he felt the tension around his eyes ease ever so slightly.

"Seriously though, how are you already dressed? We drank a lot last night."

"Having children is pretty much like having a permanent hangover. You're tired, dehydrated and in desperate need of a fry up or a day in bed most of the time. You get used to it." He smiled. "Talking of parenting, Mum's literally been waiting for you to wake up all morning. She's desperate to see you."

"She let me come and wake you up," Amy said, nodding against his chest. "She said she hoped you didn't still have a beard."

Charles let out a huff of laughter. "Charming."

"She was worried you might have to dash off." Daniel shot a stern look at Amy.

"Day off."

"Think that's what you were trying to say to me last night but the slurring got in the way."

Charles winced and took another long sip of his coffee.

Daniel had been his plus one to a new restaurant opening and he hadn't really been paying attention when the waiters had continually filled up their glasses. The food had been great from what he could remember and the atmosphere inside had been brilliant. It had been a restaurant dedicated to the 70s and the wallpaper had been made up of famous musical artists from the era, ranging from Elton John to The Rolling Stones. But, what had really stood out to Charles was how long it had been since he had seen his brother.

Daniel looked different. There were more tired lines around his eyes and a slight grey to his skin that hadn't been there before. He was only a few years older than Charles but it looked as if he was stressed and worn out. He had tried to ask him about it but Daniel had brushed him off, simply stating it was work. His eyes had said it was something else.

"Are you going to try some of the pancakes Nanma and I made?" Amy asked, eyeing his coffee dubiously. He pretended to hand it over to her, pushing the mug further and further towards her nose. She pulled a face, backing away from him.

"Who was the head chef?"

"Nanma."

"Okay then." He winked at her.

Downstairs Charles tried to untangle himself from his mother's grip and laughed as she refused to let go of him.

"You've grown so much!"

"Don't think I have."

She finally pulled away but kept her hands on his shoulders, looking into his face with a wide smile across her own.

Maria Williams was nearly as tall as her sons. At six foot she towered above most women but there was something about her kind expression and warm eyes that cancelled out quite how intimidating she could appear with her broad shoulders and pointed features. Her hair was already grey and fine lines fanned out from her eyes as well as the corners of her mouth. She didn't care, always referring to them as her signs of living.

"I'm so happy to see you," she said softly, her eyes tearing up as she took him in.

"Oh, Mum, stop it!" He said, laughing as he pulled her into another hug. "It hasn't been that long."

"The last time I saw you there was ice on the ground, it's been forever."

"Sorry," he said, more sincerely.

"Don't be silly," She replied with genuine warmth. "You're just busy, being brilliant as always." She finally let go of him and walked towards the kitchen worktop.

There was flour everywhere, milk out on the side, plates stacked beside two frying pans, and four egg cartons out and empty to the left. It was a far stretch from his own kitchen, which was always kept in immaculate condition and polished within an inch of its life. He didn't remember the last time it had even looked remotely untidy, let alone messy. However, his family home had always been a bit of a chaotic mix.

Maria had to be so careful, hygienic and organised at work that it felt like the moment she came home her messy chaotic side came spilling out of her, unable to be contained for any longer than it had to be. Kenneth Williams was the tidier one in the relationship, walking around after Maria, picking everything up. Despite the fact he would appear to moan about it, there was one thing Charles had never doubted in his life - his parents loved each other. If Kenneth didn't have Maria to tidy up after, he could imagine his dad would be pretty lost.

Something stirred at the back of his mind, like a memory of a bad dream. He shook it away.

"Can I help?"

"No, sit down over there and tell me all about work. What's happening? What are you working on? How's Jennifer?"

Charles sat down at the kitchen table in the middle of the room. Six tall stools surrounded it and he easily slipped onto the one that had always been considered 'his'. Next to it was Lottie's. His little sister had actually labelled hers. She had scratched her name into the top of the stool one day after school with her compass. A familiar lump formed in his chest at the sight of the small smiley face within the 'o'.

"Work is good. Finished the few episodes I was doing of the *Justice for Mars* spin-off about a month ago, been recording for a new animated movie over the last few weeks…and that's about it. I'm about to start a new biopic."

"Are you excited?"

He smiled. "Yeah, actually, I am."

"And how's Jennifer?"

His eyes flicked to Daniel for a moment. "She's fine."

"You two have been together a long time now," Maria said brightly.

"Yep." Charles suddenly found his hands especially interesting. He didn't like discussing Jennifer with his parents. It came so naturally to him to talk about his relationship in any other circumstance but to them, particularly with Daniel looking on disapprovingly from the side, it was much harder.

"Is there any chance of maybe hearing wed-?"

The doorbell rung loudly through the house, the old fashioned 'ding dong' sounding slightly more weathered than he remembered, and a wave of relief washed through him as he fingered the lines on the wooden table.

That had been close.

"That'll be Dad," Daniel said, shooting him a look that Charles pretended not to see.

"I'll get it! I'll get it!" Amy screeched, running from the corner of the room and over towards the corridor.

The doorbell went again. And again.

"Is he in a rush?" Charles asked, sitting up slightly straighter as the ringing continued.

"More likely he's messing around," Daniel said, pouring hot water into individual drinks as he made everyone's regulars.

"GRAND- oh. Hello."

Before any of them could even enquire as to who it was, the person in question came marching into the kitchen. Amy was just behind her, her young smile looking slightly stuck to her face.

"Charles, I need to speak to you."

"Patricia." Charles frowned.

Patricia Williams was the eldest of the four Williams siblings. She had silver hair that was styled into a sharp bob, longer at the front than it was at the back, pointed features like their mum and her lips were barely a line across her face. She was sharp, to the point, rarely got emotional and never seemed to relax. She was also the sibling Charles spoke to the most as he had employed her to deal with his public relations when she had been out of a job eight years ago.

It had been a decision he had come to regret.

"How did you know I was here?"

"Oh please, I have a tracker on your phone."

"That sounds healthy," Daniel said, dipping his head down to take a long sip of his tea as he walked around Patricia to pull Amy into a half hug. She was watching her aunt with curious, wide eyes. Now that Lottie was gone and Helen had passed away, Patricia and Maria were the only two females in her life. Daniel had mentioned before how much it annoyed him that Patricia treated Amy more like a family cat than a child.

"Patricia!" Maria said delightedly. She opened her arms and pulled Patricia into an awkward side hug that the eldest Williams sibling clearly wasn't enjoying but returned anyway. She wiped at her grey trouser suit.

"Hi Mum, you're absolutely covered in flour." She leant over and tried to wipe down the sleeves of her mum's red jumper but Maria shook her off.

"I know! It's part of the fun. Are you going to stay for breakfast?"

"Already had breakfast, Oscar and Scott were up at the crack of dawn. They had tennis camp at nine and I've got to pick them up in an hour and a half." She turned back to Charles and papers had miraculously appeared in her hands. "I've got to talk to you."

"About?"

Daniel handed him his coffee and he smiled at him gratefully.

"*Censorship*. It is being filmed at Lightswitch Productions now."

"I know," he said simply. "Gemma told me." His agent had told him last week and, although it was an odd decision, it was going to be very convenient working there when he lived barely a twenty-minute walk away. He'd never actually been to Lightswitch Productions despite it being so close.

"Did she now?" Patricia raised her eyebrows. She'd always had a weird kind of rivalry with Gemma, despite the fact they did different jobs. Gemma, very professionally, ignored it.

"Yeah, odd location but suits me."

"And tell me, did Ms Bicknell inform you of the cast and crew?"

"Yes." He glanced at Daniel but his brother was now finding something really fascinating in his tea. A couple of years ago Daniel had tried to ask Gemma on a date, but he'd asked her so formally that she had thought it was an event and had proceeded to bring her boyfriend. Daniel had never lived it down, refusing to ever come to Charles's agency with him again. Nor had he asked out anyone else.

"Charles, are you listening?"

He turned his head to look at his sister. "Yes. Lightswitch Productions. Got it."

"So, you know then?"

"About Lightswitch Productions? Yes?" He laughed, his brow creasing in confusion.

Patricia's gaze narrowed. "About Lizzie?"

Charles stilled, his eyes locked with his sister's and he felt as if the air had been sucked out of the room. It was surprising how big of an effect a simple name could have on him after all this time. He pressed his palms harder into the table.

"Lizzie?" He repeated the word back to his sister, the two syllables feeling a lot heavier on his tongue than any other word had that morning.

"Lizzie Cartwright is the bloody Production Coordinator." Patricia slammed the papers down on the table in front of him. "So, you didn't look at the crew list then?"

"Not yet, no. I was…" Words escaped him as he reached forward for the papers, seeing her name jump out at him as he held it up. It felt strange. A name so familiar to him amongst his work things, slap bang in a world he had never associated her with. A name that still caused a ball of pain to lodge itself between his lungs.

"I had no idea."

Daniel walked around behind him to look over his shoulder. Lizzie's name, telephone number and work email were on the sheet. Contact information just staring out at him. He felt something lock in his throat.

It annoyed him that just her name was having such an effect on him. It had been thirteen years. The news that his ex was working on the same production that he was should be as much interest to him as who was providing the catering. He shouldn't care. It shouldn't mean anything. And yet his heart had picked up its pace and his jaw had tightened.

His whole body had reacted at the sound of her name.

The last time he had seen her, her arms had been around his neck and she had been telling him how much she loved him before he'd had to leave for his grandmother's birthday party. She had been invited, of course, but she had been feeling sick so he had gone on his own. Lizzie had pressed her lips to his, pushed her body into him and had run her hands through his hair. The fact he could remember it so clearly sent darts of aged pain through his chest.

That night she had texted him telling him they were over.

He had never seen her again.

Matt had stopped talking to him too.

But he had seen him again… eighteen months later.

Charles 23

It was Christmas Eve, the bells were ringing behind the Williams family as they exited the church, and a small murmur of laughter followed them. Charles pulled his coat further around him and tightened his scarf. It was an icy, cold evening and the air bit at his cheeks. He turned his head to glance behind him. His mum was being wished a Merry Christmas by yet another family - she had delivered their grandson just two days before. The church service had actually finished thirty minutes ago. They hadn't even been able to move off the steps because Maria continued to get stopped and thanked by more, and more people.

"Can we just go?" Helen whispered, her arm looped through Daniel's. She was shivering, despite having her coat, Daniel's coat and Lottie's scarf wrapped around her.

"You two can go ahead if you like," Kenneth said jovially, smiling at the two of them. "Honestly, she won't mind."

Daniel looked uncertain, clearly not wanting to leave them but at the same time, Helen was practically quaking next to him.

"Go," Charles said with a smile. "We'll wait."

The streets around them were quiet, many people having rushed from the service in order to get home and back to family activities or recorded films. The street lights cast long shadows across the road whilst fairy lights strung between the buildings created a beautiful cobweb-like effect overhead. A pub close by was playing Christmas music loudly and it was filtering out into the street, making the air dance and excitement build in even the most cynical of people.

There was always something so magical about Christmas Eve.

"We'll see you back at the house," Daniel said with a sharp nod. He and Helen walked across the road, one shape merged together, and despite the fact Charles was quite used to it, he felt something pull in his chest.

It was harder at this time of year.

Being back in Tring brought back so many memories of Christmases spent with Lizzie, even before they were a couple, that he felt the empty space next to him more than usual. He didn't even remember Christmas Eve last year. It had been his first without her and he had gotten so drunk he had tried to go and talk to her. Daniel had found him holding onto a tree in the Ashridge Estate and brought him home. Apparently, he had been mid conversation with an imaginary friend called Leo.

Pa-thet-ic.

He turned back towards Kenneth and Lottie. Patricia was the only sibling not there and that was because her and Simon had decided to fly to Lapland that year. It had stunned them all. Not because she had left them, but because Patricia had always stated how much she hated Christmas so going to the home of it made no sense. They all smelled a proposal on the cards - from Patricia, not Simon.

"How long do you think Mum will be this evening?"

Kenneth grinned. "I'd say another half hour and then we will be able to go home. She's a popular woman."

"Half an hour!" Lottie groaned, scraping her feet against the floor. Her purple, woolly hat was pulled down over her hair and her nose was bright red.

"You know what your mum is like," Kenneth said warmly, turning his head to look at his wife fondly. Charles could see the pride in his eyes.

The squeak of gates caught their attention and they all turned around to see a young figure climbing over the locked, black railings that surrounded the church graveyard. For a second, it was almost like something out of a horror film. That was until the figure swayed.

They didn't seem to realise they were being watched and made no attempt to try and move quietly, their feet smacking against the black iron to get some grip and then landing heavily on the ground. Despite the hood pulled over their head, Charles recognised the shape of the person instantly.

"Matt?"

The figure turned to look at them and Charles inhaled sharply. He heard his dad swear behind him and Lottie took a few steps forward.

Matt's eyes were bloodshot, his face drained of colour and his lips trembled. He looked as if he had lost a lot of weight since they had last spoken, his body less muscular and broad, and his shoulders sagging over his frame as if he was being pulled down by some invisible force. He looked vulnerable and broken, two words Charles would never have associated with him. As their eyes met Charles saw so much hurt and pain behind Matt's green ones, that even though they hadn't spoken in over a year, he couldn't help but take a few steps towards him.

"Are you okay?"

A door slammed over the vulnerability Charles had seen in his expression and Matt straightened up.

"*Are you okay?*" He sneered, stumbling to the left slightly. "Don't you dare act like you're fucking concerned. Don't you dare act like you care."

"What's wrong?" Lottie asked gently. She made to step closer but Charles reached out an arm to stop her. There was something dangerous in Matt's eyes that he didn't want his little sister getting near to.

"Come on, son, why not let us take you home?" Kenneth said.

Matt didn't appear to hear him. His green eyes flicked towards the church and then back at Charles.

"Were you in there?"

"Yes."

Matt laughed. It came out hollow and forced. "You fucking hypocrite."

"We always go to church on Christmas Eve," Charles said, carefully. "You know that."

"Trust me, I'm trying to block out everything I knew about you." He glanced again at the church. "You were in there this whole time and he's just outside."

"Who's outside?"

Matt's eyes snapped so quickly back to Charles's that his head seemed to tremble in the aftermath. The anger slipped from his expression for just a second.

"Talk to me, Matt."

Matt stepped forward, his expression still crushed and for a split-second Charles thought he was going to hug him. Instead Matt's hands swung forward and closed around his windpipe, crushing it.

"Break it up!" Kenneth bellowed, reaching for them both but Matt spun the pair of them away, his hands tightening around Charles's throat.

"Talk to you? Talk to you? All I've wanted these last eighteen months was to talk to you and where the fuck were you?"

Charles tried to call Matt's name, bringing his hands up to pull Matt's away from his throat, but despite Matt's smaller height and skinnier than usual frame, there was a huge amount of power behind his grip. Charles pulled harder at his hands as he felt all the air slowly being sucked from his lungs. Matt turned them again and Charles felt a sharp thud as his head was slammed back into the black railings.

"Matt! Stop!" Lottie screamed. Charles saw a flash of blonde curls as Lottie tried to grab Matt's arm, but his grip didn't weaken.

"Get off me, Lottie."

"Let go off him!"

Taking advantage of the distraction, he pushed hard and managed to dislodge Matt's grip and put some distance between them.

The relief was instant. Charles doubled over, holding his knees and coughing painfully as his lungs screamed for air. A second passed before a knee connected with his groin and a fist punched into his solar plexus. He fell to the ground with a sharp grunt.

"Matt, stop it!" Kenneth shouted, but even his ex-rugby star father was unable to hold Matt back as suddenly he was on top of him. Matt's right fist smashed into Charles's face so hard his head smacked against the concrete and his vision blurred.

He tasted blood.

"STOP IT!!" Lottie screamed.

Charles tried to reach up to block him, but in truth, he was too shocked to properly react. He managed to catch hold of Matt's wrist but before he could even try and do something with it, Matt slipped from his grasp and pinned Charles's arm under his knee.

He was stuck.

Matt's fist connected with his eye socket and his whole head shook with pain. More people were yelling now, and for some reason, he thought he could hear the music from the pub even louder than before. He managed to connect his free hand with Matt's chin, but it didn't feel as if it had any force behind it, and Matt didn't so much as slow down. Instead, his own throws got faster. When Matt's fist found his jaw Charles let out a yell of pain. Something crunched and searing pain shot up towards his ear.

"Matt, please!" His mother's voice. "It wasn't his fault. You know what happened wasn't his fault."

For a second the punches stopped. It was like her words had paralysed his former friend. Charles took the opportunity to punch Matt in the stomach.

"Charles!" Maria sounded aghast. Why was she angry at him?

"You piece of shit," Matt snarled.

"Turning out to be just like your dad then, Matt?" Charles barked.

Hurt flashed in Matt's eyes and despite everything, Charles felt a flicker of guilt in the pit of his stomach.

Matt leant forward, his face mere inches from Charles. His eyes were now filled with such hatred that Charles felt trapped by it.

"My dad was right about you all along,"

"What the hell are you talking about?"

For a second Matt seemed unable to speak, his jaw tensing as they stared at each other.

"I guess there is one good thing about having been your friend. I know your fucking weak spots." Matt turned and slammed his foot into Charles's right knee.

Charles screamed, his old rugby injury exploding in pain.

"That's enough!"

Suddenly Matt's weight was lifted off him. Kenneth had finally managed to hold Matt in some sort of lock and was pulling him backwards, away from him.

"Charles, are you okay?" Maria said softly in his ear but he ignored her, instead staring into the hateful eyes of Matthew Cartwright. His face was murderous and Charles was pretty sure that Kenneth had only been able to grab him because Matt had let him.

"I trusted her with you, you filthy shit. I trusted you!" Matt shouted and as the streetlight caught his face, Charles realised he was crying. The sight shocked him out of his anger. He didn't think he had ever seen Matt cry. "You were my best friend!" Matt yelled at the top of his voice and the words echoed down the small street.

"Matt, I-" but he realised he couldn't quite form the words because blood was seeping out of his mouth and down his chin.

This made no sense. The only thing Matt could be referring to was Lizzie and Lizzie had broken up with him, not the other way around. He hadn't done anything wrong.

"You're just a coward! You should have been there! You should have been there!" Matt bellowed.

Been there?

"Lizzie did this, Matt, not me!" He yelled back.

A fresh wave of anger contorted Matt's face into someone he barely recognised. "It takes two people you piece of shit! I'm going to kill you just like you did her. Just like you did him!"

He had to be on something, Charles thought. He wasn't making any sense.

Out of the corner of his eye he saw Lottie, who had been crouched down beside him, stand and turn her head. And then she was running...running towards Matt, her head snapping sideways to say something to their father as her hands landed on Matt's chest. What was she doing? She needed to get away from him, Matt could hurt her!

She said something and Matt's eyes locked with hers, his anger momentarily torn away from him. Something unspoken passed between them.

"Get-get away!" Charles managed to say before his body slumped backwards.

Pain ricocheted around his brain and he heard sirens in the distance.

Please don't be the Police, he silently begged.

His eyes were beginning to feel heavy and things were beginning to blur at the edges. Maria was talking to him but he couldn't hear her.

A memory filled his mind before he closed his eyes, something he didn't recognise, something he had never seen.

A small hand.

The tiniest of hands he'd ever seen wrapped around his finger.

A fistful of grief and pain balled into his chest. It was so painful that it eclipsed everything else and he cried out.

"Leo," it was his voice, *"Please open your eyes. For me. Please."*

Leo?

Why did that name feel so familiar?

And then, Charles blacked out.

CHAPTER FIVE

Only a week had passed since Lizzie had been stood arguing in Tyrone's office and already she felt as if she was being crushed by the sheer amount of work that needed to be done.

She was working on *Censorship*. There had been no escape.

She had found herself tied to Neil, and working on the production, from practically the moment she had walked back to her desk.

Tyrone had taken great pleasure in telling the heavily delayed production that Lightswitch Productions had the capacity to get it everything up to speed before filming began.

They didn't.

Some of the film's production team were still working on *Censorship*, but many of them had taken other jobs due to the delay and therefore, as well as doing their own jobs, Lizzie and Neil were expected to fill those roles too. It meant a hell of a lot of work. They had worked into the night nearly every day, planning schedules, sorting out studio turn arounds, sending off reports for financial approval, setting up people's access to the studios and moving from job, to job, to job.

It had been hard work but Lizzie didn't really mind that: she liked hard work. What she hated was having *Elevenses* taken out of her hands so quickly. It was as if someone had pulled a rug from beneath her feet. She was still trying to stay as involved with the production as possible, even if it was slightly pissing off Annie who had taken the reins on it.

Today was their first meeting with the producers. To save time it was going to be a whistle stop chat of everything that was going to happen and a basic run over the schedules, rules and finances. Lizzie had been in since 5 a.m. preparing for it and had decided to take her breakfast late in the dressing room Bex was working in with Chloe and Maxine.

"Okay, so repeat again, what don't we do?"

"We don't offer to do any more jobs," Lizzie said, rolling her eyes.

Bex bashed the end of her blusher brush over her nose. "Don't roll your eyes at me, I know what you're like. Tyrone will have at least five extra jobs with your name on them that he should have employed someone else for. You are not to volunteer."

"I won't."

"Because he's a bastard."

Lizzie laughed. "Don't think you're meant to say things like that in front of the talent." She tipped her head towards the other two women in the room.

Bex was one of the senior make-up artists at Lightswitch Productions. She worked predominantly on *Jack and Jill's Breakfast Show* and was both hosts chosen make-up go-to. They had such a good relationship that they would leave Bex in their dressing rooms whilst they did the show and simply texted her if they wanted a top-up. They weren't fussy. And it meant on days like today, when Bex had been asked to stay on to help *Elevenses*, she could help whilst her show was still broadcasting. Now, Lizzie and her were both sat in Chloe's dressing room whilst she got her make-up done. Maxine was sitting in the corner.

Chloe raised her eyebrows. "You know I agree. That man is a bloody idiot."

"And yet he still gets a credit on our show and you don't," Maxine pointed out.

"Last week, when he bumped into Jill, he kept calling her Jillian. As if by pronouncing her full name he would come across as more professional."

Bex snorted with laughter. "I heard about this."

"But her name isn't Jillian? It's just Jill."

The two *Elevenses* hosts exchanged looks.

"Exactly!" Chloe said.

"Idiot," Maxine agreed.

"Bet Jill didn't take that too well."

"Don't think she was too bothered till he asked if she was going home at all this year."

Lizzie gasped, slamming a hand to her mouth. "No!"

"Yep!" Chloe and Maxine said at the exact same time.

"When Jill told him she still lived in Clapham, he hastily backtracked."

Lizzie swung her legs off the worktop and stood up, tightening her ponytail and throwing back her shoulders.

"What an idiot." She glanced at the clock on the wall. "Right, I promise I won't volunteer to do any more jobs, okay?" She held up her hands. "I promise."

"Good," Bex yawned. "That is the right attitude."

Lizzie glanced at her. Bex always looked good. Hair done, clothes perfectly put together, and the number of hours she spent at the gym meant her physique was toned and athletic. She was the kind of girl that turned heads as she walked past. She was nearly five foot eleven, had long blonde hair, feline blue eyes and she radiated confidence and power the moment she walked in a room. But, recently, she had started to appear drained and tired. A yawn wasn't alarming. The slight discolouration under her eyes was. Concealer covered it well, especially with Bex doing the application, but Lizzie still noted it.

"You okay?"

Bex shrugged. "Long week."

"It's Tuesday."

"Just been having some trouble sleeping." Bex shrugged. "Bad dreams."

"Bad dreams?" Lizzie couldn't remember the last time she'd had a nightmare. It was something she associated more with being a teenager. "What kind of bad dreams?"

Bex shook her head. "It's not important."

"Surely dream guy can help you with that?" Lizzie said, teasing her friend with a small smile.

Bex's lips twitched weakly.

Bex had broken up with her boyfriend of eight years a few months ago.

Thank, God.

Ryan was probably the subject Lizzie and Bex had fought most about. He had never been there for Bex, constantly late back to their flat, borrowed money off her only to never gave it back, and then he had started cheating. She had kept taking him back because of how long they had been together, and the fact he kept making grand gestures as ways to apologise. In their past life Bex had broken up with Ryan the Christmas before Lizzie's thirtieth. Lizzie wasn't quite sure why it had taken her nearly three years longer to do it this time around.

Dream guy was...a saviour? That or he was a sign Bex was about to lose the plot.

Much to Lizzie's annoyance, Bex hadn't dumped Ryan because he was a poor excuse of a man. She had dumped him because, in her eyes, she had been having an affair.

A dream, not-happening-in-real-life, kind of affair with a figment of her imagination that came to her in her sleep.

"Some things even he can't fix."

Bex's tone was so sad even Chloe and Maxine looked up in alarm. She caught everyone looking at her and quickly shook her head.

"See, it's crazy. Bad dreams. That's all it is. I'll go and get some hard core sleeping tablets and be back to normal in no time."

"Bex-"

Lizzie's phone beeped in her pocket and she took it out to see a message from Neil.

"Shit!" She hissed.

"What is it?"

"Apparently another producer is going to be coming to this meeting now. Better go."

"Call me later," Bex said, throwing Lizzie a look. "Tell me how it goes."

"Sure."

"And-"

"I got it, Bex! No volunteering," she said, laughing.

Lizzie rolled her coffee cup between her palms, staring at the way the barista had spelled her name on the side of it as if it was fascinating. They had been waiting for nearly half-an-hour. No one had texted them, no one had emailed them and no one had rung to tell them they were running late. Instead, Lizzie, Neil, Tyrone and Karen - Head of Finance - were simply sitting there. Waiting. Lizzie eyed Karen's laptop and seriously regretted not bringing her own down. She was too scared to go and get it in case that was the moment the producers turned up.

They were sitting in one of the boardrooms on the second underground level. Like her office, one wall was made of glass to look out into the corridor. It had been so long since anyone had walked past however, that the overhead lights had gone off and it looked dark and ominous, reflecting their ghostly shapes back at them on the surface. The room they were in was grey. Grey table, grey carpet, grey light fittings and black-turning-grey swivel chairs. Neil was very much hating the fact his squeaked every time he moved.

"Is this as glamorous as you imagined?" Lizzie turned her head to look at him, raising an eyebrow.

He threw her an exasperated look. "Fuck off, Whiskers."

"No really, was all of this worth it?"

"You two, don't!" Tyrone snapped through gritted teeth. "I don't want any bickering when the producers come in."

"*If* they come in," Neil mumbled.

As if hearing him, the light in the corridor flashed on and they all turned to look as two men in jeans and white shirts, both around their late fifties, walked down it. They were smiling and they sped up as they saw they were being watched. When they entered the room they laughed as if seeing them all sitting there was some sort of hilarious joke. Lizzie's mood dropped even further.

The taller one was bald, whilst the other had hair that had been very clearly dyed black. Lizzie automatically stood up and Karen followed her. Neil gave her a look before she kicked him and he rose to his feet too.

"Hello Tyrone!" The taller one said, thrusting out a hand for him to shake and smiling around at them all. "I'm Paul, this is Lee." They both smiled genuinely and Lizzie felt her preconceptions of them shift slightly. They seemed nice enough even if they hadn't yet apologised for being late.

"Good to see you again." Tyrone shook both men's hands. "This is my team, Neil, Lizzie, and Karen."

They all began crossing hands over the table, up and under one another so that they could all shake hands with each other. As the men took the two seats opposite Lizzie and Neil, she felt something prickle up her spine, like a warning.

"Is err," Tyrone gestured at the empty seat next to Lizzie, "joining us?"

"Charles got held up at the doors, told us to go on without him and he'll be down in a second. Not to worry, he's just sitting in to see how things are done. Fancies tackling production later on down the line."

Something hard replaced the heart in Lizzie's chest and began to bang repeatedly against her ribcage. Carefully, she slid her gaze across to look at Neil. He wasn't looking at her, his eyes suddenly fixed on his hands, but the smallest of smiles was on his lips. Something bitter felt like it had just locked around her lungs.

She moved her gaze over to look at Tyrone who was very deliberately shuffling his papers. He glanced up once, caught her eye, licked his lips and looked away far too quickly.

No.

They hadn't-

They wouldn't-

Lizzie felt all of the air rush out of her lungs.

"So, Paul, did you have a chance to go over the schedule we sent out last week?"

She reached for her ponytail to tighten it and felt herself shaking as her fingers brushed against one another. It made her grit her teeth.

Maybe it wasn't him. Maybe it was someone else entirely. Charles wasn't the most uncommon of names-

Her head jerked to the side as she saw a tall figure through the glass walking towards their door.

No. No. Fuck. No.

"So sorry I'm late. Had to say hello to some…friends."

His voice almost pulled her head up but she managed to stop it, instead staring intently at her notes as if they were about to open up into a door that she could escape through.

"Not to worry Charles, just sit down at the end there and we will continue."

At the end.

Next to her.

He was going to be sitting *right next to her.*

"Don't worry, we all have adoring fans standing outside too." Lee laughed heartily. He turned back to the table. "One of his fans waited outside of our production office for an entire night to see him."

"He wasn't even due in but he came to see them when Duncan, our security guard, texted him about it," Paul added. He rolled his eyes playfully and gestured, once again, for Charles to sit down.

Charles laughed awkwardly.

"Sounds like a really rude guy," Neil muttered low in her ear.

She snapped her head around to look at him, nearly head-butting him in the process. The fear that had her firmly in its grip didn't give her the energy to come up with a retort but she saw it physically hit Neil. The smug smile on his face dropped and his eyes sharpened.

Lizzie looked back at the table as she felt his responding alarm. He nudged her foot with his own, trying to get her to look at him again, but she ignored him.

If he really cared about her, maybe he should have thought about that before planning whatever hell this was. A surprise ambush?

She felt Charles walk around the table towards her and she deliberately turned her head at an almost uncomfortable angle to look at Tyrone, again avoiding Neil's eye. Her heartbeat was in her ears, she could feel it drumming against them, pulsing through her body, and the room suddenly felt unbearably hot.

As if Charles had put a microphone on himself she heard the chair next to her scrape back, and the sound of his clothes rustling slightly as he sat down. The smell of his cologne reached her, the one Kenneth bought him every Christmas no matter what, and it made her chest ache with memories.

She still didn't dare to look, didn't turn around to face him even though she could now feel the heat of his leg centimetres away from her own. She tilted her body even further towards Tyrone and curled her hand into her lap.

Get a grip.

She had survived thirteen years without Charles Williams. She could survive for a further few hours just sitting in his company.

CHAPTER SIX

The meeting finished roughly two hours later. It had just been to go over the finer details, to make arrangements for certain necessities that Lightswitch Productions hadn't been aware of and to schedule all of the important upcoming dates. There had been a brief talk with Karen about the financial aspects and then the subject of the crew had come up. Due to the film being delayed, delayed, and further delayed, it meant almost a quarter of the crew had moved onto different projects. Tyrone had agreed Lizzie and Neil would continue covering more roles than their own and they would also help to provide freelance staff. He had looked at Lizzie at this point, no doubt waiting for her to jump in and offer her assistance as there wasn't a freelance crew member she didn't know, but she managed to keep quiet, Bex's voice shouting at her with such force she could have probably been in the room.

Instead she had smiled at Tyrone as if she was blissfully unaware at what he was getting at and had quite enjoyed the fact he looked slightly off balance by her response. Neil had sniggered and given her a knowing look. She'd ignored it pointedly.

As everyone got up to leave, Lizzie pretended to find something truly fascinating in her rucksack which required her to duck down under the desk and sort through it. She'd had planned this move roughly forty minutes earlier, hoping it meant she could avoid even looking at Charles.

Throughout the meeting, she hadn't been able to concentrate properly. Not at all. She hadn't made notes, she hadn't corrected

Tyrone when he had misquoted how large their studios were, and she hadn't been able to lower the heat in her cheeks for the entire two hours. She was pretty sure that meant she was likely to have the flu.

Man-flu.

Literally.

She could hear Tyrone saying goodbye to the producers, their booming voices reaching her easily under the desk as she proceeded to pretend she was looking for something inside of her rucksack. Luckily there was a lot in there so the rustling sound she was making sounded convincing enough. Well, it did to her ears anyway.

The producers stopped by the doorway, still talking to Tyrone. She tried to count their shoes to distract herself, spotting Karen's small black dolly shoes slipping past them and leaving the room.

Take me with you, Karen, take me with you.

From where she was positioned she could see three sets of shoes. Tyrone was wearing trainers but the rest were in smart brogues.

But three meant Charles wasn't over there yet.

"Neil Grayson?"

She slammed her head into the bottom of the table and inwardly swore.

Charles's voice was as distinctive to her as a birthmark. She cradled her head in her hands and tried to crouch down even lower under the table.

Not that he could see her.

She turned back around as quietly as she could to see her side of the table and instantly spotted the legs of Neil and Charles. Neil had stepped into her spot and now, the two men were roughly a metre apart.

"Hello Charles, nice to meet you." Neil's voice was louder, she could hear the humorous edge to it and if she had been able to do so she would have kicked him hard.

"So sorry for being late."

"Think you said that at least five times during the meeting, why not mix it up a bit and try it in a different language?"

"Sorry." Charles laughed awkwardly.

"I have a friend who apologises as much as you."

Lizzie's cheeks flared red. If Neil dared-

"Is this the first film Lightswitch Productions has worked on?"

She felt simultaneously grateful to Charles for changing the subject, but equally angry that he had started another conversation. He needed to leave.

Now.

"Yeah, but I'm sure we can handle it. How are you feeling about the project?"

So, she was going to have to just stay under here, was she? Whilst they had a bloody chinwag. What was Neil doing? Was he trying to make her life even more unbearable?

Probably.

She would just have to wait until everyone left and then reappear with a dramatic flourish to an empty office. That would probably be best. She would be happy doing that... if not for the fact her leg was beginning to cramp. The pain had started off as a slight twinge but it was beginning to grow up through her calf, her muscles linking their strands together and making it feel as if her leg had got trapped in a vice.

"Ow, ow, ow," she whispered to herself, closing her eyes.

She was stuck. If she moved back slightly she could just about stretch her leg out.

Maybe she could then rest her head down, have a nap and look completely insane if anyone caught her.

She tried to breathe away the pain like her mum used to tell her to when she was younger.

It hadn't helped then and it didn't help now.

She was going to have to stand. She was pretty sure if she didn't that her leg would straighten whether she wanted it to or not and send her head through the table anyway. Biting down hard on her lip so not to audibly yelp in pain, she pushed herself out from the under the table. She aimed for Neil's now vacant spot and stood up, twisting her body so her back was to the pair of them.

And then she forgot about being discreet.

Her leg was in agony. She hopped away from the desk, shaking her ankle around as much as she could to try and stop her calf seizing. It was like every small muscle in the back of her leg had been twisted around the wrong way and then someone had decided to crush them.

"Ow, ow, ow." She was almost singing as she hopped toward the wall.

"You alright, Whiskers?"

"Cramp!" She hissed, solely focusing on her leg now.

"That's what you get when you hide under the table."

"I wasn't hiding!" She snapped.

"You should put it against the wall."

That voice.

For the briefest of moments, she had forgotten where she was and why she had, in fact, been hiding under the table. It hit her like a boulder but the pain quickly took the moment away and she almost fell as her leg seized again. A strong hand gripped her upper arm and helped her to the wall.

"Like this." He pressed the tip of his shoe just above the skirting board and planted his heel down in a diagonal to the floor. Lizzie copied and couldn't think about anything else until the pain began to ease up. She swallowed hard as her leg began to feel normal, part of her mind wishing for more pain so she would have more time before the inevitable. Slowly, she turned her already flushed face towards him.

The sight punched the air out of her lungs.

Charle.

It was like her whole body was singing it.

The man she hadn't been able to shut out of her head for the last thirteen years was inches from her and it caused her emotions and rationale to freeze momentarily.

He was classically handsome. Thick, dark, blonde hair, broad shoulders, a slim figure and a jawline that could cut glass. But it was his eyes that had always been her downfall. They had a way of seeing right through whatever walls she put up.

She had seen those eyes filled with warmth, laughter, playfulness and amusement. She had seen them filled with fear, sadness and loss. For the past thirteen years, when her brain had wandered, she had clung onto the memory of them filled with love. Time was meant to be a slow death for memories but Lizzie couldn't quite believe how well her mind had kept hold of him. He looked exactly the same.

"Thanks," she said, realising his gaze was still on her and his foot pressed up against the wall.

"You're welcome."

They stared at each other.

Words, responses, time, places, names, all vanished from her mind. Thirteen years. Thirteen years since they had been face to face and she could barely speak a sentence.

Charles lowered his foot and turned his body fully around to face her. He was wearing black trousers and a light blue shirt that hugged his frame nicely. His face was clean shaven and now she was close to him again the smell of his cologne hit her hard.

She flicked her gaze up, attempting to force a smile over her lips, but it momentarily froze on her face. With the force of a slap, she truly registered what she could see in the blues of his eyes.

Indifference.

She felt as if she had been punctured. The slight rush she had got from seeing his face for the first time, the quickening of her heart as she had realised he was beside her, trickled away and left an empty shadow in its place.

Since she had begun working on *Censorship,* she'd imagined it would be awkward for her to see him again. She had imagined how he might react, what he would say, or if they would both pretend they didn't know each other. Only once or twice had she considered he may not even recognise her.

A sense of stubborn satisfaction settled inside her gut. If she was so forgettable she can't have meant very much to him at nineteen, which meant she had been right.

She was right to have left him this time around.

Right to have not told him about Leo.

Right to have not hit the first domino in the chain that would end in their marriage.

This time around they had dated for two years. *Two years.* It clearly hadn't even been enough for him to think of her as remotely memorable.

"Are you alright?" He asked, frowning, but his eyes were still bland and emotionless.

Lizzie felt panic flood through her. What the hell was she going to do? If he didn't recognise who she was she could hardly introduce herself. It would be completely humiliating.

Which was why she panicked.

Panicked and said, "Hello, I'm Patsy Whiskers."

What are you doing?!

Neil snorted to the left of her, not very successfully disguising his laughter but it definitely could have been a weird sort of sneeze. For a moment she had forgotten he was even there.

"Patsy Whiskers?" Charles repeated slowly.

His face gave nothing away but there was definitely something suddenly different in his expression. The indifference had faded and there was something hard behind his eyes that even in the past she hadn't seen. It changed his entire face. Suddenly, he wasn't so handsome, he wasn't so charming, he didn't automatically look approachable...he didn't look like Charles.

Lizzie slowly pulled her leg away from the wall and turned around properly to face him.

"Yep."

She held out her hand and after a second's hesitation, he took it, his palm brushing against hers.

Once upon a time those hands had cupped her face when he was about to kiss her, they had comfortingly rubbed her shoulders when she had been stressed about work, they had stroked her hair when she cried for Leo and held her waist when he had tried over and over to teach her how to dance. Now, there was something even in his grip that was different, that separated him from their past... that made him a stranger.

You don't know him anymore.

It was like every second in his company the world was trying to remind her of that.

"Nice to meet you." They shook hands and then quickly let go of one another.

"Ah yes, our very own Irish gem, Patsy Whiskers!" Neil said. His eyes were practically glowing with laughter, the corner of his mouth so heavily upturned it was as if he was attempting to be a caricature of himself.

She stared at him, her eyes trying to create physical craters in his face with her gaze. He continued to smile.

"Irish?" Charles repeated.

She swallowed, still glaring at Neil.

"Aye, y yes."

She turned her head back to look at Charles. He had crossed his arms over his chest and was assessing her, his eyes still weirdly unfamiliar as they pinned her to the spot.

"Funny." He stepped forward and Lizzie had to stop herself from stepping away in response. "I can't place your accent. My dad's Irish you see, played for the rugby team, so I've been there a few times."

She knew that. She *bloody well* knew that.

Lizzie glanced at Neil, begging him to interrupt and rescue her. He smiled at her innocently.

"Dublin."

"Which part?"

She licked her lips, desperately trying to think of an Irish name. "Gleeson Road."

He blinked. "Gl-ee-son Road?"

"Like Domhnall Gleeson, the actor?" Neil asked cheerfully.

Lizzie resisted the urge to stab him with her elbow. "Yep. Tat te one. They liv'd neabye like."

Neil pretended to look interested. "Do they do that in Ireland? Name their roads after the actors living on them? Saoirse Avenue? Brannagh Lane?"

She smiled at him blandly but tried to communicate with her eyes that after this, there was nowhere he could hide where she wouldn't find him and kill him.

Very slowly.

The look egged him on.

"And what happens to the road where Brendan Gleeson lives? There can't be two Gleeson roads, surely?"

"Don't think I've heard of it," Charles said, forcing her head to come around and look at him again. It made her lungs ache.

"Doont expect ye to know all te roads."

It was actually making her mouth hurt having to keep this up, and she was pretty sure if her cheeks got any hotter she was going to faint. She tightened her hairband and saw Charles's clock the movement immediately. Something about the way his eyes lingered on her hands as they adjusted her hair sent a warning shiver down her spine.

"I'll look it up next time I visit."

"Please do!" Neil interjected.

"Charles!" One of the producers called across the room.

Charles waved at them and mouthed 'two minutes'. He turned his blue gaze back towards them and again, she felt something shift in his expression. She daren't analyse it further in case he noticed.

"Well, nice to have met you." He moved his hands to his hips. "You know, I was hoping I could introduce myself to the other Production Coordinator, Lizzie Cartwright?"

Lizzie felt her heart stutter in her chest.

The man who she could pick out of a crowd, whose voice still sent goosebumps up her arms when he spoke, didn't even notice when she was right in front of him. If she wanted a clearer sign that what she had done had been the right thing she wouldn't find it. The knowledge stabbed into her chest.

"She was busee t'day so she was," she said, trying her hardest to mask the pain from her voice.

Something ticked in his jaw. "Right. We've actually worked together before. Maybe you could pass on a message?"

"Sure," she nodded.

Charles paused for a second, his eyes running over her and she hated the fact that despite the fresh blanket of hurt that was now suffocating her, her cheeks simultaneously burned with heat under his gaze and nervous butterflies began to flap in her stomach. He stepped closer, making her back stiffen and she saw his keen eyes note the reaction. Inwardly, she swore at herself. She needed to say neutral. She needed to pretend she was Patsy Whiskers.

Play. It. Cool.

He leaned closer, dipping his head so he was level with her.

"Could you tell her she's still just as bad at accents as she always was?"

What had he just said?

Their gazes collided and Lizzie flinched. He had dropped the mask he had been hiding behind and within the pools of his blue eyes now, there was pure anger.

Shit.

He had known. He had known the entire time.

"Charles-"

He stepped away, refusing to look at her, turned and quickly followed the producers out of the room. She felt stuck to the floor, watching his back disappear from view and feeling her stomach lurch.

Neil let out a low whistle. "You're such an idiot, Whiskers."

CHAPTER SEVEN

"Hello!" Charles called as he walked into the hallway of his home. Everything was spotless, everything was white, and he could virtually see his reflection in the floor beneath him. The house felt too big and too grand for just the three of them, but his sister had insisted he needed a home that made a statement and a house in the centre of London with a drive as big as peoples' flats definitely made a statement. Situated right next to Regent's Park, with more rooms than he would ever be able to fill and windows that often looked into empty spaces, Charles felt at times he was playing make-believe in his own home.

"Hi gorgeous," Jennifer called back, her Portuguese accent making her tone low and soft. "We're in the living room."

Charles moved down the white-walled corridor, dropping his satchel onto the floor and kicking his shoes off before turning into the living room. Jennifer and their personal trainer, Kristina, were spread out over the long cream sofa. Jennifer was watching a film whilst Kristina had her feet up on her lap and was lying back against the arm of the sofa, not really paying any attention to the television and instead flicking her thumb up her phone as she scrolled through her Instagram feed.

"Hello ladies."

"How is my handsome boyfriend today?" Jennifer asked, holding her hand out behind her for him to squeeze. He did so, leaning down and kissing her on the cheek.

"Okay, thanks."

"How was the meeting?" Kristina removed her eyes from her phone to look up at him.

"Good." He nodded. "Yeah, great."

She swung her feet off Jennifer's lap and stood up elegantly. She was Charles's height and could make practically any movement look effortless and elegant. At home, she never wore anything other than a sports bra and tight leggings, and her body looked more photoshopped in real life than it did when photographed. Her hair was dyed black, worn in a 1920s bob, her skin was pale and unblemished, and her eyes were dark brown and seductive.

Now those eyes were running up and down him. She leaned her weight back on her hip and folded her arms, her gaze narrowing. Before she could assess him further, he ducked his head and walked towards the kitchen, trying his best to ignore the burning sensation in the back of his skull. Nearly all the bottom floor was open plan so it wasn't like he could easily escape from her gaze, but at least putting some space between them might throw her off whatever she had seen in him.

"What's up?"

He flinched, her voice in his ear.

"Nothing," he said. "I'm getting a drink, do you want one?"

Kristina turned her head to look back at Jennifer in the living room.

"Oi, you're the one dating him, you should be the one noticing when something is wrong."

"Nothing is wrong," Charles said quickly. He opened up the fridge and took out a beer, placing it behind him on the central table and now feeling both women watching him suspiciously. He could feel their eyes following him and he subconsciously cracked his neck as he used the edge of the granite to pop the lid off his beer. It flew across the worktop and Kristina skilfully caught it before putting it in the bin.

"Beer?" Jennifer said, sounding alarmed. She sat up slightly straighter and turned her torso fully to watch him.

"On a weekday?" Kristina remarked, folding her arms. "Well, you might as well come out and say it, you've pretty much admitted to something being the matter. That or you are just trying to deliberately mock the diet plan I have set up for you." She narrowed her gaze. "And if you're doing that to my face then I'm going to warn you, I will kill you for it."

He glanced up at them, trying to quickly weigh up in his mind if telling them was worth it. They were his closest friends. Having lived together for years it was hard to keep secrets from them. He took a long, slow breath.

"I saw my ex today."

Jennifer jumped to her feet, her black braids swinging out behind her head. She practically skidded over towards the pair of them in the kitchen, her face filled with excitement. Charles inwardly winced.

"Oh, my, God!" She squealed, clapping her hands together.

"Which one?" Kristina asked, looking disinterested.

Which one? He almost laughed.

Seeing Lizzie had been enlightening from the very moment he had walked in the door. He had known she was going to be there but judging from her red face and the way her eyes kept flicking at her boss, she hadn't known *he* was going to be there.

He had been aware of her constantly.

Ashamedly, he had liked the fact she had been flustered to see him. He had enjoyed her discomfort and the way her face had flushed red, the way her hands had twisted over themselves in her lap when he had sat next to her and the fact that she refused to meet his eye until she had to. He had wanted her to be embarrassed. Embarrassed for what she had done and how she had behaved when they were younger. Leaving him with no explanation and then whatever that had been with Matt outside of the church. It was all to do with her. The fight had left him with two fractures in his jaw and a dislocated knee.

But there had been something in those green eyes that he couldn't shake from his mind. Part of her expression had been terrified, like she feared him or what he was about to do, and it unnerved him. Unfortunately, even after thirteen years apart it seemed part of his genetic code was to always be protective over Lizzie Cartwright. Thinking he was the thing that scared her had sent little worrying niggles deep into his consciousness.

Kristina cleared her throat and raised her eyebrows at him. "You coming back to us anytime soon?"

"I've only had one ex really. Just the one," he said quickly, his cheeks flushing red as he placed his beer down.

Silence followed his statement and when he finally glanced up, he saw Jennifer and Kristina looking at one another, silently communicating something he couldn't read in that way the two of them always could. Jennifer felt his gaze and turned to look at him, her soft, brown eyes finding him and sending him a warmth he hadn't realised he needed. She had this effect on people, it was why she was so liked.

"Lizzie, right?" She said softly.

He closed his eyes and ran a hand over his face. He had told Jennifer about Lizzie one drunken night at drama school, when she had been pressing him again as to why he was so happy about their...arrangement.

Jennifer had liked the story a lot more than Charles had anticipated but, then again, Jennifer was a hopeless romantic. To her, him telling her he had fallen for his best friend's little sister had been the equivalent of a night in with a romantic comedy. She had pressed him to disclose every detail and in his drunken state he had told her...too much.

Once upon a time, he had considered himself a romantic too.

Now, he looked back at his actions with a prickling sense of embarrassment.

"Yes," he said curtly. "It was Lizzie."

"What was it like seeing her again?" She said softly.

"Weird," he admitted with a shrug. He took a swig of his beer. Jennifer was watching him carefully, her eyes full of concern, and

Kristina was watching him like he smelled bad. He wasn't sure which look he detested more.

"Was there any tension?"

He choked on his drink and threw Jennifer a *'don't go there'* look. A grin grew across her face and she began to talk faster.

"Did you like seeing her? How did it feel? Did you keep thinking about the last time you were together? What was she like? Did she act bothered?"

Luckily Charles was used to her thick Portuguese accent, so even as she spoke faster, becoming more enamoured with the topic, he understood what she was saying.

He took a long swig of his beer and eyed her, refusing to deign any of her questions with an answer. After a few seconds, she pulled her bottom lip out into a sulk.

"Who is this?" Kristina asked, sounding annoyed.

"Her name was Lizzie and she was Charles's best friend's little sister," Jennifer said before Charles could pull the beer away from his lips.

"Oh, Charles," Kristina said, shaking her head. "What a cliché."

"But she was really cool. She made all the first moves on Charles because he was too scared to –"

"I don't ever remember saying I was scared!" He interjected quickly.

Jennifer smiled at him. "I know you."

"Better to be because you were scared than because you were lazy. Like most men."

Charles glanced at the wall in the kitchen. "Well done, Kristina, you lasted five minutes without man bashing. Think that's a record."

Kristina grinned. "It's not."

"Excuse me!" Jennifer said, irritated and giving them both a look that made Charles want to laugh. "You're interrupting the story."

"It's not a story!"

"It's an epic story."

"Lizzie broke up with me," Charles said, turning to look at

Kristina. "That's the basic gist. End of *story*."

"Charles!" Jennifer moaned.

"We were together for two years and out of nowhere, she ended it. By text." He arched his eyebrow at Jennifer, challenging her to try and turn that into something romantic. She looked away, rolling her eyes and saying something very colourful in Portuguese. "Jenni, we have been together for over ten years, I know Portuguese and I know what you just said."

Kristina laughed, winking at Charles as Jennifer face darkened in annoyance.

He didn't want excitement. He didn't want his supposed girlfriend to start day-dreaming about setting him up with Lizzie again. For the first few years of their agreement she had often asked why he didn't reach out to Lizzie, why didn't he try and find her. After she had found Kristina, her need for him to find love had got worse. Jennifer had started trying to send him on dates with friends of hers. That had gone down like a lead balloon. Jennifer hadn't quite understood why he might not want to go on a date with a friend of hers who 'really wouldn't care' that he was supposedly taken. She had insisted they were lovely people just with shaky morals.

"This Lizzie sounds like a bitch," Kristina mumbled, breaking through his thoughts.

A flare of protectiveness beat hard inside his chest but he pushed it away. "Something like that."

"What was it like seeing her again? Did she look the same?" Jennifer pushed.

"Exactly the same."

She no longer had a fringe that wasn't really a fringe - as a teenager she had always cut it herself and it had always been a bit haphazard as a result - but she was exactly how he remembered. Slightly scatty looking with thick, brown hair that she tied up behind her. Oval-shaped, green eyes that tried to pull him closer and a small button nose that was so unlike his own.

She was still beautiful. When he had first caught sight of her, for a split second, he had felt like a young teenager again.

No, that was a lie.

He had felt like he was nineteen. Nineteen and completely taken aback when one of his best friends suddenly straddled him in her kitchen and pressed her lips against his.

His grip on his beer tightened.

"How did she react to seeing you?" Jennifer asked. She was talking in that hushed voice again. He gave her a look at the exact same time that Kristina did. At least one person was on his side.

"She pretended she didn't know me."

"What! Everyone knows you!" Kristina said.

He shook the neck of the bottle in his hand. "Not in that way. She pretended she didn't know me outside of all that. She gave me a fake name and spoke to me in an appalling Irish accent."

Another long pause stretched out between them before Kristina broke it with a snort of laughter.

"Looks like you dodged a bullet there, Charles. She sounds absolutely mental."

Why had she given him a fake name? What had been the point?

And, more importantly, *why did he still care?*

She had put him in hospital. He should still be furious at her but his mind couldn't stop trying to dissect what he had seen behind her eyes that morning.

"Sweetheart," Jennifer said softly, placing her hand on top of his and bringing his attention back to the kitchen. "You look upset."

"I'm fine."

"Honestly?"

He took another long sip of beer. "Honestly. She's just an ex-girlfriend."

Kristina tilted her head to the side and surveyed him. "Just an ex-girlfriend who hurt you enough for you to agree to be in a fake relationship for your entire adult life?"

"Yeah." He moved around the side of the kitchen table and put his bottle in the recycling box by the door.

"Charles-"

"Honestly," he cut Jennifer off quickly. "I'm fine. It was a long time ago. I don't care anymore. She can do whatever she wants."

It had been so hard trying to pull up his mask of indifference when she'd looked at him. It had taken every acting skill in the book for him to pretend he was completely unbothered about the fact she had been hiding under a table to avoid him. It had been even harder to hide the alarming kick to the chest he had gotten when he had properly seen her.

Jennifer's warm arms wrapped around him and she pressed her face into his back.

"It was just a teenage fling, Jenni," he said quickly.

Jennifer sighed. "Okay, handsome, you keep telling yourself that."

Lizzie 17, Charles 20

"You're my best friend, you know?" She whispered softly.

She was lying on her front, Charles pressed into the side of her, his fingers skimming down her spine. He smiled and kissed her shoulder tenderly.

It had been six months since she had kissed him in her kitchen and since then, she didn't know if she had ever felt so happy in her life. He was still at university so they didn't get to see each other as often as either of them would have liked but it meant that when she did see him, she could barely stay away from him.

Which made things difficult as their relationship wasn't exactly public yet.

Tonight, Charles had been around to see Matt, the two of them finally having reading weeks that matched so they were home at the same time. Charles was studying in Durham and Matt in Loughborough, so neither of them got to see each other much.

It had been the first time Lizzie had seen Charles since she had been to visit him in Durham at the end of September, and when Matt had opened the door and pulled Charles into a hug full of back claps and jostling, Charles's eyes had met hers over his shoulder and she was quite proud she hadn't melted on the spot.

They had spoken to each other but it had felt weird and alien pretending to just be friends so Lizzie had left the boys to it. An hour after everyone had gone to bed Charles had snuck into her room.

"Lizzie," Charles hesitated for a second, his palm pausing over her lower back.

"Yep?"

"I…I want to tell Matt."

She froze, her body locking.

"No."

"Lizzie, come on-"

"You promised."

He closed his eyes and shifted onto his back. She felt the loss of his touch and the warmth of his body against her side as deeply as if he had got out of bed and walked away. She watched as he ran a hand across his forehead and she could practically feel the million different thoughts coursing through his temples.

"I couldn't bear not being able to say hello to you properly today. I love it in Durham where we don't have to hide, where I can hold your hand when we go out, where I can be with you. Properly."

Her heart swelled at his words but she forced herself to push the emotion away and think rationally. Charles was a romantic. He always had been. He made this stuff sound so easy because he really felt it would be. But she knew better. If Matt found out, he'd be cross. He'd be angry that she had taken his best friend away from him and he might make Charles choose.

Her breath hitched at the thought and she turned her head on the pillow to look the other away.

Charles would choose Matt.

They had been best friends for God's knows how long and she knew their bond was unbreakable.

And when Charles did choose Matt, it would break her.

She pushed back the tears in her eyes and stared stubbornly at the wall.

Seconds later, she felt Charles's knuckles brush the dip of her waist and she flinched, hating the fact her body reacted so strongly to his touch even when she was upset.

"What are you thinking, Cartwright?"

Her lips trembled so she refused to open them.

"Look at me."

"No."

"Look at me."

At the slight roughness in his voice she slowly turned her head back around on the pillow. He was back on his side, his face momentarily unreadable as he took in her tearful expression.

"What is it?"

"Nothing. I just don't want you to tell him."

He raised his eyebrows at her. "You are a rubbish liar."

A small laugh escaped her lips but she smothered it by pressing half of her face into the pillow.

A couple more seconds passed.

"You'll choose Matt," she whispered, trying to swallow hard to stop the sob in her throat. "Everyone chooses Matt."

His gaze sharpened in understanding and his arm wrapped around her tightly, pulling her into him so fast that she turned and her chest collided with his. The look he was giving her was so intense that she felt her cheeks heat under it and her stomach dip.

"I want to tell Matt because I am in love with you."

Her breath halted as his words hit her. "What?"

A playful smile crossed his lips as he stroked a few loose strands of hair out of her face.

"I love you."

The smile that broke out across her face was almost painful in its size. Warmth, happiness and utter adoration exploded inside of her like a firework.

"I love you too," she whispered. Charles's grin grew wide and she felt tension she hadn't noticed ease out of his torso. She frowned. "Were you worried?"

"No, course not." He shook his head, his eyes gleaming cheekily, but it quickly turned into a nod and Lizzie laughed, affectionately punching him on the shoulder. "Such an idiot."

He threw back his head and laughed, the way he'd always done since he was a child. Lizzie adored that laugh.

"LIZZIE!"

Lizzie and Charles froze at the sound of Matt's voice. Their eyes locked with one another and whatever Charles saw in Lizzie's expression made him pull her closer to him, running a reassuring hand over the small of her back.

"TIP FOR YOU! IF YOU'RE STILL TRYING TO KEEP THIS A SECRET, YOU NEED TO FIND A WAY OF MAKING CHARLES LAUGH LIKE A FUCKING NORMAL PERSON!"

Charles burst out laughing and Lizzie closed her eyes in pained annoyance, her cheeks burning red.

"MATTHEW CARTWRIGHT, HOW LONG HAVE YOU KNOWN?" She bellowed back.

"ABOUT SIX MONTHS BEFORE EITHER OF YOU TWO DID PROBABLY!"

"Charles, stop laughing!" Lizzie muttered darkly, shoving at his chest. He didn't, instead pulling her closer to him and soon it turned infectious. She covered her mouth, trying to smother her own laughter as Charles buried his head into her shoulder, his whole body still vibrating. Relief, like no other, surged through her.

Matt hadn't made anyone choose.

Matt didn't care.

CHAPTER EIGHT

It was finally the end of the week. As a way to solve the fact that her mind kept going over and over her meeting with Charles she had thrown herself into work, letting it completely consume her and spending every hour she could inside of the office. On Wednesday, she had even gone to sleep in one of the dubbing theatres - they always had the best sofas - as she had stayed so late that there was really no point in going home.

However, sleep was when it got worse. The moment she closed her eyes, the memories started. Charles's face, the cold indifference in his expression, followed by the sinking sensation she had felt in her stomach when she'd realised that he had known it was her all along. The memories kept her brain ticking over and over, unable to rest.

It meant that, by Friday, she felt as if she was constantly blinking her eyes open and trying her hardest to combat a headache. By the time the clock hit 7 p.m., all she wanted to do was crawl home and try to sleep. She planned on drinking at least a bottle of wine to make sure she completely dozed off, before spending the weekend trying to sort out her mess of a flat. But then Matt rung, asking her to come and meet his girlfriend and her brother for a quick bite to eat.

The idea had temporarily floored her enough to agree to it. Matt never asked her to meet his girlfriends. She only met them by accident, if they passed in the hallway or just outside of the house. She knew all of their names, Matt had no qualms in talking about them, but there was never a need for her to actually meet them as none of them were serious. The idea that Zoey could be, excited her. Selfishly, it lifted some of the guilt she had always felt about the fact that maybe Matt shied away from relationships due to her massive failure in one particular one. He hadn't had a long-term girlfriend last time either, but still…she worried.

Now, as she stared into a mirror bigger than the ones in the studio's dressing rooms, in a room that smelled of lavender, she severely regretted it.

"I'm going to kill him," Lizzie snapped, her head slanted to the side as she trapped a phone between her shoulder and her cheek.

Bex laughed down the other end of the phone. "I think he's a genius. I've been trying to get you on a date forever."

"He didn't tell me! I came straight from work and I'm in this posh restaurant where even the waiters wear tuxedos and there are only three things on the menu! I was going to order a glass of wine but then I noticed for one small glass it was eleven pounds! Eleven pounds, Bex!"

"Surely if Matt has tricked you into this he's paying. I'd take advantage if I were you. Order the lobster or something."

Matt had failed to mention that the 'Regent's Prince' was a five-star restaurant and not a pub like she had presumed from the name. It was the type of restaurant that had different types of forks for different courses, napkins that looked too expensive to get dirty, and lights so low that walking between the tables was a precarious act.

The night had more of a double date vibe than a 'meet the family' vibe and she knew Matt had done it on purpose. Positioning them so that he was opposite Zoey and Lizzie was opposite Kieran, Zoey's brother, he had spent the evening so far focusing all of his attention on Zoey. He had barely asked Kieran a question and had changed the subject anytime anything long-term or serious came up.

What was worse was that Zoey hadn't been expecting her. It was obvious she had wanted to introduce Matt solely to her brother, and Matt had taken the situation and turned it around so it was less important. Usually, Matt would have broken up with a girlfriend had they suggested meeting a sibling. Clearly, he wanted to hang on to Zoey for a bit longer and, therefore, had orchestrated the situation to suit himself.

Lizzie had seen the frustration behind Zoey's own green eyes and felt so sorry for her that she had almost poured the jug of tap water in the centre of the table over Matt's head. She hadn't - the restaurant would have probably charged her more than her month's rent for making a scene.

Matt's charms, however, had slowly eased Zoey's upset. Meanwhile, Lizzie was left faced with Kieran. He was a good-looking man, roughly the same age as Matt, with cheeks that had dimples when he smiled and short, black hair. Like Zoey, he had an Irish accent which, well, even she couldn't deny was sexy.

Nothing like hers had been the other day.

Lizzie stared at her pale pink jumper. It had frayed sleeves and definitely looked more of a sickly skin colour than the blush it had originally been when she'd bought it two years earlier. Her hair was tied up in her usual low ponytail and she hadn't a scrap of make-up left on her face from that morning. She felt completely out of place. She dried her hands on one of the fluffiest towels she had ever felt and then moved to hold her phone properly to her ear.

"I'm wearing jeans!"

"Why didn't you Google the place?"

"Because it is Matt. He hates these kinds of places."

"True." Bex clicked her tongue down the phone. "Well, I could come and bring you some clothes?"

"That's so sweet of you but that's out of your way, and I think it would be even weirder if I spend the next forty minutes waiting for you in the toilet." She glanced around. "Although it is a very nice toilet."

"Do they have folded up towels?"

"Yep! And the end of the toilet paper has been shaped into an origami swan."

Bex made a high-pitched noise that dogs would probably have struggled to hear. "Oh, I would so much rather be where you are. A date with a gorgeous guy in a fancy restaurant. Sounds perfect."

"How do you know he's gorgeous?"

"Matt's shown me pictures of Zoey. She is stunning so just makes sense for him to be. Am I right?"

Yes. Lizzie knew Kieran was good looking even if she didn't feel anything towards him. He passed the eye test too. Maria Williams had once told her you could see someone's true nature if they smiled through their eyes.

"Yes."

"Well then, what's the harm in getting to know him a bit? You never know."

"You never do."

She did know but she didn't want to completely stamp on Bex's optimism. She also knew the only reason Matt would have ever set up this double date was because Kieran lived in Ireland – therefore, no chance of anything serious ever happening between the two of them. Matt had never set her up. Sometimes it felt like he trusted men less than most women did.

Lizzie hadn't been with anybody since Charles. At first, it was due to the fact she'd had to go through losing Leo all on her own: she'd been in no fit state to even think of being with anyone. She'd been twenty-two when she had next kissed someone and it had felt like she was cheating. She had cried the entire taxi ride home and Bex had banned her from ever drinking rum again – she'd presumed that was to blame for her hysterics.

And what was the point? She'd been in a relationship with her best friend. He had made her laugh, held her when she'd cried, and told her she was beautiful with her hair like a birds nest and her make-your-own retainer hanging half in, half out of her mouth first thing in the morning.

Nothing was going to top that. She hadn't done any of this for a new relationship so she'd never felt the need to go out and get one.

"And if you don't like him, at least let me have his number," Bex said, bringing her thoughts back to the present.

"You wouldn't like him, he's actually a nice guy."

He had stood when she joined them at the table, and had complimented her on how she looked even though she knew she looked completely out of place.

"Touché. So, is your hair in its traditional ponytail?"

"Maybe."

"First port of call, take it out. At least attempt to look different from how you do at work. What make-up do you have on you?"

"Lip balm and concealer."

"I'm impressed, that's more than usual. Have you taken out your hair yet?"

Lizzie pulled out the hair band and let her hair fall down behind her shoulders. It had a slight wave to it and the fact it was third-day-washed hair made her feel even more self-conscious now it was down. It could definitely have looked nicer. She ran her hands through it, trying to give it some sort of boost. Feeling it on her shoulders felt wrong. She felt naked with it down and her hands yearned to reach behind her head and put it back the way it had been. She gritted her teeth and stopped herself.

"That fancy toilet not got any free make-up in there?"

Lizzie laughed. "No."

"Don't laugh. That Polish lady is always in The Boatyard's toilets selling make-up. Their wine is only four pounds a glass."

"That's a club, Bex."

She sighed. "Well, I think you're beautiful anyway, just go out there and be you."

"Someone's watching *Queer Eye*."

"Hey, it's the second-best way to spend your Friday night, after a date in a fancy restaurant being paid for by your mega rich brother."

Lizzie winced. "Never call him that to his face."

"It might make him work harder in boxing."

"But you love beating him."

"Yeah, but it would be nice if he was more of a challenge. Anyway, stop distracting me. Go out there and practise your flirting - it's bound to be a little rusty. Just see it as something to enjoy.

Nothing serious."

"Since when has flirting been enjoyable?"

Bex groaned. "Since forever. I even do it in my dreams."

Lizzie's heart softened. "Dream guy still coming to visit? Despite the bad dreams?"

Bex had told her that morning her bad dreams had eased off since the beginning of the week. She had looked fresher and brighter, and her eyes had sparked, but it still worried Lizzie somewhat.

Bex sighed. "Thankfully, he stepped back in to take their place."

"You still absolutely positive he doesn't go to your gym?"

Despite everything Bex had said, Lizzie was pretty sure the man must go to her gym. The only men Bex ever met were from her gym - it was where she spent most of her free time.

She laughed. "Positive. Did I tell you what his hands did to me last night?"

"No, no, no, no, none of that! Not whilst I'm sat in a fancy toilet. Work, yes, fancy toilet, no. Feels like a massive trap door might open up beneath me and I'll be thrown out." She paused and tapped her foot against the ground. "Although-"

"Haha, no way, Lizzie. No running away. No trap doors. You're doing this!"

Lizzie huffed, leaning closer to the mirror and turning her head from this way to that to see if she needed to rub off any pen marks from her face. "I'd better get out of the toilet before they start to think I've actually done a runner." She threw her shoulders up and down and tried to shrug off the worry gripping them. "Okay, I can do this."

Bex laughed loudly. "It's a date, Lizzie, you're not going to war."

"It had to be red, didn't it?" Charles said, using his napkin to try and mop up the wine he had accidentally spilled on the tablecloth. Despite the awkward start to the dinner, whereby Patricia had been late and pointed out that she hadn't known children were welcome -

staring daggers at Daniel as Amy sat grinning next to him - it had turned into quite a lovely evening. The four of them had chatted, eaten, and Amy seemed to be trying to drink as many pints of milk as she could fit into her tiny little body. It was nice going out as a family. After he had been down to Tring a couple of weeks ago he had mentally told himself he had to make more of an effort to see his family.

"Tu es maladroit, Charles," Amy said, shaking her head at him as the red began to seep like blood through the white tablecloth.

"Since when did she start speaking French?"

Daniel laughed. "Maladroit is her new favourite word." He leaned over the table. "And I think you're making it worse."

They were sat on a square table at the back of the restaurant which meant Daniel was across from him, Amy was on his right and Patricia's empty space was on his left. It also meant that because he had stained his own spot, he'd pretty much reddened the entire table.

"Just because you didn't get a single one of the clumsy genes," Charles huffed, now trying to cover up the spill with his plate and knife. "I swear you did this on purpose to avoid the conversation."

"Yes, I forgot to tell you, I recently became an X-Men and now have the power to move things with my mind."

"Shut up!"

"When Patricia gets back from the toilet she's going to kill you."

"Here you go," Amy said, pushing her own plate towards his to help cover up the red stain. It looked like it was getting even bigger despite Charles's best attempts.

"Thanks Amy. Now could you please tell your dad to stop avoiding the question?"

"Dad, stop avoiding the question."

"Look, it's a no. I'm not dating, I don't have time. And anyway, you can't talk, you've been single for the last God knows how many years."

"Daniel!" Patricia hissed, catching the last few words as she returned to her seat. "Can you keep your voice down please? We don't discuss these things in public." She narrowed her eyes at Charles's plate. "What's happened to the table?"

Daniel sighed. "We aren't in public. Hate to break your silver bubble but this restaurant is far from public. I'm pretty sure I spotted the Prime Minister in here and some of these bottles of wine are as holidays."

"Well, smaller ears might be listening." Patricia's eyes darted towards Amy who was looking between them all curiously.

She smiled toothily. "I know. Dad told me."

That surprised even Charles.

"You told your child?" Patricia said, aghast.

"I told Amy, yes."

"Might as well just ring up *The Daily Mail* now then." Patricia threw her hands in the air, angrily glaring at her brother. "Put it out on *Sky News*."

"It's fine," Charles said gently, shaking his head softly. "Amy's a good secret keeper."

"She's known for the past year so evidence would suggest that."

"It's not fine! She's a child!"

"And she has known for the past year," Daniel repeated, drumming his fingers on the table rather than looking at Patricia. Patricia, meanwhile, was getting redder and redder.

"Why did you tell her? Why did you have to say anything at all?"

"It's fine!" Charles repeated, firmly.

Amy put her hand up.

Patricia's nostrils flared. "Put your hand down-"

Charles stood on his sister's foot. "Yes?"

"Would it be okay to leave the table?"

He threw Patricia an irritated look. "I trust you, Amy. You can stay at the table if you want to."

She smiled. "I know, Dad always tells me to ignore what Aunty Patricia says anyway."

Charles tried his hardest not to laugh as Daniel swore softly under his breath.

"He does what?" Patricia snapped.

"I just wondered if I could go and say hello to Lizzie?" Amy continued.

"A friend from school?" Daniel asked, frowning, and pretending not to notice Patricia's glare.

"No." Amy shook her head like he had asked a stupid question. "Aunt Lizzie." She pointed to her left.

"You don't have an Aunt Lizzie." Daniel followed Amy's gaze as Charles watched in amusement. Maybe this was some sort of game Amy was making up to distract them all from arguing with each other.

She was a smart kid.

Daniel's eyes caught who Amy was looking at and his face stilled, something akin to confusion flickered behind his pale blue eyes and his mouth parted.

"Charles." He swallowed. "I am pretty sure Lizzie Cartwright is sitting three tables behind you."

CHAPTER NINE

Charles stared at Amy, the hairs on the back of his neck lifting.

"You don't know Lizzie," Daniel said cautiously.

They were all looking at Amy now and Charles knew what they all must be thinking.

She sounded like Lottie.

Amy had never met Lizzie. She had been born five years after they had broken up. Charles glanced at his brother and he saw worry etched along his expression. He looked wary and tired.

"Yes I do." Amy turned to look at Charles. "We used to build tents together." She leaned forward and grabbed his arm. "Don't you remember?"

"You've made this tent near impossible for adults to enter." Charles used his elbows to pull himself the last few feet into it. When he finally sat up, his jumper had ridden halfway up his stomach and his feet were still poking out the end of the tent.

Amy was asleep, curled up on a pile of cushions, and Lizzie was sitting just beside her, felt tip pen on her face and some kind of glitter around her eyes.

"Amy was giving me a make-over," she said catching Charles's expression. "And since when did you start calling yourself an adult?" She leant forward and pulled his jumper back down.

"Slip of the tongue."

"Big mistake." She pressed her lips against his softly and he felt the worry in his chest ease slightly.

"Won't happen again." He smiled, pulling away and reaching an arm up to loop around her shoulders. "It got too much in there, didn't it?"

He felt Lizzie relax into his side, her smell so familiar and her hair so soft it felt much more like she was comforting him than the other way around.

"I just don't like it when Patricia starts asking me if I've tried all manner of things to get pregnant." She adopted a slightly higher pitched voice than her own. "Have you tried this app to track your ovulation? Have you tried not eating such and such? Have you been exercising regularly? *Like she genuinely thinks after five years I haven't given everything my best shot."*

He kissed the top of her head gently. "Sorry."

"It's okay. She's your sister, I should be apologising to you."

He laughed gently into her hair, before moving his hand down to lift her chin up towards him. She wouldn't meet his gaze.

"Lizzie?"

"It's just...she always makes me feel like..." Her eyes caught his and she stopped herself, running her tongue over her lips as her gaze danced back and forth over his face.

"What?"

"Nothing."

"Lizzie?"

"Honestly, it's nothing. I'm thirty-two, I can handle your sister." She leaned forward and placed another soft kiss against his lips. "I'm fine."

"Lizzie," he tried to lean away, knowing full well it wasn't nothing but she pressed her lips tighter against his own and, as her hand threaded through his hair, what he'd been about to say slipped from his mind.

Charles pulled his arm away from Amy violently, his eyes widening in shock and his heart racing. Hurt flashed across the young girl's face.

"Sorry," he said quickly. "Static shock."

What had that been? A dream? A mini stroke? It looked like no time had passed but the vision had been so strong Charles felt like he had been there. He had felt her skin against his, her warmth tucked into his chest, her hair against his lips.

Her lips against his lips.

"She sounds like Lottie," Patricia said softly, breaking through the panic that was building inside his chest. The name of his youngest sister brought him back to the present and he quickly risked a look at Daniel. His face looked calm but he could see the stiffness in his shoulders and his cheekbones looked sharper than usual.

Patricia continued. "Has she been having many of these kinds of episodes? I have a really good child psychologist I've been meaning to send Oscar to on my Instagram." She picked up her phone as if to write something down.

"Amy's not like Lottie," Daniel said firmly, shaking his head but the fear in his eyes was giving him away. What was worse was that Amy was starting to pick up on it. Her head was flicking between the adults as they spoke about her, her eyes becoming guarded.

"No, I must have mentioned her," Charles said quickly, knowing full well he hadn't. He waved his hands in front of him as if it was nothing. "Must have said something or other."

He would talk to Daniel about Amy later. In private. Without her little ears listening. If she was like Lottie he was determined not to make the same mistake with his niece as he had with his little sister.

"Why would you be talking about Lizzie?"

"Because I bumped into her recently."

The table stilled. All eyes now on Charles and he realised slightly too late he may have just shot himself in the foot. "It was at the start of the week, the production meeting I tagged along to. She works at Lightswitch Productions."

"I know that, I was the one who told you that!" Patricia hissed, her interest in Amy completely gone as she leaned across the corner of the table towards Charles. "Why didn't you tell me this?"

"It's not important."

"Are you joking?" A surprised laugh left Daniel's lips. "Why were we even discussing my dating life when you had that gem to tell us?"

Charles threw him an aggravated look and his brother tried to correct his amused expression by lowering the corners of his mouth, but his eyes still danced.

Charles straightened his hands out onto the table cloth. "It was nothing."

"Nothing?" Patricia's hand reached out to him, it felt like her nails were trying to pierce his wrist. "Nothing! What happened? Amy, stop looking at her."

Charles hadn't even realised his niece had turned her head to watch Lizzie again. He resisted the pull to do the same.

"It's fine. We are past the awkward first meeting again stage and now, we will just have to act professionally. I doubt we will even run into each other. She isn't the Production Coordinator for the actual film, she is the Production Coordinator for the studios. And anyway, most parts of production never see each other until the wrap party." He caught Patricia's angry expression and quickly added. "Not that I will be going to that anymore."

"Why was it awkward? What did she do?" Her nails were really starting to hurt.

"She pretended she didn't know me."

"She what?" Daniel glanced over Charles's shoulder again far too obviously.

"Stop looking at her Daniel!" He snapped.

"Well, if she doesn't remember you she won't have a clue who I am."

Charles lowered his voice. "No, she does know who I am, she just… she put on a fake Irish accent and called herself Patsy. She pretended to not know me outside of this." He held the hand Patricia wasn't clawing into off the table in a weak impression of Jazz hands.

Daniel stared at him for a second, his face a picture of calm before it crumpled in on itself as he tried his hardest not to snort with laughter.

"It's not funny."

"It's ridiculous!"

"Keep your voice down!" Patricia snapped.

"She doesn't seem to have clocked we have been here for the majority of the evening, why would she notice now?"

"Because your laughing is hardly discrete."

"It's the most discrete of all of us."

"That's not saying much," Charles interjected.

Daniel looked straight at him, a smile still playing across his face.

"Must have been hard. Her pretending to be someone else to your face."

"Well, who wants to bump into their ex?"

Daniel contemplated the question, his expression serious. "I don't think I'd care after a decade or so. Wouldn't be top of my 'to-do' list but wouldn't be so awful that I'd try to pretend to be someone else."

Charles shrugged. "She did."

His brother glanced behind Charles's shoulder again with a gleam in his eye that Charles hadn't seen in a long time. If it had been any other situation, he would have welcomed it.

"She looks good."

Charles hands tightened on the table, his palms no longer feeling relaxed.

"Daniel," he said in warning.

"She looks really good."

"What are you doing?" Charles and Patricia said at the exact same time.

"Pity, she seems to be on a date."

Patricia pried her hand off Charles's wrist and instead jabbed a finger into Daniel's arm. "Are you out of your mind? Shut up!"

"This game-" Charles gestured between the two of them, "-isn't going to work."

"Judging by your attitude, it already is working."

It *wasn't* working. Daniel's words weren't making him want to turn around. They weren't causing his blood to heat. They hadn't triggered a scratching feeling in the back of his skull which was begging him just to take a look.

Shit.

"So, back to the dessert menu-"

Daniel's mouth formed a surprised 'O' and he sucked in a small amount of air audibly enough for Charles to swing his gaze back up towards him. He felt the back of his neck tingle uncomfortably. He shook it off. Whatever his body was doing right now clearly wasn't anything sensible.

"What is it?"

"Oh, that's interesting."

"What is?" He said, between gritted teeth.

"I'm the one staring at her but she ends up spotting the back of your head." Charles's back stiffened and the prickles along his neck intensified. He still refused to turn around.

"Daniel, stop it," Patricia hissed.

"I'm not falling for it," Charles said.

Daniel smiled slowly, raising an eyebrow. "Nothing to fall for, I'm telling the truth." He took a very obvious, lazy look behind Charles's shoulder again and Charles felt a prickle so sharp along his back it felt like it was in his bones. "I forgot how much she used to blush around you."

Charles's body whipped around before his mind had time to put up a single 'Stop' sign. It acted out of instinct, out of memory and when his gaze collided with Lizzie's he felt an unexplainable jolt in his chest. Their eyes met for just a fraction of a second, but it was enough for him to see the fear that had been in them before, dancing on the surface. Her face was a dark shade of crimson. She looked away, her hands flexing at her sides and he saw a slight tremor in her shoulders.

Daniel's description hadn't even come close to the truth: she looked absolutely incredible. Just like she had the other day. Her blush deepened as she felt him watching her and she brushed a strand of hair behind her ear self-consciously.

Her hair.

It hung in loose waves around her shoulders and a knife of jealousy stabbed through him that was completely irrational. When they had dated the fact that she had worn her hair in a ponytail around everyone else but him had always made him feel...well, a bit smug if he was honest. It had been such a small thing, but to him it implied that she trusted him enough to let that wall down. He had picked up on the fact it was a defence mechanism long before that. Whenever she had been stressed or anxious, she would pull at it or tighten it.

Once upon a time he had been able to read her so well.

Seeing her without said ponytail was messing with his emotions and causing memories he had buried to come rushing to the surface.

She glanced back up at him, flinching in her seat as she realised he hadn't stopped staring and once again, he got a good look at the fear behind her green eyes. He instinctively leaned forward.

What are you hiding, Cartwright?

She'd always been so easy to read so why was he finding it so hard to do now?

He felt a strong, hot glare upon in his face and his eyes flicked up to look at where it came from. He presumed it was from her date but when his eyes met the person on Lizzie's left his mouth dried and his jaw tensed.

"Matt," he said simply, turning back to his brother and feeling both of the Cartwrights' eyes on the back of him. "She's out with her brother. Not a date."

Daniel pursed his lips. "So, you didn't notice the gentleman opposite her? You just thought she would sit adjacent to Matt for dinner?"

"I-er-" he ran his tongue along his bottom lip and caught his brother's smirk. "I'm glad you're finding this funny."

"I am."

"Matt, look at me."

Finally, he turned his gaze towards her and she felt the angry heat of it burn across her skin.

"Was that Charles Williams?" Zoey said, her voice one of awe and she saw the green in Matt's eyes darken even further.

Zoey, don't go there.

If Matt found out Zoey admired Charles in any way they wouldn't be together in the morning.

"Yes, it was," Matt hissed out, without moving his glare away from Lizzie's face.

"What's this about then?" Kieran asked curiously, leaning over the table and brushing Lizzie's arm with his fingertips. She jerked it away, feeling instantly guilty about having done so but she couldn't help it. She didn't want to be touched, she didn't want to be talked to, she was completely unprepared for this situation.

"Nothing." She tried to offer Kieran a comforting smile without letting her gaze stray from her brother. She was scared if she took her eyes off him for a second he would be up and over to Charles's table. "Matt's just passionate about his films."

"Excuse me?" Matt snarled, glaring at her. Lizzie silently begged him to calm down, her eyes desperately trying to reach out and appease him. "If I'm so passionate about his shit films I better go over there and ask for his fucking autograph." He made to stand up but Lizzie grabbed him by the arm and pulled him back into his seat.

"Stop it. You're making a scene."

His green eyes practically sparked at her angry tone. He leant towards her.

"I can make a much bigger scene if I want to," he whispered darkly, quietly enough so that Zoey and Kieran couldn't hear. "Maybe I should reveal to this whole restaurant what kind of man Charles Williams really is."

"Do not threaten me."

"I'm not threatening you!"

"Yes, you are. What you are referring to is a threat to me. It's my business not anyone else's."

"What he did to you is my business too. I am the one who had to pick up the pieces, I am the one who had to pry you back from that bloody ledge."

"You're being dramatic. I was nowhere near a ledge!" She hissed.

"Weren't you?" Matt raised an eyebrow at her. It was mocking and cold, and Lizzie felt a shiver run through her. She glanced around the table and realised the other two were staring at her and suddenly she felt overwhelmingly trapped.

"Can we get the bill please?"

"We have just as much right to be here as -"

"I didn't say we didn't. I just don't want to be here anymore."

"Ouch." Kieran placed a hand to his chest but his expression was soft and there was a cheeky tilt to his smile.

"Sorry," Lizzie said quickly, glancing at him. "It's not you, I promise."

"We could go for drinks somewhere else?" Zoey asked softly, her eyes were kind.

"That would be lovely but I think I should go home."

Her legs were trembling, she could feel them shaking under the table. Her body was still acutely aware of the fact Charles was metres away, and that he had been staring at her with such a curious intensity that she could still feel the shadow of it across her skin.

Matt pulled out his phone and wallet. "I'll go and settle the bill."

Kieran quickly began to try and find his own wallet but Matt brushed him off. "Don't worry about it, mate, I'll get this one."

"Thank you, Matt," Lizzie said, warily watching him as he got to his feet.

He didn't look at her, but he nodded.

They both knew she wasn't thanking him for getting the bill.

CHAPTER TEN

Outside the restaurant, Lizzie groaned at the feeling of the cold air against her skin. It acted like a bucket of cold water, calming her nerves, straightening her vision and slowing her pulse. She took two deep, calming breaths, threw a smile at the doorman and walked forward, her eyes scanning the street for the orange glow of a cab.

"So, I'll leave you guys to it," she said, trying her hardest to give the other three her most earnest smile. They had been much slower to leave the restaurant than her. "Thanks for such a great night."

"I'll walk you home," Kieran said, straightening up and smiling at her.

"No, no, that's fine. I'm not really a walk away so I am going to get a taxi."

Kieran glanced at Matt and gave him a look that Lizzie couldn't read.

"What?" She asked.

"Nothing," Matt said slightly too quickly. "Kieran, if you could just get her home, I'd really appreciate it. I'll pay."

"I am honestly fine to get in a cab home by myself."

"Humour me, Lizzie," Matt said, sounding tired. "Please?"

Lizzie met his gaze and felt guilt swirl in the pit of her stomach at the expression on his face.

She owed him.

She always owed him for what she had put him through.

"Fine," she whispered.

"Don't get one from outside of here though, they'll probably charge you extra because of the restaurant. Go around the corner."

"Lovely meeting you properly," Zoey said, wrapping her arms around Lizzie and momentarily distracting her from trying to analyse her brother's body language.

"You too."

They all pleasantly said their goodbyes and the individual pairs began to walk off in different directions. Lizzie shivered, bringing her arms up around herself and trying her hardest not to turn and stare at the restaurant they had just walked out of.

Of all the chances.

Twice in one week.

Thirteen years and she hadn't even caught a glimpse of him but now she had seen him twice in one week.

"Sorry," she said, turning her head to look at Kieran. "I acted like a right nutcase in there."

"It's fine. It's understandable."

"Understandable?"

"Matt told me Charles Williams is an ex of yours."

A stab of fear flared up inside her and she recoiled away from him. "What? What did he say?"

"Hey, hey," Kieran soothed. "He just said he was your ex and it ended badly. Don't be angry at him, he refused to divulge anything else."

"When did he tell you that?"

"When we were getting our coats."

Coats. Damn.

"I forgot my coat!" She turned on her heel, the restaurant now out of sight and the streets around them more empty.

"Matt can go back and get it," Kieran said. "Let's just get you in a cab and text him."

He put his hand on her lower back and began steering her away

"No, honestly I don't actually want Matt having any excuse to go back in there."

"I'll text him." Kieran's grip on her back intensified.

She frowned. "Like I said, I really don't want Matt going back in there."

"Well then, you stay here and I'll go."

His voice was edgy, distracted, and Lizzie felt the hairs on the back of her neck stand up. She took a step away from him.

"What's going on?"

"Nothing's going on, I'm just trying to stop you having to see your ex again."

"I'm fine. It was just a shock."

"It didn't look like that."

"Well, it was." She took another step away from him and turned to go back to the restaurant.

Kieran reached out and grabbed her wrist. "Lizzie, don't."

His grip wasn't painful but the touch of his hand made her body lock. She swallowed hard.

"What's going on?"

"He's your big brother, okay? I get it. Honestly, I do."

"What do you *get* exactly?"

Kieran refused to answer so Lizzie ripped her hand out of his and began to make her way hurriedly back to the restaurant. What was going on? What did Matt being her big brother have to do with her going back for her coat? She rounded the corner and the restaurant came back into view. Nothing seemed different, nothing had changed and nothing was immediately odd apart from the fact Matt was still on the corner with Zoey. They were deep in conversation with one another. Matt with his arms crossed defensively over his chest and Zoey gesturing wildly. She was shaking her head over and over at him, her cheeks flushed.

A movement caught Lizzie's eye.

The line of cars parked to her right of her looked odd; larger, misshapen and bulky. Slowly, her eyes began to clock the cameras and the people hunched behind them, and her heart began to jump in her chest.

She heard Kieran's foot steps behind her and turned around to face him.

"What's with all the cameras?"

"Come on, let's get you away from here before the drama happens." Kieran reached for her arm again, but she moved it behind her back.

"Before the what happens?"

"Matt didn't want you to be here. I'm supposed to make sure you leave, so come on!"

"Be here for what?" She turned back to stare at the restaurant.

Her heart slammed even harder into her ribs as she saw Charles, Daniel, Amy and Patricia coming down the stairs. A swell of nostalgia rose in her stomach. She hadn't even noticed they had all been there. Her eyes had only noticed Charles. Now, she took them all in, their familiar figures and the way they all seemed to move like a well-oiled machine. Charles and Daniel were close together, talking to one another animatedly, Amy was under her father's arm and Patricia hovered behind, talking to someone on her phone.

The cameras remained hidden and silent but, like crickets in the night air she felt them buzz, excitement running along the line of them as they spotted Charles.

She felt sick.

"What's Matt done?"

Kieran didn't reply. Instead he made one final attempt to grab her arm and pull her away. She slammed her feet into the floor again and sharply elbowed him in the side. The sound of the door reached her and she glanced up to see the four leave the restaurant, yet still the cameras did nothing.

Matt was moving around the corner. He had passed his suit jacket to Zoey, who had her hands over her face, and he was rolling back his sleeves.

Her stomach dropped.

"He set this up. He's going to hurt him," she whispered, turning her horrified look back towards Kieran. He didn't say anything.

Before she had time to stop herself, she was running towards her brother, desperate to get to him before he got to Charles.

"Charles!" Matt yelled, a look on his face Lizzie had never seen before.

Charles turned and instantly, like a switch had been thrown, bright flashes of white smashed into the side of Lizzie's vision as a chatter of clicks shuddered through her. It was nearly blinding and she wasn't even in front of them yet.

"Matt, stop!" She yelled, but her voice was easily drowned out. "Matt!"

He wasn't looking in her direction, he hadn't even noticed her moving towards him. His eyes were fixed on Charles.

She needed to stop him, to stop whatever the hell this was. But as Matt surged forward a sickening clamminess filled her chest as she realised she wasn't going to make it.

Matt looked terrifying. She had never realised it before but with his broad physique and his gym toned body, he looked like he could tear a person apart. He could tear Charles apart.

And Charles wouldn't fight him.

Lizzie knew that. If Charles was still anything like the man she knew, he would try and prevent a fight for as long as he could.

She yelled Matt's name again, but he was already only a few metres away from Charles and the sounds from the cameras were still drowning her out. Charles put up his hands in what looked like a calming gesture, his eyes fixed on her brother.

It all happened within the space of three seconds.

Matt reached Charles and with a burst of panicked energy, Lizzie reached Matt. She slipped into the small space between the two men, shoving Charles behind her just as Matt swung his fist upwards. A second blow cracked between her eyes.

Pain exploded through her skull and something sharp stabbed into her arm.

Shit.

"Patricia!" Someone yelled.

White.

That was all she could see and all she could taste was blood, pooling in her mouth and slipping out of her lips. The noise of the photographers became deafening as they screamed for her to turn and look at them, screamed for Charles to do something, and screamed for Matt and Charles to continue fighting. She couldn't think straight. All she could do was feel her face pulsing rapidly and she stumbled back into something solid.

"Lizzie, shit, Lizzie." Charles's concerned voice found her but she couldn't tell where it was coming from or remember why he was talking. Her mouth was ringing and she was starting to panic about the sheer amount of blood she could taste. She ran her tongue along her teeth.

Okay, at least they were still there.

Was her face?

And then everything sped back up. As her vision finally returned her legs crumpled beneath her, only to be swept up at the last second as a strong arm lifted her back up. There was blood everywhere, running down her face, seeping out from her lips and pouring from her nose as if it were an open tap. Her left arm was throbbing with pain.

"Oh, God," she whispered, bringing her hands up to cover her face as the cameras continued to snap away greedily. The blood seeped through her fingers onto a bright white shirt next to her head and she snapped her head up so fast she smacked the person holding her in the chin. Charles didn't even notice, instead he was turning with her and being ushered by the waiting staff into a side entrance as quickly as they could as they created a barrier from the paparazzi around them with their suits and bowler hats.

"Lizzie! Is she alright? Is she okay?" Matt's voice called out frantically to her amongst the noise but it sounded as if it was getting further and further away. "Let me go! She's my sister, I'm not going to hurt her!"

Someone was screaming and Lizzie shut her eyes to try and block out the sound. Despite herself, she tucked her head into Charles's chest. She just wanted it all to go away. All the noise, all the fuss, all the light.

And then she was being lowered onto metal stairs and the sound of cameras and yelling was cut off as a door swung shut.

"Lizzie," a hand cupped the back of her head, thin fingers brushing through her hair. "Lizzie, sweetheart, can you hear me?" It was Daniel. His calm, collected voice was so familiar and comforting, she just managed to stop herself sighing at the sound. Lowering her hands slightly, she opened her eyes.

Daniel was crouched down in front of her. He looked even paler than usual. His hand was the one she could feel on her head and his other was on her shoulder, his medical eyes running across her face. She nodded but more pain ripped through her forehead as a result and her lips parted in a groan. Amy stood at the bottom of the stairs, her eyes wide and shiny and her arms wrapped around herself. Lizzie itched to comfort her.

They were in a stairwell. Paint was peeling off the walls, the stairs underneath her felt cold and damp, and two of the waiters stood like guards by the black door they had come through. Patricia was just in front of them. She looked between Lizzie and Amy and quickly stepped forward, bringing the young girl under her arm and turning her head away. One of Patricia's shoes was in hand and Lizzie noted the red stain on the heel.

"Sorry." Patricia winced as she looked at Lizzie's arm. "I was aiming for your brother."

Lizzie tried to shake her head as if it didn't matter but it instantly began to throb harder.

"Don't do that," Daniel said sternly, stilling her with his hand.

Lizzie tasted more blood between her lips and forced herself to swallow to stop herself retching. She could imagine just what a state she was in by the concern in Daniel's eyes. He turned to talk to someone, asking for a first aid kit and whether an ambulance had been called.

"I don't need an ambulance," she managed to mutter but even speaking those few words sent a shudder through her head. Daniel ignored her and stood up.

"Just in case." Another familiar voice said behind her.

Shit.

For a few moments she had forgotten why she was there, what exactly she had been doing to get herself into this mess and who must be very close by.

She wasn't alone on her step.

The heat against her back was breathing. She cast a glance downwards noting another pair of legs, one either side of her own. Charles shifted himself so he was at a slight angle to her, and she felt his piercing gaze move over her face. She quickly covered it.

"Lizzie, look at me."

"I'll get blood on you."

He laughed softly.

"Think you've already managed that, are you okay?"

A bang made them both jump as a door further up the stairwell swung open and people came rushing down. The stairs shook with their pace and Daniel ran up to meet them, his long legs passing Lizzie's vision.

"Cartwright, look at me."

Cartwright.

The name slammed into her. He had always called her that. At first, she had thought it was because he couldn't be bothered to remember her name and was simply putting her in a category with her brother, but then she had started to realise he only said it when it was just the two of them. When Matt wasn't around. On their wedding night, she had asked him about it and he had laughed at her ridiculous theories, telling her it had just become a term of affection more than anything else.

It shocked her how strongly that one word made her feel and she found her eyes taking advantage of her momentary paralysis by flicking upwards and drinking him in. He was breathing heavily, his eyes dark with concern and she could feel a sharp tension in his body.

She dropped her gaze as her face began to heat and the dark, scarlet marks across his shirt quickly acted like a bucket of ice. She sucked in sharply.

"Charles, I'm-"

"It's nothing the dry cleaners can't fix," he said quickly.

"I'm so sorry-" She tried to recoil away from him but he didn't let her, one arm coming up to loop around her shoulders and pull her back against his chest.

"Lizzie, stop."

"No, no, no!" She reared back again, looking between them at the utter mess she had created. "I can fix it, I can get stains out with this thing I bought online. Well, Bex bought it and I borrowed it once and still have it. It's really good, I promise. But blood comes off in the wash sometimes, doesn't it? Maybe I could just stick it in with some of mine and bring it to you, I'm sure I-"

"Lizzie, stop," he said calmly, watching her in amusement. She quietened as she saw the warmth in his gaze. His blue eyes tracked over her face again and she felt him squeeze her shoulder softly. "You shouldn't have done that."

"He was going to hurt you. I had to."

Something unreadable passed behind Charles's eyes.

Daniel returned and sat himself down next to Charles, a first aid kit in his hand. He glanced between the two of them, a smile at the corner of his lips and Charles quickly looked away.

"Someone tipped off the papers that there was going to be a fight. Patricia has just gone outside, she's screaming at them," Daniel said softly, opening up the small green box and quickly removing any contents he didn't need. He took the ice pack and scrunched it up in his hands before handing it to Lizzie. "Place this on the bridge of your nose."

She did as she was told. "Thanks."

"This thing is a mess," he said, shaking his head as he pulled more contents out of it. "Why does no one ever check their first aid kits?" He passed her what looked like a bandage. "Not what it's meant to be used for but just try and stop the bleeding. Lean forward, don't lean back.”

Amy appeared at his side to help. She began putting all of the useless stuff he had emptied out back into the box neatly, her curious eyes swinging up to look at Lizzie. She smiled at her when their eyes met.

“Your arm looks like a bullet wound.”

Lizzie couldn’t help but laugh.

“Amy!” Charles said, but he couldn’t disguise the laugh from his voice.

“It’s a flesh wound,” Daniel said quickly. “It’ll heal. No scar and no bullet wound. I didn’t realise Patricia’s shoes were so lethal.” He turned his gaze to admonish Amy. “And don’t scare her.”

She just laughed.

Lizzie swallowed. “It was Matt, I am so sorry I had no idea.” The brothers exchanged wary looks. “I promise it wasn’t me. I would never, ever do anything like that.”

“I know,” Charles said. “It’s more than your job’s worth.”

“It’s got nothing to do with my job. I wouldn’t do that to you.”

Their eyes locked for a fraction of a second and for a moment, she saw a flicker of confusion pass behind his eyes.

A loud bang made Lizzie flinch and Charles’s grip around her shoulders tightened momentarily as paramedics surged into the stairwell, accompanied by more blinding white light.

“I really don’t need all this fuss,” she said quickly, trying to pull herself up off the step but her body swayed. Charles was instantly at her back, steadying her. She grabbed the bannister to stop herself completely leaning into his touch.

In a swam of green, the paramedics crowded her, taking away the bandage, handing her tissues, tilting her head further forwards, taking away the ice pack, giving her a new one, and assessing her face for damage. She bit back cries of pain as they moved her head this way and that and one of the men placed a comforting hand on her shoulder. It felt cold and small. Too late she realised the heat behind her had gone and she could no longer feel Charles’s gaze on her skin.

"Ch-" She stopped herself just in time.

He wasn't her husband anymore, she reminded herself, and the pain in her head seemed to intensify. He couldn't just drop everything and come to her rescue. He wasn't the person she was meant to want in these situations.

He wasn't even a friend.

She swallowed and leaned more into the paramedic's touch, trying to seek the comfort she wanted from it. The taste of iron was still strong in her mouth and the throbbing in her ears increased as the stairs seemed to swim underneath her.

It was strange how even though she was surrounded by people, she suddenly felt utterly alone.

Lizzie 19, Charles 22

Lizzie and Charles sat side by side in the study, their sides touching and their backs resting against the bookcase filled solely with Daniel's medical textbooks. Sound filtered up from downstairs, soft music and people's voices floating through the floorboards and lingering around them. Lizzie was playing with a toy giraffe in her hands, her fingers stroking over the soft yellow neck and her eyes staring off into the distance.

"Do you think we'll ever feel normal?" She whispered.

Charles's chest tightened and he turned his head to look at her. He itched to reach out and hold her, but she hadn't let him touch her since they had come back from the hospital. She had shied away from any type of contact with anyone, which was particularly hard when it was what he needed. He needed to hold her. He needed to feel her chest rise and fall against his own. He needed to press his face into her hair and breathe her in.

"Of course," he said briskly, "absolutely." He tried to give her a reassuring smile but she looked away as if upset by what he had said. Charles looked down at his hands, the gold wedding band still looking so fresh and new on his finger.

It had been one of the happiest days of his life. A bright October day full of family and friends. They hadn't stopped laughing and smiling all day.

Little had they known that just a couple of months down the line their life was going to completely derail.

Charles had proposed to Lizzie when she had told him she was pregnant. It hadn't been quite the way he'd ever planned to propose, but he already had a ring and had talked to Matt two weeks before that ridiculous warm night in June. He just hadn't yet found the right moment to get down on one knee and ask her.

Leo intervened.

They had managed to sort themselves out quickly and were married a few short months before he was born. Despite it being October, Lizzie had sweated like it was the summer for the entire day and Charles had dropped literally the first thing he'd dared to put in his mouth down his suit. He'd got drunk and sung ABBA loudly and appallingly whilst Lizzie had found herself in a cutlery orchestra with Daniel. They'd danced. Lizzie stepping on his shoes more than once, and he'd laughed so hard he couldn't breathe when she got stuck during a twist under his arm.

It had been magic.

Yes, Leo hadn't been planned.

Yes, it was probably not the best timing.

Yes, they were young.

But they loved each other and had been prepared to give this baby everything.

But now, two weeks after he had been born, they were upstairs.

Hiding from their own baby's wake.

He felt tears on his face again and he quickly wiped them away, taking a slow and steady breath. He couldn't break down. Not in front of Lizzie. He needed her to know he was there for her when she was ready to be with him again. He needed her to think of him as strong and safe, just like everyone was telling him –

The brush of her fingers against his startled him and he turned his head sharply to look at her. Through slightly blurred vision he could see she was looking up at him, her eyes glassy and in her other hand she offered him the giraffe. He took it from her, emotion swelling his throat as he closed his hand around the small toy. It had been the first toy he had bought Leo. He'd bought it only a week after Lizzie had told him she was pregnant. At the time she had rolled her eyes at him and told him he was an idiot. But it had become the toy they had taken to every doctor's appointment.

Now, even its soft fur felt cold in his hands.

"Please stop pretending you're okay," Lizzie whispered. Her voice croaked out of disuse and he turned his head away from her momentarily, swallowing hard.

"I have to."

There was a slight pause. "Not for me, you don't." She sighed. "Especially, not for me."

He still couldn't turn his head back around to look at her, scared his emotions would give him away. "I can't-," he paused, fearing he was about to break.

Slowly, Lizzie rested her head against his shoulder. He closed his eyes, tightening his grip around her hand as the weight of her on his shoulder sent crippling waves of comfort through him.

"Lizzie?" His words caught in his throat.

She nodded against his shoulder.

"I'm not okay." He sniffed sharply, trying his hardest to stop his chest from shaking. "I really wanted to be a dad." He dropped his chin to his chest and for the first time, let the weight of grief utterly consume him. He felt Lizzie wrap her arms around his neck and bury her face into his neck.

This time, he didn't stop to wipe the tears from his cheeks.

CHAPTER ELEVEN

Lizzie had ignored both of her alarms. She didn't want to get out of bed, she didn't want to open her eyes, and she didn't want to face reality in any shape or form. Sleep had been brief, interrupted regularly by sharp pulses of pain running down her face and a constant feeling of dirt in her mouth.

Bang. Bang. Bang.

She pulled the blanket up and over her head. It was a Saturday. She didn't have to work and she didn't have to get out of bed. She was allowed to be as lazy as she wanted, especially when she had been in hospital till 3 in the morning.

Bang. Bang. Bang.

She ran her fingers over her face as gently as possible, flinching the moment she placed the slightest bit of pressure on her bruising. The doctors had said nothing appeared to be broken but she had to go back for tests in three days. One of her eyes, however, was nearly swollen shut and the cut on her arm stung. She felt like she had decided to run into a brick wall.

At the sound of the front door being thrown open Lizzie sat up and the sudden sharp spike of pain in response almost knocked her down again. Two people had keys to her flat - Matt, who she didn't want to see, and Peggy, her landlord who lived upstairs, who she also didn't want to see when she looked like this. The old lady might have a heart attack.

"Who is it?" She yelled.

The bedroom flung open and Bex stood angrily in her doorway, hands on her hips, hair pulled up into a high ponytail and her glare causing Lizzie to slink back under the covers of her bed.

"I have been banging on your front door for the past half an hour!" She snapped, dropping two large tote bags onto the bedroom floor. "You look like shit."

"It's not that bad-"

"It's horrific. It looks like you're one of those creatures David Attenborough finds in the depths of the Mariana trench."

Had she rung Bex last night?

She looked like she had just come from the gym. She was wearing bright red leggings, a black t-shirt that said the words 'Bring It' on the front, and she'd wrapped a jumper around her waist. Despite her attire, her face looked blemish and sweat free whilst her hair was styled perfectly.

"Thanks."

"I am being serious," Bex bent down to open one of the bags she had by her feet and took out a large packet of salt and vinegar crisps. "I thought these might be needed."

"Did Matt call you?" She went to frown but pain flickered around her eye sockets and made her head reel.

"No."

"Did I call you?"

"Oh, hun." She laughed, throwing her head back and practically cackling. "No. Even with blood all over your face I would recognise you anywhere!"

She threw back the corner of the duvet and pulled herself into the bed, rearranging the cushions so she could sit up.

"Recognise me?"

Bex was still not making any sense but then again, maybe Lizzie still had concussion - the doctors had warned her it would be a possibility judging by the force her brother had punched her with. Her best friend leant over the side of the bed to grab the same bag she had got the crisps from and tipped it up. A bunch of heavy papers fell from it, spreading their pages like open wings over the dark purple duvet. Lizzie stared down at them, her eyes slowly adjusting and seeing herself over, and over again; her with her hands over her nose; her lifted up into Charles's arms; her with blood running down her face.

"You!" Bex said, stabbing the pile of newspapers with a perfectly painted nail.

"Shit," Lizzie whispered. She sat up and grabbed at the papers, staring at her face and the words underneath them but not really reading them, instead her eyes scanned back and forth across the pictures.

"Shit indeed." Bex leant down to the side of the bed and reached for the other tote bag. She took out two tall dark black bottles. "So, I brought the sparkly stuff as I thought it would taste best with a hangover."

"I don't have a hangover."

"No, but your face is smashed." She laughed at her own joke.

Lizzie continued to flick through the newspapers, picking up one after the other, over, and over again. What had she done? What did this mean? Would work find out? Could she be fired for this?

Questions flew through her head but, despite the seriousness of the situation, her eyes kept being pulled to the look on Charles's face as he'd realised Lizzie had been hit. Her stomach did a weird kind of drop thing: he looked terrified.

There was one photo that showed Lizzie scooped in his arms. What surprised her was it looked as if Matt was going for another punch but Daniel and a waiter had managed to grab his arm. Charles hadn't noticed. He was just staring at her as she had rested her head against him. He didn't seem to have even registered the fact she was getting blood all over him.

Emotion clogged inside her chest.

A loud 'pop' from just by the side of her head made her drop the papers and a black bottle was thrust in front of her face.

"Drink!" Bex commanded.

"It's the middle of the morning!"

"It's actually lunchtime."

"What?"

"Yeah, it's one-thirty in the afternoon."

"I-I-no." Lizzie dragged a clammy hand across her head, pushing her hair back against her scalp and trying to make herself relax. "I never sleep in." Even when she tried to she was rubbish at it.

"Clearly your head injury knocked you out for the count. Did you go to hospital?"

Lizzie nodded and took a sip of sparkling wine. The fizz made her cough as it hit the back of her throat.

"And what did they say?"

"I had a scan," she gestured at her face. "I'm fine...well, they think I am fine. I have to go back in three days just in case. The swelling might be hiding a fracture."

Bex opened up another bottle of sparkling wine. The cork flew across to the other side of the room and landed by the side of the dressing table. She took a lengthy sip and managed not to smudge her lipstick.

"So… are you going to tell me what happened or am I going to have to read about it?"

Lizzie fell back onto the pillows and groaned. She didn't want this. She didn't want any of this.

"Do you think I'm going to get fired?"

Bex snorted with laughter. "No. Come on, you're barely recognisable and the newspapers haven't named you yet. So far, you are a mystery woman who jumped in front of Charles Williams." She wiggled her eyebrows. "Exotic."

"It's not exotic at all."

"It is. Now spill."

She closed her eyes and tried to calm the churning nerves in the pit of her stomach. Before now, she hadn't even thought about the newspapers or the fact she would be plastered all over them. All she had been focused on in the hospital was over analysing all of the emotions she had felt when with Charles. "It was Matt."

"Matt?"

"Yep, Matt."

"Matt, what?"

"Matt hit me."

"Matt, Matt? Our Matt?"

"That's the one."

Bex took a small sip of her wine before replying seriously. "Do you want me to kick his arse?"

Lizzie laughed but it quickly turned into a groan as it sent shockwaves of pain vibrating through her skull. She put a hand to her forehead.

"No. I don't think that will be necessary, but thanks. I think security took him away."

"He's in prison?"

"I don't know." She shut her eyes. "Does that make me awful? I just came back here and fell asleep - hang on, how did you get in here?"

"Peggy gave me her spare key. I've always loved her. I was banging on the door for ages."

Everyone loved Peggy. She was in her eighties, with short, wispy, white hair and freckled skin. In her youth, she had been a professional tennis player. When Peggy's husband had passed away she had decided to convert her house into flats as she missed the sound of other people. She had become a surrogate family member and had a particular soft spot for Matt. She was whacky, insisted on living on the top floor despite her age, and was always wearing bright pink ankle skirts.

She had been a big part of the reason why Lizzie had agreed to move back here despite the memories of her past life.

"That was you? That banging woke me up."

"Clearly not straight away because I wouldn't have had to stand there banging. Now, why were you, Charles Williams and Matt in a fight?"

"Matt was aiming for Charles."

"Ya-uh. I got that part." Bex fixed her with a sharp stare. "This is about the Banned List, isn't it?"

Lizzie looked away. All these years she had managed to not say anything, kept the past hidden well away, skirted around questions about past relationships and managed to finally stop Bex setting her up on blind dates. Bex had never even asked about why Charles was on her Banned List, so not talking about it had been easy enough. However, all of a sudden, she could feel the truth pushing down on her chest with such a force it was beginning to hurt.

Lizzie couldn't tell Bex everything. Obviously. But maybe she could tell her a slightly blurred version of the truth.

"The reason he is on my Banned List, and why I acted like a fool on Tuesday, is because Charles and I used to date."

Bex paused, nodding slowly as if taking this on board before turning, picking up the nearest newspaper and rolling it into a tube. Lizzie watched her curiously, wondering what she was about to do, when Bex turned back and proceeded to smack her over the head with it.

"Ow, face!"

Bex ignored her and did it again but harder.

"I don't care about your stupid face. Can you repeat that again please, because I think you just told me you used to date a celebrity and hadn't told me about it?"

"It's not really the first thing to spring to mind."

"Oh, don't give me that bullshit! Dating a celebrity? Really? Not the kind of thing you'd tell the person you're supposedly closest to? After all the dates I've tried to set you up on?"

Lizzie groaned. "Okay, when you put it like that it sounds awful."

"It is."

"I'm sorry-"

"Don't apologise. It's too late." She threw her a haughty look.

"Come on-"

"Just!" Bex held up a hand, put her bottle of wine down on the bedside table, and scooted herself down further into the bed. "Tell me everything."

Lizzie blinked. "What do you mean?"

"What do you mean, what do I mean? How you met, how you got together, how long were you together, why did you break-up?" She raised an eyebrow. "All the things you're meant to have already told me."

Lizzie blinked. "Right, well, um…" A brief summary. That's all she needed. And she needed to say it fast, like ripping off a plaster. "He was Matt's best friend. We had known each other for a long time, grew up together, that sort of thing." Even just the basic facts stung. "And I started to fall for him." *Understatement.* "And one day, I had enough of fancying him, and not knowing where I stood, so I kissed him."

"How old were you?"

"Me, seventeen. Him, nineteen."

"Knew it."

Lizzie frowned. "What?"

"You were drunk, weren't you?" Bex said, her lips tilting into a cat-like grin.

She scowled. "Only a little bit."

"Exactly, you would never just kiss a guy. I like this young Lizzie's confidence. She going to be making a comeback anytime soon?"

"I can be confident!"

Bex raised her eyebrows at her and didn't bother to respond.

"I can be confident, Bex!"

"How long did it take you from realising you liked Charles to kissing him?"

She licked her lips and pushed a strand of hair behind her ear. "He could have made the first move, you know?"

"How long?" Bex repeated more firmly.

Lizzie took another swig of sparkling wine. "Three years."

"Points to me."

"Anyway," Lizzie said pointedly. "Mum interrupted us and sent us to bed."

"Ooo, how unorthodox of her!"

Lizzie smacked the back of her hand across Bex's arm. "Not like that! Charles was always staying around because of Matt. Mum sent us to sep-ar-ate bedrooms and I was humiliated, dying inside, nothing like your mum grabbing you by the hair and ripping you off a guy's lap-"

Bex choked on some of the wine she had just taken a generous swig of. "You were straddling him!"

Lizzie flushed red. "I was drunk, okay?"

Bex clapped her hands delightedly. "So, nooowwww you admit you were drunk! I'm so asking Jean about this next time I see her."

"I'm not proud of it!"

"You should be! Women taking charge." Bex punched her free arm into the air. "We need more of that."

"Well...well, anyway, Charles followed me to tell he that he had feelings for me too."

"Had he not kissed you back?"

"Well, yeah, but I still got scared maybe I'd imagined it or he was just being nice."

"Just being nice?" Bex snorted. "Guys don't kiss you back just to be nice. Especially if they are your older brother's best friend."

The ghost of a smile crossed Lizzie's lips. She remembered the night so well. The way Charles had suddenly walked into her room. She had been throwing her dress in the wash bin, her huge men's size pyjamas hanging off her, and she had forced her hair back into a tighter ponytail. Mascara had blotted her cheeks, making her look like something from a Halloween film, and her eyes had been red and raw. But he had looked at her...well, he had looked at her like she was the most beautiful thing he had ever seen. She hadn't had the chance to ask him what he was doing before he had strode up to her and kissed her. She remembered the way her breath had caught and she had gripped his arms extra hard, expecting him to disappear like he was a dream. But he hadn't. He'd been very, very real.

"We dated from then on. Kept it a secret for a little while but Matt apparently knew the whole time. And then we broke up."

She sat up and pushed the blanket further away from her chest. Suddenly everything felt too warm and too close. She shifted trying to get comfortable and the packet of crisps on the duvet rustled.

"And you broke up because…?"

"We just did. We fell apart. He went to University and I stayed at home."

Bex didn't even question her response and Lizzie didn't know whether to be pleased at just how well her lie-telling had improved, or to feel guilty for not telling the truth.

"And Matt hates him because you were his little sister?"

She nodded, focusing on Bex's shoulder as she did so, playing with one fine piece of brown hair in her fingers. She would have tied it up but she had no clue where any of her hairbands were. Usually she woke with one around her wrist but not this morning.

"Matt never approved of us dating. He didn't like the idea of Charles and me being together. Protective brother versus best friend kind of thing."

Bex pulled a face. "Matt never came across as such a hot head."

"Boys," Lizzie said with another shrug, the pain in her face making her feel only the tiniest bit guilty for painting her brother in such a way. The ache around her nose was slowly starting to increase again, and she wasn't sure if it was her imagination but she swore she could taste blood. She reached for the packet of salt and vinegar crisps.

This seemed explanation enough for Bex, she nodded and rubbed her hands together, the wine bottle cradled in her elbow. Lizzie sunk lower into the mattress, trying to box all of her emotions back down inside of her. Unfortunately, no matter how hard she tried, a wisp of pain and longing still managed to escape. She forced the packet of salt and vinegar crisps open and scooped a handful into her mouth, the taste biting down on her tongue sharply and distracting her.

In the brief snatches of sleep that she had gotten the night before, she had dreamed of Charles, of being in his arms, of being cared for by him. Nothing explicit and nothing passionate, but just the feeling of being held had made her feel so content and warm. She reached for another handful of crisps as she tried again to push her feelings away.

She could do this, she could get past this, it was just a blip. She had pushed away thoughts of Charles Williams for over a decade. She could do it again. The box had opened but she could shut it again.

She could.

"So, if you two broke up amicably, and you two knew each other from when you were children, why did you pretend to be someone else? Back in the studio."

Lizzie swallowed, staring up at the ceiling. "I thought he didn't recognise me. I panicked."

"You thought he wouldn't recognise you?" Bex repeated slowly, like she was stupid.

"Yeah, and I was nervous."

"And that's why he is on your Banned List? Because you didn't want to be nervous around him?"

Lizzie hummed in agreement. "Yep."

"You realise that sounds like utter bullshit?"

Lizzie jerked her head around to look at her. "No, it doesn't!"

"It really does. Why would you care if you were nervous?"

"Think of how unprofessional it would look if I was nervous around one of the talent?"

"Surely you'd just be nervous for your first meeting? After that it would be fine. Not a big enough deal to ban the poor guy. I got nervous around Margot Robbie and she was a bloody angel. I didn't ban her from the studios because of it."

"I could have made a complete fool of myself!"

"You did."

"An even bigger fool! I might still do! If I act like that for the entire film, who on earth is going to take me seriously?"

"You know I'm a girl's girl, first and foremost, but even I don't think that's a good enough reason to ban him."

"Would you want to work with your ex?"

"Fair point." Bex pursed her lips and took another sip of wine. "You never get nervous around men."

"Yeah I do."

"Never. I have envied you so much for that. A cute guy comes to talk to you and you're pleasant but cool. Helpful, disinterested, unbothered." She scrunched up her nose. "I mean Neil's a good-looking guy, attractive if you're into smug arseholes, and yet his flirting and his charms never made you so much as smile, which is why you two are now such good friends."

"He never flirted with me."

"Hun, that boy sleeps with anything with a heartbeat. Yes, he did."

"He hasn't slept with you."

"He tried. I made it perfectly clear I would dismember him in his pursuit." She shuddered. "I might date some pricks but I never date younger than me. If guys my age are too immature, what would the younger generation be like?"

Lizzie laughed, wincing again as the pain in her nose reminded her it was still there.

"Is dream guy older than you then?"

"You're trying to distract me."

"Well, is he?"

Bex smiled softly. "Thirty-eight."

"Specific."

"I told you." She tapped her head. "This is not a joke. I genuinely think this is the universe's way of telling me there is someone out there that I'm just missing."

"And you're sure you haven't seen him in the gym?"

Bex elbowed her hard. "How many times do I have to tell you and Matt he doesn't go to the gym!"

Lizzie laughed. "Okay, okay!"

"Anyyyyyywwwway, back to you and Charles Williams."

Lizzie groaned dramatically. "Do we have to?"

"People don't usually get that nervous over a guy who they

haven't seen in…what was it?"

"Thirteen years."

"Thirteen years. I mean it's weird you'd even – oh, my, God!" Bex raised herself up slowly onto her elbow, her eyebrows so high up her forehead they were almost hidden. "Lizzie Cartwright, have you dated anyone since him?" The question hung in the air between them.

Lizzie held her gaze for a fraction of a second before looking down at her hands. "What do you mean by date?"

"Jesus Christ!" Her best friend shook her head, throwing her arms up dramatically before sinking down lower in the bed so that she was side by side with Lizzie. "Well, it doesn't take Einstein to figure out that you still care about him."

"I don't."

"Yes-," Bex took a crisp and crunched loudly on it as if to make her point. "You do. One thing in particular makes it painstakingly obvious." Bex tapped her nose, eyeing her friend cheekily. "I don't think I know anyone who would take a punch to the face for their ex." She brushed a few hairs back from Lizzie's face. "Especially a punch from Matthew Cartwright."

Lizzie smiled. "Don't know how you always end up looking fine after kickboxing with him."

"Oh, he wouldn't dare aim for my face. If he tried he wouldn't be able to have children." She grinned, winking at her.

Lizzie's chest tightened with emotion and she dug her fingernails into her palms, praying Bex wouldn't notice her sudden locked muscles. She let out a fake bark of laughter and flipped onto her back.

For a few, short, peaceful moments she'd forgotten the real reason Charles and her had broken up.

…Or, more accurately, why she'd made sure they had broken up.

Lizzie 28, Charles 30

Charles was sat on the sofa, marking spread out around him in a fan formation. His eyes felt gritty with tiredness and he could feel the ache in his upper back protesting against how he had been sat nearly all day.

When had he gotten old?

Next to him Lizzie was still staring at her phone, her finger scrolling back and forth across the screen and her eyebrows furrowed.

"You okay?"

She made a sound between her lips, which he wasn't sure to take as a yes or a no.

"Something wrong at work?"

She looked up, her frown dipping for a fraction of a second. "What?"

He nodded at her phone.

"Oh, no. I just…" She turned to look at him, crossing her legs up under her. "Do you think it's weird?"

"What's weird?"

"Weird that I'm not pregnant yet."

He started, a smile almost breaking across his lips until he caught her serious expression. "No," he said quickly, shaking his head. "Hadn't even thought about it. It's been two months."

They had decided at Christmas they wanted to try again. It had been Charles's suggestion, and God, how he had fretted over bringing it up for months before, but on Christmas night they had lay in bed and discussed it properly. To his relief, Lizzie had been feeling the same.

"I know but last time I got pregnant when we were using protection. So, I just thought that without it, it would just...happen."

"I don't think it works like that."

"No?"

He reached over and placed his hand on her knee. "I really don't think we need to worry."

"Really?" She thrust her hands behind her head to tie up her hair and he eyed the movement cautiously, worry tightening in his chest.

"Honestly."

She pulled sharply at her ponytail and let out a sigh. "Okay." Charles saw some of the tension leave her shoulders but her eyes remained distant. "I guess Daniel did say coming off the pill messes with your hormones for a while."

He shifted in his seat, a frown appearing across his forehead. "You talked to my brother about this?"

She shrugged. "He's a doctor."

"He works in A&E."

"Still a doctor." She sighed, leaning her side against the back of the sofa.

"You talked to my brother before you talked to me?"

She looked up, her eyes soft and he saw her cheeks tighten as she swallowed. "Sorry. I...I didn't want to bother you with it and I thought maybe I was overreacting...which I guess I am doing now. In both senses."

"Lizzie, you're my wife, I *want* you to bother me with everything," he said, fixing her with a mock-stern stare. "Especially if it's about us having a baby."

"Sorry... I was just so worried."

"I promise you don't have to be." She still didn't smile so he moved his work off his lap and reached out a hand to hold hers. She didn't look at him, instead her gaze was focused on their hands and even when he squeezed hers, she didn't look up. "Why don't I leave the rest of this marking and we can go out? See a movie or something?"

"You don't have to do that."

He leant across and kissed the top of her head. "It's rare you get a Saturday off these days. I should be making the most of it." He frowned, realising he was actually making a good point. "Sorry."

She sighed dramatically and a genuine smile flickered across her face. "I know, you used to be such a romantic, I've clearly been rubbing off on you too much." She rolled her eyes jovially before finally meeting his gaze, her features relaxing somewhat.

Guilt flickered in the pit of Charles's stomach. When was the last time he had done something romantic? Lizzie always pretended she didn't need him to be, but he liked the way she smiled when he did something spontaneous. He liked the way her eyes would light up as she chastised him for doing something extravagant. He liked showing her just how much he loved her.

"Charles," she said gently, bringing his attention back to her. "It was a joke, I don't expect you to drop everything just because I'm home for a whole weekend." She pressed a sweet kiss to his lips and squeezed his hand back.

"I know, but still, I miss you. A weekend off is once in a blue moon moment. We should make the most of it."

"We've been married nearly ten years, I don't think it's in the rule book to make the most of weekends together anymore."

"Clearly, we have different rule books." Charles winked at her and Lizzie gave a short bark of laughter, her eyes lighting up as their gazes met. "So, movie?"

"I'll go get showered." She stood up, leaning over to kiss him on the forehead before she left the living room.

Charles watched her go, his brow furrowing as she turned her back to him, her ponytail swinging out of sight. Slowly, his eyes were pulled to the mobile she had left on the sofa. Despite himself, he picked it up and the page she had been reading lit up as he lightly touched the screen. At the top of the screen was what Lizzie had typed into the search bar.

Does stillbirth affect fertility?

He swallowed.

Is that what she was really worrying about?

The article she had been reading stated there was no link between stillbirth and the ability to conceive. But even so, the words did little to ease the new ache in his gut. He believed it - he wasn't one to question science - but he knew Lizzie wouldn't have. The fact she had searched it showed him she had probably already made up her mind.

CHAPTER TWELVE

Turning up for work on Monday was less embarrassing than Lizzie had anticipated. It was raining so she had taken the tube to work, and, typically, nobody gave her bruised face the slightest bit of attention. Or, if they had, they had hid it well in the 'look up, look down' British fashion. As more and more people piled into the office and didn't ask her about it - even Annie hadn't flinched when she asked her if she wanted a cup of tea - she felt calmer and more relaxed. Maybe it was similar to spots, the way everyone always thought theirs stood out with red angry arrows pointing at them whereas no one else actually noticed. Even so, she still kept one of Bex's old caps pulled down low over her head.

At around 10.30 a.m. Neil slipped into the seat beside her. She turned to smile at him and he physically recoiled away from her.

"What the fuck have you done to your face?"

Silence descended in the office and she felt the hungry curiosity of her fellow colleagues turn towards her.

So, it was noticeable then.

They had all just been bloody waiting for Neil to arrive, knowing full well he didn't give a damn about being polite or subtle when it came to her.

"I had an accident." She pulled the cap down lower, which simply triggered Neil to lean over and pull it off completely. "Hey!"

"Do you have an abusive boyfriend you haven't told me about? Because that's not fair, I told you I need a text the moment you break that century long dry spell."

"Neil," she snapped, looking around, embarrassment burning at her cheeks.

"I'll make sure I give him a thank-you card before I punch him. What happened?"

"I tripped that's all." She sank lower in her seat.

Neil paused, his eyebrows knitting together into a frown. "Okay, I was joking about the abusive boyfriend, but now you're making me think there is some truth behind it."

"I got into a fight, okay?"

Neil snorted. "Okay go back to the tripping, I believed that more."

"My brother was in a fight and I tried to break it up. I ended up getting punched in the face."

"Whiskers, you're a right idiot sometimes, you know that?" He leant forward to examine it closer. "It's some pretty bad bruising you've got there. You took quite a punch. I'm impressed." He turned back to his desk. "You're lying though."

"No, I'm not!"

"Yes, you are."

"No, I'm not!"

"Why bother with the 'I tripped' if you actually broke up a fight involving your brother? Why lie in the first place if that was the truth? It's hardly embarrassing, is it?"

"I-"

"Don't even try it, Whiskers. No point." He still didn't look at her but his smile grew as he entered his password into the work computer. She could feel he was itching to say something else.

"What is it?" She snapped, irritated.

"Must have hurt, getting punched by your brother."

"Well…yeah." She tried to reach past Neil for her cap. Without even looking he moved it further out of her reach.

"Wasn't he on the rugby team at school?"

Lizzie froze, her eyes fixed on Neil and something uncomfortable crawled up her spine.

"How do you know that?"

"He was going to be quite a big deal, wasn't he? Till he got suspended from school for breaking another kid's collarbone during a rugby match." Neil's smile grew. "Apparently the kid deserved it though. Five minutes before that he had dislocated someone's knee on Matthew's team during an illegal tackle."

Lizzie remembered the day well. She had been watching them from amidst the crowds. She had seen Charles go down and saw the twisted mask of pain cross his face. The sight had caused her heart to slam to a halt in her ribs. She had wanted to rush out of the stands to see if he was okay but the amount of people pressed around her made it impossible. And then her eyes had caught Matt. The relief she had felt as he'd reached Charles had made her sway. The fury pulsing through Matt's body had been obvious to everyone. He had practically vibrated with it. A weird hush had fallen over everyone watching as he had pinned his gaze on the boy who had done it.

It hadn't been an accident.

Later, they found out that the team they had been playing had placed bets on who could bring down Kenneth Williams's son.

Matt had known it wasn't an accident straight away.

Either way the boy from Hemel Boys School hadn't stood a chance. Lizzie wasn't quite sure why Matt had even bothered to wait for the game to restart. The moment the whistle was blown he had slammed into him. His collarbone had broken as he'd hit the floor and Matt had been suspended from school.

"I told you I'd find out, Whiskers."

She turned back to her computer, trying her hardest to push her shoulders back and look somewhat sure of herself. "I'm not exactly sure what you think you've found out."

Neil finally looked at her. He watched her as she brought her e-mails back up and under his gaze she felt her face get redder. Slowly, he moved his chair closer to hers. "Tell me, friend to friend, did your brother's best friend bully you? Is that why you're terrified of him?" His eyes traced across the side of her face mischievously. "Or, and I think this is more likely, did you fancy him?"

She snapped her head around to glare at him. "I know you think your journalistic skills are amazing, but you're wrong."

Neil wasn't riled by her response. He leant back in his chair and regarded her with a smug smile. "You're right. Fancying him wouldn't be enough of a reason to put him on your Banned List. So...?" He waited, his eyes scanning over her face.

"So, what?" She snarled.

He remained still, barely looking like he was breathing as his gaze grew more intense and assessing. "You were in love with him."

Anger rushed through her. "Where the hell did you get that from?"

He simply smiled in response. "You tell me."

She ducked her head even closer to his. "I'm not in bloody love with him, are you insane?"

"Did I use the present tense?"

"Shut up!"

His eyes ran across her face. "You dated him, didn't you?"

"This is not work appropriate conversation."

"Oh fuck off, Whiskers."

"I will report you to HR."

"Go ahead, Katherine wouldn't dare tell me off."

The type of smile changed on his face for a split second. Lizzie closed her eyes painfully, she knew that smile all too well. "Oh, my God, you slept with her."

"Yep." He gestured from his mouth to hers. "See how easy that was? To admit the truth?"

"You slept with our HR representative?"

"Means I never have to worry about getting told off. Win, win." He leaned forward. "And stop trying to distract me."

"I'm not."

"I will find out, Whiskers, I'll find out whatever it is you are hiding. I'll find out everything."

Well, that was categorically not true. He would never be able to find out everything. No one could.

No one would believe her even if she told the complete truth.

Her shoulders hardened and she witnessed the first flicker of doubt she had ever seen cross Neil's expression.

"No, you won't."

"Lunchtime." Neil nudged her arm.

"I'm not that hungry," Lizzie said. She hadn't had much time to check her e-mails at the weekend, it had been too painful to do anything but lie on the sofa staring at the ceiling and consequently, she had a lot to catch up on.

"That's not true. Your stomach has been making disturbing noises for the last hour."

"No, it hasn't."

"Trust me, Whiskers, it has. Come on," he reached for her arm and tried to physically pull her from the chair.

"Neil, stop it!" Lizzie couldn't help but laugh as she wrapped her legs around the bottom of her chair and tried to clamp her hands to the desk. "Get off me!"

"We have to give you sugar or you get grumpy!"

"Neil! You can go to lunch by yourself."

He let go of her. "Fine, bloody workaholic. Want me to get you anything?"

"No, I'm good."

"Go on, call it my charity for the ugly faced."

Lizzie laughed, shaking her head at him.

"Honestly I have a can of soup in my bag if I get hungry."

"How very exciting. Well, if you're sure." He shrugged and left the office.

Lizzie smiled after him before turning back to her desk. She was alone in the office, the only sound coming from the radio in the corner of the room and the clock. She glanced around, wondering what they had all really thought when they had seen her that morning resembling Will Smith in *Hitch* after his allergic reaction. How had Annie managed to keep such a neutral face when she had spoken to her? She tried to catch sight of herself in her laptop screen to see if the swelling had gone down at all but she couldn't make out anything.

Her face was really starting to throb, the painkillers she had taken that morning had faded a long time ago and her stomach was, now she thought about it, rumbling quite loudly. What she really fancied with her soup was a piece of bread. She pulled out her phone to text Neil but when she sent it she heard a ping on his desk - he had left his mobile. The door opened behind her and she tutted loudly.

"Actually, I've changed my mind, could I get some bread?" She turned around waving his phone at him before her amused expression slackened.

Charles smiled at her. "I think that's a fairly easy request."

CHAPTER THIRTEEN

Her heart shot into her throat. Charles's tall, strong figure stood in her office, smiling down at her. She quickly stood up, dropping the phone back onto Neil's desk.

"Hello."

"Hello."

"What are you doing here?"

She wasn't prepared for this. She really wasn't prepared for this. Why was she never prepared for this?

It was like being back at the restaurant again but a hundred times worse. Her body was humming at his proximity, her blood heating at just the sight of him, and she was grateful her face was more a purply puce colour so she could hide how strong a blush had risen in her cheeks.

He scratched the back of his neck. "It was the only way I could think to check on you without breaking all data protection regulations. May I?" He gestured at Neil's empty seat and she nodded, wincing as the movement caused a bullet of pain to shoot through her skull. He was dressed in dark black jeans and a light blue jumper that looked practically mundane compared to his eyes, his hair was in its natural wavy state and he looked somewhat unsure of himself.

"How are you?" He scanned her face carefully as he sat down and she ducked her head self-consciously, wishing she had put Bex's cap back on.

"I'm okay." Her chair squeaked awkwardly as she sat too.

"Is anything broken?"

"They can't be sure yet but I'm sure it's fine."

He leaned further towards her and his cologne hit her. The spike of lust it shot up her spine forced her to bite down on her lip to stop herself from outwardly reacting. Why did he have to smell so good?

"He really went for it, didn't he?" Charles winced.

"Honestly, it's much worse than it looks- I mean better! It's much better than it looks."

Charles laughed as she flushed even redder. The sound did nothing to stop the new nervous flutters in her stomach or lower the uncomfortable warmth in her face.

If she really thought about it, she actually preferred it when he had been angry and aloof. That she could deal with. Whatever this was, she couldn't.

"I'm so sorry, Lizzie."

"It wasn't your fault." Could he please just leave? Every part of her body was so aware of his closeness that it was making her skin prickle uncomfortably.

"I should have done something. I'm sorry we didn't stay. Patricia said we should leave you to it."

"It's all fine. Really." The look of concern in his bright blue eyes pushed at some of the walls she was holding up.

"I wanted to stay."

Lizzie felt emotion tug at her throat and she pressed her palms into her thighs to make it subside.

"Honestly, you really didn't need to have done. I'm fine. I'm just going to look like the elephant man for a couple more days."

"It doesn't look that bad."

She raised her eyebrows.

"Liar."

His face broke into a laugh and his eyes danced with mirth. "I'm being serious."

"No, you're not, you're being Charles." She rolled her eyes at him, with her bruises even that was a struggle.

Their eyes met and an unreadable emotion passed across his face.

"Can I?" he gestured with his hand towards her face.

She swallowed. "Sure."

What was he doing?

No, seriously, *what was he doing?*

He didn't need to examine her face. He wasn't a doctor! Yet he had asked the question and now he had to go through with it. She flinched slightly as he took her chin in his hands and he quickly apologised for the firmness of his touch. She had looked away at his comment, her face reddening.

She felt thinner beneath his hands, her face smaller than he remembered and her eyes looked so much bigger. He tried to look at the bruising as if he was actually examining it, but instead his eyes were taking her in, focusing on the woman he had miss- not seen properly in over a decade. He still couldn't believe that a woman he thought despised him, had taken a punch for him.

And not just any punch. Two punches from Matthew Cartwright.

Instinctively he wheeled himself that bit closer to her, his eyes raking over her skin. She was blushing. Even under the bruising he could tell that and he wasn't too sure what to make of it. Was she embarrassed he was there? Their knees knocked together and his stomach tightened involuntarily.

Really?

What the hell was his body doing?

"Do you think I'll live?" She said, her lips quirking into a smile whilst her eyes avoided his.

How had this happened? How had his anger towards her turned so swiftly into concern? The moment he had realised she was in front of him, a split second before Matt's upper cut hit her, it had vanished as if it had never really been there. Instead, something more real had flared up inside him, and it was yet to go away.

"Charles?"

Their eyes met and he realised he had ignored her question.

What had she said?

Shit, how was he suddenly so close to her?

"Close call, but you might just make it." He let go of her chin and sat back quickly. "Does it hurt?"

She considered his question. "Do you want me to lie?"

"No."

"Then yeah, it does."

She pulled a face and he laughed at her expression, feeling a warmth and familiarity settle in his bones that he didn't want to analyse.

"I'm sorry," he said, unable to shake the guilt he felt at the sight of her.

"Stop apologising." She nudged his leg with her knee affectionately. Instantly her smile dropped, and she pulled back quickly, rolling her chair at least half metre away. Fear, once again, threaded itself through the backs of her eyes. It was like she was meant to be playing a role and yet the real Lizzie kept breaking through it, in her smiles, in the way she had protected him, in the way her eyes met his, but what was the role for? Why was she putting on a front in the first place?

That wasn't all he wanted to know. Since the anger had cleared, curiosity had also begun to stir within him. He wanted to ask her questions. About everything. From when they'd broken up until now. He wanted to pry open the shell she was clearly caught inside and find all the answers to his questions.

He thought back to Patricia on Friday night and the telling off he had received the moment the chaos had cleared.

His sister was right. He *should* want nothing more to do with Lizzie Cartwright. His mind just hadn't registered the message yet.

He cleared his throat. "I also came to warn you that my PR agent is releasing a statement that the incident was because of a drunken, jealous boyfriend." To his surprise his words were transforming her nervous expression. Her eyes met his with a slight glint behind them and she rolled her lips together. "What?"

"No continue, please go on."

Charles pulled the collar of his jumper away from his neck.

"Well, the story is you were a fan getting slightly too excited - are you laughing?"

"Sorry," Lizzie said, her shoulders had started to shake and her cheeks had pinkened again beneath the purple. She wiped a tear away from her eye and flinched slightly as she brushed over her bruising. "Go on?"

"You got slightly too excited over the fact I was there." He couldn't look at her, she was shaking with laughter and he could feel his face reddening. Why had he agreed to this? "And your boyfriend got jealous."

"And?"

"Well, that's it really."

"So, because I was a crazy Charles Williams obsessive fan, I was frantically falling all over you and all of your fantastic-ness and my boyfriend got pissed off."

"Yes."

"My boyfriend who's actually my brother."

"Yes." He couldn't look at her, instead rolling his foot to the side and looking down at the sole. Heat rose higher in his cheeks. "Just to clarify, I don't think anyone would be falling all over themselves because of me. Patricia thinks it'll make the whole thing more masculine so-"

"Patricia?"

Charles winced. "She's my head of PR."

"Patricia is the head of your PR?" Now she wasn't even trying to disguise her laughter.

"Yes."

"Why?"

"Unfortunately, she is actually pretty good."

Lizzie laughed and although embarrassed, Charles found himself beginning to smile. "Lizzie, stop it."

She shook her head and her eyes sparked even more. "And she thinks this will make you look more *masculine*?"

She said the word as if it disgusted her.

"Apparently, a woman taking a punch for me isn't quite the image she wants us to go for."

"Wow, she really hasn't changed much, has she?" Her eyes ran up and down him and he shifted uncomfortably.

"She thinks it will attract more roles."

Lizzie shook her head. "You should have hired Lottie. At least she would have been pleasant to work with!"

His good mood dropped at the name of his little sister, his heart beating harder in his chest. "You know why that wouldn't work."

Everyone had known. Guilt fisted tightly around his chest. Lottie had been a good distraction in the end from thinking of Lizzie, but slowly, she had gone further and further off the rails. She'd never been the same since the night of his grandmother's party.

He hadn't been able to save her.

"Charles?" Lizzie leaned forward, resting her arms along her thighs. "What is it?"

"Lottie and I don't speak anymore." He raised an eyebrow. "Surely, you knew that?"

"Why would I know that?"

"I thought everyone in Tring knew."

She stared at him, her brow dipping. "No. What happened?"

"She doesn't speak to any of us."

"No, that's not-" She stopped herself. Concern flared across her eyes. "Why? When?"

"It's a long story."

But for some reason he felt a pull inside his chest to confide in her, to tell her, to bring her back into his life when he really shouldn't.

She broke that need as she quickly leaned back away from him, a new tension in her body that hadn't been there before.

"Of course, sorry."

And like that, she reminded him that she was no longer part of his life. Not a friend, not a close friend and definitely not a girlfriend.

Just a colleague.

"I better be going." He stood up and flattened his hands down his jumper. "I got you something." He opened his battered leather satchel that Patricia had specifically banned him from keeping. "Patricia suggested a big payment as a thank you-"

"Excuse me?"

"Don't worry, don't worry." He laughed and looked up to see her horrified expression. "I knew you wouldn't accept that. And you hate flowers -"

"I don't hate them -"

"You just kill them."

Lizzie smiled shyly. It made his heart quicken in his chest and he quickly ducked his head.

What the hell was wrong with him?

"So, I got you...," he pulled out a large jar of peanut butter. "Just in case it was still your thing."

She stared at the item in his hand, her eyes round and her lips ever so slightly parted. He had thought it had been a great idea, buying something she would actually like but not big enough to embarrass her but now...now he was starting to feel very, very stupid. His cheeks reddened again and he wished he could rewind the last two minutes.

Why had he got something so personal? Why had he chosen to get something that would so evidently point towards their shared history? Their long nights of sitting in his conservatory, their legs entwined as she ate from a tub of smooth peanut butter and he would eat from a crunchy one. The many times he was in the Cartwright's kitchen and he would grab the tub off Lizzie so her mum didn't catch her eating it - Jean Cartwright thought anything with a high calorie count was the equivalent of cocaine. The way she'd always bring a jar for him and a jar for her when she had come to see him in university. They'd sit up late discussing everything that the other had missed over the past few weeks until their spoons hit the plastic bottoms. Charles shifted on the spot, the memories causing a whirlwind of longing and regret to stir in his chest. Lizzie still hadn't moved.

Charles cleared his throat. "But obviously if you hate-"

"No, you," she licked her lips nervously. "You guessed correctly." She took it from him and continued to stare at it for a couple of seconds. He saw her visibly swallow and push back whatever she was thinking before she looked at him. Was she remembering the same things? Did she even remember anything so specific about their relationship? She'd always joked that he was the romantic one in the relationship. Was he simply being an idiot? "Thank you."

"No problem." He nodded, still trying to figure out what was behind those dark green eyes. A part of him that he couldn't push away really didn't like the fact she had got better at hiding her emotions. "Thank you again. See you soon."

He turned to the door and his head jerked back slightly as he realised they weren't alone. Neil Grayson was stood in the doorway. His hands were resting on his hips and there was a smirk across his face as he surveyed them both.

CHAPTER FOURTEEN

"Sorry to interrupt, I forgot my phone." His tone was lazy and relaxed but his bright eyes showed he was anything but sorry.

"Neil!" Lizzie said, sounding startled.

"Hey, Whiskers," Neil replied. His eyes, however, didn't move from Charles.

"Hi," Charles said curtly. "How are you?"

"Good," Neil responded simply. Something glinted behind his eyes and he took an obvious glance between the two of them. "Remind me again how you two know each other?"

Charles swallowed. "Old friends."

"Neil," Lizzie said, standing up. Her tone was warning and low.

"Old friends," Neil said casually, as if Lizzie hadn't just barked his name across the room. "So, what was with the whole Patsy Whiskers thing?"

"Ignore him, he thinks he's funny." Lizzie's hand briefly touched Charles's elbow but by the time he turned his head to look at her, she'd slapped it down to her side.

He was still curious about the Patsy Whiskers thing too but he'd already spent too long in Lizzie's company for today. He needed to try and squash whatever the hell was happening inside his chest every time she smiled or her eyes caught his, and to do that, he needed to leave.

"I'll see you around, Lizzie. Thanks again."

"No worries," she said quickly, still not looking at him, but instead staring at Neil as if he were a bomb about to explode.

Charles nodded at him as he passed and Neil smiled back. There was something careful about his expression. Charles had studied human faces a lot, trying to perfect emotions and hidden secrets as best he could. Behind Neil's smug exterior there was a protectiveness he was trying to hide.

Charles left the office, hearing the door shut behind him, but as he walked down the stairs he heard it open again and Neil call his name.

He sighed, running his hands through his hair as he turned up the stairs to face him.

"How can I help?"

Neil was fast. He was just one step behind him.

"I know you two used to date," he said simply, not even bothering to keep his voice down. Luckily the staircase seemed as empty as Lizzie's office. People swarmed the corridor below but it was humming with so much noise that they couldn't be overheard.

"Right."

Was this part where Neil warned him to stay away? Or told him that they were a couple now so Charles had no chance? Something folded deep inside him and he furiously ignored it.

He did not care if Lizzie had a boyfriend.

Good for her.

"Look," Charles said, desperate to get this over with, "I have a girlfriend if that is what you're concerned about."

"Concerned about?" Neil repeated slowly, the corner of his mouth lifting into a sardonic smile. "Oh, you think I should be threatened by you?"

Charles's felt his ears burn with embarrassment. "No, I was just letting you know in case Lizzie and you are…" He gestured with his hands.

"Are what?"

He was laughing at him. Charles could see it in the quirk of his lips and the spark behind his eyes.

"Are together."

Neil crossed his arms across his chest. "Are together when? At work? Yes, all the time."

Charles gave him a cold stare. "Are together as a couple."

Neil tilted his head to the right. "Would that bother you?"

"No, like I said, I have a girlfriend. So, if you two are together…?"

He didn't give him an answer. "Look, feel free to come in here, make your move, give her all the peanut butter you like. Honestly. Flirt, whatever-"

"I have a girlfriend."

"Yeah, I heard you," Neil shrugged. "My sources say otherwise-"

"Excuse me?"

"Just don't hurt her again, okay? Simple, really. Don't be a prick."

"Hurt her?" The words took him off guard.

Neil eyed his surprise.

"Yeah. Hurt her. She hasn't dated anyone the entire time I've known her. And I've known her over six years. And seeing as you are the first guy I've seen her act completely loony over, I'm guessing you're the one who hurt her." His eyes grew more serious and his tone less cheery. "Trust me, I get it. I don't do relationships either, but there's women who can handle that and there's women who can't. Lizzie can't. So, if that's what you're looking for, look elsewhere."

For a second Charles was speechless, a fist of anger formed in his chest and his eyes narrowed. He fixed Neil with a hard stare.

"I think you'll find, Mr Grayson, that your sources aren't completely valid. I didn't break up with her."

A beat passed.

"You didn't?"

"No."

Charles waited for Neil's reaction.

Instead of a frown or surprise, or even an apology, the other man's face broke out into what looked like fascinated delight. "Well, well, well, the plot thickens." He rubbed his hands together excitedly and Charles's anger was replaced momentarily by disbelief. "You'll be very pleased to know then that I've now switched sides. Let me know if you need my help!" Neil winked at him and began to move back up the stairs.

"Help with what? Neil, I have a girlfriend!"

"Sure you do!" Neil said, turning away from him.

"I do not feel-," he flicked his eyes around them, checking no one was around. "I do not feel that way about Lizzie."

"Sure you don't."

"I don't!"

Neil stopped at the top of the stairs, teetering slightly and then, with almost the elegance of a dancer, he spun and walked down the stairs again, taking two at a time. When he was back in front of Charles he stared at him for a couple of long seconds, a smile across his mouth and an intensity in his eyes that made Charles uneasy.

Just as Charles was about to ask him what he was doing Neil's hand came out of nowhere and grabbed him by the chin.

"What the hell?" Charles said, trying to shrink his head back but finding Neil's hold was actually rather strong.

It tightened. "What? I thought this was a friendly gesture?"

"What are you talking about?"

"It's quite intimate really, when you think about it. Wouldn't you agree?"

Charles didn't respond this time, the hairs on the back of his neck standing up as it finally clicked into place what Neil was referring to. Neil moved Charles's chin side to side, as if examining his face before bringing their faces closer together.

"Wouldn't you agree?"

"Yes." Charles bit out.

The snake-like grin was back. "So, why did you do it to your ex just now?"

Charles shoved Neil's arm away.

"How long were you watching us?"

"Long enough that if you both weren't completely absorbed by each other you'd have noticed." Charles face flushed red and he opened his mouth to protest but Neil didn't give him a chance to interrupt. "You might be better dressed than me," He flicked his head up to the top of Charles's, "and taller, but you're still a man. Holding a girl's face is a move and you know it." He raised his eyebrow. "And examining her face is an open invitation."

Lizzie 28, Charles 31

She was trying her hardest not to cry, letting her nails bite into the skin of her thigh as hard as she could, welcoming the sting of it. The white stick dropped into the bathtub and she dropped her chin down onto her chest, closing her eyes in pain.

Not pregnant.

Again.

They had been trying for nearly a year and still there was nothing. She thought it would be easy. Last time they hadn't even been trying, they had both had some form of protection, they had been careful, so, why on earth couldn't she get pregnant when they were actively trying? It made no sense. She ran her hands through her hair, pulling it into a tighter ponytail to try and stop herself from crying.

What is wrong with me?

It was the happy ending. It was the formula. Films, books, theatre, all showed people getting married and then having babies. It was just the next step, right? It was just the next rung on the bloody ladder. So, why wasn't her body doing it?

She stood up, put the thing she had come to despise in the bin, washed her hands, and headed back into the corridor, trying her hardest to stop her frustration and sadness seeping out into the flat. A few months ago she had stopped telling Charles when she was late, instead trying to wait till she had done a pregnancy test before getting their hopes up, but unfortunately her soul didn't seem to get that message. It always hoped no matter what. For the five days leading up to her period and every day after she was due, she was convinced that this time was different. That this time it would happen.

But it never did.

"Do you want a coffee?" Charles called from the kitchen, his voice sounded heavy with sleep.

She gritted her teeth and tried her hardest to not snap her response.

"No, thanks," she called, "I don't drink caffeine anymore, remember?"

She had told him a million times. Why didn't he listen? He should remember these things! She had given up coffee because all the websites told her she should stop drinking caffeine if she wanted to better her chances of conception. She had showed the websites to him. Why the hell didn't he bloody remember?

Deep down, she knew she wasn't really angry with him, but he just didn't seem to have the same sense of urgency as her. Charles wasn't bothered that she wasn't pregnant yet and that....frustrated her. Why didn't he care? Why didn't he get just as angry as her? Why didn't he want to do something about it?

Instead of walking into the kitchen she turned and walked towards the living room, wanting a bit more space away from him, but at the same time wanting him to hold her and tell her it was going to be okay. Her mind was a constant mix of changing emotions, like someone was shaking a bag of pic-n-mix around in there and couldn't quite get it sorted.

The one thing that was constant was the heavy feeling of failure on her shoulders. Her body was failing them.

Again.

She ran her hands through her ponytail. It was all going wrong. She was tired, more stressed, more anxious, snapping more at Charles, having less patience at work, feeling drained and sorry for herself constantly, and it was all because of her stupid bloody body.

Again.

She curled her arms around her waist, trying her hardest to keep everything within her, trying her best not to make a sound. The taste of salt on her lips let her know she was crying and she pressed her eyes together to try and stop it.

Just get over it, she told herself firmly. Onwards and upwards. If she let it stress her out or upset her, there was even less of a chance of them conceiving and she would just waste another good month.

Strong arms wrapped around her and pulled her into a warm body. She whimpered and slammed a hand over her mouth, simultaneously grateful for his comfort but resentful that he had found her like this. Turning, she pressed her face into his bare chest and he rocked her gently, dipping his head to press his lips against her hair and holding her to him.

"I'm really sorry," she managed to choke out.

"You have nothing to be sorry for."

His words made her grip him harder.

"I'm not...it's just...I really thought..."

He stroked his hands up and down her back.

"It's fine, honestly, Lizzie, it's not your fault."

But it wasn't fine. She knew it. In the depth of her soul she knew something was wrong. She pressed her face harder into his chest and a memory flickered strongly inside her mind.

Charles's heartbroken expression as he had held the toy giraffe in his hand. The moment he had finally stopped pretending he was coping fine with the fact they had lost Leo.

"I really wanted to be a dad."

She squeezed him tighter, her breath feeling painful in her lungs. What if...what if she couldn't give that to him?

CHAPTER FIFTEEN

Lizzie opened the door with almost a dramatic flourish before stopping sharply at the sight of the scruffy haired man in the hallway.

"Wasn't expecting you." She went to close the door but Matt caught it.

"I'm sorry, I'm sorry, I'm sorry, I'm sorry!" He raised his hands up high. "I didn't let myself in using my key this time! I knocked, see?"

It had been three weeks since the incident at The Prince's Regent and Matt had tried to come and apologise twice. Both times he had simply let himself into her flat. The first time Bex had been there, and he had backed out pretty fast at the murderous expression on her face. The second time he'd started off his apology really well but then had started trying to claim it wasn't his fault and that if Charles hadn't been there it wouldn't have happened.

They both walked into the living room in silence.

"Who were you expecting it to be?"

"Bex, she's meant to be coming over in a bit."

He winced. "Is she still mad at me?"

"Furious. I would avoid seeing her until at least the month mark."

He sighed. "Lizzie, I am really sorry for what happened."

She cast her eyes across her older brother's face.

It was her fault he hated Charles.

It was her fault they weren't the best of friends. Last time, they had been inseparable, Lizzie often having to fish Charles back from Matt's flat after work.

She knew the day she had sabotaged that connection had been

one Matt would never forget. A bit like with an embarrassing memory she had hoped the sting would fade over the years, but guilt had a timeless quality to it.

"It's okay." She held out her arms. "Hug?"

"Men don't give hugs!" Matt said in a gruff, deep voice. A smile broke out across his face as he scooped her into his arms and crushed her into his scruffy t-shirt. For a few seconds he simply held her. His shame was strong enough for her to taste and her anger towards him faded away completely.

"It's okay, Matt."

"I'm so sorry. I just- what he did - I-," she felt him sigh into her frame. "There's no excuses for what I did, but honestly I see him and his fancy lifestyle, and how well he has done for himself, and it makes me so angry."

"We've done well for ourselves too."

He squeezed her tighter. "Absolutely, but...but he doesn't deserve to have done well. You know what I mean? He doesn't deserve good things. He isn't a good person."

Guilt spilled into her chest and she made a non-committal hum between her lips. He let go of her slowly, stepping back and putting his hands on her shoulders.

"I'm your older brother, Lizzie. No matter what, I'm never going to forgive him."

"I know," she said softly. "Matt, I think you should sit down. I need to tell you something." She gestured at the sofa.

The sofa in her living room dipped more one end than the other, and the back was slightly frayed, but it was so comfortable Lizzie couldn't part with it. It was the kind of sofa that sucked a person into it once they had taken a seat.

"Spill," he said, doing as he was told.

She took a deep breath in. "I'm working with Charles."

Matt's easy expression fell and his jaw locked. She could see the amount of different emotions battling it out behind his eyes and she desperately wanted to reach forward and hold his hand, but she didn't dare move.

After a few painful seconds he managed to open his mouth. "What?"

"I'm working with Charles." She closed her eyes briefly. She really hadn't meant it to come out so bluntly, she had wanted to ease him into it, preferably with a beer in his hand. "*Censorship* is being filmed at Lightswitch Productions. I am the Production Coordinator for the studio."

He jumped up, his neck strained and his body tense.

"You're working with him!"

"I have to."

"But you said," he swallowed. "Ages ago, you said about your list…"

"Tyrone decided the film was more important."

Matt's eyes darkened. "Well, that's bloody outrageous!"

"That's what I said."

"Is this because of the restaurant? Did he force you to work with him?"

His words made her smile briefly. "No, it doesn't work like that. The restaurant didn't make a difference, it had already been agreed. And Charles isn't like that."

Matt's eyes narrowed. "I think the guy who left you, supposedly the love of his life, when you fell pregnant is capable of anything, actually."

Lizzie flinched.

And there it was.

The lie.

She tried not to show the sting of it flicker across her face.

It had been the only way.

The only way to stop Matt simply going to Charles and telling him the truth. The moment Matt had peeped his head into the family bathroom to find her at nineteen-years-old, screaming and surrounded by pregnancy tests, she had known she had to lie.

The world had given her the second chance she had asked for.

The chance to do the right thing and to let Charles go in the kindest way possible.

Unfortunately, Matt had been part of the collateral.

"He wouldn't have done that, Lizzie, you must have got it wrong. I'll go and talk to him." He made to walk towards the door, a small amused smile across his face. She grabbed him, her desperation rising.

"He told me I had to get rid of it, Matt. Told me he didn't want to be with me anymore and that he didn't want the baby. He didn't even give me a choice."

Matt shook his head, still looking amused. "But Charles would never do that. This must be some side effect of your pregnancy hormones. Jesus, he's going to have his hands full. I thought the crazy stage was later."

"He said he couldn't be seen getting a Cartwright pregnant!"

Something stilled behind Matt's eyes. The usual jovial dance behind his green eyes stopped. "…What?"

"It's just like Dad said. He's a wealthy dickhead who never really thought we were worthy of him anyway. He told me he was disgusted and for me to get rid of the baby and get out of his life."

It had been the first time she had witnessed heartbreak face to face.

She had delivered a low blow, knowing that her brother would never recover from her words, knowing her dad had said similar things often enough that Matt would believe it. The only way she had stopped him going over there and killing Charles was by insisting she wanted no one to know. She had told him it was embarrassing – Charles's rejection and the baby. She had begged him to stay inside and not to give Charles another thought. In the process, she had gutted her brother. The scars were still evident.

She'd done a horrible thing but for the right reasons. And a huge part of her still hated herself for it.

Matt sat back down and gripped one of her hands between his own. "Lizzie, promise me you'll stay away from him."

She blanched. "Of course I will! It's a film. It's work. I'm hardly going to be top of his friends list, am I? After you tried to punch him in the face?" She tried to make her tone light hearted and cheerful but Matt's expression didn't change.

"I know what you're like around him."

"Knew, you knew what I was like around him."

"Makes no difference. Who exactly have you dated since? Who have you trusted?" He arched an eyebrow.

"Who have you?"

Matt shook his head. "Don't try and make this about me. Yes, Charles is just another reason why I don't believe in long term commitment. Yes, if my best friend, who I thought was a stand up, genuine guy, is capable of fucking around my little sister, then anyone in this world is capable of anything." He let out a long breath. "They call it love but it means fuck all."

"Matt," Lizzie said, leaning towards her brother. "You can't mean that."

His jaw tightened. "I do."

"That's awful-"

"Promise me you won't go near him, Lizzie?"

"Matt, really-"

"Promise me." His grip on her hand became vice like.

"I promise, okay? I promise," she said softly. The tension eased ever so slightly from his frame. "Neil is dealing with the cast side, I am dealing with the crew. I've sorted it out so I never have to speak to him anyway."

That was true. Neil hadn't been pleased at first, but she had managed to finally annoy him enough to convince him it was for the best. She was dealing with any issues or circumstances revolving around the crew and he would do the same for the actors.

"Fine." Matt sighed. "But just remember whatever charm he puts on, he isn't a nice person."

"Matt-"

"No, wait, just listen. He wasn't there for you, he didn't look after you, he didn't care. It was all an act. All the time. Just like Dad said.

Just remember that."

She looked away. "I'll remember."

He raised his eyebrows at her.

"I mean it!" She stressed.

"Okay."

"Matt…" She hesitated, part of her wanting to shuffle away from any conversation containing the Williamses but part of her knowing Matt might be the only one able to answer her query. It had been buzzing in her head since Charles and her had spoken.

"Yes?"

"Do you know what happened to Lottie?"

He sat up straighter, his shoulders locking near his ears and she saw a pulse just by his right eye.

"Lottie Williams?" He clarified, even though they both knew who she was talking about.

"Yes."

He looked away and then back again, dropping her hand and pushing his palms along his thighs. "Why do you want to know?"

"I - I overheard Charles saying they no longer spoke. He was talking to Neil. I wondered if you knew why."

Matt smiled ruefully. "Just another good person he screwed over."

That's not what it had looked like to her. She knew what it looked like to hide painful memories. She had done it most of her life. In that moment, in her office, Charles had been doing the same thing.

"Lottie went a bit," he swallowed, "crazy."

"Crazy?"

"She believed she was from a different time. Believed she had already done this life. Like some overextended Groundhog Day."

No.

A cold anxious dread closed sharply around Lizzie's heart and she flinched. Matt gave her a puzzled look so she tried to make her face as expressionless as possible. Her heart was beating so fast she was surprised her whole body didn't vibrate with it.

"Go on."

"It made her do stupid things, risk her life all the time, act crazy." He looked away. "I found her once."

"Found her?"

"She was going to jump into the lake. It was freezing cold, around February time, and she was just in shorts and a vest thing. I told her she would die and she laughed at me." Despite what he was saying, a fond smile broke out across her face. "Quite mad."

"Did you stop her?"

"Try to stop Lottie Williams doing something?" He raised an eyebrow at her.

"She didn't do it!"

"She did." He shook his head. "I stayed with her. It was the middle of the bloody night, she needed someone there to make sure she didn't drown."

She stared at him. "And this...this was after...?"

"After Charles showed me who he really was? Yes." He shrugged. "But Lottie was too crazy to be mad at. She seemed separate from it all, you know? Like she was some kind of ghost who was simply hanging around and observing everything." He clicked his tongue. "Maybe not a ghost, like a really loud, annoying one. What are they called?"

"Poltergeist?"

"Yeah, a poltergeist."

"You kept her safe?"

He avoided her gaze. "She wasn't exactly in any immediate danger."

Lizzie leaned forward and squeezed Matt's hands. "It was good of you, Matt." He stared at the action and she saw a flicker of hurt cross his face.

"Lizzie, I'm not the bad guy here. Charles is the bastard, not me." He shook his head at her and pulled his hand away. "Sometimes I think you forget that. I would never have just let Lottie dive into that lake with no one around. She was sixteen."

"I know, I just meant...sorry. I know you wouldn't have."

He eyed her and she knew he didn't quite believe her. Hurt and frustration merged in his eyes.

"Please, go on."

"Fast forward a few years and the Williams decided they were going to send her away to a mental institution. Get her out of the way. Bit like what he tried to do to you. Send away the embarrassment. Get rid of anything that might tarnish the blessed Williams reputation."

Lizzie frowned. They weren't like that. She knew they weren't. They must have been really concerned about Lottie.

Matt continued. "She saw the emails. She was going to get picked up the moment the place had space for her. I was twenty-five by this point and we were already in London. She reached out to me."

Surprise rippled through her. "What?"

"Well, she knew how much I hated Charles. If she had turned to anyone else and asked for help, they would have probably told her family. Crazy or not, I didn't care. She was a nice person. So," he broke eye contact for a moment or two, "so, she came to stay with me."

"What!" She stared at him, her mouth wide open. "You're joking!"

"She stayed for six months tops. Till she got enough to save for her own rent."

"She was downstairs! You were hiding her? Here? The whole time?"

"I wasn't hiding her, don't be so dramatic, I was helping her out."

"Six months isn't long enough to save for rent."

"She went to Australia first, to see the Polleys. Worked out there a bit and...well, I helped her out."

She did a double take. "Are you serious?"

He shrugged and refused to meet her gaze, something unsaid hiding behind his expression. "I'm sorry if you feel like that was a betrayal."

"A betrayal? No, of course I don't think it's a betrayal." She stared at him, realising with a swell of love for her brother why he looked so uncomfortable. "Oh, you idiot! I loved Lottie, remember? Of course, it's not a betrayal. Don't ever think like that. I'm just…surprised. Really surprised." She swallowed. "Where is she now?"

"I have no idea. We lost touch over the years. We were never really friends, just bonded over a mutual hatred of her family."

She raised an eyebrow. "You weren't friends after living together for six months?"

He glanced at her, his expression sheepish. "Yeah, okay, we were friends."

"Matt." Lizzie shook her head with a laugh. "You don't have to hate the Williamses by default for me."

Especially not for her. She thought back to being cradled in Charles's arms, being looked after by Daniel, and then the few minutes in her office where every part of had seemed to spark at Charles's proximity.

Back in their old life Matt and Lottie had always got along. They liked to wind each other up constantly. Felix, Lottie's boyfriend, hadn't liked it at all.

"She…she knew about Charles."

Lizzie swallowed, her body growing cold again. "She did?"

"Yeah. I told her."

"Why would you do that?"

"Don't look so alarmed, she didn't tell anyone. It just confirmed her suspicions that "this time around", as she called it, Charles was an awful person. She kept going on about how "last time" he was a good person. I got a bit annoyed about it actually. Last I heard from her was when she sent me all the money I had ever lent her. It was just in an envelope." He leaned back into the sofa, shrugging his shoulders. "She left me a bit extra too. Told me to bet on Jodie Whitaker being the new Doctor in that show she used to love."

"*Doctor Who*, Matt, don't pretend you don't know what it's called."

He laughed and the sound caused Lizzie to have a small respite from the guilt and horror that had crept back into her body at the reminder that Lottie had remembered. All of this time and she'd had a friend that had remembered. A friend who would have been more confused and scared than even she had been.

Lizzie felt a desperate pull to talk to her. She wanted to see her, to ask her if she had any idea what had happened...to ask her if she blamed her. Part of her always wondered if it had been completely her doing. If it had been her wish that had been answered. But a larger part of her couldn't believe she would have that kind of power.

Lizzie 29, Charles 32

She picked up the pace, her feet almost falling over themselves as she dragged them across the sodden ground, her brain was too far away to really register her body was moving. Despite the slightly darker colour beneath her feet hinting at the fact rain had just been falling from the sky, all above was blue. Bright blue. As if it had absolutely no sympathy or remorse for how she was feeling. She pulled her sleeves further down her arms and shivered. She had left her coat in the room with no windows.

"Lizzie!"

She sped up, almost tripping over her shoes. She didn't remember how long she had run for or when she had stopped, but she hadn't expected him to find her so quickly. Upon hearing his voice, she didn't turn around. It wasn't till a large hand wrapped around her elbow and pulled her physically in the opposite direction that she dared to face him. Charles's eyes were filled to the brim with concern and the pity in his expression made her yank her arm away. She hated it.

"What? I'm fine!"

Something dark flickered in his expression. "Don't do that."

"Don't do what?"

His gaze penetrated her. "Don't shut me out."

She stared at him, her mind stubbornly determined to argue back but inside everything crumbling. Tears invaded the sides of her vision and she took a step away from him as he reached for her again.

"How did you know where to find me?"

"Because I know you."

She had walked far enough that trees now fanned overhead, their branches reaching for one another and the blue sky had to try to break through. Primrose Hill smelled of rain and newly cut grass. Most people were at work at this time in the morning, but there were still many people passing through the park. Happy, smiling, going about their day.

None of them looked as if their world was collapsing.

"Can we talk about this?"

"Nothing left to talk about." She turned and started to walk away but Charles quickly fell into step beside her.

"Yes, there is-"

"No, there isn't. It's my fault. Just like we always expected. Just like I predicted. It's my fault." The words felt heavy in her mouth, her lips barely making it around them.

His hand curled around hers and he pulled her to a stop again, not letting her continue walking until she looked at him. For a short while she simply stared at their feet. Her old trainers versus his old cap toe Oxfords.

Was she old now too?

Was that part of the problem?

She looked up at the sound of her name. Charles was blurred. A blob of blonde, blue and pink. When he pulled into his arms this time she didn't protest.

"It's not your fault." He repeated over and over, bending his head so his lips touched the top of her ear. She could feel the warm tickle of his breath against her but his words did nothing to ease the cold ache inside her chest.

It *was* her fault. The doctor had said Charles was all good to go, all boxes checked, and she...well, she wasn't. Low egg count, some sort of hormonal issue in her brain, some scar tissue from mild endometriosis in her tubes.

Not just one thing. A lot of things.

"At least we can identify the issue," the doctor had said.

At least.

She hated those two words.

At least you got nine months with Leo.

At least you now have an excuse to have lots of sex.

At least you had the chance to see your baby.

At least modern technology is now available to help.

She had run from the doctor's surgery. Not the moment he revealed the results or even when they were told to leave. It was when Charles was making another appointment for them to come back and talk through options. She had simply put her hand on the door and bolted. Truthfully, she hadn't even thought about it. Her legs had just moved on their own accord.

A question, one she had been forcing back, and back, and back as the doctor had spoken, reared up its head. She swallowed away her sobs, trying her hardest not to make a sound as Charles held her. She felt like she could smell the doctor's surgery on his clothes and it made her want to scream. The voice crept into her head once again as his hands ran up and down her back reassuringly.

If she had this much wrong with her now, how could anyone tell her what had happened to Leo wasn't her fault?

She pushed herself away from Charles, feeling her emotions crack inside of her chest.

"Lizzie, please-"

"Why did it have to be me?"

He stared at her, his eyes shining in the morning light. His mouth opened, then closed, then opened again as he tried to come up with something to say.

"Why couldn't it have been you?" She said tearfully, shaking her head and hating herself for having voiced the thought out loud.

"We would still be in the same position."

"No, we wouldn't." She took a step away from him. "Because I wouldn't be the problem all over again. I wouldn't be the one holding you back."

"You never -"

"I'm always the fucking problem!"

"That's not true! Lizzie, listen to me-"

But she didn't stay to hear his protests. They meant nothing. He could say whatever the hell he liked but she wouldn't believe him. Her feet slapped against the path and she felt a fresh wave of nausea run up through her as for once in her life, she wished she had stayed well away from Charles Williams.

CHAPTER SIXTEEN

September had slipped into October discreetly, the warmer days being blown away by browning leaves and scattered rain. Lizzie spent most of her time inside, surrounded by paperwork and without seeing the changing weather outside. Filming had started which meant early mornings and later nights. Her head practically rung from tiredness but she pushed it back, along with her hair, and forced herself not to slow down. Well, she tried to force herself. One night Neil had unplugged her laptop when she had gone to grab more coffee, he'd gone home with it on purpose just so she would go home.

The heated argument that had followed had definitely been one of their worst but it had ended with Lizzie asleep by midnight for once. She had felt better for it the next day but she hadn't admitted that to Neil.

The thing was, there was always more that could be done.

And she still wasn't quite happy with Annie supervising *Elevenses*. She was great at the job but Lizzie couldn't help but check in every night and simply...oversee what was going on. Annie was slowly getting more and more pissed off with her. She couldn't blame her, Lizzie would have felt the same had it been the other way around.

"Morning," Neil said, sitting down next to Lizzie as he got into work.

He handed her a coffee which she took gratefully, warming her hands around it, and he smiled at the croissant she had left on his desk from her own breakfast run.

"Thanks."

"Back at you." He stripped a piece away from the pastry. "So, what do you think the meeting's about?"

"Another day, another meeting I am not told about."

Neil raised an eyebrow. "Again? Have you checked your junk folder?" She threw him an incredulous look and he laughed. "Okay, sorry, course you have. Meeting. 8.30 a.m. Tyrone's office."

He spun his chair around to his laptop and began typing at the keys, after a few seconds he nodded slowly. "Oh, you were missed off the sender list." He frowned. "But it's about the crew so I am guessing that's a mistake."

"Even if it wasn't about the crew I should be in all the meetings," Lizzie said, giving him a cold side-eye as she turned back towards her own laptop.

"Chill out, Whiskers, I know that! All I am saying is that because it is about the crew, you especially wouldn't have been missed."

"It's 8.20 now."

"I know. Better get going."

Lizzie sighed, tightening her ponytail behind her. "If Tyrone really thought I was so important that this production couldn't miss me, why the hell does he keep not including me in things?"

Neil shrugged. "You'll have to ask him yourself."

"Maybe it'll prove a point if I don't go."

"Or maybe it will mean I just have to walk my arse back down the four flights of stairs to come and get you again."

She smiled. "Is that really that bad?"

"Yes, I'm knackered. Come on."

Rolling her eyes, she batted his arm away as he reached for her and stood up, grabbing for her coffee and closing her laptop. "Another late night?"

"Yep." Neil took another bite out of his croissant.

They walked together out of the room, their strides falling in unison.

"What was her name?"

He looked uncomfortable for a second. "It was Kacey actually."

He pointed at her quickly before she could reply. "And don't!" Lizzie grinned. "No, Whiskers! I refuse to let you go there."

Lizzie's grin widened. To see Neil actually worked up about something gave her immense pleasure. He gave her a filthy look as she continued to grin at him.

Kacey was a four-year-old girl with a mass of curly, black hair and the darkest eyes Lizzie had possibly ever seen. She was also the only female on the planet who had Neil wrapped around her little finger. When he had first moved to London, he had rented the spare room of Lara and Rupert's house. A year later Lara had fallen pregnant, so Neil had been set to move out when Rupert was hit by a car on his way home from work. Neil had stayed. He'd liked Lara and Rupert, and despite Lara telling him he would hate living with a new-born baby, he had stuck around to help. It was why he never brought women home and also part of the reason Lizzie knew, despite how frustratingly annoying he could be sometimes, underneath it all, Neil really did have a good heart.

"Was Lara in?" She asked, mock innocently.

Neil groaned. "I told you not to go there."

"Why not?" She asked, batting her eyes exaggeratedly at him.

"You know why."

"I like her. She kicks your ass."

"Yeah, she's great, but we're friends. Don't make it weird. Whenever you talk about her like this, I act weird around her when I get home. You put thoughts in my head."

"Thoughts that are just already there. I'm just unwrapping them."

He gave her a sardonic look. "How poetic of you."

"And you know the two of you are destined to be together."

"Rupert was my friend for God's sake."

"He was your landlord. And he liked you." She grinned at him as they began ascending the stairs.

"Don't think he'd have liked me very much if he thought I was going to screw his fiancée."

"Should I go all Neil-logic on you?"

"Neil-logic?" He raised an eyebrow but didn't fully turn to look at her.

"Far-fetched, annoying, but somehow turns out to be true."

He smiled slightly but didn't respond.

Lizzie continued. "So, you and I are friends. Right?"

"Debatable."

"And people make comments about us being together all the time. You never get weird around me."

"Where is this going?"

"But me teasing you about Lara makes you weird around her because you secretly do like her, you just haven't admitted it to yourself yet. Neil-logic."

"Neil-logic," he repeated, sounding disgruntled.

She shouldered him jovially. "You know I'm right."

"Shut up."

"You know it!"

"Change the subject, Whiskers."

"So, when are you going to ask her out? I'll babysit."

"I'm warning you."

"Neil and Lara, sitting in a tree," she took a swig of coffee, "K-I-"

"Have you got off with Charles yet?"

She choked on her coffee, grabbing hold of the stair's handrail and trying not to spit her drink all over Neil.

On second thought, maybe that wouldn't have been a bad idea...

He laughed loudly, the sound echoing around the stairwell, and when she turned her reddened face back towards him, his usual smug expression was back. "I did warn you."

"I hate you!" She gasped, trying to regain some composure but failing miserably. Pulling herself up, she straightened her clothes.

"I'll take that as a no or you wouldn't be so uptight."

"Neil!"

"Probably hasn't stopped you dreaming about it though."

"Shut up, now!" She snapped at him, trying her best to look as serious as possible. Neil raised a comical eyebrow at her.

"Might want to get in some practice beforehand, Whiskers, he's a celebrity now. Will have probably screwed tons of people."

"Just stop it." She walked away from him, pushing away the stupid feeling of hurt that had curled into her chest at his words. She didn't want to try and guess how many people Charles had probably slept with.

Neil didn't follow her. "When did you last sleep with someone?"

"We are at work!" She called over her shoulder.

"That's why I said slept and not fu-"

"Neil!" Lizzie snapped, stopping four steps up from him and looking around in horror. "Keep your voice down. Come on, we have a meeting to get to."

He didn't move. "You have slept with someone since Charles, right?"

"That's really not your business," she spluttered.

"Oh, dear God, it's worse than I thought."

"Shut up!"

"How many years has it been? Is this why you're a moody bitch most of the time?"

"I'm not a moody bitch! And I don't have to talk to you about my sex life." She turned and walked away from him again but he caught up quickly.

"So, no one since Charles?"

"I won't mention Lara again, okay?"

"Too late for that now."

"How would you even know if I've dated or slept with anyone, full stop?"

He raised an eyebrow at her. "Would that be whilst you're at your desk or *whilst you're at your desk*?" He whipped his side fringe higher out of his eyes and she literally saw the second epitome cross his eyes. "When did you two get together?"

She ignored him and kept walking.

"I SAID, WHEN DID YOU TWO GET TOGETHER?"

"Neil!" She shouted angrily, spinning on the stairs to glare at him.

Her eyes quickly ran over the space around them as panic flared in her gut.

"Well?" He said, lowering his voice to a normal level again.

"I was seventeen. Now, come on."

Neil's eyes sparked. "So, was he your first then?"

Her face was burning with so much embarrassment that she could feel the heat travelling down her neck and into her chest.

"We are at work," she hissed, motioning up and down the stairs. "Anyone could hear us, would you please shut up?" She turned away and began to walk up the stairs but Neil, once again, simply fell into step beside her.

"I totally get it now."

"Get what?"

"He was your first. Explains all the gaga-googooness."

"Gaga-googooness?" She hissed. "What the hell are you talking about?"

"Taking a punch to the face for him, putting him on your Banned List, all those times you are randomly on set."

"I am on set because I have a job to do!" They turned another corner of the staircase.

"But do you really have to go down there that often?"

"Yes!"

"I don't."

"You don't do your job properly!"

She had told Neil the truth about the punch to the face after he had caught Charles and her together in the office. He had practically put the dots together anyway. For the rest of that afternoon, he'd kept coming up with different scenarios and asking if she would ever take a punch to the face for him.

"So, not even a one-night stand? Was he just *that* good?"

"Neil, for the love of God, shut the hell up or I will throw you over these stairs."

They turned up the third set of stairs. Lizzie tried again to quicken her pace to get away from him but he managed to increase his own without even looking like he was trying to. She could see the landing to the floor just below Tyrone's office ahead and she knew the post room was up there. If they were going to bump into anyone on this walk up, they would be there, and she really didn't want anyone overhearing this conversation.

"Can't believe I didn't figure this out before," Neil said loudly.

"It doesn't make a difference. Can you please keep your voice down?" She pointed at the landing ahead.

Neil ignored her. "Really, Whiskers, you don't think that this has some kind of significance?"

She stepped onto the landing and her heart slammed to a stop. So did her body guessing by the fact Neil smacked into the back of her a second later. The coffee she had just swallowed threatened to come back up.

"Oh, hello Charles," Neil said, sounding gleefully. "How are you today?"

Charles's blue eyes met hers.

He had heard them. Every word. Of course, he had. The moment he had heard Lizzie's laughter coming up from the stairs he felt it zing through his entire being.

God, he was getting pathetic.

Over the last few weeks he had seen so much of her and yet none of her at the same time. She was everywhere. On every call sheet, cc'd into every e-mail, at every meeting, walking around set at least four times a day, and yet he hadn't *seen* her. There had been no one-on-one conversations, other than a very awkward moment when he had found her 'not hiding' - as she had stated - in between two prop bookshelves. Apparently a cameraman had been trying to find her to ask for the fifth advance she had given him that month.

'You never saw me' she had mouthed and they'd shared a smile before she had gestured to his hair and said, "It suits you".

The compliment had made him far too cheerful.

His hair had been cut very short to fit in with *Censorship*'s time period. He wasn't too sure if he liked it, he kept running his hands through it only to find there wasn't as much hair on top of his head as he was used to. But it had to be done, rules were rules. And if Lizzie liked it...well, it couldn't have been that bad.

Part of him felt awful for eavesdropping, the other half had been wondering how close he could get to the edge of the stairs and not be noticed. He'd tried to do the gentlemanly thing; cleared his throat, looked down at his phone and pretended not to hear any of the conversation. Unfortunately, his ears seemed tuned into them. No one else in the queue knew the Charles they were referring to was him, but he still felt his cheeks redden as he saw colleagues stop talking and exchange interested looks as they listened.

When he had heard Lizzie and Neil coming up the final set of stairs towards the post room, part of him had contemplated hiding behind the plant pot stood in the corner - it was too short.

"Hi, Neil. Hi, Lizzie."

He clocked Lizzie's blood coloured cheeks and wide eyes. She wasn't looking at him. Instead, she nodded quickly, her lips jerked into a half-arsed smile, and then she said, "Well, we must be going. Come on now, Neil."

Neil stood still, taking a lengthy sip of his coffee and meeting Charles's eye. "Did you enjoy being Lizzie's first?"

What the hell?

How did he literally have no filter? Something hard tightened in Charles's chest as Neil's gaze became challenging – the man knew what he was doing.

Lizzie choked beside him, sweat now beading along her forehead, and a flare of protectiveness sparked inside of him.

"Excuse me?" He said coldly.

He felt Lizzie's gaze slam into him and then felt its immediate loss. He wanted to reach out to her, to take away some of her embarrassment. He wanted to growl at Neil that it was none of his business. But right now, he was determined to win whatever weird staring contest this was.

Neil looked away first.

"First fist fight," he said, looking between the two of them innocently. "Sorry, is that a sore subject?" His eyes landed on Lizzie and his smile turned more gleeful. "Whiskers, you've dropped your coffee on the floor."

"Shit," Lizzie hissed, ducking down as the cup indeed was rolling away from her. It had splashed coffee all up her jeans and over her shoes. Charles hadn't even noticed.

"Are you alright?" He said quickly, walking over to her.

"Fine, fine, fine!" She said, her voice unnaturally high pitched. She still refused to look at him for longer than a second. "I'm all good. Don't worry." She raised a hand in the air to stop him crouching down to help. It also acted as an extra shield to hide her face. Taking a packet of tissues out of her pocket, she began to try and dab at the brown liquid now seeping into the carpet. It didn't look like it could be saved.

"Still waiting on an answer here?"

Charles turned to look at Neil. They were inches apart.

He straightened himself up, deliberately squaring out his shoulders before he folded his arms and pushed any embarrassment he had out of his expression.

Neil clocked his actions but it just made his smile widen. God, he was infuriating.

"Definitely helped to have her there. I still owe her for that."

Neil's eyes brightened. "How *much* do you owe her?"

Did he really have to make everything into an innuendo? He saw Lizzie try and subtly punch him in the foot. He pretended not to see and Neil pretended not to feel anything, although Charles noted his lips pinched ever so slightly.

"Quite a bit," he said, calmly, refusing again to look the least bit bothered by Neil's words. "Could have done with her help the first time. Matt's a strong guy."

Lizzie stood up so quickly it was like she had never been crouched on the floor. A damp tissue was in one hand and her empty coffee cup in the other. "The first time?"

Shit.

He hadn't meant to say that. Her face had paled but the colour of her eyes seemed to have intensified.

"There was a first time?"

"It was nothing."

"When was this?"

"A long time ago."

"When?"

"Lizzie, it's not important."

"When was it?"

He swallowed, casting a glance at Neil who, of course, at this moment in time, had nothing cocky to say.

"I was...twenty-three, I think."

"And Matt punched you?" He noted the way her hand was flexing around the damp tissue.

"Honestly, it's not-"

"Where?" When he said nothing she took a step closer to him. "Where was this, Charles?"

"Tring. Christmas Eve. Outside the church." He ran a hand through his hair. "Sorry, I didn't mean for you to find out. I realised it probably hadn't been your intention for him to do that."

"You thought I'd set my brother on you?"

There was a short silence. "For a little while."

"I thought you knew me better than that."

"I thought I knew you better than anyone," he replied roughly.

They stared at each other, Lizzie's breathing getting heavier as her gaze pinned him to the spot. There was hurt shining through from the backs of her eyes but she was trying to hide it.

What did *she* have to feel hurt about?

"Were you injured?" She asked, taking a step back. It did little to ease the new tension in the air.

"No."

"Matt didn't hurt you?" She raised an eyebrow. "At all?"

He ran a hand over his jaw and thought back to the two breaks and the dislocated knee. "No."

"You're lying."

"Lizzie-"

"You know I can tell when you're lying. I always can."

His lips settled into a stubborn line. "Touché, Patsy Whiskers."

They stared at each other, her angry gaze bored into him but he refused to tell her what she wanted to know. He hadn't wanted her to find out. Especially after she had been forced to take Matt-sized punches for him. A Matt who had been a lot bigger than he had been at twenty-three. Her anger was evident and a small part of him...God, a small part of him liked it. Liked that she was being protective over him. Liked that she cared enough to be angry with her brother. He pushed the feeling away, refusing to let it blossom or appear in his expression.

It felt like the temperature around them was rising. Lizzie was becoming all he could focus on, like everything else had been blurred out, and all he could see was her.

There was a loud slurp to their right.

Neil.

Shit.

"Hate to break this reunion up but we have a meeting."

Lizzie dropped her gaze, her cheeks flushing again and her hands soared up to tighten her ponytail. Charles pretended not to notice that the action caused the dregs of her coffee cup to soak into her hair.

"See you around, Charming," Neil said, with a smile.

He winced at the nickname – it just made Neil's grin broaden.

"Bye," Lizzie said curtly.

"Come along, Whiskers, before even I get turned on from all this tension," Neil said loudly.

"Neil!" Lizzie snapped.

Charles spluttered, completely losing any of the cool, intimidating bravado he had been trying to possess before.

"I'm so sorry, he doesn't mean that," Lizzie said desperately, her face now crimson.

"I do."

"Don't worry about it," Charles said, feeling his own face blush red and trying his hardest to stop it. "It's just Neil's way." He inwardly frowned at his response.

What the hell did that mean? He barely knew the guy.

But it appeared he'd said the right thing. Lizzie's face softened, her shoulders relaxing somewhat. "Isn't it just?" She threw him a grateful smile which caused something warm to settle in his chest.

Neil placed his hand on the small of Lizzie's back, throwing a wink at Charles as he did so, and began to lead her up the stairs.

He watched the pair of them go, seeing Lizzie pull away from Neil's grasp about four stairs up and start sprinting upwards.

She didn't look back.

Charles swallowed, trying to push what had just happened and the whole new bunch of emotions jumping around inside of him away. He turned back to the post room. There was no longer a queue and James behind the counter was reading a magazine.

"Hi," he said quickly, stepping forward. "Any post for Charles Williams?"

"Aye," he said. "Always is."

He turned and the moment Charles did not have to maintain eye contact with him, his mind jumped back to what he had overheard before Lizzie and Neil had come into view.

Had she *really* not been in a relationship since theirs? How was that possible? Why would she do that?

"Fancy seeing you here."

Charles turned his head to the right to see who had spoken. He recognised their voice but the cogs in his head didn't click until he laid his eyes on the man. He couldn't hide the shock on his face.

CHAPTER SEVENTEEN

Lizzie's back locked. Blood was thundering around her body with such force that her head was beginning to ache. The abused coffee cup was still in her right hand, squashed to such an extent it had now become a simple, soggy square of cardboard.

Tyrone wasn't looking at her.

It hadn't been a mistake. She had deliberately not been called into this meeting and Tyrone had looked extremely awkward when she had entered the room. His eyes had flitted to Neil in a panic. Lizzie had known that look.

Their scenic supervisor, Jayden Turin, had broken his leg. Tyrone had decided to take the issue into his own hands and find a replacement.

No one had informed Lizzie.

No one had informed Lizzie because Tyrone already had a pretty good idea who might be available for the job.

"He was the only Scenic Supervisor available," Tyrone said, looking tired.

Lizzie didn't feel an ounce of sympathy. She just felt angry and terrified, her stomach clenching hard at every thought of him.

"He's a carpenter."

"Was. He was a carpenter. Recently promoted so that's why he's free."

"That's what he says."

"I tried everyone."

"Why didn't you ask me to sort it?"

"Because I knew if every single person on this planet was busy you still wouldn't call him, you wouldn't even consider him and we need him."

She shook her head. "Promote someone else already on the team."

"No." Tyrone sighed heavily. "See, I knew you'd act like this. This was why I just wanted Neil in this meeting. So we could discuss this like adults and sort out a way to do this so that you wouldn't have to know."

The barb stung.

"This was the only option," Tyrone finished.

"But it wasn't. If you had let me do my job this wouldn't have been an option."

"Yes, and instead you'd be even more stressed, fretting over finding someone. This is the better solution."

Neil cleared his throat. "With all due respect, Tyrone, Lizzie's already been forced to work with one individual on her Banned List-"

"I am well aware of that." He laughed, looking at Neil as if expecting him to laugh with him. "She hardly made it easy for us, did she?"

Neil said nothing. He simply looked as if he were curiously inspecting Tyrone's face, finding it suddenly fascinating. There was something unnerving and serial killer about that look.

"I can't work with Craig," Lizzie said, firmly.

"You said the same thing about Charles."

"That doesn't matter, I won't work with Craig."

"Neil will deal with the finance side of things, the correspondence, any issues like that, and you can pretend your dad isn't even here."

But he would be there. The man she hated most in the world would be in her studios, in her space, in the place she had worked so hard to build herself up within.

And he would be working with Charles.

"He said he would be happy to put the past behind him."

Rage reared inside her chest. "Of course he did! He has nothing to put behind him! He was the problem!"

"There are two sides to every story."

She stared at him and felt something crack ever so slightly inside of her.

Tyrone was her boss.

She had trusted and looked up to him for so long but now…now, she just saw a selfish, inconsiderate man who didn't much care for his employees. Not someone to be trusted, not someone to be respected, not someone she should have looked up to.

"Yeah." She jutted out her chin and resisted the urge to tighten her ponytail. "And I told you my side of the story in confidence." She wanted to stir up some kind of response from him; a flicker of guilt or a remorseful comment or *something*.

His expression remained somewhere between tired and pissed off.

Was she going crazy? Was it ridiculous of her to have taken these lists seriously? Were they broken all the time and she just didn't know about it? Was she being unprofessional? Doubts, questions and uncertainties flitted through her brain and she suddenly felt very, very lost.

She felt about seven-years-old, sitting on the stairs and realising that no matter how many times she begged, Craig was never going to forgive her.

"He is your father," Tyrone said, leaning forward and placing his hands in front of him. She presumed he believed this would give him the look of an empathetic person but it came across patronising. "But don't we think it's time, at twenty-eight-years-old, you put this squabble behind you?"

Neil swore under his breath. "She's thirty-two. I'm twenty-eight."

A flicker of red crossed Tyrone's cheeks. "It doesn't matter. Look, we have no other choice. It's already done."

There was silence in the room.

Lizzie stood up slowly. "Okay then."

"If there was any other way, I'd follow it. You understand?"

"Sure," she said, because there was nothing else she could say.

Neil stood up beside her. She didn't look at him. She'd told him about Craig a long time ago. They'd both been drunk and he'd questioned her Banned List. She hadn't said anything about Charles, but she had told him about her dad. If anyone could sympathise about disappointing parents it was Neil.

He turned to her. "Lizzie, I need to have a quick word with Tyrone. I'll meet you back in the office."

Her eyes scanned his face. He wasn't going to leave with her. Even if he did have something to ask Tyrone, surely it could wait. Surely, Neil could look like he sided with her for once. Disappointment crunched inside of her gut.

"Sure."

"I work here."

Charles was struggling to keep his emotions under control. "You work here?"

"Yes."

"Does Lizzie know?"

The smile across Craig's face made Charles feel slightly nauseous. The man's teeth were still tinged yellow, his lips badly cracked and his face looked so much older than the last time they had crossed paths. His skin practically sagged into his skull.

"I'm sure she will find out soon enough."

"Parcel, Charles."

Charles turned to look at James as if he was talking a completely different language, before quickly gathering himself.

"Of course, sorry." He took the parcel and the dozen or so letters that James was offering him, thanked him, and grabbed the pen to scrawl his signature into one of the boxes. He wasn't really paying any attention to what he was doing, his mind was too fixed on the person next to him.

"Didn't think you'd really care anymore if Lizzie knew I worked here or not."

Charles didn't respond, trying to gather himself before any form of red mist descended over his face. It always did when Craig was around. Leaving his post on the side, he turned to face him.

Craig still had that stupid smile across his face. His eyes, however, were far from happy.

They both hated each other.

That had been obvious since Charles had become friends with Matt. Craig had made it clear that Charles was not someone he wanted his son hanging around with, and when he had started dating Lizzie, Craig's hatred of him had got worse. Not out of protectiveness or fatherly love, but out of the fact his daughter was dating a Williams.

"What are you doing here?" Charles asked.

"Like I said, I work here. I'm the new Scenic Supervisor for *Censorship*."

"For *Censorship*?" His eyebrows soared to the top of his head.

"Yep."

"What happened to Jayden?"

"Bet you think you're so wonderful to remember the crew's name."

"What happened to Jayden?" He repeated, more firmly.

"Like I have a clue. All I know is that Tyrone gave me a call last night and asked if I were free." He sniffed. "Luckily, I just had a job fall through. And also lucky for me, Tyrone doesn't listen to Lightswitch Productions Banned List crap." He smiled that creepy smile again that did everything to Charles that smiles were not supposed to do. It made him feel worried, like a shadow had crawled under his skin. "Lucky for the both of us, ey?"

Charles felt a sharp pain enter his ribs, but he deliberately kept his face emotionless.

Surely Lizzie hadn't put him on her-? But then again, hadn't Neil mentioned something about her Banned List when they were walking up the stairs earlier? He racked his mind trying to recall what she had said but it was all mixed up and blurred; it hadn't been the part of the conversation he'd been focusing on.

But if he had been on Lizzie's Banned List surely he wouldn't be here? Surely Lightswitch Productions wouldn't have accepted the film commission? His mind went back to Gemma, his agent, when she had contacted him about the new location and new studios. He remembered the slight irritation to her voice.

"I mean, quite frankly, I'm shocked you've never been asked there before. Jack and Jill should have had you on their show years ago."

"Ooo, your mask slipped there for a second, bud," Craig said with an insincere smile. "How does it feel knowing my daughter classes us in the same category?" He reached over and slapped Charles's arm and an image slammed into Charles's head. He tasted beer on his lips.

"How's the barren wife?"

Despite being mid-conversation with his brother, silence curled around Charles's throat and ice-cold anger coursed through him. He turned slowly. He and Daniel were stood in the corner of the pub. Both of them had seen Craig when they had walked in but had chosen to stand on the opposite side of the room in order to not have to exchange eye contact.

They were meant to be meeting Bex and Matt here later as they had all come down to Tring for a pre-Christmas weekend. Bex and Matt, naturally, had to find some kind of fitness class to do in between the drinking, celebrating and house decorating. Lizzie was at home, taking the opportunity to sleep whilst she could: they'd had a false positive two weeks before and the emotional rollercoaster of it all had drained her. After they had been told it was incorrect they had fought, a lot. Even on the way to Tring they had argued. A jumble of emotions rallying back and forth between two people boxed within a small car.

He was exhausted.

There were plenty of people in the pub - it was December - and all of them had been smiling and conversing with one another. At Craig's loud shout, everyone had stilled.

He slipped off his bar stool and grinned as he realised he had got both Williamses attention.

"She not here?"

Charles glanced at the two people behind the bar, silently begging them to get involved.

They didn't.

They were barely eighteen, mouths hanging open, eyes alert and excited at the prospect of drama.

"Craig, I think you're drunk," Mr Fletcher said. He had been Charles's old History teacher. He threw Charles a supportive look. "Maybe it's best I get you in a taxi."

"Why's Lizzie not here, Charles? Have you finally dumped her ass for being a failure of a woman?"

Charles surged forward, heart slamming into his ribs as he felt the edges of his vision blur red.

Daniel grabbed onto the back of his jumper and yanked him back.

"Don't!" His brother hissed quietly in his ear.

"I feel sorry for you, I really do," Craig continued. Charles's anger only seemed to have pleased him even more.

"That's enough, Craig," Daniel barked. "You're drunk, go home."

"You got yourself kind of stuck, didn't ya, Charlie-boy?"

"Go home, Craig," Charles choked out, his teeth practically trying to smash into each other as he clenched his jaw shut. How did this man even know anything about their life?

Jean?

Had to be. She still held a torch for Matt and Lizzie's dad even living in Spain. Apparently he'd been out a few times to visit her. It had to be through her, Matt had stopped talking to him years ago. Charles had sat with him as he had downed whiskey and told him how'd he'd finally turned his back on him. He'd actually been rather proud of Matt for it, even if it was a few years late. Matt had slowly come to realise how badly Craig had acted when they were children, and how much poison he'd worked into Lizzie's head when he'd acted the way he had when they had lost Leo. However, Matt had still talked to him, still given him the benefit of the doubt. He'd never told Charles what had happened on his twenty-seventh birthday, but a few days later Matt had declared he would never talk to him again. He said he had done something so terrible it had opened his eyes.

Craig walked up to them and Charles felt his anger heighten. He detested the man so much he didn't even look like Lizzie or Matt to him. He was simply dirt.

"You're not denying it though, are you?" Craig sneered.

"He doesn't have to," Daniel said.

"It is her fault though, yeah? That's all been confirmed."

"We're not getting into this with you."

"I think you should leave," Charles said, surprised by just how calmly the words came out. Inside, everything was carnage. He wanted to slam his fist into Craig's face until he was unrecognisable. This man had caused so much pain in Lizzie's life, set up so much doubt about her worth in her head, poisoned her confidence and tried to manipulate her in so many ways. He'd broken Matt too. Matt had once confided to him that the reason he never let himself get into any serious relationships was because he was scared he would turn out like Craig.

And yet, Craig was still here, in their home pub, saying spiteful, hateful things.

And Maria wasn't.

If the world was fair, it would have been the other way around.

"That's basically the advice I was giving you. You should leave!" He threw back his head and laughed at his own joke. He was now close enough that Charles could smell the alcohol coming off him. It mixed unpleasantly with the stale smell of cigarettes. "I'm sure your dad could find you a perfectly suited match for you to get pregnant."

Charles's jaw was wound so tightly it was beginning to ache. A dull pain was running through his head and he knew his eyes were smarting from anger.

When he refused to respond, Craig pushed on. "Isn't that how it works usually for your type. You find your well-suited match, get your heir and that's that." His eyes flicked to Daniel. "Even if she's sleeping with someone else."

"Get out!" Charles shouted, taking a step forward so he could tower over the smaller man.

Craig still had his eyes fixed on Daniel. "How many affairs did Helen have in the end? Although, no one can blame the poor girl. We all know how boring the eldest Williams boy turned out to be."

"Just be quiet, Craig," Daniel said, his tone disinterested.

"Doesn't it even bother you?"

"It's none of your business."

"Oh," Craig smirked. "For a while it was."

Charles made to step forward again but Daniel grabbed him back. "You punch him, he'll go to the Police," Daniel said darkly in his ear. "He wants a reaction."

How could he be so calm about this? Craig had just implied he'd been sleeping with Helen and Daniel simply looked unbothered.

Craig cocked his head to the right, still watching the oldest Williams brother. "Does it ever bother you that Amy looks nothing like you?"

This time Charles felt Daniel's body lock next to him. They both turned their heads back to face Craig. Charles could feel Daniel's body shaking and he was pretty sure his was too.

"Keep my daughter out of this."

Craig smirked. "Is she your daughter though?"

Before either of them could verbalise a response Craig's face disappeared and the sound of something solid being slammed into wood vibrated through the pub. Charles flinched as Craig yelled out in agony. The back of his head was grabbed again and practically thrown into the bar, his cheek painted with flecks of wood.

No one moved to help.

"Get out of here, you piece of shit!" Bex hissed darkly, her blonde hair tied up in a bun on top of her head. She was wearing her gym kit with a huge blue duffel coat over the top, and Matt was stood behind her. He looked shell shocked, his eyes dark with complicated emotions and he was staring at his dad as if he didn't recognise him.

"You fucking bitch-"

"Don't call her that!" Daniel snarled making to step forward but Bex simply slammed Craig's head down again, harder. Blood was smeared across his mouth and slowly filling the grooves around his teeth. No one moved to stop her. Everyone just watched.

She leant down lower to speak in Craig's ear. "I said, get out."

He straightened up, forcing her to let go off his hair and his eyes locked onto her with such hatred it could be felt in the entire pub. Before anyone could move his hands were around her throat.

Charles started forward but Daniel was quicker, grabbing hold of the back of Craig and sending him spiralling back into the bar and onto the floor. Matt, the stronger of all three men, hadn't even had a chance to step forward. Craig yelled out, placing his hand on the small of his back where he had hit the bar.

"Daniel!" Bex snapped. "I totally had that covered."

Daniel didn't appear to have heard her, instead he moved so as to put a barrier between the two of them, his eyes blazing with anger.

Charles, for a moment, was completely stunned. His brother had never partaken in sports, or been confrontational, but he'd just flung a 190 pound man into a bar and to the floor.

"Don't you ever touch her again," Daniel said darkly, his eyes pinned on Craig.

"I'm fine!" Bex insisted, trying to twist Daniel around to look at her. He didn't move. "Daniel, look at me, I'm fine." Her tone turned gentle but Daniel kept his gaze pinned on Craig.

"Don't insult my family, and yes, Lizzie is my family, don't try and pick fights with my brother, don't lay a finger on Bex and don't - I don't care what stupid rumours there are in this small town - ever imply Amy is not my daughter."

"Glad to see you have some sort of personality, Daniel," Craig sneered.

Bex surged forward and it was Daniel's turn to grab her. "Don't."

"But he just-"

"It's fine."

Something silent seemed to pass between the two of them, both staring at each other. Bex with a stubborn ferocity to her features and Daniel much calmer and serious. Bex gave in first, resting back on her heels. She turned her head to look at Charles, concern etched behind her eyes.

Charles knew instantly. He knew that look straight away.

"Lizzie was here?"

"We bumped into her as she was leaving. Think she came down to get a change of scenery."

"Go," Daniel said quickly.

CHAPTER EIGHTEEN

Charles yanked his arm away from Craig as the image faded around him. That time he had felt the vision through to his core. Every single emotion was still pumping through. Anger was still hot in his blood, a deep grinding ache low in his ribs, and he felt bruised. A dream or not he felt something worrying tilt in his core, like he was missing something.

Something important.

Craig raised an eyebrow. "You on something? Your eyes have gone all weird."

"I'm fine." Charles could barely talk, hatred was curled around every word and it was taking so much effort not to shout at the man in front of him. "You do not deserve to be here."

"Woah, was it something I said? Or are you just sad my daughter put you on her Banned List too?"

"Lizzie is not your daughter!" He snapped. "Real fathers are actually there for their kids. You gave up the right to call her daughter when you left her."

A surprised huff of laughter left the man's cracked lips. "That's all very rich coming from you."

Charles stared at him, his brow dipping and his hands curling at his sides. "What's that supposed to mean?"

"You're hardly a role model yourself."

"What are you talking about?"

"Push me too far, Williams, and I will go to the fucking papers. I was trying to be the bigger guy here. I was trying to put everything behind us. I should have realised a Williams is always going to think he is so much better than everyone else."

"Mr Rosswool, I'll kindly remind you talking to talent like that could give me grounds to fire you."

Both men's heads snapped to the side to see Lizzie standing next to them. Charles immediately ran a concerned gaze over her, taking in the pale face, the extremely tight ponytail, and her stiff posture.

"Talent?" Craig sneered, looking as if the word tasted unpleasant in his mouth.

Charles didn't really care for it either but it was better than 'celebrity'.

"Yes. Frankly, you come far lower in the pecking order when it comes to this production than Charles. Insult him again, and I'll have you fired."

"Don't worry, love, I'm well aware you always put him on a fucking pedestal." He turned fully around to face Lizzie and Charles resisted the urge to step between them. "Ever since you were a snivelling kid who fancied the pretty boy."

The insult barely touched him but he saw Lizzie's jaw tighten. She took a step towards Craig, fixing him with a steely glare.

God, I'm proud of you.

He didn't question his emotions this time, or try and push them away. He could see the pain in her eyes, the scars in the way her posture was so defensive and the child behind her stubbornness. He'd never seen Lizzie stand up to her father.

"Whilst you are working here you cannot talk to me like that either." She drew herself up even higher. "You've managed to get on this production, well done." She stepped forward again so that her and Craig were only a few inches apart. "But don't, for one second, think that means I am going to make this easy for you. Now, if you don't mind, I've got to get back to work. No more squabbles in the hallway."

"I wasn't squabbling," Craig sneered.

Lizzie ignored him, instead her gaze flicked to Charles. "I'll see you on set Mr Williams, let me know if this man bothers you again."

"Of course." He nodded once, making sure he held her gaze. "Cartwright." He didn't say anything else. Not in words.

A flicker of a smile traced her lips but in front of Craig he saw her push it away. With a slight kick, Charles realised he was reading her again. Either she was letting him or something had changed and he simply was able to. A blush coloured her cheeks.

Both men watched her turn and walk down the stairs.

"Fuck this, we'll see what Tyrone has to bloody say, shall we?" Craig threw Charles a dirty look before storming up the stairs that Lizzie had just come down. Charles watched him before turning back to pick up his post.

James was sitting in the corner of the room, a pencil between his teeth and a newspaper in his hand. Admirably, it seemed he hadn't listened in on what probably would have been great work gossip.

As Charles walked down the stairs he took a shaky, unsteady breath. His insides were still charred from his earlier anger and this time, unlike the other vision he'd had when Amy had touched his arm, he could still picture everything so clearly.

He could hear the audible gasp of the fellow pub-goers, and feel the burning anger churning in his gut. He could even feel the shadow of Daniel's hand knotted in the back of his jumper and recall the exact northern twang to Mr Fletcher's voice. He ran a hand through his hair, trying to come up with some sort of explanation, and something smooth caught against his forehead. He brought his hand down to see what it was.

The sight made him stumble. He grabbed the bannister and dropped his mail on the floor, not feeling the burn of splinters in his palm, or the pain of rolling onto his ankle. He didn't even realise some of his letters had spilled through the gap in the stairs to the floors below.

A gold band was looped around his left ring finger.

Lizzie 29, Charles 32

Charles sat up. The bedroom was dark, the only light that was coming through was from the bright streetlight just behind the curtain. He glanced at his mobile on the side of the bed. Lizzie had been gone for a good fifteen minutes.

"Lizzie?" He called out.

No response.

He dragged his legs out of bed, shuddered as his feet hit the floor, and quickly pulled on a pair of jogging bottoms before padding across the bedroom floor.

"Lizzie?" He called again, sticking his head out of the bedroom.

"I'm just in the bathroom. Don't worry, go back to sleep."

He frowned, grabbed a grey hoodie off the back of the door, and walked through the kitchen into the corridor. There was no tell-tale orange glow around the bathroom door frame and he frowned at the peculiarity of it. He knocked quietly.

"Come in if you promise not to judge!"

Without hesitation, he pushed the door open.

"Hi," she said, sheepishly.

"Hi." An affectionate smile crossed his face. "What are you doing?"

She was lying on the bathroom floor, slotted between the toilet and the bath with her legs up against the wall. Her head was closest to him. She had thrown on freshly washed, pink pyjamas and had pulled her hair back into a ponytail.

"I know it's an old wives' tale but there might be some sense in it. It was on this documentary I watched earlier." Even in the darkness he could see her face was flushed red. "Sorry, I thought you'd fall asleep before you realised."

"Wait there." He turned and left the bathroom.

When he came back, she opened her mouth and began to laugh, her eyes running across the things in his arms and even from upside down, her joyous smile gave him a little kick to the stomach. It had been harder and harder to make her laugh recently.

"What are you doing?"

"Thought I'd come and join my crazy wife."

"Don't call me crazy!" She jabbed a finger up in the air, her tone only half-joking.

He handed her the first item he had grabbed from the kitchen - a jar of smooth peanut butter. She took it from him, a smile creeping back onto her face.

"Peace offering?" He said, with a wink.

"Did you bring a spoon?"

"I am not a savage." He passed her a teaspoon and she happily took it from him, her eyes watching him as he proceeded to take the next few bits and pieces out of his arms.

First, he placed the blanket from their bed over her, tucking in the edges before lifting her head and placing a pillow beneath it. He placed one next to her for himself. He couldn't lie down beside her because either side was blocked by the toilet or the bath, so instead he lay the opposite way, their heads aligned but their bodies in totally different directions. He had to bend his legs in order to fit in the room before rolling onto his side to look at her. Finally, he grabbed his own jar of crunchy peanut butter and pulled a blanket he had plucked from the living room up and over himself to keep warm. She turned her head to look at him and smiled affectionately.

"You're going to be such a great dad."

He smiled bashfully, avoided her gaze and instead grabbed his own spoon for the peanut butter. His embarrassment made her chuckle and soon after, he felt her fingers brush through his hair.

He cleared his throat. "So, this documentary, was it Mumsnet by any chance?"

She flushed an even darker red and he laughed. "How did you know?"

"When do you have the time to watch a documentary?" He shifted slightly on the pillow. "Correction, when are you here and watching television when I'm not?"

"Okay, you have a point." She pushed her spoon into the jar and took a bite before turning her head to look at him. Their noses brushed. She hesitated, a tiny smile spreading across her lips as her eyes searched his face.

"What?"

"This is quite romantic really."

He laughed, rolling onto his back. "Two tired people lying on the bathroom floor?"

"Yeah!"

"I've clearly been slipping with my romantic gestures if you think this is romantic."

A flutter of laughter left her lips. "I like it."

They continued to dig their spoons into their individual jars for a while longer, both staring up at the ceiling and occasionally glancing at one another. After a few minutes passed, he placed his jar to the side and shuffled his head closer to hers. "How long are we staying in here for?"

"Bored already?"

"No."

"I have no idea. I was just going to stay here till I fell asleep. If you need to go back, seriously, you can. I know this is mad. You have work tomorrow."

"So do you."

She shrugged.

"I'll stay." He reached up and took her ponytail gently in his hand, running his fingers through the brown soft strands and frowning ever so slightly.

"Thanks," she whispered.

"For what? Being a clingy bastard who can't sleep without his wife in the bed with him?" He waggled his eyebrows at her and she laughed again.

"No, for coming to find me and putting up with, well up with *this*. And me."

He frowned. "Lizzie, I don't *put up* with you, I love you." He ran his hand across the top of her head and something moved behind her eyes so quickly he didn't catch it.

A flicker of alarm passed through him as she closed her eyes, a slight scrunch to her nose.

"Hey, hey, hey," he whispered gently, running his thumb back and forth across her hairline. "What's wrong?"

She didn't respond, she simply screwed her face up even tighter and a tear escaped down the side of her face. He pushed himself up and kissed her forehead gently. She felt warm and soft, but something cold settled in his stomach as he saw more tears on her cheeks. He pulled away.

She opened her eyes slowly. "I don't want you to ever feel like you have to."

"Like I have to what?"

"Come after me."

"Lizzie, what are you talking about?"

"I just...I feel so guilty." She took a sharp breath in. "All the time."

"You have nothing to feel guilty about."

"I know you say that but I do. I held you back. What if I'm always going to hold you back?"

His breath caught in his chest. What was she even talking about? "Lizzie, come on-"

"I found the drama leaflets."

He dropped back onto the pillow, staring up at the ceiling. His mouth suddenly felt dry and something hard pressed down onto his lungs. "Ah," he said simply.

"When were you going to tell me?" She whispered and he flinched as he heard her voice catch. Guilt swirled at the bottom of his stomach.

"I didn't...I didn't even know if I was going to apply."

"You did apply. You have audition dates."

"Lizzie, you can't just go through my post!" He tried to keep his tone under control but he heard the bite to it.

Lizzie's body locked next to his and he reached out instinctively, his fingers just brushing the top of her head.

"I'm sorry," she whispered.

"Why did you do it?"

"I saw that they were all from drama schools and I got…" She swallowed and didn't finish her sentence.

He ran his hands over his face. "It was just a thought. A pipe dream. A 'shit-I've-turned-thirty' moment."

She played with the jar between her hands. "You turned thirty a while ago."

"I know. I've been thinking of it since then. I probably wouldn't get in anyway."

"You would."

Her words should have made him smile but her tone was sad.

"You think?"

"You got in last time."

"That was a rather long time ago."

She fiddled with her hands. "Do you hate teaching?"

"No." He let out a long sigh. "Of course not. I just…I just miss acting. That's all. And I'm always thinking 'what if?', you know?"

She didn't respond straight away. He turned to look at her.

"Lizzie?"

"You're always thinking that?" Her voice was barely a whisper.

"Well, not always. Just, sometimes." He thought about it when the kids were being extra rowdy or the head teacher was making them stay late for another school meeting.

It had been an idea. Just a little niggling idea in the back of his brain. Nothing more than that. He liked his job. It had just been…something. An itch to scratch.

"I get it."

He turned to look at her and his heart tugged as he noted her glassy eyes.

"Lizzie, honestly, don't worry about the post thing. It's fine. And don't worry about my job, I love my job."

She nodded but he could still see the pain in her expression. He wanted to take it all away. All the pain, all the remorse, all the guilt in those gorgeous green eyes. Once upon a time he had thought he would have the power to do it by himself but, over the years, he'd realised more and more he couldn't take it all away. Some of it… but not all of it. Some, only Lizzie could make disappear.

CHAPTER NINETEEN

The weather had shifted. It was colder, coats had become thicker and people began to invest in new scarves and hats for the oncoming season. Fairy lights lined the streets of London, waiting to be turned on once Halloween was over. Orange pumpkins glowed in windows, children got into fights over what character they were going to dress up as, and more hoaxes flooded the internet stating clowns were going to be stalking the streets once again. When it rained, people smiled as the cold water lashed their faces and bounced back from their boots, enjoying the cold, wet weather while it was relatively new. Restaurants were filled with people who hadn't seen each other in months and people spilled out of the seams of pubs, clutching their drinks to their chests like they were emitting heat.

Winter set London alive.

Lightswitch Productions was a hub of activity with people in and out of the building no matter what time of the day, and everyone was investing more in their coffee habits than they were in their weekly food shops.

Lizzie was shattered but she had finally managed to do enough work that she could take a full Sunday away from her laptop, which was why at 8.15 a.m. on a Sunday morning, she found herself boarding a train to Tring. There was a strange melancholy in the air as the train pushed away from the station, taking its inhabitants out of London when everyone else in the world seemed to be desperate to be in it.

Lizzie tried to visit Tring as often as she could, which hadn't been too often over the last few months. Her mother no longer lived there, having instead decided to move to Spain to set up her own Yoga and Wellness retreat in the sun, and most of her friends had left the area after university called them to different ends of the country but, Lizzie still enjoyed her visits back, enjoyed the way the village just went about things at its own speed and the way it looked pretty, even when it was grey and miserable.

The train picked up speed and she thought back over the last week. She had bumped into Charles a few times since the hallway incident, and they had actually started to speak like normal human beings. It was all professional and superficial, however. Lizzie found it easier that way, easier to push away the butterflies in her stomach, to ignore the fact that her mind kept trying to make her remember their past in vivid detail, and to hide the fact that whenever his blue eyes caught hers, her skin would warm and her heart would stutter.

It was sunny in Tring, the light bounced against the autumnal blanket of leaves across the roads causing everything to shine like a fresh painting. Outside the memorial garden, there were people selling poppies and opposite, there were small stalls set up in front of the Saint Peter & Paul's Church selling flowers, clothes and trinkets. It was busy everywhere. Families, friends, colleagues, bustling this way and that as they made the most of the fair day.

Lizzie bought a small bunch of Paperwhite Narcissuses from a French lady who stood behind the third from last stall. She always smiled at her as if Lizzie were her favourite customer, and gave her a can of Diet Coke whenever she bought a bouquet. Taking a purple ribbon she had bought from London out of her bag, she wrapped them slowly around the stalks, droplets of water slipping from the ends of them and onto her boots. The flowers looked very similar to yellow daffodils except for their white petals and thinner stalks.

Her therapist - she had actually been to one this time around - many, many years ago, had told her it was good to get into a routine when grieving. It was meant to make things easier to handle, but, as she passed through the gates to the cemetery, even with the sun in the sky and the flowers in her hand, she still felt a small wave of panic wash over her.

Her mind cast back to Charles and she felt the ghost of his hand in hers. Her heart tugged. They had always done this together. When they lived in Tring, every Sunday after they had finally got out of bed, they would walk down to the cemetery and see Leo. They would talk to him, tell him all about their lives and what they had been up to that week, and then would walk to Cathi's Cakes, the small bakery a few streets away, where they would have drinks and whatever new baked goods Cathi had made. They tried to have a different thing each time, which was easy as Cathi got bored frequently and created new things nearly every single day. When they moved to London their visits had become rarer.

Lizzie reached the small grave and sat down, forgetting to unfold the waterproof mat she had brought with her to sit on, and instead just using her coat. There were other flowers upon the grave, small clusters of Roses as well as tiny notes. She glanced at some of them, recognising Maria's swirly handwriting and smiling gently before placing her own flowers down upon the stone. Matt had never mentioned the fact he must have seen Maria's notes and flowers.

When it had come to Leo's birth this time around, Matt had been at a stag do in Scotland and her mum had still been in Spain. It had been the exact same before except for this time she also didn't have Charles holding her hand. Just as she had been told to push, and her heart had been breaking apart inside of her chest, she had felt someone's hand grip hers and a familiar comforting voice had started whispering in her ear.

Maria.

She had come in to see another patient and had seen Lizzie's paperwork.

Maria had been strong, reassuring, and kind. The memory was a bit of a blur for Lizzie, her brain having censored parts of it out for her own good, but she remembered she had clung to her, crying and apologising over, and over again. Maria had simply held her head tightly to her chest, not letting go until she had to.

And then a whole new set of problems arose. Lizzie had begged her not to tell Charles. In her emotional, confused state, she had almost spilled the entire thing about time travel and a past life to her. Instead, she had told Maria something that was still very true.

She would have only held Charles back.

If he had proposed to her and married her before Leo, he'd have lost everything.

Maria had disagreed, point blank refusing to do as Lizzie said.

"It would break Charles's heart to know you were here, by yourself. He loves you."

"We broke up."

"He still loves you, Lizzie. The break up ruined him."

She hadn't believed her, knowing fully well that Charles was hardly going to be hung up over losing her. He was an attractive, intelligent, young man who would have moved on fairly swiftly. They had stopped talking when the midwife had handed her Leo to hold.

Last time she'd refused, unable to bear the idea of holding her son and instead, Charles had done it to the side where she couldn't see. This time, she was so distracted by Maria and begging her not to tell Charles, that she had taken him without thinking.

And he'd been the most beautiful thing she'd ever seen.

Inside of his many blankets, for just a few moments, she could pretend he was breathing, see life stirring behind his closed eyes and curl his little hand around her finger.

She had fallen even more in love with him in that moment.

"He's beautiful," Maria had whispered, not reaching over to touch Leo but letting Lizzie have this moment.

"He is," Lizzie had agreed, holding him closer to her chest as her heart swelled with affection.

She had let herself imagine him having Charles's blue eyes and her brown hair. She'd let herself breath in the smell from his forehead and imagined a life full of standing out in the rain at football games, of demanding who had eaten the chocolate out of the fridge, of pillow fights and a boy who was as loving and kind as his father.

His life flashed before her eyes just like it had so many times before. The life she so desperately wanted for him. The life she had been going to be a part of.

It was in that moment, she knew everything she'd done leading up to that point was correct. She could tell Charles the truth and they could start their life all over again, or she could leave him to have the life he deserved. The one she had set him on when instead of telling him about her pregnancy, she had dumped him. A life filled with someone who could give him children, who didn't work every hour under the sun, who didn't force him to give up his dreams to look after her.

She wasn't able to give her son a life, but she could give his father the one he deserved.

She had made a bargain with Maria. If Maria went and got a smear test and it came back negative, she could tell Charles. If it came back with abnormal cells, she could not. Maria had been reluctant at first, but Lizzie had insisted, stating that the news of Leo was only going to hurt Charles anyway.

What Maria hadn't known was the huge advantage Lizzie had.

They'd never spoken again but the notes and flowers on the grave had continued.

Charles didn't know. He was in a loving, happy relationship.

And, by some miracle, Maria Williams was alive.

A cold breeze ran up through Lizzie's hair and a shiver walked down her neck, bringing her back to the present. She closed her eyes and dropped her chin to her chest.

"I've seen your dad," she whispered, tracing her hand across the grass.

People passed, church bells rang and Lizzie remained seated on the grass, silently telling Leo everything that had happened, from the fake name to being punched in the face.

"I did the right thing though. It goes to show I did the right thing," she whispered. A shadow passed behind her, tingles ran across her neck and for a second she felt like she was being laughed at. It was the strangest sensation and made her turn to see if anyone was watching her.

There was no one.

She stared at the graveyard, trying to see if anyone was watching her when she heard another laugh. A weird sense of recognition shot through her.

"Stop it, I did the right thing."

Sure thing, Mum.

Lizzie's back stiffened and her eyes darted around her again. Another whisper of laughter drifted towards her on the wind as sunlight managed to peer ever so slightly around the white clouds overhead. The moment was broken as someone's phone went off nearby, 'Lucky' by Britney Spears breaking out across the air. She rolled her eyes at herself, and quickly settled down for a chat.

Cathi's Cakes was as toasty as ever. Lizzie managed to grab a coffee and a slice of cake described as a mix between a Victoria Sponge cake and S'mores. Positioning herself in the corner with her back to most people, she pulled out her book from her bag and began trying to read it. Alas, the words swam before her eyes and her mind kept getting pulled back to the last few weeks.

Craig had stayed out of her way. She had felt so proud of herself for standing up to him but it had been short lived. A shard of fear was constantly digging into her spine whenever she walked into work.

At least Craig didn't know about Leo - her brother had reassured her of that a long time ago. But there had been something about seeing him, something about the way he was talking to Charles that made her...she shook her head.

She trusted Matt. He wouldn't have told Craig. He would know how much that would hurt her.

Awareness danced along the back of her neck, pulling her out of her thoughts.

"Lizzie?"

God, she was turning into an utter clown. Was she imagining voices now? Was that a new thing? Just like she had imagined the voice earlier? Was she going mad? Imagining voices when there weren't people? She ran a hand along her forehead and tried to bring her focus back to her book.

Someone tapped her shoulder and she turned automatically in her seat.

"Hey," Charles said, a smile breaking out across his face as shock passed through her own.

Not madness this time then.

"What are you doing here?"

Charles was wearing a dark green jumper, his short hair looked more ruffled and relaxed than normal, and he was so tall his head skimmed the ceiling.

"Promised Mum I'd come down more often, so I drove down yesterday when I realised we had the whole weekend off filming." He pushed his hands into his pockets. "What about you?"

"Visiting old friends."

He frowned. "Thought Yasmin moved."

"I had other friends!"

He grinned. "Oh, yeah…there was Matt…and then there was me."

"Stop it! I had more friends than Yasmin!"

Charles eyes creased with laughter and the sides of her mouth tugged into a smile.

"Mum has tenants in the house too so it's always good to come and check everything is okay."

Charles scrunched his nose up. "Doesn't feel right people being inside your house."

"We haven't lived there for a while now."

"Still...just," he shrugged. "Weird. Do you think they've found the recorders?"

Lizzie burst out laughter, covering her mouth as a few people turned to look at her. "Oh, my God, I'd forgotten about that."

His eyes twinkled. "We hid them under that slate in the kitchen."

"Just so we didn't have to do the school concert. You were such a bad influence, I was actually okay at the recorder."

"I have no idea what you mean." Charles's smile turned to a grimace. "They made us use the lost property ones."

"I can't believe I forgot about that." She pointed at him. "I can't believe you remembered that!"

He gave a slow smile that made her heart rate triple in speed. "I remember everything, Cartwright."

She ducked her head as sudden, unwelcome pain decided to muscle in on all the nice, giddy feelings that had been flooding through her.

He definitely didn't remember everything.

"How's your weekend been?" She asked, trying to mask her emotions.

"Weekend's been good, thank you. Daniel and Amy came down and Amy's been running me around silly. I am absolutely knackered. Oh, Amy's my niece. You met her in the infamous stairwell." He pulled a face. "Although concussion might mean you have zero recollection of that."

"Course I do."

"Yeah?"

"I don't think I'm ever going to forget getting blood all over you. I still owe you some dry cleaning."

He grinned, his eyes sparking at her comment. "I think we settled that one. The punch to the face was payment enough."

"You sure? That plain, white shirt of yours was probably worth more than a month's rent for me."

He winced. "God, you make me sound awful."

A bright eyed, pinched face appeared beside Charles's shoulder and Lizzie's breath caught in her throat. Joy and surprise caused her lungs to feel like they were expanding at the sight of Maria Williams by Charles's side.

"Lizzie Cartwright!" She practically boomed, reaching forward to grasp her hand. "How are you? What are you doing here?"

"Hi Maria!' Lizzie tried her hardest to stand up but there was barely any room between the tables and with Charles behind her, it made it an almost impossible squeeze. His hand settled on her shoulder and he smiled at her reassuringly with a small shake of his head.

It's fine.

But-

Honestly, it's fine.

"I was just visiting," she said, settling back in her chair but still shaking Maria's hand. There was even something in just the touch of her skin that was comforting.

Understanding passed behind Maria's eyes and she squeezed her hand fondly. "How lovely, have you had a nice time?"

"Yes, thanks."

Maria's eyes dropped to Charles's hand, which was still on Lizzie's shoulder, and then back up towards her son.

Lizzie felt him swiftly remove it.

"It's good to see you," Lizzie said earnestly. "Are you okay?"

"Very well." She paused. "Thank you."

Was it Charles's imagination or had there been more behind that question than he realised? The way the two women were looking at each other appeared like they were talking in secret code, yet their words were fairly normal.

He had been surprised to see Lizzie. So much so that he'd been hesitant to approach her at first. As if his legs had a mind of their own, however, he'd been behind her before his brain could come up with any reason not to be.

He'd liked the way she had been herself. In Tring, her barriers seemed to be less iron solid. For a couple of minutes it had been deliciously familiar.

"Thanks for…" Lizzie trailed off but Maria nodded as if Lizzie had said a full sentence.

"Of course," she said. "And thank you for the heads up."

What?

Before he could open his mouth to question what they were talking about his mum straightened up. There was a gleam in her eye that he recognised. It was the same one Lottie had used to have when she was up to something.

"Lizzie, what are you doing for the rest of the day?"

He tilted his head away from Lizzie and gave his mum a hard stare.

Which she ignored.

"Oh, um, nothing really."

"Come and spend the afternoon with us! What time is your train?"

"I don't want to be a pain-"

"No pain, whatsoever -"

"Mum, maybe she doesn't want to-" Charles started, turning to look at Lizzie.

"- Honestly, I don't want to be in the way -"

"- You wouldn't be in the way, but I totally get -"

"- But it's so last minute –"

"- I wouldn't mind at all-"

"- And I'm sure you wouldn't want-"

"Children!!" Maria said, and they both turned to look at her obediently. Charles could feel a slight sweat along the back of his neck. "That's it sorted then. Kenneth would love to see you too, I'm sure, so you'll come and spend your afternoon with us. Unfortunately, I brought the smaller car with me, packed it full of the weekly food shop so there isn't any room, but you two can walk back, right? It's quite a nice day still." She glanced out of one of the windows. "When you've finished your tea of course."

Charles stared at his mum. She was telling an outright lie. She had driven them here in her jeep. The shopping filled up most of the boot but that was it. Her brown eyes flicked up to meet his and he saw the smile behind them. A huff of laughter left his lips as he very slightly shook his head at her. Not enough for Lizzie to spot it out of the corner of her eye, but enough for his mum to know he knew exactly what she was doing.

"That sounds nice," Lizzie said, her voice slightly higher than normal.

He turned to look at her but from her profile he couldn't tell what she was thinking.

Maria left barely minutes later, scooping up the tray of gluten-free cakes she had ordered for Dr Heins, and shooing him away as he offered to carry it back.

"Sure I can't help you to the really small car?" He'd whispered in her ear.

Maria had merely laughed, before striding away confidently.

"Sorry about that." He said as Lizzie got to her feet and managed to make her way out towards him from between the long tables.

"Don't be, your mum's sweet."

"That's one word for it."

Meddling was the other. A brief frown crossed his face. What made it worse was that she believed Jennifer was his girlfriend and she was still meddling. Why would she do that? She liked Jennifer. His mum would never encourage cheating. Unless…unless the fact he had been with the same woman for ten years and he still hadn't asked her to marry him had started to make Maria suspicious.

Jennifer's nervous expression filled his head and he felt in his pocket for his phone. She hadn't texted him yet. This weekend was *the* weekend. The weekend she was going to come out to her parents and tell them the truth. He needed to ring her later and check she was okay, but he was trying to take it as a good sign that she hadn't rung the day before. She was brave. He couldn't even find the courage to simply tell his parents the relationship wasn't real.

Outside, the sun was still shining in the air but it felt colder and more windy than before. Long shadows stretched across the street and people around them pulled their coats closer and their hats down lower.

He eyed her shoulders and a smile tugged at his lips. "Some things never change."

"What?" She said curiously, glancing behind her. "What are you looking at?"

"Your lack of coat." He began to shrug his own off his shoulders, the warm familiarity of the situation causing any thoughts of his mum or Jennifer out of his head.

She went crimson, her eyes flicking between what he was doing and his face as if he had just wielded a knife. "I did have one." She patted her arms as if this was evidence. "I promise, I did have one!"

"Yeah, yeah, I didn't believe you a decade ago, and I don't believe you now," he teased.

"I did! I promise!" But she was laughing, staring around still as if someone might magically appear with it in their hands. "I had one!"

"Turn around, Lizzie."

"No, honestly, you don't have to do that!"

"Arm," he said in mock annoyance.

She waved her hands in front of her frantically, but she couldn't stop bursts of laughter slipping out from between her lips. "No."

"Arm, Lizzie."

She grinned and then covered her face as if trying to suppress it. He really wished she wouldn't.

"Cartwright, come on."

A triumph flare sparked in his gut when he saw the effect the name had on her.

So, she *did* remember that.

Reluctantly, she turned. As she threaded her arms through the coat, he felt a stab of nostalgia. He swallowed it away but the embers remained burning in his stomach as he pulled the coat up and over her shoulders. When she turned back around she was so close to him that he could see the red of her nose and the tiny brown fleck in her right eye. He could smell mint on her hair and a perfume on her skin that he didn't recognise... but at the same time, he did.

"Your collars askew." He brushed his fingers around it, making sure it lay correctly against her neck before pulling it tightly together at the front.

Their eyes met and the atmosphere around them tightened.

"Thanks."

"You're welcome."

She dropped her gaze and he dropped his hands as she began to do up the buttons. He watched her as she did and felt so many things he wanted to say clog up in this throat. He wanted to ask her about her family, he wanted to ask her how her life had been…he wanted to ask her if she ever thought of him.

He wanted to reach over and do up the buttons for her, going back over the two she had got wrong in a completely Lizzie fashion. He wanted to let his pace slow as he got to the top, tilt her chin up towards him and-

Fuck. He looked away sharply but it was like his eyes could only be apart from her for a second.

She looped the final button through its hole and looked up, catching him staring at her. Surprise flickered across her face.

Still, she didn't look away.

She was so close.

His eyes dropped to her mouth and he saw her take a sharp quick breath.

Words, Charles.

Words.

Now.

"Right, then." He took a sharp step away and turned to the right, brushing his hands against his jeans and hoping to wipe his sudden urge for her away. "Home?"

"Home," she agreed, shoving her hands into the coat's pockets. She jumped slightly and then began to laugh.

"What?"

She lifted up her hands, clutching a handful of marbles, a satsuma, a pair of goggles and a mini calculator. "You still keep everything random in these. I guess some things never do change."

He swallowed away the sudden tightness in his throat.

One thing definitely had changed.

God, he wished it hadn't.

CHAPTER TWENTY

Lizzie turned over in the bed for what felt like the hundredth time.

Maria hadn't let her go home on the train as it was 'too late'. She had come close to physically blocking the door, instead telling Lizzie she should simply go along in Charles's car the next morning. Despite her protests, Lizzie realised she had been fighting a battle she had lost the moment she'd stepped foot in the house.

The afternoon had been wonderful. She had been welcomed back into the Williams's household with hugs and smiles, and for that afternoon, which turned into an evening, she had let herself forget. Forget that she had given all this up, forget that she had sacrificed these kinds of Sundays, and forget that this was a one off, never to be repeated. Seeing Maria had been the most rewarding part of the day, her kind smile and energetic eyes pushing all of Lizzie's fears about coming face to face with her again out of the window.

Maria was healthy.

She was alive.

She was happy.

The sound of rain against the window caught her attention. Smiling, she slipped out of bed, grabbed her hoodie off the side, and made her way downstairs. Her feet knew automatically to miss the noisy last step on the staircase and not to put any weight on the bannister - it would groan louder than Matt getting out of bed.

The Williams's conservatory had always been a place she had loved. It looked out onto their impressive garden, which was kept in tip top shape due to Kenneth's love of gardening. With a backdrop of Ashridge Estate's forest, it made it look even bigger and more impressive. There was greenery for miles around, trees entangled so closely together they sometimes merged into one and different coloured flowers that still shone brightly even in the darkness. Lizzie sat down on the rug just in front of the central, lime green sofa. She leaned her back against it and stared out into the garden, enjoying the steady drum of rain falling upon the glass walls. Even in her worst moments, coming in here had made her feel safe. Especially in the rain.

She ran her hands along the soft rug beneath her, stroking the white strands delicately and feeling her heart grow heavy. It had literally been a lifetime since she had done this.

During the afternoon, sitting next to Charles had felt so deliciously normal. He had always been tactile and today had been no exception. His fingers brushed hers as he took her plate, he squeezed her shoulder affectionately when Kenneth had teased her about no longer having a fringe, his ridiculously long legs had been so close to hers beneath the table that they had kept brushing her own. The annoying thing was that he probably hadn't been aware of any of it, not tuned in to her inner turmoil due to the fact he wasn't interested in her in any romantic way whatsoever - he was dating Jennifer, after all - and yet, *she* had slowly become more and more frazzled by the second. When Daniel had joked about Charles's clumsiness when he managed to spill the wine he'd been tasked to pour, she had so nearly reached out to squeeze his knee that she ended up slamming her own hand up into the table to stop herself.

They had all turned to stare at her.

A shiver shot up her spine and caused her to open her eyes; she hadn't even realised she had closed them. She could feel his presence, her whole body reacting to it before she had even seen him.

"Couldn't sleep?" Charles asked softly, placing himself down on the floor beside her.

She nodded, inwardly scolding herself at how much she loved the feel of his warm body next to hers. She really needed to nip whatever these stupid emotions were in the bud.

They couldn't be friends, she reminded herself. This was more than just two exes being close, this was much more serious than that, and she needed to take a step away. What if her proximity meant he started to remember? What if she fell for him all over again and forgot why she had done this in the first place? What if she made a move on him, forgot about poor Jennifer, and embarrassed herself?

She had Googled his girlfriend over the years…many a time. She was not only gorgeous but also intelligent and possibly the nicest person in the world. She had been on *Jack and Jill* twice and, through the grapevine, Lizzie had heard great things about her each time.

She turned, opening her mouth to say she needed to go to bed but her words stuttered to a halt before they reached her lips. He was holding something out to her.

"You didn't!" She reddened at just how loudly she groaned those two words.

"Smooth for you, crunchy for me." He waved his own tub at her, an infectious smile on his lips as he handed her a spoon.

"But how did you even have these ready? Please don't tell me these are actually over a decade old."

"I bloody hope not!" He laughed, shaking his head. "It wasn't me. I was in the kitchen just now, getting some water. I heard you come down the stairs and suddenly I spotted them out on the table, just sitting there."

"Odd." Something cold danced across the back of her neck and she brushed it away.

"Maybe it was Mum. Nice surprise though." He groaned softly as he took his first spoonful, closing his eyes and resting his head back against the the sofa. She watched the dip of his Adam's apple as he swallowed and had to fist her free hand into her lap.

She'd had too much wine at dinner. She had known she should have stopped Maria filling up her glass. She should have actually made an effort to say 'no'. Alcohol was the only explanation as to why, in that moment, the desire to lean over and press her mouth to Charles's neck was overbearing.

Stop it.

"I think it's been years since I've had peanut butter."

"Yeah?" She was surprised she even managed to force out that one word from between her lips.

"Sadly." He opened his eyes and caught her watching him, a curious smile crossed his lips and she quickly looked away.

"You're not on some mad celebrity diet, are you?" Lizzie said hurriedly, trying to push the heat away from her face.

"First, I am not a celebrity and secondly, yes. Kristina doesn't let me keep peanut butter in the house."

"Kristina?"

"Our personal trainer. She lives with us."

"You have a personal trainer who lives with you and you say you're not a celebrity?" Lizzie laughed, shaking her head but something sharp slid under her ribs at his words. She hadn't missed the fact he had said the words 'our' and 'us'. Jennifer's face flickered to life in her mind, reminding her that despite their easiness around each other, and the way he appeared to look at her, Charles was just being friendly. The stupid shivers, the butterflies, the blushes were all one-sided.

That had always been one of the hardest things about liking him.

Even as a teenager he was just so bloody nice to everyone it had been hard to tell if he was being nice to her out of obligation, friendship, or something more. It was why she finally made her move at seventeen.

He nudged her in the side and upset the newly settled butterflies in her stomach. "Okay, it is a bit extravagant I'll give you that."

"Do you have your own gym?"

"Maybe."

She laughed.

"Okay, yes, I have my own gym but that's more a privacy thing. I get told off for not using it."

"By Patricia or Kristina?" Lizzie raised her eyebrows.

"Both."

She waved her spoon at him. "Got to keep up that *masculine* image."

He shook his head, laughing. "Sadly, I think my body rejects building muscle. Never going to get those hero roles so might as well enjoy this. Cursed to be a bean pole my whole life." He pushed his spoon back into his own peanut butter.

"You've gained muscle," Lizzie said, shaking her head. "I mean look at your shoulders-" She turned to look at him and stopped at the look he was throwing her, her tongue suddenly getting stuck. He raised his eyebrows teasingly and she inwardly scolded herself as her cheeks burned. Seriously, why had she drunk so much? "And besides you look great with or without it." She finished quickly, turning her head away.

"What was that about my shoulders?"

She nudged her leg with his. "Stop it!"

"No, please, keep going."

She tried to suppress a laugh and threw him a look. "Don't pretend to act all cocky, you're blushing!"

There was a pink tint along his cheeks that sent a bolt of nostalgia rushing through her. He never could take compliments.

Charles smiled and tilted his head ever so slightly to the right. "As are you."

The change in his tone sent shivers running up her spine. She looked away, unable to hold eye contact with him for any longer as she was scared the fizzing feeling in her stomach might make her explode.

"Well, Jenni likes the gym anyway. She had been saying for ages she wanted one so seemed like the perfect opportunity. She's really into her fitness."

And there she was again.

Charles had probably done that on purpose, maybe he had realised just how close they seemed to be getting and was establishing boundaries again.

She should be pleased and grateful for it - he was doing a much better job at distancing them than she was - but instead it felt like something heavy had latched onto her heart, and the happy, peaceful feeling that had been settling in her stomach, splintered.

"What was Jenni up to this weekend? Would have been nice to have met her." She forced her tone to be breezy.

Charles's body stilled, like he had been caught off guard, and his hand slipped slightly causing him to drop his spoon.

"Her...um, her parents. She needed to talk to them."

"You two look good together."

He didn't reply straight away. A painful silence settled between them and Lizzie pressed her knees together, inwardly squirming with the uncomfortableness of it all.

"Thanks."

"I'm happy for you."

"Thanks." He still looked awkward. His body rigid and his eyes not looking in her direction. "How about you? Are you seeing anyone?" He turned to look at her this time, his eyes looking more of a diamond blue in the darkness and his shoulder brushed hers.

"No," she said. She wanted it to come out as a laugh but it was more like a soft whisper. "There's no one." Her fingers itched to fix her ponytail.

This time the subsequent silence was gentle and calm. They both sat back further into the sofa, their legs out in front of them on the ground, barely touching, eating their peanut butter slowly.

"I'm sorry if my mum was a bit much today."

"It was lovely to see her again."

He smiled wistfully. "She always liked you."

Guilt curled over her heart.

"Your dad's still exactly the same."

"I don't think he will ever change."

"Nor should he."

She put down her peanut butter as what sounded like a new fresh wave of heavy rain struck down against the glass above them. They both looked up and then glanced out of the sides of their eyes at each other. The symmetry in their movements made Lizzie blush and Charles's eyes shine with...well, with something that made her blush deepen and her breathing suddenly become difficult.

"You made me re-enact *The Sound of Music* in here once," he said out of nowhere.

A loud laugh escaped her lips and she quickly smothered it with her hand. It had been a brilliant night. She had managed to persuade Charles to dance with her, jumping on and off the sofas and using them as makeshift benches. She had been surprised at just how well he could dance and suddenly, the way he had held her hand, the way he looked at her, the way he lifted her up, all of it, had felt more significant. It had sent her face scarlet and butterflies soaring in her stomach.

She had gone over, and over, that night in her head for weeks. Another case of her teenage-self trying to figure out if Charles might have caught the same kind of weird feelings she had, or if he was just being nice.

She turned her head around fully to look at him. "You knew all the words already. How old were we?"

"You were fifteen and I was seventeen. I kept changing the words over to our actual ages and you hated it."

"Hated you reminding me I was so much younger than you."

"So much?" Charles raised an eyebrow.

She laughed and put her hands up in mock innocence. "Hey! You were the one who kept over-emphasising the age difference."

He grinned jovially, brushing her side with his own. "We had fun though, right?"

She smiled at her hands. "Always."

"Good." He took a breath. "That's good, I...well, I always had fun whenever I was with you."

She looked up to find him watching her and an electric shiver tapped its feet up any bit of skin it could find.

God, he was beautiful. There was no other way to describe him. He was simply stunning. From the lanky, wavy haired teenager to the thirty-five-year-old actor sat next to her, there had always been something about Charles Williams that Lizzie couldn't help but be drawn to and find undeniable attractive. His high cheekbones, his strong jaw, his bright eyes...his soft mouth.

She was suddenly desperate to change the topic. "I found out about Lottie."

There was an awkward pause and the tension around them eased its heated hold. He leaned back slightly. "You really didn't know?"

"I wasn't really in a fit state to listen to town gossip around then." He frowned. "Why?"

"I asked Matt in the end. He told me," she said quickly.

He eyed her for a second, his keen eyes running over her face before he looked away and sighed, his body sagging in on itself. "I'm sure he didn't sugar-coat how I let her down."

"He didn't say that."

Charles raised an eyebrow at her.

"Okay, maybe he did." She looked down at her lap. "You...you think you let her down?"

"I did. She was unwell and I just...I became too focused on my career. Forgot that family was more important. I was selfish. She ran away." Fresh pain crossed his face, his eyes far away, and without thinking she reached over and threaded her fingers through his own. He didn't stop her. His hand was warm and soft and she felt the slightest fraction of tension leave his body. She squeezed it comfortingly.

"It's not your fault."

"But it is." His eyes found hers. "It really is. Lottie was always closest to me, she always told me everything and I just...dismissed her. I just ignored her and believed what everyone else said. I called her crazy. I didn't go after her." He looked down at their clasped hands and she followed his gaze. His hands had always been so much bigger than hers. Given their difference in heights it was to be suspected but in the darkness, the sight of them made her stomach lurch. For a second, neither of them did anything. Ever so slowly

Charles lifted his thumb and ran it along the back of her hand. She had to stifle a gasp and quickly tore her eyes away, her skin hot as something she hadn't felt in a very long time drummed through her body.

"Seems to be my trademark." His voice was barely a whisper.

"What is?"

He hesitated, pulling her gaze back to him. There was an internal struggle battling it out behind those blue eyes and it made Lizzie want to lean in even closer. He didn't answer straight away so after a couple of seconds, she asked again. "What's your trademark, Charles?"

His eyes scanned her face.

"Not going after the people I care about." His hand tightened around hers and this time, when his thumb traced over the back of it, her stomach dipped like she had been on a roller coaster. "Cartwright, I should have come after you."

She needed to reply, she needed to say something, anything, but the distance between their faces was becoming increasingly smaller and it was making it harder for her to think straight. She felt herself being pulled towards him. She could see just how long his eyelashes were, the fact there was a small dip in his nose and his jaw looked ever so different to before. His eyes were no longer blue, but black, and torturously slowly, they dropped to her mouth.

She pressed her knees together and her breath stuttered in her throat as she felt his hand brush her cheek, dipping his head closer, and closer -

A scream sliced through the air.

It pierced through the dark. Lizzie pulled away from him, almost falling back onto the floor. Charles blinked rapidly, as if he had been coming out of a dream, and his chest rose and fell rapidly.

"Lizzie, I-"

A second scream cut through the air.

"Amy!" she gasped and in less than a second, she was pushing past him and sprinting towards the stairs.

Lizzie 32, Charles 35

It was late. Lizzie had gone to bed earlier than the others because she felt so tired. She always felt exhausted for weeks after egg retrieval. Her body would feel sluggish and bloated, her head would ring and she would feel sick most of the time.

Like being pregnant, the doctor had joked.

Hilarious.

She wasn't sure how much later it was but the house felt still, the sound of music from downstairs had ceased, and her mouth was feeling particularly dry. Turning, she saw Charles's side of the bed empty. Beneath her fingers it felt cold and unslept in.

She loved being in Charles's old bedroom. His parents hadn't changed it since they had moved out and they had kept all his old theatre posters on the wall. Picture frames were scattered along the sides and she smiled as she caught sight of many that were of just them.

Swinging her legs out of the bed she headed to make her way downstairs. She could hear Kenneth's soft snores from down the corridor and she briefly stopped, listening to the calming rhythm of it.

A beam of light highlighted the bottom of the stairs, it was shining out of the living room and with it came the sound of voices. Slowly she crept towards it, hoping not to disturb Kenneth and thinking once she got some water she would go and find Charles. Today would have been tough on him – it was Maria's birthday. The whole family always came together to celebrate it. It was with the hope that it would be a happy, joyful day to remember her by, but every year it inevitably turned solemn.

Maria would have hated that.

The voices reached her ears as she stepped onto the ground floor, three feet away from the living room door.

"So, none of the IVF rounds have even worked? No usable eggs at all?"

Lizzie froze, her hands reaching out to grip the bannister as her heart slammed against her ribs and woke every single part of her up. It was Daniel who had spoken. His soft, gentle voice recognisable instantly.

"No," she heard Charles sigh.

"That sucks," Lottie said. "But onwards and upwards, right?"

Typical Lottie. Always optimistic about everything. Optimistic and feisty. An odd combination but Lottie was an odd combination of everything. Clothes, likes, appearance. She was the only Williams child who looked like both her parents, split down the middle, fifty/fifty, unlike the others who looked more like one than the other. She had blonde curly hair like Kenneth but brown eyes like Maria, she wore trousers with dresses, odd shoes, enjoyed Math's but also excelled in Art and loved to learn but found school boring. She was like a jigsaw puzzle that didn't slot together.

Charles sighed again. "It becomes easier when you are just prepared for bad news all the time."

Bad news.

All the time.

Lizzie leant on the bannister, not trusting her legs to keep her upright. She felt sick. Sweat prickled along her arms and suddenly the air felt humid and stifling. Was that what he thought? Had he just given up on her completely? She felt the bruises along her stomach ache as if to answer. Months and months of egg removal had left patterns on her skin.

"It'll happen one day," Daniel said.

"At least you know nothing's wrong with you!" Simon said, sounding cheerful. He was Patricia's husband.

Lizzie looped her arm around her stomach as the words cut through her.

Those kinds of comments shouldn't still hurt but they did. Her mind flashed back to what she overheard her dad say at Christmas in the pub. Maybe those kinds of comments would always hurt.

"Not the most helpful comment, Simon," Daniel replied curtly.

"Do you ever regret it?" Patricia asked, her words slurring ever so slightly.

"Regret what?"

There was a pause.

"Don't you sometimes wish you two had never got together? Like properly? In the grand scheme of things."

Lizzie's torso jerked like she had been shot and her breath caught sharply in her throat. At first, her body reacted but she felt nothing. Her mind unable to process what Patricia had said.

But what hurt the most came next.

The deadly silence.

It crept inside of her and iced her from within. The sweat cooled on her neck.

Charles said nothing. Not a word. He didn't protest, he didn't sigh angrily, he didn't swear. He remained silent.

"I would," Simon added.

"No one asked you!" Lottie snapped. "Patricia, that's a fucking awful thing to say."

"I was just asking hypothetically. Charles has always wanted to be a dad. Remember how cut up he was about Leo."

"Think Lizzie was quite sad about that too," Daniel said, coldly.

"I'm actually ashamed to be related to you right now!" Lottie snarled. There was a sound like she'd kicked the sofa.

"He wouldn't have married someone who didn't want children so-"

"That's very different," Daniel snapped.

"I think Mum would have even slapped you for that if she was here. She'd be appalled."

"I know Charles loves Lizzie, that's not what I was saying-"

"Stop," Daniel cut across. "Just stop."

Lizzie waited at the bottom of the stairs for a couple of seconds, her eyes burning with tears and her head swimming with a head rush of different emotions. She needed to hear Charles deny it. She needed to hear him tell Patricia that she was wrong. She needed him to say…something.

But, he didn't say anything.

CHAPTER TWENTY-ONE

Amy was sobbing uncontrollably, doubled over in her bed, her arms wrapped around her knees and shaking. A few of her pillows were scattered along the floor.

"Lizzie?" She managed to gasp through a sob and without thinking Lizzie threw her arms around her.

"It's okay, you're awake, it's fine." She pulled Amy in close to her, feeling her small body shake in her arms.

"Hey Amy," Charles whispered, kneeling down in front of the bed and placing his hand on her shoulder. "What happened?"

"Dad...Dad died." She began to shake even more and Lizzie felt her small hands fist into her back. "He died and there was so much blood and I-" she began to cry even harder, her body shaking in Lizzie's grip. "It was all my fault."

Get Daniel, she mouthed at Charles who with a quick stroke of Amy's hair did as he was told.

"Charles is getting your dad, Amy. He's fine. He's just sleeping."

But Amy was inconsolable. She continued to cling onto Lizzie, her small hands fisting into her hoodie, muttering under her breath until she was being pulled out of Lizzie's grasp and hauled up into the air.

"It's okay, Amy, I'm here, I'm here," Daniel whispered quietly into his daughter's ear as she wrapped her arms and her legs around him. His hair, for once, was askew, there were dark circles under his eyes and he looked weathered. Holding Amy made some of the tension in his face relax. She knew it was the middle of the night but she felt a flicker of alarm at seeing him in such a state.

Even after Helen had died, she had never seen him look quite so defeated.

"It was-," sob, "so real," sob, "this time. The car was so loud. You weren't listening to us, you wouldn't open your eyes. We asked you to but you wouldn't."

"I'm here, darling, I'm here."

"Every time. You never open your eyes."

Daniel's eyes were open now and they gleamed slightly in the darkness. "I'm so sorry, darling. I promise, I'll open them next time. I promise."

It took Daniel a while to settle Amy. Charles stood in the doorway, promising her he would stay until she fell asleep again. Lizzie had left soon after Daniel had arrived, telling him it was probably best for her to go. He'd seen her face, however, and it had very much shown she hadn't wanted to leave. He'd almost asked her to stay, but instead he had simply reached out and squeezed her hand.

She hadn't squeezed his back, instead looking suddenly even sadder and her eyes hiding more than they were showing. Every part of him had wanted to follow her, to simply hug her to him out in the corridor and check she was alright. But he had stayed still, reminding himself of just how close he had been downstairs to doing something incredibly stupid.

He watched his brother sitting on Amy's bed, whispering in her ear and stroking her forehead. Her eyes were closed and her slight breathing suggested she had finally fallen asleep but Daniel held onto her.

He looked broken.

He hadn't opened the door when Charles had knocked initially so Charles had walked into the bedroom. The sight that had greeted him had made his blood run cold. Daniel had been thrashing this way and that, his hands clawing into the duvet and he had been mumbling 'No' and 'I'm sorry' over and over. When Charles had shaken him,

Daniel had first grabbed him by the front of his shirt, gasping as if he had been dragged up from underwater and his eyes had shone with unshed tears. Worry had instantly clawed at him but Daniel seemed to recover quickly, jumping out of the bed the moment Charles had said Amy's name.

"Sorry," Daniel whispered, tucking Amy more tightly under her bed covers before standing up.

"Nothing to apologise for." He nodded to the hallway and they both walked out, not letting the door close fully behind them. "Are you okay?"

"Yeah." He let out a long breath before flicking his gaze up to look at Charles. Whatever he saw in his expression made him change his answer. "No. No, I'm not."

"This has happened before, hasn't it?"

"Yeah." Daniel sighed. "Once a week for the last two months, I'd say. She wakes up screaming and I can't...I can't do anything to stop it. She dreams I'm hit by a car."

Charles folded his arms. "Is it a delayed reaction to Helen's death? She's scared she will lose the both of you to the same thing?"

"I thought so. I talked to someone at work about it but...Helen died years ago. Amy was three, the likelihood of her having any trauma from that is slim. And Helen barely had any time for her anyway." He winced and closed his eyes painfully. "Sorry, I shouldn't have said that. Forget I said that."

Although it made him feel bad to even think it, Charles was pleasantly surprised. It was the closest Daniel had ever come to talking ill of his late wife. Charles had been convinced for years there was something Daniel wasn't telling him about their relationship but his older brother was too honourable to say. He'd stayed with her despite the cheating, despite openly trying to belittle him, and despite the fact she had run his credit rating into the ground. For some reason, he had refused to walk away. Helen had chipped away at Daniel's confidence for years. When she had died, Daniel had still refused to hear anyone speak badly of her.

The night she had died, Helen snuck out of the house whilst Daniel had been at work to meet up with one of the many men she had been sleeping with. Before she got in the car, she'd put Amy to bed and drunk at least half a bottle of gin. Helen hadn't had her driver's licence or any form of identification with her when the car was found, and the car had been registered to Helen's mother who'd had her phone switched off at the time. Amy had been left alone until Daniel had come home. She'd managed to climb out of her cot and bang her head so hard on the side that she'd had bruising for weeks. He hadn't a clue where Helen was until the police had arrived that evening.

Charles still didn't understand why he'd never appeared angry about that. Instead, Daniel had blamed himself.

"It could still be worrying her, she might have some memory of it? And it would make sense. She doesn't want to lose both parents. And kids freak out about their parents dying all the time. Do you remember Lottie?"

They shared a tired look.

When Lottie had started to lose track of reality, stating she was in fact a twenty-nine-year-old woman stuck in a sixteen-year-old body, she had also been adamant Maria was going to die. At first, she had kept crying every time she had seen her, and then slowly, she had begun begging her to go to the doctors.

Maria had refused, stating she wasn't going to give Lottie's delusions any kind of power over them. His little sister had grown more terrified.

It had scared them all.

Finally, around Christmas time, Maria had gone and got a smear test. The results came back stating that she had stage 1 cervical cancer. Within half a year it had been treated.

The day Maria had announced she was cancer free, Lottie hadn't stopped crying. She had used the information against them all, saying it proved she was right.

"I worry about her."

Charles swallowed and shook his head out of the past. "Who, Amy?"

Daniel shifted on the spot. "Of course, but…Lottie too. We still have no clue where she is." He ran a hand through his hair. "We're her big brothers, we should have done more."

Charles thought back to his conversation just an hour ago downstairs. "We should have."

They stood in silence for a short while, their shared guilt almost tangible..

"It looked like you were having a pretty bad dream yourself."

Daniel looked away, his grey eyes darkening.

"I dream of the crash too. Of the same car accident that Amy does. There's three of us. Amy, me and -"

"Helen?"

He swallowed, something hesitant passing behind in his eyes. "Yeah…yeah, Helen."

Charles studied Daniel. "What happens?"

"We are walking together. Amy runs off ahead and I just…I know she's in trouble. I can feel it. I see a car." Daniel ran a hand over his head and Charles noted the sweat on his brother's face. "I run out into the road, I push her out of the way and I get hit. And then I'm on the floor. Dying. And… Helen begs me to talk to her. I can hear Amy screaming and all I'm thinking about is the fact I'm going to leave Amy all on her own and that I am going to lose…well, just lose them. It's suffocating."

Charles didn't know what to say. He took in his brother's broken posture and sunken expression and quickly strode forward, pulling him into a hug. "It's a dream. It's just some weird, traumatic dream brought on by you losing Helen. That's all it will be." He didn't know if he was trying to reassure himself or Daniel. "Amy must have described it to you one night and now you're getting it. Sympathy nightmares."

"Sympathy nightmares?" There was a snippet of laughter in Daniel's tone.

"Yeah, did they teach you anything in medical school?"

"I must have been ill that day." He squeezed him back tightly.

Charles tried to laugh but it sounded fake and forced. It made no sense at all but this didn't feel like Daniel was describing a dream. The way he looked when he spoke about it, the way he sounded, it made it all seem very, very real. Part of him was worried that this was some kind of mental health trauma that Daniel really needed to look into but wasn't doing for Amy's sake. He hoped his brother knew what he was doing. He also hoped he knew he would be by his side no matter what.

Charles wasn't going to make the same mistake with two siblings.

As they parted, Charles glanced at Daniel's face. There was a slight far off look to his eyes and Charles could see his mind was back there. With the car crash. With Amy. And with someone else.

Charles knew how to read faces.

Helen wasn't the woman Daniel had been dreaming about.

Lizzie 32, Charles 35

They were arguing. Again.

"It's never romantic. You can't say what we do is out of any desire or want for each other. We have sex according to your calendar. Whenever I try to initiate things, you go and check the fridge to see if we should be saving ourselves. Everything is done by the book or a diagram. You're never here anyway! You're always busy doing overtime so we can afford another round of IVF. IVF that I have already told you I don't want to do anymore! This baby is taking over our life and it isn't even real." He threw up his hands. "I'm sorry I missed dinner. Matt asked if I wanted to go for a drink and seeing as I am so used to you coming home after I've gone to sleep, I said yes! Don't stand there acting like I am the bad guy because the one time you try and make a romantic effort I'm not here to see it!"

Two plates of untouched food were placed on the table, a candle between them and Lizzie looked exhausted. Her hands were shaking but Charles was tired. He could feel weariness pulling down his shoulders and the guilt that he had missed what looked like a really lovely evening made him angry and frustrated.

He shook his head angrily. "We can't have children, Lizzie. You need to grow up and accept that. No amount of fancy dinners or positions we try is going to change that. Five years of trying, two years of IVF, this isn't going to happen. And you need to actually listen to me when I say I don't want to do this anymore!"

His words rung through the kitchen, bouncing off every surface. Lizzie's shoulders dropped.

"I was just trying to make an effort."

He pinched the bridge of his nose and tried his hardest to lower his voice. "Then don't yell at me when I come in late from the pub. Don't get angry at me when I didn't know tonight was going to be the night my wife didn't spend stuck to her laptop at work. Why tonight anyway? Why is tonight special? The calendar you've installed on my phone didn't send me a notification to say you were ovulating like it normally does. You didn't write it all over my school planner for my colleagues and me to see. Did Neil not want to spend another late night in the office with you?" He knew he was being git. He knew he should simply excuse himself and go to bed but it was like the meal between them was taunting him, the candle flame flickering like some kind of joke.

Lizzie frowned. "Neil's a friend-"

"I know he's a friend but you spend more time with him than you do with me!" He slammed his hand on the table and the cutlery shook. "I never get to see you!"

"I was here tonight!"

"And you didn't tell me! You just expected me to be at home waiting for you! Once again, Lizzie, why tonight? Why is today so special?" The words were still spilling out of him. At the back of his mind a million different voices were trying to stop him but they couldn't halt his rage. Hurt, pain and grief were spilling out of him.

He missed Lizzie and he felt wretched that he had missed an evening with her. He felt guilty, he felt sick, he felt annoyed. Annoyed at the fact that a night with her was now a rarity. Annoyed at the fact that going to bed alone had become normal. Annoyed that she only woke him when she got in from work if she was ovulating and consequently, wanted to have sex with him.

He wanted her to come home at a normal hour to see him, at least once a week. He wanted to talk about something other than fertility.

He wanted her to wake him in the middle of the night because she wanted him in that moment.

He wanted his wife back.

And he felt like a git for wanting it too. He could never voice his concerns out loud because it officially made him a dick. He'd been the one who'd suggested trying for a child again. He'd started this. Guilt and anger fused in his chest. Right now, he didn't even know if he wanted a child anymore.

"I'm a week and a half late," Lizzie said.

"And?"

She looked a bit taken aback. "Well, that's a good thing."

He looked upwards at the ceiling, grinding his teeth together in annoyance. A laugh very nearly escaped his lips but he managed to swallow it back.

"For fuck's sake!"

"What?"

"It means nothing. We both know it means nothing. A week late, two weeks late, a day late, it never happens, it never works."

"It might! You're not a doctor!"

"Lizzie, you can't have children, okay? Your body doesn't work like that!" He shouted and a weird ringing sound filled the room.

The expression changed on her face and it punched him the stomach.

Shit.

What had he just said?

Lizzie's body sagged, like she was a puppet and someone had cut the string above her. "That's the first time you've finally admitted it's my fault." She sounded so young.

"Lizzie, I- I didn't mean that, I'm sorry. I've had a bit to drink, I-"

But Lizzie wasn't listening. She was turning, moving towards the front door, tightening her ponytail as she moved.

No.

"Lizzie, please."

She turned to look at him, her eyes shining with pain. "You were the one person," her voice broke, "who never said it was my fault."

"It's not. It's not, shit, Lizzie, I-" he said, hastily, moving around the table as quickly as he could.

"The only person." Tears ran down the side of her face.

He'd made her cry. He'd *never* made her cry.

"Lizzie, please-"

She took a few more steps away from him, holding up her arm to make sure he didn't come any closer. "Do you blame me too?"

"I don't blame you for anything-"

"For Leo."

His body ran cold and he stared at her. "What?"

She shook her head and choked back more tears. "I do. All the time. Like you said, my body just can't have children." She gave one last sob and then ran to the front door.

"No, Lizzie, wait! Lizzie!" His foot caught the side of the table leg and he tripped forward, just managing to catch himself before he fell.

The front door slammed, the sound piercing through him like glass.

Shit.

What had he done?

CHAPTER TWENTY-TWO

As the director called cut, Charles felt his whole body slump into his chair in relief. It had been a long day and with little to no sleep the night before, it had been a struggle. Before anyone took a breath he straightened himself up, not prepared to let anyone see that he was tired, especially not Damien Reading sitting opposite him. He was theatre royalty, known for his strong work ethic and his no-nonsense attitude. He worked hard, hated attention and was often reported as being a bit of a grump, but Charles loved working with him. He wasn't actually rude, he simply didn't try to run around after anyone or feel he needed to get involved in cast politics and the like.

Charles looked up at the crew, his eyes unintentionally scanning for a certain brunette's figure behind the glare of the lights and huge black cameras. Lizzie often came down to the studio at the end of the day. He was used to seeing her weaving in and out of people, wires, and equipment, and being bombarded with questions everywhere she went. Her hair was always tied back into a low ponytail and a clipboard would be in her hand, ready to write down her new list of things to do once she returned to the office.

"Can I get you anything, Sir?" Brooke asked. He jumped slightly, not realising she was at his shoulder already. Brooke was the runner assigned to him when they were filming inside the studios. She was timid, with a thick Australian accent and still called him 'Sir' despite how many times he had said she was welcome to call him by his name. She worked hard though and he liked that.

"No, I am fine, thanks, Brooke."

"I've got your phone here, Sir, it kept going off inside your trailer.

I thought it might be important."

"Thanks," he said, frowning as he took it off her. His mind went straight to Daniel. He and Lizzie had left too early that morning for Daniel or Amy to be awake and he hadn't had a second to ring him and check he was alright once he got into work. The memory of his brother's fitful sleep flickered into his mind and he felt his chest tighten. The bad dreams were affecting Daniel more than he had let on. Charles had tried not to see his brother's hands shaking as they'd said goodnight, or at his glassy eyes as they had checked on Amy again. When he had left that morning, Charles had popped his head into Amy's room and hadn't been surprised to find Daniel asleep on the floor.

The missed calls, however, were not from Daniel but from a variety of numbers. The most being Patricia and Jennifer. He quickly walked to the side of the soundstage and clicked on Jennifer's name first, knowing that, out of the two, she was the one he would prefer to talk to first.

She answered after one ring. "Charles, thank God-" And then she promptly burst into tears, the sounds tearing down the phone.

Fear raced down his spine.

"Jenni, what is it? What's wrong?"

But she couldn't answer him, instead her sobs kept getting caught up in her speech and she could barely string syllables together, let alone a sentence. He heard someone else take the phone from her.

"Hey, Charles."

It was Kristina.

"What's wrong? Is she okay? We've just wrapped for the day so I can come straight home. Was it her parents? She said they were okay with it."

She had texted him the night before, after he had tried to ring her twice. She had been happy. A weight had lifted off Charles's shoulders that he hadn't even known was there when her text had eventually come through.

"They were. Two seconds." Kristina must have pulled the phone away from her mouth because her voice became distant. "Jenni, go and sit down. Make a cup of tea. Go on." There was a long pause and Charles suspected Kristina was waiting for Jennifer to move far enough away before she spoke into the receiver again. "They were happy. We had a great weekend. Got back this morning and thought everything was fine."

Charles hadn't even had time to go home. He had come straight to work from Tring. Lizzie had sat in the passenger seat but as far away from him as she possibly could, her arm pressed up against the door and her head turned towards the dark windows. The car journey had been silent, filled with unsaid things and memories of what had almost happened the night before.

"So, what's happened?"

"Apparently, Malli was not so happy."

Malli was Jennifer's younger sister. The last time Charles had met her she had just tried out for drama school for a second time.

"What do you mean?" His stomach turned and he began to notice how many eyes were suddenly watching him. Cameramen glancing at their phones and then between themselves, the lighting guys with their heads together but looking in his direction, and he could have sworn Brooke had tears in her eyes. He turned his back to all of them and faced the wall.

"She's gone to the papers," Kristina said, sounding defeated. "Made out as if I've come along and turned Jennifer gay. She's made me out to be a right home wrecker." He could hear she was trying her best to be jovial but there was a shudder in her voice that he had never heard.

"Shit," he whispered, closing his eyes. "I'm so sorry, Kristina."

"It's okay, it's fine. Jennifer's distraught. It came out online about half an hour ago and it will be in *The Evening Standard* tonight. Full interview with Malli about the personal trainer who snuck into her sister's perfect relationship and destroyed it."

Anger stirred in his stomach. He lowered his voice and stepped further away from anyone potentially trying to listen. "This is going to sound patronising so I apologise, but you did tell all of them that our relationship was fake from the start?"

"Of course we did! We told them everything. How you were in no fit place to be in a relationship, how you two were friends, how you made the arrangement with the idea of it only being short-term and it kind of ran away from you a bit. All of it. Malli seemed to be fine with it but she had a weird look on her face the entire bloody time. I should have known. I should have bloody known. I face this kind of shit all the time! When clients discover I'm gay and suddenly think I'm going to start coming on to them." She sniffed angrily. "She...she took pictures of us. On the sofa after dinner. Arms around each other. That kind of thing. And...well, we thought everyone had gone to bed and Jenni was so happy that her parents knew and didn't care that we got a bit heavy handed on the sofa. She filmed it."

"Bloody hell!" He snapped, forgetting he was trying to be quiet.

"Exactly." Kristina sighed. "It's all a bit of a shit show."

There was a long pause. Charles had no idea what to say. His chest felt extremely tight and his emotions were torn between empathetic pain and utter fury.

Jennifer and Kristina were his family. Jennifer was one of his oldest friends and he knew just how sensitive and vulnerable she was. No wonder she had been a mess when she had called him. He hadn't known Kristina for as long but he did know that despite her tendency to appear strong and unbothered, she loved Jennifer and she did care what others thought of her. This would have hurt her to the core.

"Jenni is convinced you're going to hate her."

"Hate her?" He spluttered, lowering his voice again. "Why would I hate her?"

"Because she's 'broken the pact'. She's convinced you're going to hate her for being so stupid."

"How the-?"

"Her words, not mine."

"Well I don't. It's not even a bloody pact. This isn't her fault. Look, I'll come home straight away and we can discuss how we are going to play this-"

"You can't. We're not there. We're at my brother's flat in Lewisham. Photographers were already arriving at the house when we left."

Charles ran a hand through his hair and cursed under his breath. "I could come to your brother's?"

"I'll send you the address but if there is any chance of you being followed, please don't come. I love you but please, don't. Jenni is...well, she's a mess."

"Can you put her on?"

"I don't think she can talk."

"Just put her on, just for a second. Please."

Kristina sighed and he heard the sound of rustling, trainers walking across a floor and then more sobs.

His heart wrenched.

"H-h-ello." Her voice was quiet and a fresh wave of sobs echoed down the phone when she had finished her word.

"Jenni, I love you. I am in no way mad at you. Do you understand me?"

A sobbed response ripped from her mouth and tenderness rose in his chest. She did not deserve this. She did not deserve a single shred of this. He fisted his free hand into the side of his leg.

"We are going to sort this, I promise."

"I'm sorry," she managed to whisper.

"Never say that again, I don't want to hear it."

She mumbled something else and it very much sounded like another apology.

"I'll see you soon, okay? Jenni?"

She gargled something back and he hung up the phone. His heart was pounding and he took two deep breaths. His phone vibrated again.

Patricia.

He ignored it and as the call faded off the screen he saw he had missed calls from his agent and his mum too.

Shit.

He clicked his tongue, not sure if he wanted to call either of them back. It was only then that he realised how silent the studio around him was. He slowly turned back to see everyone's eyes on him. Everyone except Damien who appeared to have left the studio.

In a film he would have probably said something tough like "got a problem?" or "yes?", but the words didn't feel right in his mouth. They felt stupid. His mouth felt dry.

Some of the crew at least had the decency to look away when caught staring. Others did not.

He looked around at them all, suddenly feeling like an animal in a zoo.

"Now, now, everyone stop staring," a familiar voice called across the soundstage. "The poor man's just found out he's turned his girlfriend gay."

Craig.

He was stood in the corner, leaning against the wall with a lighter in his hand. Lazily, he flicked it on and off, the small flame appearing and disappearing over and over as he smiled that ever so creepy smile at Charles.

"I'm going to take you to make-up, Sir." Brooke was by his side, her glare piercing into Craig deeply. She began to steer him backwards. At any other time he'd have been impressed by her confidence but right now he was too busy staring at Craig Rosswool.

"He did the same to my daughter."

Brooke stumbled and Charles felt the silence around the studio grow hungrier. He wasn't sure how many people were aware that Craig was Lizzie's father: neither of them offered the information to anyone and they never spoke to one another.

Susannah, the director, looked up and her keen golden eyes told him that she was definitely aware of the information.

The noise of Craig's lighter grated into the side of Charles's head. Open and shut. Open and shut. Charles fists clenched at his side.

"Turned her off men for life."

"You have no idea what you're talking about," Charles snapped, unable to stay silent for any longer. He took a step forward but Brooke's hand was still pressed into his chest. It reminded him he needed to act professional.

It reminded him of where he was.

Craig's smile grew and he looked around at his audience with a glint in his eye. He was enjoying this far too much.

"Everyone thinks you are Mr Nice Guy, but I wonder, would they still think that if they knew?"

"Knew what?" Charles could feel the anger vibrating through his entire being.

Craig opened his mouth to talk but instead he suddenly yelled out, screaming in a high pitched wail as he disappeared from sight.

"Gee, I'm so sorry!" A blonde head came into view to Craig's right. "My bad, Mr Rosswool is that you? I just came in and thought I saw fire."

"What the fuck?! You stupid idiot!" Craig yelled, furiously wiping foam away from him and gasping as if he had just jumped into cold water. He looked as if he had fallen into an upright bubble bath.

"God, I'm so terribly sorry, I saw fire and acted out of instinct." Neil didn't sound sorry at all.

"It was my bloody lighter!"

"I just saw a flame! Very safety conscious, me. And we do advise no lighters near the set. Never know what kind of accidents could happen." Neil grinned. He flicked a glance behind him towards Charles, meeting his eye and winking. "I'm doing Lizzie's rounds today. Make-up are looking for you, Charming. Brooke, could you take Mr Williams there?"

CHAPTER TWENTY-THREE

Having his make-up taken off had been awkward. The usually talkative Emily had been quiet, her stares intense and even her body language felt careful around him, like he was a bomb about to explode. When he had got to his trailer it had been a relief to be left alone.

He hadn't looked at his phone since. He didn't want to hear Patricia's angry tone or deal with his mother's concern. If he was honest, he had no idea what to do. They'd been found out. It would be all over the news and internet that Jennifer and him were not together. What the internet didn't know was that they never had been together in the first place. They would think Jenni was a cheat.

When they had first started they had both been super conscious of their act; going out together, holding hands, meeting each other outside of work almost daily to convince their fellow actors and the media that they were a couple. Nowadays, they no longer tried so hard: they didn't need to. Ten years after their agreement Jennifer and Charles were successful in their own right and no one questioned their relationship. They were both so much happier than they had been when they had come up with the plan.

Jennifer had found love in Kristina, and Charles had...well, there had been a few people he'd been interested in getting to know better over the last decade. He'd not trusted any of them enough though, preferring to let them believe he was a lousy cheat than put Jennifer's secret in jeopardy. He'd never dated them for very long, hyper aware there was something missing with every single one of the handful. He had never been able to be himself around any of them.

Now it was out, what was he to do? Play the part of the wounded boyfriend?

No.

He wouldn't. He would not paint Jennifer and Kristina out to be bad people. Patricia would want him to, he knew she would want him to try and gain the sympathy card but he'd refuse. There had to be another way. He just hadn't figured it out yet.

His phone buzzed again in his pocket. He glanced at the screen. *Mum.*

Charles closed his eyes and chucked it onto the sofa.

What the hell was he going to do about his parents? He'd have to tell them truth. He ran a hand through his hair. It would hurt them. A lot.

"Shit," he hissed.

As his brain filled with images of his mother's tearful face and his father's disappointment, he looked up to see a piece of paper had been laid out on the coffee table next to the sofa. The main room of his trailer was both a kitchen and a living room. It was a bit of a mess and he knew he should have really tidied it up the previous Friday when they had been allowed to go home early. He just hadn't had the energy. He loved the two women he lived with but they hated mess, and he was a naturally messy person. Like his mother in her role at the hospital, his natural messy side exploded when it could.

He picked up the piece of paper and unfolded it. Trepidation trickled down his spine. Part of him suspected it could be someone's well wishes, left in his trailer whilst he had been having his make-up taken off. Maybe it was from Brooke? She had keys to his trailer after all and would have been the kind of person to write him a letter. Another part of him feared it might be an article from that evening's news or photos of Jennifer and Kristina printed off by Craig and left to taunt him.

It was neither of those things.

Instead, the piece of paper had the name 'Leo' painted across the top in blue thick paint and underneath it were two blue, impossibly small footprints.

A lump he couldn't explain formed in his throat.

The paper was only A4-sized but it felt larger in his hands, its importance heavy. He ran his eyes over the name again and felt a punch of pain so strongly in his gut he almost cried out.

Leo.

Protectiveness rushed up inside of him so fiercely he bent with it. The name felt so familiar. He moved his lips around the word, unable to speak it aloud for a reason he couldn't explain.

My Leo.

The footprints were so small that he could have put both feet comfortably in his palm. He turned the page over in his hand. The creases looked dark and wrinkled, like the page had been folded and unfolded hundreds of times. Fan mail? He had been sent some crazy stuff in his time but not quite in the same category as a baby's set of footprints.

"Please breathe. Please be a mistake. Please, for me, just breathe."

His own voice ran through his head and he blinked as tears began to burn in his eyes. In confusion he laughed at himself, wiping them away hastily as the lump in his throat grew.

Something moved out of the corner of his eye and he jerked around in time to see...nothing. Laughter. Playful, young laughter reached his ears but there was no one there. Grief curled up inside of his gut and suddenly, his problems with Jenni and his fear over confessing his lie to his parents felt so small and insignificant. Everything did. It was nothing compared to this.

He felt more tears on his cheeks and hastily tried to wipe them away, trying to continue laughing at himself but the sound wouldn't escape his lips. Instead there was just silence. A thick, suffocating, isolating silence that somehow seemed familiar. The piece of paper fluttered to the floor and under the coffee table. He bent down to retrieve it, not knowing why he desperately needed to see those little blue footprints again but simply knowing that he did.

There was nothing under the table.

"No!" he yelled. "No, no, no, no!" He knelt on the floor, his fingers running through the fine hairs of the carpet, looking around desperately to see where it could have gone.

Not *that*. He couldn't lose *that*.

He mouthed the name again, feeling pain slice across his tongue and his eyes burned with a stinging heat.

Dad, it's okay.

"What?" He shouted, looking around him desperately and slamming his head into the table. The voice had been so close to his ear he had felt breath on his face.

"Charles?"

His head flicked to the door. For a second, the wave of relief was so strong it felt like it was going to knock him to the ground. Lizzie was standing there, wearing jeans and a purple jumper. She had changed from that morning and even though he felt so relieved to see her, something strange was stirring in the back of his mind. He didn't know how he knew it but that jumper wasn't hers.

More voices flooded through his head.

"Daniel, why's Bex's jumper in your living room?"
"Is it?"
"Yeah, it's the purple one with blue stars along the bottom."
"...No idea."

"Charles, I'm so so sorry," Lizzie said, her gaze roaming over his face as he pushed himself off the floor, trying to blink back his tears as fast as he could. He wasn't fast enough. In a blur, she was in front of him, wrapping her arms around his waist and pressing her cheek against his chest. He still felt shaken, the image of the painted footprints still in his mind and he automatically wrapped his arms around her.

The sense of calm her embrace brought him made him tighten his grip, loving the feeling of her in his arms, loving the way despite her lack of height and her smaller frame, he felt so much strength and comfort from her touch. Despite the misunderstanding, he couldn't bring himself to interrupt the moment. He hadn't hugged her since the night of his grandmother's party.

He bent his head down so his chin was resting on top of her head and wave of nostalgia flowed through him. She smelled like home.

A home with a purple kitchen.

He swallowed and pressed his face into the top of her hair.

"It'll be okay," she whispered gently.

He opened his mouth to speak but couldn't say anything, distracted by her completely and not sure what to say to make the situation right.

He should tell her the truth.

But it wasn't all his truth to tell. It was Jennifer's too. He hadn't trusted anyone but Daniel with it. Patricia had only found out when it was her job to know. He'd refused to tell her initially, saying it wasn't any of her business so Jennifer had gone behind his back and told her instead. She had claimed it was a safety precaution.

"I know," he replied simply.

He felt her begin to tug away and reluctantly he let his arms drop.

"How are you feeling?" She craned her head back to look up at him.

"I'm okay." He caught the look she was giving him. "Honestly."

"There's about fifty people with huge black cameras outside the gates. If you want I can try and sneak you out the caterers' entrance."

He raised an eyebrow at her. "Load me in the meat van?"

"Something like that. I know Allery very well, she would probably let me."

He laughed. "Thanks but I think I'll pass."

He noticed the tenderness in her expression and guilt, once again, wound itself up tightly inside him.

"You could stay here? I can let security know?" She said softly.

He ran a hand through his hair. "That's actually not a bad idea."

There was a slight pause and he deliberately avoided her gaze, instead looking out of the window into the car park. Two people passed and he saw them gesturing at their phones before looking towards his trailer.

"How are you doing? Really?"

"I'm okay."

"I'm so sorry about Jennifer. I feel terrible."

"Please, don't be."

"I just…I can't believe she would do that. I got the impression she was lovely…I was so happy you found someone nice." Her tone pulled his gaze back to her. "If you need me to redo the schedule or sort out something with production so you can have a few days to process this, I can. I can say it's our fault. Gas leak or something."

He laughed slightly at her suggestion. "Lizzie, if it were a gas leak wouldn't that put every production on halt?"

"Yes," she said, completely seriously.

Affection clawed up his chest as he stared at her. She would do that for him?

"Really, Lizzie, that isn't necessary."

She looked at him hard and something that looked vaguely like irritation flickered in the backs of her green eyes.

"It was a ten-year relationship."

"Honestly, it's fine."

She let out a huff of frustration. "You know you don't have to be strong all the time! Despite what Patricia says, you don't have to put across this whole macho masculine image."

"I'm not being strong, I just-"

"Honestly, it's the twenty-first century, you're allowed to be upset!" She gripped his arms and shook him slightly. "You don't have to lie!"

"I'm not lying," he answered tersely.

"I saw you crying!" Her voice turned from annoyed to soft. He wasn't sure if it infuriated him more or less.

"That was about something else."

She raised an eyebrow. "Charles, come on."

"That wasn't about Jenni."

"Sure!" She lifted her hands up in exasperation. "Jesus Christ Charles, it's me! You don't have to lie!"

"I'm not lying!"

"Of course you are."

"No, I'm not."

"You always have to be 'strong', don't you? Always have to pretend nothing's wrong!"

"Am I lying?" He snapped.

"Obviously-"

"Cartwright, am I lying?"

She hesitated, either his tone or his words catching her off guard. Charles waited, watching her eyes run across his face. Ever so slowly, her brow began to furrow. He took a step forward and lowered his voice. "Lizzie, am I lying?"

"Well, you are an actor now-"

"Answer the question."

A couple of seconds passed where neither of them spoke.

"No," Lizzie finally whispered. Shock was written through every fraction of her expression. "I don't understand."

"I'm just not upset."

"Charles, you're the biggest romantic I know." The ghost of a smile passed her lips and he felt something squeeze inside his chest hard. Once upon a time he might have been. "Why aren't you upset? Jennifer cheated on you! Why are you being so heartless about this?"

He flinched but didn't say anything, firmly keeping his lips pressed together.

It all came down to did he trust her or not. The woman who had broken his heart and destroyed two of the best friendships he'd had. Did he trust her?

His mind said one thing.

His heart said the opposite.

"I knew," he said quietly.

The words caused her head to jerk backwards. "You knew?"

"I knew about Jenni. I knew about Kristina." He clicked his neck to the right. "I knew from the start. It's been fake. The whole time. The whole relationship. It was a lie."

"The whole time?"

"The whole time. Jennifer is gay. She was having a hard time at drama school. Thought her sexuality, her size, her ethnicity would hold her back and I was not ready for another relationship so, we agreed to pretend to be together and it kind of escalated."

Her eyes flared and her teeth slammed together. He'd anticipated many reactions from Lizzie. Anger had not been one of them.

CHAPTER TWENTY-FOUR

"How could you be that stupid?" She snapped, the softness around her vanishing. "A fake relationship! A fake -" For a moment it appeared she was too angry to even speak. "You're meant to be happy, you're meant to be living your best life!" She stepped forward and jabbed her finger into his chest. He warily looked down at her, completely taken aback. "I'm so angry at you! You're thirty-five! What the hell do you think you're doing? What about loving someone? What about a family? Don't you want all that?" She paused as if her anger had momentarily run out of steam. "I thought you wanted all of that."

"For a second, I thought you might be about to say what a nice thing it was we had done for each other."

She gave him a horrified look, the sadness gone and the anger back. "Absolutely not. I think it's awful. What the hell were you thinking? What about being happy?"

"I am happy," he said firmly. "I'm fine."

"Fine isn't good enough." She shook her head and he realised the anger had now shifted into some sort of desperation... and fear. Dancing just out of reach behind her eyes, like she didn't even realise it was still there. "Why did you do this to yourself?"

"It was a joint decision. We were helping each other."

She felt like she was on the verge of a panic attack. It was getting harder and harder to breathe and her stomach felt as if it was crushing itself.

It had been fake. The whole time.

He wasn't happy.

He wasn't in a loving, brilliant relationship.

He wasn't any closer to having the family he'd always wanted.

And she was furious at him for it.

He had messed *everything* up.

"Don't you miss it? Miss being in a relationship? Miss being close to someone? Miss not being alone?"

He raised an eyebrow at her. "Do you?"

"I'm not alone." Her tone returned to mildly outraged. "I have Bex, I have Neil, I have Matt. I am fine."

"Thought you said fine wasn't good enough?"

"It's good enough for me."

"What the hell is that supposed to mean?" There was an annoyance to his voice that made her angry. He didn't get to be mad at her.

"Exactly what I just said!" She snapped, before raking her hands through her hair and tightening her ponytail, pulling so sharply on the hair band she could have cut off blood supply. She had done all of this for him. For him to be happy. Yes, he had got the career he had always wanted but family had always come first to Charles. He'd wanted to be a dad more than an actor. And now he had done this.

She turned and began to walk towards the door. "You're a bloody idiot, Charles!"

She needed to get out of there, she needed to breathe, she needed some time to process what he had just told her. She needed to leave before she said something she regretted. The rage inside her was practically burning at her seams and she could feel the threat of angry tears at the backs of her eyes.

Why were men such idiots?

She pulled open the door but it was suddenly slammed shut as Charles's placed his hand above her and she felt the heat of him at her back.

"Why did you put me on your Banned List?"

How the hell-?

"Did Neil tell you that?" She spun around to face him.

"Does it matter? Why was I on it?"

"That has nothing to do with this!"

"Well, I think it's fair. I've told you my secret, now you tell me yours."

Bastard.

"That's not how it works!" She shouted angrily.

He was so close to her. His body heat was like a furnace but her own anger was burning through her. She didn't think she'd ever been so livid at him in her entire life.

"You put me on the same list as Craig, I deserve to know why!"

"For completely different reasons."

"What reasons?"

"Stop it!"

"What reasons, Lizzie?"

She pressed her back into the door, glaring up into his thunderous gaze. He had left his hand on the door above her head, whilst his right was next to her waist. His whole body had her caged.

"I-," suddenly she was finding it hard to speak. He really was too close, his eyes too dark, his mouth too close. She needed to come up with some sort of passable lie but his proximity was making her brain short-circuit. "I-"

Think of something.

He raised his eyebrows and cocked his head to the right. "Yes?"

"I couldn't risk seeing you again."

He stared at for a good long second before slowly repeating, "Couldn't risk seeing me?"

His tone was patronising and it ignited more irritation inside of her. She tried to get her brain to say something sarcastic but he was still so close she felt as if he was taking the air she needed to breathe properly. She shoved at his chest but he didn't move. "Stop it, Charles!"

"Stop what?"

"Stop this."

"What do you mean you couldn't risk seeing me?"

"I just couldn't risk seeing you!" She shouted, fear and desperation flapping their wings inside of her. "I didn't want to see you. I didn't want the emotional hurricane that would come as a consequence. I didn't want to get hurt! I didn't want to put myself in that position. I knew if I saw you I'd..." She cut herself off, pressing her lips together tightly.

His body stilled. "You'd?"

She shook her head.

"You'd what, Lizzie?"

Her eyes met his and for a fraction of a second, she let him see what she meant. She let him read it for himself.

Charles looked momentarily lost for words, his chest heaving with every breath as his eyes pinned her to the spot.

With a growl that was so unlike him, he pushed himself away from her almost violently and turned his back to her. Her body slumped against the door, her own breathing heavy as if she had just run there. She couldn't believe she had just said that, that she'd admitted...she'd admitted *that*. Humiliation tried to ripple through her but her sudden exhaustion eclipsed it.

Charles was stood a few feet away. His back was too her and his shoulders were locked by his ears. He was wearing a grey shirt tucked into dark blue jeans. They looked so simple but the way they fitted him like a glove emphasised their expense and reminded her of just how different their lives had turned out to be.

"I should go," Lizzie whispered, resting her head back against the door and staring up at the ceiling.

He didn't turn to face her and when he spoke all the anger had gone from his voice.

Instead he sounded deflated.

"Maybe you should."

Lizzie nodded, reaching behind her for the door handle. As her fingers closed over steel, he spoke again.

"Why is it that you seem to have forgotten you broke up with me?"

She stared at his frame. "What?"

"Why is it that everyone seems to have forgotten that you broke up with me? Your brother, your dad, you. All that Patsy Whiskers nonsense. All of that fear I see behind your eyes every time I see you. Your dad said I abandoned you. You brother put me in hospital-"

"Matt put you in hospital?" She said, her eyes widening.

Charles turned around to face her. "In Tring. The first fight. He broke my jaw in two places and dislocated my knee."

Horror cinched at her waist. "God, Charles, I'm so sorry."

"Don't apologise." His eyes locked with hers. "Not for that."

She shook her head and looked up at the ceiling, taking two heavy gulps of air as she fought back the multitude of emotions building in her chest.

"I agreed to fake a relationship with Jenni because the last time I fell in love with someone it didn't end well for me," he said, coldly. "I promised myself I wouldn't let it happen again."

For a second she felt like she had been punched. A raw hurricane of emotion whipped up inside of her but she ignored it. She had become better at that over the years.

"When was that?"

As much as it hurt maybe this was a blessing. She would find this person. Find them and try and set the pair of them up again. Maybe this could work. Maybe she could still salvage this and fix the problem. Men could become dads whenever, right? Rock stars in their eighties were always reported to be fathering yet another child, weren't they? Maybe there was still hope. Neil could help. He would be able to find them.

She imagined asking Neil to help to find Charles's long lost lover. And then, she accurately imagined his response.

Absolutely fucking not.

"You're kidding?" Charles said, bringing her attention back to him. His gaze made something prickle along her skin but she fought against it. After a couple more seconds he wiped a hand across his face. "You're not fucking kidding." His voice sounded hoarse. "Cartwright, come on."

"Heather?"

His first girlfriend. She had been beautiful and lovely. They had separated after they had gone to different universities but they hadn't ended on bad terms.

"Heather?"

Was he laughing at her?

"Heather, really?" There was definitely humour in those eyes but there was a bite to his tone that she had rarely heard.

"First girlfriend, first love."

"I didn't love Heather, Lizzie."

They stared at each other.

"I-," he pulled his bottom lip into his mouth and looked away.

Lizzie didn't dare speak. There was a weird kind of tension surrounding them which felt like it shouldn't be broken. It was causing her heart to race and her cheeks to redden. She flattened her palms against the door, hoping the cold surface would calm her down.

It didn't.

"You have no idea what I am talking about?"

"No!"

He took two strides forward, his jaw rock solid and he looked as if he was barely breathing. "No idea at all?"

"No!" She craned her neck up to look at him.

"Okay then," he swallowed, blinking a couple of times before looking away. Even without his gaze on her, the air around them felt heavy, like there were a million unsaid things woven throughout it. "I don't know how you did this," he said quietly.

"Did what?"

He turned his head to look at her. "And you were only seventeen. I'm a thirty-five-year-old man."

She frowned. "What did I do when I was seventeen?"

When he didn't reply, she curled her hand around the door handle again – she didn't remember when she had let go.

"Charles, I'm going to go."

"Please, don't." It wasn't his response that caused her to freeze. It was the look he was giving her. "Jesus Christ Lizzie, how can you not know?"

He closed the space between them and crushed his mouth against hers.

Lizzie's body locked, her heartrate rocketing to some lethal speed and her nerves exploding in surprise.

Charles was kissing her. Charles was *kissing her.*

And she was kissing him back, pressing her lips against his and pushing herself off the door to be closer to him. She felt his arm slide around her waist, pulling her up against his chest whilst his other cupped her face. All of her thoughts and reasoning disappeared into smoke. All she could focus on was him.

She slid her hands up the front of his shirt, her fingers digging into it and pulling him closer to her whilst she teetered on the tips of her toes. She had forgotten the taste of his lips. She had forgotten the shape of them. The way just the touch of them could shoot heated tremors of excitement soaring through her.

She began to lose her balance and he pushed her back against the door. Before she had time to feel the loss of his strong arm around her back, his hands traced up her body, sculpting over her hips and pressing in to hold her waist. Even through her jumper his fingers left electric trails and she gasped against him, jumping slightly as they stopped just below her ribcage. She could feel the heat of his chest, the muscle of his thighs, the pressure of one of his legs as he pressed it hard between her own. It felt good. Too good.

She whimpered and almost tore her mouth away from him in embarrassment. Both of his hands moved to cup her face and he refused to let her, instead smiling against her lips.

"You have no idea how long I've wanted to do this," he whispered, coaxing her into letting him kiss her again but this time deeper. His tongue ran along the seam of her mouth and she was utterly powerless to it. He kissed her as if she was something to be explored.

It had been so long. So long since she had been kissed, but fundamentally, so long since Charles had kissed her and she was overwhelmed by the amount of emotions it was firing up inside of her. She felt consumed by him. Like he was taking up every single sense of hers. His body seemed ten times bigger than it was, smothering her in heat and need. Her hands reached up to the back of his head and he whispered her name as she ran her fingers through his hair.

The way he said it made her sound needed.

Wanted.

Charles broke away first, resting his forehead against hers. The sounds of their heavy breathing were the only thing to fill the empty space around them and she knotted her hands in his shirt to steady herself. Her eyes dipped to his mouth again, she really wanted to kiss him again.

"Same."

Their eyes locked and Lizzie felt a blush rise in her cheeks. "I didn't say anything."

"You didn't have to."

She laughed gently and he closed the gap between them again, kissing her lips affectionately before whispering. "It was you, Cartwright. It was always you."

Her body locked. Any sparks that had still been coursing through her died out as what they had actually been discussing before their kiss came rushing back into the forefront of her mind.

No.

Lizzie let out a breath she hadn't even realised she had been holding.

No, no, no, no.

This couldn't be her fault.

Not again.

Please, not again.

"Lizzie?" Charles lifted his head back, sensing the sudden change. "What's wrong?" He pulled away from her.

"I didn't do this! I didn't make you!" She pushed past him, stumbling forward towards the middle of the room. "I didn't make you do this. This can't be my fault!" She whirled around to face him. The sight almost knocked the air out of her lungs. The blue in his eyes had nearly all turned to black. He was still breathing relatively hard and his hair was a mess.

Had she run her hands through it?

She couldn't remember.

She choked back the rush of desire that bulldozed through her and instead focused on her anger. Focused on her horror at what he had just said. What he had implied.

"I didn't make you do this."

"I never said you did, I was saying that I loved you."

"We'd only been together two years!"

"So? We still loved each other!"

"You were a child, you didn't know what love was."

"A minute ago you were trying to tell me I was in love with Heather, who I dated before you!" He frowned. "Wait, are you saying…are you saying you didn't love me?" He looked so young all of a sudden, something painful flickering across his eyes.

Lizzie refused to let it get to her.

"Of course I did! How can you ask that?"

"How can you say that I didn't!"

"You never came after me!" She shouted, shaking her head at him. "If you'd been heartbroken, if you'd been so put off love that you never entered another relationship again, you'd have tried to stop me. If you had truly loved me, you'd have stopped me! You'd have begged me to stay! Charles, you never even yelled! You didn't put up a fight. Your response to me breaking up with you was just 'okay'. A text. Just a single text response. You can't say this was my fault!"

"I never said it was your fault." He straightened up, taking a step forward and crossing his arms.

"You literally just said you were too hurt by our relationship to move onto another one so you faked one. For ten years."

"Jenni and I were perfectly happy with the arrangement. It wasn't a hardship."

"I'm sure she is wonderful but you weren't in love with her, Charles."

"No, I wasn't. And it wasn't a problem for me. For either of us." He ran a hand through his hair. It did nothing to flatten it. "You wanted me to come after you?"

"Of course I did!" The words left her mouth before she could stop them. She winced as his eyes widened. As much as she'd tried to tell herself over the years that she hadn't wanted him too, that she wanted to get on with her plan of giving him a better life, clearly her sub conscious still thought differently.

"Then why did you break up with me?"

"I-I-" She stammered over her words.

"Was it some kind of game?" She could see the anger behind his expression growing hotter and hotter. His eyes were practically sparking with it.

"No, of course not."

"Then I don't understand!" He turned away, as if he couldn't bear to look at her, running his hands through his hair and pulling at the ends in anguish. "If you wanted me to come after you then how can you deny the break-up was some kind of sick test?"

"I was doing you a favour," she snapped angrily. "And a stupid bloody part of me hoped you'd realise that. I gave you up, Charles!"

He froze. Even though his back was to her she saw the tension in his shoulders and the slight shift as his body locked into place. A warning shot up her spine.

A couple of seconds beat between them.

"What did you say?" He turned his head a fraction to the right.

What had she said? *Shit.* What had she just said?

The kiss had loosened her tongue. She had never meant to say that. She'd never meant to say *any* of that.

"I...err..."

He turned around and she felt the force of his anger crash into her. It took her completely by surprise. Charles's usual calm expression had been stripped away and suddenly his face looked as if it were filled with hard edges and sharp lines. She took a step back.

"Tell me you're joking." His voice was dark and his stare glacial.

Lizzie swallowed and stubbornly stuck out of her chin. "I did the right thing. I did what was best."

"For who?"

"For you."

A muscle twitched in his jaw and Lizzie resisted taking another step away.

"Then why didn't I get a say in the matter?"

She swallowed, trying her hardest to push away the tightness in her chest. "Because you'd have made the wrong choice."

"Right," he said darkly, taking a step forward, "so, you know I'd have chosen you."

"You didn't."

"You didn't give me a choice!" He shouted.

She flinched.

"It was the right thing to do."

"What does that even mean?"

"You're a Williams, Charles. Put that brilliant brain of yours to use. Different classes, different leagues, different-"

"Am I talking to Craig or am I talking to Lizzie?" He snapped.

"Maybe Dad was right-"

Charles took two determined strides forward and grabbed her by the arms. Her words faltered in her mouth.

"Don't you dare." His words were clipped with anger. "Don't you dare say your father was right. Craig has never been right in his entire life. The way that man treated you when we were kids..." She tried not to shudder as his palm brushed her cheek. The memory of their kiss was still burning on her lips and now he was so close, it was all she could focus on. "He made you feel worthless. He made you feel not good enough for anything."

Or anyone.

"It was a long time ago," she said softly.

"I don't care. I will never forgive him for that."

Silence stretched between them. It was full of unsaid things and shared pain. Lizzie felt emotion choking at her throat as she noted the tenderness in Charles's expression. The urge to kiss him again began to rise in her belly and she had to inwardly yell at herself to push it away.

She cleared her throat. "I would have held you back. You'd have never gone to drama school, you'd never have been doing a job you love, you'd have been stuck with me, no family, no children, nothing."

He stared at her incredulously. "And how do you know any of that? How do you know any of that would have happened? My family hated the fact I wanted to go and do drama after university. You were the only one encouraging me to the entire time. They wanted me to settle down and get a more secure job. You told me I could do it." His thumb crossed her cheek. "When would I have been stuck with you? I loved you. Life with you would never be nothing. It would have been a hell of a something."

It had been. She remembered their walks through Regent's Park, their determination to put up the Christmas tree on Dec 1st, their lazy nights in, the way he would always make them both a fort of pillows for their movie days, the pick-n-mix he'd pick up from the cinema when she'd said she'd had a bad day, the way he listened to her, the way they'd played Dean Lewis's 'Hold of Me' and danced around the living pretending to play guitars. All of it. Her chest lifted with the memories.

It had been a hell of a something.

"And, if we wanted to have a family, what would have stopped us?"

His final question slammed into her with the power of a car and the happy memories shattered before her eyes. She yanked herself away from him, unable to speak, emotions and hurt flooding every part of her. Old scars, old arguments, yelling, pain, disappointment…oh, the constant disappointment wrapping around her like an old dressing gown. The shame and guilt made it harder and harder to breath.

"Lizzie?" He whispered, reaching for her but she pushed his arms away.

"You have no idea what you're talking about," she snapped, her vision blurring. "I wanted you to find someone, Charles! I needed you to find someone else!"

She pushed past him, grabbing at the door and flinging herself out into the cold November air. He was calling her name, she knew he was, but it felt like it was on from a television screen or distant radio because her brain could barely register it.

She was outside, her feet pounding against the car park floor as she ran towards security and the exit. Once she got there, her body went into automatic. She signed Charles in for staying the night and left the front as calmly as she could, hoping not to draw anyone's attention and shouldering past the photographers and fans all waiting outside. Some held signs up with 'We Love You Charles' and many looked as if they had been crying. She ducked her head and pulled at the front of Bex's jumper. Coming from Tring she'd had no clothes to change into when she had got to work. Luckily, Bex was far more organised than her and kept clothes at work so she could fit in workouts if she had the time.

The cold seeped through to Lizzie's skin thick and fast despite the burning hot anger and humiliation raging through her. Wrapping her arms around herself she made a steady exit down to the right. She didn't have to run. Even without the photographers and the media waiting to watch Charles's every move she didn't need to run.

He wouldn't have come after her.

She turned down the first corner away from the building, keeping her head low and trying to stop her body from shaking so much. Out of the corner of her eye a flash of dark blonde caught her attention and for a second she thought the unbelievable had happened. She stumbled, disbelief flooding through her.

He hadn't actually come after her, had he? He hadn't risked facing the cameramen and fans outside for her?

She hoped he bloody well hadn't! Her protectiveness over him flared up inside as her body jerked around to focus on what she had seen that had felt so recognisable.

The blonde someone was watching her from across the street.

It wasn't Charles but the sight still made her eyes widen and her heart stutter.

She had dark blonde curly hair that fell down to her waist, dark brown eyes, a small nose, and clothes that looked half nineties and half cameo sports chick.

"Lottie."

CHAPTER TWENTY-FIVE

Lottie seemed as stunned as she was. Her round eyes stared at her across the street, cars passed between them in angry brake light blurs and the weather demanded it was too cold for them to stay still for long. Yet they did. Simply staring at each other.

Lottie made the first move, her face breaking out into her infectious smile. She leant back her head and laughed at the sky. Lizzie couldn't hear it over the traffic but the memory of it rang through her head. The youngest Williams sibling glanced left and right before running over to her.

"Lizzie Cartwright!" She said, enthusiastically throwing her arms around Lizzie's body and hugging her tightly. Lottie smelled of paint and ginger, and her body felt like a mini inferno against Lizzie's shivering one.

She hadn't realised how much she had missed her until she was right in front of her. Tears built up behind her eyes again and she buried her head into the side of Lottie's, her curly hair scratching against her face and helping shield her from the icy November wind.

"Little Lottie."

She let out a bark of laughter. "I haven't been called that in years!" She pulled away and her face stilled. "What's wrong?"

She gestured at her. "What are you doing here?"

"I…" Lottie winced, looking behind Lizzie and then back at her. "I saw the news about my brother and I was near the area and I just," she let go of Lizzie's shoulders, "felt I needed to check in on him." She rolled her eyes at herself. "Even after all these years I still get defensive over my big brother. Stupid, I know."

"I don't think that's stupid at all."

Lottie chewed her lip. "It is. He's not really my brother anymore." She glanced at Lizzie. "We don't talk."

"I know, Matt told me."

Lottie's eyes scanned Lizzie's face for a second, something passing behind her big brown eyes that Lizzie couldn't quite catch. "What did he tell you?"

"About you running away, about you staying with him for a while…about you thinking we had done this life before?"

Lottie physically relaxed. "Ah, the basics." She grinned. "No offence, Lizzie, but you look like you've seen a ghost."

Lizzie pointed at her. "I feel like I have!"

She grinned cheekily and shook her mass of blonde curls, her face full of boundless energy. Lottie had always had this ability to look as if she hadn't aged past twenty. Her face was naturally youthful and she barely wore a scrap of make-up. Instead, despite the fact it was November, freckles were scattered across her nose and cheeks. "Well, I promise I'm real."

"Do you want to go and speak to him? To Charles? You can use my pass." Lizzie moved to grab it out of her back pocket.

"No," Lottie pulled a face. "I don't think so. I don't think I was actually ever going to go in. I just…I don't know. It's stupid." She physically shook her head as if wiping away her thoughts before looping her arm around Lizzie's shoulders. "Come on, why don't we go back to yours and we can have a chat? You look like you need a cup of tea. Or a hot chocolate." Her eyes widened in excitement. "Oh my God, let's pass a shop on the way and grab some hot chocolate! There's that twenty-four-hour place down your road! Let's go there! They have that own brand hot chocolate stuff which tastes like heaven! You still live in Kentish Town, right?" She was talking fast, her face animated and her eyes bright. "I love that place. Is Peggy still there?" She glanced at Lizzie, feeling her watching her. "What is it?"

Lizzie felt herself smile affectionately. "I've really missed you."

Lottie grinned. "Likewise."

An hour later they were tucked up either side of Lizzie's sofa, hot chocolates in their hands and Lottie had, so far, been talking at a million miles an hour.

Lizzie felt somewhat shell shocked by her presence. Just like she'd used to Lottie had somewhat crashed into the Lizzie's flat, her energy and excitement lighting up the room. There was something about Lottie that was so incredibly alive it was hard not to be drawn to her and feel warmed by endless upbeat manner.

"I loved this flat. I have missed it. It's so you." She pulled a face. "Charles and you, unfortunately. Can't stop thinking of him here too, like some unwelcome ghost, but I'm sure I'll get used to it." She sipped her hot chocolate, getting a small marshmallow stuck above her lip. It fell onto the blanket covering her legs and she happily picked it up and plonked it back into her drink. Her eyes flicked up to Lizzie. "Oh, sorry. I should have warned you, I don't dial down the crazy. Never have, never will."

"You still believe we've done this before?"

Lottie pulled a face. "It's not like a dream. It hasn't just disappeared over time. It's a memory. I remember the basics and I know we've done this before."

"And you tell everyone this?"

"Well, anyone who's important." Lottie glanced at her. "Don't give me that look."

"What look?"

"That worried look you're giving me right now. I'm fine. Honestly. I only talk like this around people I trust." She shifted in her spot. "Don't want to get sent down the loony bin again."

Lizzie looked away, guilt beginning its usual climb inside her chest. "They really were going to send you there?"

"I saw the e-mails."

"But that doesn't sound like your parents at all."

Lottie shrugged. "I might have pushed them a bit. I really didn't even try to fit in. Some would say I should have kept my head down." She rolled her eyes. "When I first moved in with Matt, he said that."

"Really?"

"Yeah, I was bit tearful when I moved in and he just looked at me and said I should have dialled down the crazy if I'd wanted to stay in Tring. His no-nonsense attitude about it made me laugh. It also made me torture him for weeks as I argued he'd kind of implied I didn't need to dial down the crazy with him as he wasn't Tring."

Lizzie smiled. "Did he mind?"

"He pretended to." Lottie took another sip of her drink and shrugged.

"You know I never knew that you thought that way. I only found out recently."

"Wow, what hole were you living-?" Lottie sucked in her breath sharply, stopping herself finishing the sentence and her face visibly paled. "I'm so sorry, Lizzie, I didn't mean- I -I know what you were going through. I am so sorry. I just didn't think."

"Don't worry." Lizzie sipped her hot chocolate, resisting the urge to groan at the taste. Lottie really did make the best hot chocolates in the world. "I was pretty much living under a rock."

There was a short silence and Lizzie felt Lottie's eyes on her. She wanted to say something and Lizzie could practically hear her hesitation like it was drumming through the room.

"He didn't do it before," she said finally, very, very quietly.

"Sorry?"

"I don't know whether this will help, but in the last life, my brother took care of you. He didn't leave you because you were pregnant." She shook her head. "Can't believe I'm related to someone so foul. How's working with him? Is it awful? When I saw *Censorship* was being filmed there I looked up your Linkedin straight away. Saw you were still working there." She scowled. "He's such a piece of shit."

It was weird hearing Lizzie's own lie in someone's mouth. The sound of it almost made her want to laugh and yet cry at the same time.

Look at the damage you've caused.

She opened her mouth. She needed to tell Lottie the truth. She needed to-

Tears were streaming down Lottie's face. She was desperately wiping them away with her sleeve and unsuccessfully trying to hide her face behind the hot chocolate.

"Lottie, what's wrong?"

"I'm so sorry, Lizzie. It's all my fault. All of this. All of this is my fault."

"What is?"

"*This!* I changed this. I made you lonely."

"I'm not lonely!"

"But no one lives here right?" She looked around the flat. "There's no one else? Matt was always talking about how worried he was. You up here, on your own."

"That doesn't mean I'm lonely."

"Still." She sniffed and turned her whole body around to face her, pulling her legs up and under her. "I'm glad I've seen you because I can finally tell you just how sorry I am. This is all my fault. I made Charles bad."

"You made Charles bad?" Lizzie repeated slowly.

"Last time, honestly, you couldn't have found a man more in love with his wife. That was you, by the way, you were married and you were -" Lizzie looked away, suddenly finding her chest tightening sharply at Lottie's words. "Oh, God, sorry, I shouldn't say that. That probably is really unhelpful after everything he's done."

Lizzie swallowed. "You didn't make Charles bad."

"I did." Lottie sat up straighter. "You don't understand, I...I made a wish. I made a wish and everything changed."

The fine hairs on Lizzie's arms stood up, goosebumps zigzagged across her skin and she felt hot chocolate splash down her arm as she jolted in her seat. "What?"

"I made a wish but I didn't realise something would have to be sacrificed because of it. I didn't realise everything would change. This is going to sound crazy, this is going to sound absurd and you'll probably think I'm just as mental as everyone else does but you have to hear me out." She put her hot chocolate down on the side table before running her hands back through her hair. She pulled slightly at the ends. It was a move that reminded Lizzie of Charles and she felt a kick pass through her chest. "I've been debating whether to come and see you for years. Once, when I lived with Matt, I came up and knocked on your door and then I ran away. I couldn't face it."

"Lottie-"

"Please, just hear me out. I've waited so long for this."

Lizzie swallowed, staring into the pleading brown eyes opposite her. She nodded.

"I know it sounds crazy but there was another life. We were all exactly the same except when you fell pregnant, Charles proposed to you. You got married, you were together, you were happy. Leo still didn't make it but you both battled through that together. I was in a relationship." She closed her eyes briefly. "We lived together, we were happy."

Lizzie had met Felix a handful of times. He was skinny, geeky and rather quiet. Painfully polite and every time he looked at Lottie it looked as if he had won the world.

"He...he was nice. Really nice. He cared a lot about me but, it got out of hand. He started to insist on knowing exactly where I was at all times. He said it was because he loved me so much. I would be five minutes late and he would argue with me over exactly what time I had got the train. I would drive to see him and he would check to see if the traffic I said was on the roads had actually been there. He would pick me up from every party, make sure I got home safely or insisted I came home with him, even if I hadn't been with him that night. He started to control every little thing I did and at first, I thought it was because he cared. I thought it was because he loved me so much. I thought that I was so lucky to have a man take that much of an interest in me. He'd get so upset sometimes when he thought I was sad or I'd had a bad day that he would smash things. If our plans didn't go to plan he would break things."

Lizzie slowly sat up, her eyes scanning over the girl she had once considered to be a little sister. Protectiveness sparked inside her torso and her grip tightened around her mug of hot chocolate. "Did he hurt you?"

Lottie shifted in her seat.

"Lottie, did Felix hurt you?"

"Twice. Only twice. And I hate myself for saying that. I always thought I was so much stronger than that. I thought I would leave the moment someone hit me but when it happens it's so much more complicated than that. I had two brothers who would never treat a woman like that, I knew it was wrong but I stayed because he loved me. And I believed him when he said he didn't mean it." She rolled her eyes. "He would apologise and cry and tell me he was the worst person in the world and I would...I would comfort him and forgive him. I felt bad that he felt so bad about it when it was just a smashed plate or a ripped book." She took a breath. "The first time he turned on me I went into hospital with a fractured wrist. Felix ran away, too upset by what he had done. I wanted to follow him but I was in too much pain so I took myself. I was in too much shock to even realise where I was. That was until an A&E doctor caught sight of me in the waiting room and recognised me. My brother was on shift that night and she went to find him."

She took a breath.

"Daniel had always been wary of Felix. The only person who seemed to clock his behaviour was controlling not caring. We'd fought about it before. And now...well, he knew. He was standing in front of me, staring at my wrist and I knew he knew. I told him some lie but...I could see it in his face. I remember wanting him to hold me and tell me everything was going to be okay but at the same time I wanted him as far away as possible. He didn't understand that Felix was sorry. He tried to come and talk to me about it afterwards and I told him I hated him. I told him he had no idea what love was or what Felix meant to me because how could he? He'd never had anyone fall in love with him."

Lizzie inhaled sharply and Lottie covered her face. "I know, I know, I was mean. I went for the heart. Talked about Helen. Brought all of that up. I only saw him once again after that and it was at Mum's birthday memorial thing we used to do. I never spoke to him on my own though and there was a frosty atmosphere between us. Even Patricia picked up on it. Few weeks later, Felix destroyed all of my paintings. He said I loved them more than him. That I spent more time painting than I did with him. He set them alight."

Lizzie reached forward and grabbed Lottie's hand. Lottie had worked as an accountant but in her spare time she had painted. Lizzie remembered walking into her room when Lottie had gone to university and stepping over easels, paints and chalk scattered over the floor. The walls had been filled with her work. She had been brilliant. It was where her true passion lay but she was good at maths so she'd followed the path every teacher had told her to.

"It's weird that that was the trigger. That was what made me step back. He could hurt my body but my work...I wouldn't let him. It made me wake up. I ran out of the flat. I tried to call Daniel, he was the first person I wanted to talk to but it went straight to voicemail. And then he called me back but...it wasn't him." Her breath hitched. "Daniel had been hit by a car. They were pretty sure he wasn't going to make it."

Hit by a car.

Lizzie's brain flashed to Amy's nightmare. The fear in her eyes and the fact she wouldn't stop crying.

Something else flickered at the back of her mind. The sound of brakes. High pitched and loud. And a scream. The scream of someone she recognised.

Primrose Hill.

Something stirred at the back of her mind. The dots weren't quite adding up.

"And I made a wish. I wished that I could take it all back," Lottie said softly, her eyes far away. "And then, everything changed."

Lizzie put down her drink, shuffled down the sofa and curled her arms around Lottie as she began to sob.

"It's okay, Lottie, honestly, it's fine."

"But it's all my fault."

"You saved Daniel. That's all that matters."

Lottie looked up at her, her bloodshot eyes riddled with confusion. "You don't believe me, do you? That's why you're being so nice."

"I believe you."

"No, you don't, otherwise you wouldn't be so nice. You'd hate me."

"Daniel's alive." She let out a long breath. "Honestly, if my life has been hit in the aftermath, who cares?"

"How can you be so calm-?" Suddenly Lottie reared her head back from her, confusion passing behind her brown, glassy eyes as a light clicked behind them. "How did you know his name?"

"What?" Lizzie shook her head in confusion. "Whose name?"

"Felix. You mentioned him first. You said Felix's name first! How the hell did you know his name?"

"You must have said it."

"No, I didn't. Not until you asked me if he'd hurt me. How did you know his name?"

Lizzie swallowed, her mouth turning dry and her heart beginning to beat a lot faster.

It was now or never.

"Because I made a wish too."

Once she had finished telling Lottie about her night on Primrose Hill and about everything she had done after then, Lottie spent a couple of seconds staring at her in disbelief. Her mouth hung almost comically open and her mascara was well and truly smeared over her cheeks. The pause felt like it lasted forever.

"Bollocks. Bloody bollocks."

She sounded so ridiculous Lizzie laughed. She stopped herself when she saw Lottie's eyes darken.

She straightened up. "You weren't there, Lottie. You don't know the ins and outs of our relationship. He wanted kids. He's always wanted children and I couldn't have them."

Both women were now at the same end of the sofa, their mugs of hot chocolate sadly empty and both underneath the same blanket. Lizzie felt as if all the years had been stripped away from them. She felt like she was twenty-one-years-old again, discussing secrets with her makeshift little sister. "You saw what damage it did to us."

Lottie sighed. "In parts. But I just thought you were going to work through it. You're Lizzie and Charles. You're *the* couple. You'd have worked it out."

"Maybe," Lizzie said. "But I'd never have got over the guilt of it. And I was given the chance to give him a better life, how could I not take it? Wouldn't you have?"

Lottie carefully assessed her. "You lied to Matt didn't you? Charles has no idea about Leo."

Lizzie closed her eyes. "No idea." Taking a deep breath she turned to look at Lottie. "I'm so sorry. I'm sorry Matt told you that. It was the only way I could force him not to go to Charles and tell him about Leo. I didn't realise he would tell you too."

Lottie was quiet for a moment. "I want to be so angry with you. I want to be furious. I want to scream and shout and pull this room apart." She threw her hand in the general direction of the television. "But I can't. Because I get it. I am still angry," she pointed her finger at her, "but I get it."

"Even though I ruined your relationship with your brother?"

"He ruined it before Matt told me. He didn't believe me. He didn't listen."

"Would you have believed him? Had it been the other way

round?"

Lottie shrugged. "I'd like to think so. I have never been the most sane of people."

A smile tugged at Lizzie's lips. "It makes you special."

A shimmer of a smile crossed Lottie's face but she looked down at her hands. "Charles was too busy focusing on his career. Our relationship became really rocky. Especially because I kept telling him to go after you."

Lizzie felt her stomach tug painfully. "Well, he didn't."

"Because he was being a spineless idiot. Mooching around the house and acting sorry for himself."

Lizzie frowned. "What?"

"Well, he was kind of heartbroken."

"But we'd only been dating for two years this time around."

Lottie raised her eyebrows. "And?"

"He wouldn't have cared enough to be heartbroken. He was a twenty-two-year-old kid."

Lizzie tried not to think about the fact she'd had this exact same argument with Charles mere hours earlier.

Lottie stared at her. "This is Charles we are talking about it, right? Two months or two years, he was always in love with you. I should know. I teased him rotten about it. Last time, he proposed to you at twenty-two."

"Yeah…because I was pregnant and Charles wanted to do the right thing."

Lottie eyed her speculatively. "Is that what you really think?"

Lizzie looked away, not liking the way Lottie's gaze was suddenly making her feel extremely stupid, as if she had missed something obvious.

"I'm not saying he didn't grow to love me. I know Charles loved me in the end. I'm just saying, at twenty-two, he was fine."

"He didn't sleep in his own room for a year."

Lizzie flinched. "What?"

"He said it reminded him too much of you."

She looked away, her heart in throat as Lottie's words tried to break through a box of emotions she had kept secure for over a decade. In less than half a day, certainties she'd once relied on felt as if they were flaking apart and her previous truths splintered.

Lottie cleared her throat. "Anyway, I'd take not talking to my family over Daniel or Mum being dead. At the end of the day whatever or whoever caused this to happen... they are alive."

"I wish you would have told us about Felix."

Lottie patted her hand. "I didn't really know how badly I was stuck until I was really stuck. Funny what perspective can do." She rolled a curl around her finger. "Talking of which, what has perspective taught you?"

"What do you mean?"

"Do you still think breaking up with him was the right thing to do? Do you think you made the right decision with your 'second chance'?"

"I don't know why what happened actually happened, but I do know that Charles is happy. He's rich and successful. He's doing something he loves."

Lottie licked her lips. "Money doesn't always equal happiness."

"Charles is fine."

"And the whole having children part?"

Lizzie pulled her knees up tighter beneath her. "What about it?"

Lottie blinked at her and then slowly raised her eyebrows. "Well, where are his children? Surely, if it meant so much to him, Jennifer and him would have an army by now?"

Lizzie hadn't told Lottie about Charles's relationship being fake. It felt too raw and personal to share just yet.

"I don't know."

But she hadn't thought of it like that. If he had been so desperate to have children, surely his arrangement with Jennifer would have become...strained? Inconvenient, even? Had they thought about having children? Had they planned to have them together?

"You guys were trying for a while. Like years." Lottie's eyes narrowed. "So, why in this lifetime does he not seem to care?"

"We don't know he doesn't care."

Or was that one of the reasons he was happy to continue his pretence with Jennifer? Did he not care? Would the universe be cruel enough to orchestrate that in this new life he wasn't so bothered?

"Ya-huh." Lottie gave her a non-impressed look.

"I don't know what you're trying to get it."

"I'm trying to get at the fact maybe he only wanted children with *you*. To have a family with you."

Lizzie closed her eyes.

And, hell, if we wanted to have a family, what would have stopped us?

Pain slashed across her chest as she allowed the possibility that Lottie was right to seep into her bones. She must have picked up on her discomfort as she suddenly changed the subject.

"How's working with him?"

"It's okay."

She felt Lottie's eyes roam over her face. They had the same ability to be just as fiercely intense as Charles. "You still love him, don't you?"

"No. Don't be ridiculous."

A flutter of laughter left Lottie's lips. "Oh, Lizzie."

"What?"

"I don't know how Matt didn't see right through you."

"What do you mean?"

Lottie's brown eyes were warm and affectionate. "You've always been a rubbish liar."

CHAPTER TWENTY-SIX

November was turning out to be a lot colder than Lizzie had anticipated. It had brought with it frost, rain, dry hands and puffs of white air every time she breathed. Any time she stepped outside it was like a silent wall had hit her, its crisp sharpness burying into her skin before she could stop it.

Her fight with Charles had been over a week ago. They had barely seen each other since and Lizzie had made sure to keep herself busy so she didn't find herself getting distracted by thoughts of him.

It was hard, especially when he was in the newspaper all the time, being regularly talked about on the radio or television, and worked in the same building as she did.

Jennifer and Charles had released a press statement together. It was only a slightly twisted version of the truth. They'd stated they had realised five years ago that they weren't meant to be together. That they were more friends than partners. When Jennifer had developed feelings for Kristina they had already separated, but, Charles had agreed to continue pretending to be her boyfriend as she was too scared to come out to her family.

Lizzie had to applaud Patricia. It did the trick. Neither looked like the bad guy and the fact they had lied to their individual fanbases for so long suddenly didn't have such a big repercussion. Charles had done it for a friend and Jennifer for love. How could anyone hate them for that?

Lizzie did. It boiled in the pit of her stomach and ate away at her thoughts whenever it could. She had thought her plan had been working: he was successful, doing a job he loved and he was in a long-term relationship. Happy and in love. Win, win. But now she knew it had all been lies. Every single bit of it. In terms of love and a family he was in the exact same spot as when they'd been married.

And if Jennifer had been falling in love, why hadn't Charles given himself the chance to?

Loyal, caring, piece of shit.

There was one huge positive to come of this week. Seeing Lottie had been incredible. Ever since Matt had told her about the youngest Williams's fate, a guilt had settled on her shoulders that she hadn't even been aware of. It was only now she realised how draining its presence had been.

Part of feared it had almost been too easy reuniting with her. Like the universe would plan something horrible in exchange.

"Got any plans this weekend?" Neil asked, scrunching up a piece of paper and aiming for the bin.

"Brunch with a friend tomorrow." Lottie was going to meet her at her flat and then take her to a place a friend of hers owned in Camden. "And then Bex is coming over for food in the evening."

"Bex doesn't have a date on a Saturday night?" Neil raised his eyebrows.

"She doesn't have to have a date on a Saturday night. Go and pick that up." He'd missed the bin.

"We are talking about the same Bex?"

"Careful Neil, might start to sound like you like her."

He let out a bark of laughter as he sauntered over, picked up his litter and put it in the bin. "I don't like the girl but that doesn't mean I'm blind. Bex is hot. And she also isn't determined to live out her life under a rock, unlike you." He reached over and painfully pinched her cheek as he took his seat again.

"Get off!" She batted his hand away.

"You wrapping up soon?"

She yawned and glanced at the clock. "Yeah. It's late enough I guess. You?"

The door squeaked behind them and being the only two left in the office they both turned to look at the visitor. Lizzie's hands tightened in her lap as her gaze slammed into her father.

He stood in the doorway, his jaw tight and his shoulders up by his ears. He looked tired and she recognised the slight gleam in his eyes - he was looking for a fight.

"Mr Rosswool," Neil said, sounding mockingly delighted.

Craig grunted in response before taking a few steps into the office. "I've come to talk to you both about my pay rise."

"What pay rise?" Neil glanced at Lizzie. "And Lizzie has nothing to do with your payments so there is no need to talk to her."

Lizzie felt a swell of affection for Neil rise in her chest. He could be the most annoying man on the planet sometimes, but right now he was showing his real side. When it came to his friends, he was fiercely protective. Well… when he wanted to be.

Craig let out a bark of laughter. It wasn't warm in the slightest. "Because she can't be a grown up? Because she can't handle working with her own father? No, I'm afraid this time that isn't a good enough excuse. This concerns both of you."

Lizzie narrowed her gaze and felt her heart pick up its pace. How did this man still have such a power over her? Why was she still afraid of him? She'd done so well cutting him out of her life and she hated the fact he still had the ability to make her skin crawl. Using Neil's support as a courage booster she jutted out her chin and looked her father directly in the eye.

"How so?"

Craig's smile was cold and unwelcome. "First," he turned to Neil, "you're going to pay me an extra £450 a week or I am going to sue you for damages."

Damages?

Lizzie looked between the two men, her eyebrows raised. Neil folded his arms and cocked his head to the left, looking disinterested.

"I don't have that kind of power. We get the funds to pay you from the production."

"You will discuss it with Tyrone and get it from the studio's finances. And second," he now turned his gaze to Lizzie, "you will give me Matt's contact details."

"Absolutely not," Lizzie said with zero hesitation.

Matt had stopped talking to Craig a few years ago. She'd never found out why because Matt changed the topic whenever she asked but she had seen the extra layer of pain on his shoulders.

Neil clapped his hands together gleefully. "Seems like none of these things will be happening. Goodnight, Mr Rosswool."

"I am going to sue you," Craig hissed.

"For what?"

"For the fire extinguisher episode."

Fire extinguisher episode?

Lizzie glanced at Neil and then at Craig. What were they talking about?

"You've been fit and healthy and in work since. On what grounds exactly are you going to sue me?" The side of Neil's mouth was lifting into his traditional grin.

"You covered me in foam!"

"I saw a fire and I put it out."

"I was playing with a lighter!"

"And I have five witnesses who will say they also thought it was an open flame."

"CCTV-"

"Does not cover that corner of the studio." Neil's grin widened before his voice dipped. "How stupid do you think I am?"

Craig stepped forward and Neil stood up. Lizzie's friend wasn't an intimidating figure but his disinterest, and the fact he was clearly enjoying the situation, put him at an advantage. It gave him an almost untouchable air and it made Craig stop in his tracks. He ran his gaze up and down Neil's body, fury burning out of his eyes before he flicked them to Lizzie.

She recognised the snap behind his gaze.

Craig knew he was fighting a losing battle with Neil, she had just been upgraded to primary target.

"You're an embarrassment."

She had already braced herself for whatever insult he was going to throw at her so it barely scraped the surface. In fact, she was surprised he had gone for something so tame.

"Only I get to talk to her like that," Neil said calmly, but she saw the sudden stiffness in his jaw.

Lizzie stood up. "You heard Neil, you're not getting a pay rise, you're not getting any of Matt's information and you're not in any position to sue us."

"Why the fuck did you feel the need to set this dickhead on me?"

Neil placed a hand on his heart. "Dickhead? That really hurt, Craig."

"I didn't," Lizzie said, still confused.

"Oh, so he was bothered about me talking about Charles's love life for his own sake, was he?"

"I take a great interest in Charles's love life, actually." He put a hand to his chin as if he was thinking and far too obviously side-eyed Lizzie. "Definitely someone I'd swing for. If you two ever need a third-"

"Neil!" Lizzie snapped. "Not the time."

"You should have been supporting me," Craig snarled, his gaze still pinned to Lizzie. "I was just giving Charles a little wake-up call. Showing him he wasn't all that."

Craig had been having a go at Charles?

Why hadn't she heard about this?

Neil sighed. "The guy had just found out his girlfriend of ten years was gay. You were being rude and insulting to the talent. It has nothing to do with Lizzie as to why I chose to shut you up."

"So, you admit to trying to shut me up?"

Neil grinned. "No. Did I say that? Lizzie, is that what I said?"

What was Neil talking about? Why hadn't she heard about any of this? Her mind tried to piece together the fragments of the conversation.

She turned to stare at Neil. "You...you used a fire extinguisher on

Craig to shut him up?"

"No, to put out an open flame." He over enunciated the last few words, the corner of his mouth lifting higher up his face. "Shutting him up was just a happy coincidence."

Lizzie felt a smile tug at her lips in response. "Very happy coincidence."

Neil winked at her.

Craig practically growled at them. "Like I said, an embarrassment. Any other normal woman would want the man who got her pregnant and fucked off to be as insulted as much as possible. But instead, you run around defending and protecting him."

Lizzie felt her body freeze. Her heart rate sky rocketed and she felt pain, pure humiliating pain, course through her. She pulled her gaze away from Neil sharply as his slammed into her.

A beat passed.

And then another.

How did Craig know? How did her father know about Leo?

A fist tightened around her heart.

Matt.

Had to be.

It was the only explanation.

He had promised her that he hadn't told Craig. He had insisted. She tried her hardest to swallow back the hurt as she felt like she was falling. She couldn't hide the shock or fear from her face and she saw Craig smile as he clocked it.

"Get out," she just about managed to say.

He took another step closer to them. "I want Matt's details."

"You've done enough to Matt, don't you think?"

"More than you? Leaning on the poor lad after your bloody child didn't make it. You should have been grateful!"

Every tiny part of her body spiked defensively. "What did you just say?"

"That kid was going to be born with no father, no money, nothing. You had no house of your own to raise it in, it was a bloody blessing in disguise-" She slapped him. Hard. The noise was so sharp it cut through the air like a knife and Lizzie flinched.

There was a pulse of silence.

Craig lifted a hand slowly to the side of his face. Shocked. His eyes wide and his mouth open in utter confusion.

He couldn't see it.

He actually couldn't see why what he had said was possibly the most disgusting thing anyone had ever said to her.

"I'll get you fired for that you bitch."

"No witnesses," Neil said, his voice sounded hoarse and when Lizzie glanced at him he avoided her gaze.

"You were right here!" Craig shouted.

"No witnesses," he repeated.

He didn't sound like Neil at all.

"Get out," she said coldly, turning back to look at her father and raising her arm to point at the door.

"I was stating fact."

"Get out!" She growled, her voice even darker as anger flowed through every word.

When he still didn't move, she channelled as much of Bex's energy as she could, grabbed him by the sleeve of his jacket and began marching him to the door. He stumbled back, his hand locking around her wrist painfully but she refused to let go. He'd done that when she was younger. Grabbed her by the wrist, squeezed it right on the bone so it burned. She'd learnt a long time ago how to pretend it didn't hurt.

"Get your hands off me!"

"Then get the hell out of my office!" She shouted, only stopping because they had reached the glass doors.

He held her gaze, looking murderous.

"You still run around after him like a fucking dog. Even after everything he did to you. Just like you did when you were a bloody teenager, gagging for it."

"Maybe I take after my mum." She fixed him with the coldest

glare she could. "How many times did she take you back?"

"Don't you dare-"

"She's found someone by the way. Did she tell you?"

For a second, Craig's anger slackened on his face. "No she hasn't."

"She has. Five months ago she met a man called Chris. Was forced by his kids to come out to the retreat to distract him from the tenth anniversary of losing his wife. He plays bridge and apparently, he's a really good dancer. Speaks fluent Spanish too. Never went home."

His anger was gone now. Instead, something had truly shattered behind her father's expression. Lizzie didn't feel the slightest bit of sympathy for him.

"Now, get out," she snarled.

Without another word, he turned and left the room.

The moment he was out of sight Lizzie's shoulders dropped, she gasped for air even though she hadn't been holding her breath and she felt the burn of tears crowd her eyes. She blinked them away.

Inside everything was crumbling.

He had known. Her father had known about Leo all this time and yet he hadn't told Charles. God, she should be grateful for that but right now, horror was all she could feel. Horror at the idea that Leo had been shared even the smallest amount with her father.

Craig didn't deserve any of him.

Without saying a word, she turned and walked towards her desk, gathering her things as quickly as she could even as she felt Neil's gaze burn into the side of her.

She zipped up her bag, the noise sounding loud and unpleasant in the office.

"Well, see you on Monday." Her voice was shaky.

"Is it true?"

Lizzie closed her eyes, swinging her rucksack onto her back and forcing the emotions that had been stirred up inside of her back down.

"Don't worry about it."

He took a step towards her. "Don't worry about it? Are you being serious?" He snarled. She turned to walk past him but he stepped in front of her, blocking her path. "Lizzie. Is it true?"

"No, of course it's not." She tried to say it jovially, pushing it away as if it were nothing. "Craig's just making up rubbish like usual." She moved to pass him again but he swung his arm out to stop her.

"It didn't look like it was made up rubbish."

She finally looked up and was caught off guard by his expression. He looked genuinely concerned. She didn't think she had ever seen Neil look concerned about anything. And behind that concern was an anger. An anger she had certainly never seen in Neil's eyes.

The lie was ready, lingering between her teeth. She hadn't said it for a while but it still felt like it might be easier to say than the truth.

But something was stopping her.

Maybe it was the look on Lottie's face when she'd realised all she had believed about Charles had been a lie. Maybe it was the fact that Lizzie knew Charles now and he was every bit as good as he'd always been.

Maybe it was because he'd kissed her and for that magical moment she had felt more alive than she had in a very long time.

The lie wouldn't come. It wouldn't move past her teeth.

Neil stepped forward and gripped her by the forearms. "Tell me the truth."

She could feel the muscles in her mouth twitching, begging to speak, to say something. Deep down she knew she couldn't bear it if someone else thought badly of Charles. For someone else to think he had done one of the worst things a man could do.

"No. It's not true." She swallowed. "I was pregnant but I didn't tell him about the baby."

Neil let go of her arms and took a step back, his eyes widening and she could see calculations swirling across the backs of them. "He said you broke up with him."

"I did."

Neil stared at her like she was crazy. "Because you were pregnant?"

"Yep." She tightened her ponytail, not stopping till she felt the band pinch hard on the back of her head.

"Why?"

She took a shaky breath in, ignoring the hurt that Neil's judgement sliced into the side of her. "Before you have any ideas of revealing the truth to him and trying to find where that child is, I should tell you Leo didn't make it. That was the blessing Craig was referring to." She slowly hid her hands behind her back: they were shaking. She tried to keep her expression calm and emotionless. "So, I protected Charles from that pain."

"You didn't know that was going to happen."

Oh, but she had. She had been optimistic but she had known.

She bit back her tears. "I'd have held him back."

Neil was silent for a few moments. "Are you telling me this is all because of some self-deprecating bullshit?"

Lizzie flinched. "You can't tell him Neil, okay? You can't tell him!"

"You really think I'd do that to you?"

"You went behind my back about him coming to work here," she bit out angrily. "What else am I to think?" Ignoring the flash of hurt that crossed Neil's face she sidestepped around him and walked towards the door.

Charles walked quickly down the corridor, side stepping around the cleaner's trolley and almost putting his foot in a mop bucket. His head really was all over the place and he needed it to settle down. Unfortunately, as he was on his way to see Lizzie, that probably wasn't going to happen. He'd spent all week trying to get a moment with her when she came to the studio, trying to catch her eye, but she had avoided him. Part of him felt deflated by it all, like maybe his mind had over exaggerated just how into the kiss Lizzie had been.

But then he would remember the way she had run her hands through his hair, the way she had whispered his name and he knew he wasn't making it up. He had kissed a lot of people over the years; on stage, on screen, in rehearsals, or Jennifer when Patricia demanded they needed to be a bit more affectionate with one another in public. It had started to become robotic, something he associated with cameras and precise body positions. That kiss...it hadn't been robotic.

He'd seen Jennifer in the middle of the week. She had come to set and despite the numerous phone calls they'd had, she'd been convinced Charles still secretly hated her.

She'd cried. A lot. He'd felt awful for her but the story Patricia put out seemed to have worked. No one was hounding her or being cruel, and online trolls quickly got shot down for their comments. Patricia had said he'd received some nasty comments but he didn't even know the password to his own Twitter account so it didn't bother him.

As he walked up the emerald stairs, nerves began to dance in the pit of his stomach. He really wanted this to go well. He wasn't even sure about what he was going to say but he just knew by the end of it he wanted him and Lizzie to be...talking? He winced at himself.

Okay, he wanted them to be more than talking but he was too cowardly to admit that even to himself right now.

He walked in through the glass doors to see Neil packing up.

No Lizzie.

No open laptop, no rucksack, no coat.

His mood instantly deflated.

Neil looked up and flinched as he saw him. His eyes widened and for a second, Charles thought he looked much younger - a teenager in man's clothing. But it was gone within a second.

"Hey Charles," Neil said. He sounded tired. "You came to see Lizzie?"

"Yeah, must have just missed her." He tried to sound cheerful and threw Neil a smile.

Neil didn't return it. He walked forward, his eyes studying Charles and his lips a thin line.

"Are you okay?" Charles asked.

"Fine. I'm fine."

This wasn't the Neil that Charles was used to. It felt like there was a completely different person standing in front of him. Maybe he was ill? Knocked out by the flu or something? Or maybe something had happened at home? The man annoyed him to no end but he had come to his rescue when Craig had been a git. And there was something about him...something familiar, and for some reason, Charles felt a rush of protectiveness for him.

"Are you sure everything's alright?"

"It's fine. I'm sorry you missed Lizzie."

"No bother." Charles shrugged and smiled politely. "It wasn't urgent."

Neil simply raised an eyebrow. "Sure."

The two men stared at each other.

"Well, see you next week," he said quickly and turned to leave. He heard rustling behind him and then-

"She loves you, you know?"

Charles stilled, his breath catching in his throat. "Sorry?"

"She loves you."

The statement hit him in the chest and for a second he couldn't think of anything to respond with. Charles turned slowly to face Neil. He had stepped closer to him and now had a piece of paper in his hand. There was the faintest of real smiles across his face. He handed it to him.

"That's her address. I'll warn you, she was quite upset when she left. Craig was here, mouthing off." Something bitter swirled behind Neil's eyes. "And on that note I need to ask you for a favour."

"What is it?"

"I have no authority over Tyrone. I can't do anything. But you, you can get Craig fired."

Charles raised his eyebrows. "Last time I looked Lizzie was handling it."

Neil smirked. "Lizzie always tries to look like she is handling it." His face turned grave. "But trust me, Charming, if you had heard the stuff he was saying to her tonight, you'd want him nowhere near her."

Worry itched at his skull. "I've wanted that for a while."

A smile tugged at Neil's lips again. "Good…well, if you could put in a word, I'd be very grateful. I really have no leg to stand on now I am leaving in a few months."

"You got a new job?"

Neil shook his head. "Not yet. I quit the day Tyrone went and hired Craig. I told him to change his mind or I would walk." Neil shrugged. "He didn't think I'd follow through on my threat. Don't tell Whiskers, I haven't figured out a way to tell her yet which won't make her feel insanely guilty."

Charles studied him. "You're a good man, Neil."

He smirked. "I'm going to love telling her you said that." He nodded towards the piece of paper he'd handed him. "Now, go get your girl, Charming."

"That's not what this is," Charles said quickly.

A huff of laughter left Neil's lips. "I just told you that she loves you and you still want to go after her. If you didn't feel the same, you'd be running a mile." He shrugged an arm of his rucksack over his shoulder and tapped his nose. "Neil-logic."

The younger man sidestepped around Charles, leaving him feeling slightly shell shocked. His insides were a mixture of emotions that he couldn't quite control. He fisted his hand around the piece of paper, trying his hardest to not let Neil's words fill his chest with hope.

"Oh, and Charles?" Charles turned to look at Neil, who was now stood with one leg out of the office and one hand resting against the glass door. His grin turned mischievous. "Go easy on her, it's been a while."

"Neil!" Charles groaned. "Do you ever give it a rest?"

Neil gave him one last wink before he sauntered out of the room, chuckling to himself.

Charles slammed down the images that Neil had just conjured up and folded up the piece of paper with Lizzie's address on it, pocketing it.

If Lizzie was upset she wouldn't have gone home.

He couldn't tell why but for some reason he knew that as clearly as he knew his own name. It was like the thought was humming through his own bloodstream.

There was only one place Lizzie would have gone.

CHAPTER TWENTY-SEVEN

Primrose Hill was still just as beautiful as always. There was something about it that elicited excitement and joy, with its spanning greenery and Victorian lampposts. But the magic trick was at the top, when Lizzie would turn back around and look down over the grass, see the glistening zig zag of lamplights and the London cityscape behind shining out from the darkness.

London never slept. Not whilst she was up here. It was only 9.30 p.m. on a Friday night so she could see people walking through the streets, hear the sounds of people cheering in the distant and practically feel the warm hues of orange spilling from pubs. There were even a few fireworks in the distance that from this angle looked far too close to people's rooftops.

She was never alone on Primrose Hill. No matter what time of day or night, there were always people around and it made the place feel that much safer. As if they'd all stumbled onto this small London haven and were appreciating it together, shut away from the metal, the chaos and the drive of the city.

At the top of the hill she was hidden in darkness, the closest lamp light a few feet behind her, and it eased the tension from her spine. She let herself take a huge breath in.

Once upon a time Charles and her would race each other up to the top of the hill. He'd even let her win occasionally - he had ridiculously long legs. It was here they would come for picnics in the summer or night-time strolls in the winter. When it had snowed one December, they had come early and made angels in the white carpet before Lizzie had turned and slammed snow down Charles's collar.

The snow fight that had followed had been of epic proportions until Charles had called it to an end when he had noticed Lizzie was shaking with the cold even before she had.

It had been on this hill she had made her wish, and somehow, the universe had heard her.

Doubt flickered in her stomach. Before a few months ago it had never dared rear its ugly head, but now, she could feel it settling.

"Maybe, I was wrong," she whispered, almost scared to admit it out loud.

A familiar shiver ran up her spine and she felt her cheeks warm.

How?

How on earth-?

"It's baltic out here, why aren't you wearing a coat?" His voice was soft and tender.

She laughed. Nearly the same words he had said the last time they had been up here together.

Nearly.

Charles stood just behind her. He was wearing a white shirt, tucked into black trousers, a blazer and a huge brown coat over his shoulders that fell to his thighs. She swallowed. He looked good. Really good.

"Are you stalking me?"

"No." He pulled a face. "Okay, maybe a little. Are you warm enough?" He made as if to take off his coat but she shook her head quickly, the butterflies now permanently living in her stomach sitting up.

"I'm wearing three jumpers. I'll roast."

"Well, at least you're being sensible this time, even if you still refuse to buy a coat," he teased.

"I own lots of coats, actually."

"I feel so sorry for them. Wasting away at the back of your wardrobe, never to be seen or worn again."

She smiled, her shoulders relaxing a little. It didn't feel as if the last time they had spoken they had been arguing. All she felt from

Charles was warmth. From his eyes, from his face, from the way he was standing. Like a cup of tea after being caught in the rain or a blanket on the sofa. Pure, gentle, warmth.

Charles took a few steps forward so he could stand beside her, his eyes on the view and she felt the loss of his gaze.

"I tried to find you at work."

"I left kind of promptly."

They stared out at the city around them, a comfortable silence settling on their shoulders and bringing a weird unexplainable hum with it. She watched his profile out of the corner of her eye and felt homesickness cloak her shoulders. It lumped in her throat.

"I come here to think too. It's a nice place to just...shut off," Charles's voice was soft.

"It's wonderful," she whispered, her mind tracing back her steps to many years ago. Why were the memories of this place so much brighter than the others? She could see their time here so vividly it was like it was laid out in a picture book in front of her. "I read the press statements, you came across well."

He let out a long, weary breath and raked a hand through his hair. It was getting longer again, naturally begging not to be as short as the film demanded it to be. It probably meant on Monday it would be cut again.

"That was all Patricia. She's annoying but she's good."

Lizzie smiled. His arm brushed against hers as he dropped it to his side and, even through the jumpers, shivers needled their way into her skin. She knew she should step away but she just couldn't.

Not again.

Not whilst stood upon Primrose Hill with Charles next to her, just like it was in their last life. Like they were married, like she had never bloody gone through with this.

Is that what she wanted?

Did she really want to change her decision?

She winced slightly at her selfishness.

"You okay?" His voice pulled her away from her thoughts and she turned her head to look at him. She took in his bright blue eyes, his soft skin, his high cheekbones, his height, the way he stood.

She wasn't homesick.

She just missed him. Missed him harder than she had ever missed anything in her entire life. Missed making him laugh, missed holding him, missed being looked after, missed being loved, missed making love. It all flooded through her so strongly she just about managed to stop herself reaching out for his hand and squeezing it as hard as she could. Instead her fingers merely twitched by her side.

He'd been there. Through everything. He'd known her better than anyone else and she had let him into every little dark thought she was having...until she hadn't anymore. Until she had started building up walls and putting space between them, thinking it would be better, thinking it would be for the best if he wasn't aware just how scared she was to lose him. Thinking it would hurt less if he then chose someone who could give him what he wanted.

"I'm sorry I didn't give you a choice.," she said, meaning it for a hundred more reasons than he could possibly know.

She felt the brush of his fingers as he stretched them out to cross through hers, each individual finger slowly slotting between her own. Not quite holding hands but feeling somehow even more intimate.

"I'm sorry you didn't feel you could talk to me."

His gaze was so intense she felt it pin her to the spot, sending thrills up her spine and her affection for the man beside her grew even more. Everything else just blurred. It could have just been them, standing there on the Pride Rock of London. Just them in the entire world. English teacher and best friend's little sister or famous actor and Production Coordinator.

Either story fit.

He insisted on walking her home.

Because of course, he did.

They'd sat on the cold inch high wall that had a quote by William

Blake carved into it and looked out upon the view. They'd talked, their hands never fully holding the other's but always touching, somehow always connected. Charles told her about the many different ways in which photographers had managed to capture photos of him that week, including waiting outside a public restroom, and Lizzie told him about the issues she'd been having studio side. At first she'd felt silly, her problems seeming so much more trivial than his, but the way he looked at her and the fact he never interrupted except to ask questions or clarify a particular point, made her realise he was just as interested in what she had to say as she was in his stories.

They moved on to talk more about their own lives.

It was easy. So easy talking with him. She didn't notice the time passing, she didn't notice anyone else leaving or entering the park. Even as they had walked back through the streets of London she hadn't looked anywhere else but at him. She wasn't even sure if he had led the way or if she had.

At the front door to the home she shared with Peggy and Matt, they stopped. The blue door looked even darker than usual, the gold numbers standing out sharply and she felt a sense of sadness descend on her. The night had passed so quickly it felt like water pouring through her hands. And now she had the weekend to assess how she was going to proceed, because at the end of the day, yes, she might still have feelings for him – she could no longer deny that - but she couldn't be with him.

As much as she might want to, she refused to be selfish.

Not with him.

Not again.

"Well, this is me." She gestured at the blue door awkwardly. "I didn't just lead you to a random house in the middle of nowhere."

"Is this whole place yours?"

"Oh, no." She almost laughed. "Bottom floor's Matt's. I'm the middle and Peggy lives in the flat above. It used to be her home until her husband died and she converted it because it felt too big."

"It sounds lovely." He said smiling.

You loved it.

Her heart tugged. All it wanted to do in that moment was to be reckless and ask him to stay. Her stubbornness stopped her. As much as she may miss her old life, she had fixed the problem in it. She couldn't hold him back again. He was only thirty-five, he might still meet the love of his life tomorrow and go off and have a house of children. He still had years and years of an acting career ahead of him. He didn't need her.

Charles reached over and squeezed her hand closest to the door.

"I better be going," he said gently. He bent his head down and his lips skated across her cheek. She inhaled sharply at the smell of him, his proximity almost becoming painful and she dug her free hand into her hip to stop herself simply turning her head and pressing her mouth against his. He pulled away and she thought she saw the same reluctance she was feeling mirrored back her.

She didn't have time to analyse it though.

A drunk, male voice carried down the street. Charles didn't react, instead dropping her hand and moving to pull his coat closer around himself. Lizzie, however, felt her back stiffen and her eyes widened.

"It's Matt," she hissed, grabbing Charles by the wrist and yanking him towards her so she could look behind him.

Unfortunately, she was right. Matt was walking down the street, his arm around Zoey, and the pair were laughing loudly, the sound echoing in the cold night air. He hadn't spotted them yet but he was heading their way and there was no way he wouldn't see Charles if he tried to leave now.

"I could say hello and explain?" Charles suggested. She stared at him incredulously and his lips twitched with laughter. "Not my best idea?"

"No!" She turned, clutching at her keys and slotting them into the door as quickly as she could. Grabbing Charles's hand, she pulled him through the moment it opened. He had the quick thinking to catch the door before it slammed shut.

"Lizzie, what are we doing?" He whispered. "We're acting like teenagers."

They were in fact acting a lot like them as teenagers, trying to sneak around behind Matt's back, trying their hardest not to get caught and running around in the dark. The only difference was that, apparently, they hadn't been very good at it as teenagers and Lizzie was determined not to make the same mistake again.

"Shut up!" She snapped, reaching for his hand again and pulling him up the stairs as quickly as she could. The lights were off and she heard him trip behind her and then hit his head on the ceiling above.

"Sorry, you're a bit too tall for the stairs."

"You think? Who lives here? Hobbits?"

A laugh escaped her lips but she slammed her mouth shut. As they got to her landing she heard the keys in the front door.

"Shit!" She whispered.

They weren't going to make it. There was no way she could open her door without Matt noticing.

She quickly pushed Charles up against the wall next to it instead, pressing herself against him and putting a finger to her mouth. From this angle, they shouldn't be seen. If Matt decided to go on a walk up the stairs, however, then they'd be screwed.

Charles bent his head slightly.

"Quick question, what are we doing?"

She moved her finger from her lips to his and glared at him. Her head jerked downwards as she heard the front door close, her back locking painfully and she found herself leaning in closer to Charles's tall frame. Fear licked up her spine. Despite straining to, she couldn't pick up what Matt was saying but Zoey kept giggling.

"Why don't we just sneak into your flat?" Charles whispered.

She pressed her finger harder into his lips and glared at him. If he didn't shut up they'd get caught.

Something sparked in his eyes and she felt his lips twitch.

No. No. No.

His chest began to shake against her.

The bloody man was laughing.

Their eyes met and annoyingly, Lizzie felt the corners of her own lips twitch in response. She pushed it away. They couldn't start laughing. If they laughed they would get caught. Just like if she tried to open her door they would get caught.

There was a loud thud downstairs. Before Lizzie could question why Matt's door closing had sounded so strange it was followed by the extremely audible sound of kissing.

Oh, dear, God.

Charles snorted and Lizzie slammed her entire hand across his mouth, trying her hardest to scream at him to shut up with just her eyes. His body was shaking uncontrollably and despite every brain cell screaming at her, she could feel her own body beginning to react. Laughter began to form in her chest like a cough. She clamped her lips shut, trying her hardest not to let it out but in the end her body was near convulsing with her attempt to stop it. She pressed her face into Charles's chest.

"Matt, babe, let's go inside."

Lizzie thanked Zoey loudly inside her head.

Matt responded with a highly suggestive alternative which made Lizzie's cheeks burn with even more embarrassment. Charles began to shake again.

"Can you hear something?"

Matt's voice.

Shit.

She stared up at Charles's face, wondering what in the hell she was going to do. He was about to laugh out loud. She could see it in the way he had now screwed up his eyes and was leaning his head back against the wall. Matt couldn't hear Charles laughing. That would be it.

Game over.

End of.

If Matt saw Charles here, he would kill him.

Without even properly thinking about what she was doing, she pushed herself up onto her tip toes, pulled Charles's head down and pressed her mouth against his.

CHAPTER TWENTY-EIGHT

It killed his laughter instantly. He stopped shaking. He stopped moving. For a second, it felt like he had stopped breathing. And then his hands circled her waist and he was pressing his lips back against hers and pulling her body into him.

Her stomach dipped violently, and her cheeks flushed as excitement zipped up her spine. How did his mouth have this much of an effect on her when they weren't really doing anything but being pressed together?

Voices came from downstairs but she barely heard them. Her mind was too preoccupied with the feel of his lips on hers as he slowly began to kiss her. It was delicate and gentle, yet the tenderness of it was causing her heart rate to rocket. In every way it was a silent, secretive kiss but that made it feel delicious.

The sound of a door shutting reached Lizzie's ears.

She pulled away instantly, ducking her head and smiling apologetically. "Sorry, just...you wouldn't stop laughing." She looked down at their feet and tried her hardest to push her blush out of her cheeks. "Good laughter killing technique."

God, she sounded so lame.

She felt the press of Charles's fingers on her neck as his thumbs guided her head back up to look at him. For a second he simply looked at her. His blue eyes stripping down the remainder of the walls that she had so carefully constructed. Whatever he saw caused him to smile and bend his head back towards her, pulling her into a second kiss.

The carefulness in which he handled her made her skin shudder, his thumbs tracing small circles along her jaw as he held her face in place. And then slowly, as if seeking permission, he began to up the intensity. She gripped helpless at his shirt, the feel of his mouth on hers causing hundreds of butterflies to erupt inside of her. He spun them around so he could push her up against the wall and she whimpered against him, suddenly oblivious to everything else except the feel of Charles's body on hers. It was unbearable and incredible, not enough and yet consuming, passionate and gentle, all at the same time.

When they pulled away she was completely breathless, her breath coming out hot and heavy as her mouth still tingled from his touch. He rested his forehead against hers and their gazes communicated a hundred messages. Without thinking, without rationalising at all, she turned and fumbled for her keys. She almost dropped them as Charles leant casually against the wall next to her, his gaze too heated for her to look at him properly.

"The door," she said quickly, trying to stop the tension around them building to an immovable level. "It would have given us away. Watch." She slotted her key into it. Shifting it a bit to the right and a bit to the left, before doing it again whilst holding down the handle, and another time pulling the door towards her. The door didn't budge. Instead it just made a racket, bouncing back and forth in its frame.

"Struggling?"

"It takes a minimum of five goes."

She was on her sixth.

"What's the maximum?"

"Fifteen has been my record."

"Can I try?"

Lizzie felt her lower belly tilt.

If he managed this, it would be too familiar. All too real.

He moved in front of the door. With a slight twist of his wrist to the left, the door audibly unlocked and he pushed down the handle with a pleased smile.

"It must like me." The door then emitted a very loud groan. He pulled a comical face. "Or not, and you were right that would have definitely given us away."

They both stared into her empty, dark flat, silence rising between them as they both suddenly seemed a little lost as to what to say. She turned her head up slowly and almost melted at the unguarded expression on Charles's face. He was trusting her. Again.

A trust she didn't deserve, a trust she shouldn't be welcoming.

"Would you like me to go?" He said gently.

She should tell him to leave. Tell him to go. But the look he was giving her…

And that kiss.

Her heart thumped painfully at the thought of telling him to leave. She swallowed. "No."

His smile grew and every nerve end tingled as he said, "After you then."

She stepped into her flat, hearing his footsteps follow her and the door close behind them. They stood in complete darkness.

Charles was just inches from her, she could feel the heat radiating off his body and she bit down hard on her lip. Now she was inside, she didn't have a clue what to do. The tension around them made it too hard to talk and yet she was paralysed to the spot so she couldn't move either.

God, she was an idiot.

Charles was an actor now. He probably had been seduced by hundreds of women. She was going to be so poor performance in comparison-

His hands pressed against her shoulders and he turned her around slowly. Their gazes met in the darkness and Lizzie's inner dialogue fell into silence. A second passed. It felt like an hour. Both of them studying each other, their breathing the only sound Lizzie could hear.

"Come here," he said roughly, hauling her against him.

Their mouths met, desperate for the other. Charles pushed her back against the wall and through his shirt she could feel his heart thudding just as fast as hers. Heat travelled down her spine.

This was Charles.

Her Charles.

Oh God, she wanted this, she wanted to give in to all the desires she had pent up inside her and she wanted to forget what she was doing and the consequences it was going to wreak on her later. She threaded her hands through his hair, tugging on the strands ever so slightly and couldn't ignore the rush of sexual confidence that flooded through her as he groaned into her mouth.

She wanted to laugh and sob all at the same time. Why had she given this up? How had she managed to? She pulled against him urgently. Trying to breathe properly was impossible, trying to think was even harder.

"Charles, please," she whimpered against his mouth.

"Bedroom," he whispered huskily against her lips and she felt another hot jolt of desire shoot through her.

This was happening, this was really happening.

Without being told where to go, he began to pull her towards the bedroom, their lips never parting as their hands roamed each other's bodies frantically.

Everything almost felt too much for Lizzie. There was too much heat in her body, too many excited nerves in her gut, too much need for Charles to never stop touching her.

Inside her bedroom, his hands dropped to the hem of her jumper and he began pulling it over her head.

And then the next.

"How many of these bloody things do you have on?"

"I told you I didn't need a coat."

"I think you've been trying to convince me of that for years." She laughed against his lips and reached up to push his coat and blazer simultaneously off his shoulders. The move made him mock grumble as she interrupted his pursuit to rid her of her multiple layers.

And then their lips were on one another once more. Lizzie tried her hardest to kiss back him with as much passion as Charles lavished on her, but it was a struggle. The way his mouth was moving on hers was making it harder and harder to stand upright. Her brain fused as she felt his hands skate over her naked skin and begin to reach for her bra. Self-consciousness lifted its head for a millisecond but, like he had read it in her lips, he let her go for a fraction of a second, his eyes travelling down her body. There were heavy with desire.

"You're so beautiful, Lizzie," he whispered. "You've always been so beautiful."

Emotion clogged in her throat and she crushed his mouth back to hers, fighting back tears behind her eyes as she kissed him to the point of pain.

He made sure to keep that self-consciousness at bay. It was in the way he was holding her, as if she was something to be cared for, looked after, admired, the way his hands ran up and over her skin sending excited darts of anticipation where her body craved them, making her feel desirable and wanted.

Her hands explored the new, unfamiliar hardened planes along his chest. At first she was hesitant, her touch a mere whisper against him but slowly she became more confident. She traced the lines and shapes, gradually letting her hand travel lower and lower. It made him groan her name against her mouth.

They toppled down onto the duvet, his palms just landing by her so that he didn't crush her. She didn't think she would care if he had. At some point he or she had taken the hair band out of her hair as it now fanned out behind her. They paused for a second, their heavy pants filling the silence, their foreheads pressed together. The feel of his skin against hers and his weight on top of her made her heart do a strange little dance. Part of her still couldn't quite believe she was naked. It couldn't believe he was naked too.

"Hello," he whispered, his eyes looking down at her tenderly.

"Hello," she whispered back.

His eyes tracked between her own. "I just want to check, this is definitely okay?"

Lizzie paused for a fraction of a second before laughing, the sound blossoming up through her and her heart feeling fuller than it ever had. She reached up and pulled him to her, kissing him hard.

His hands traced over her as he deepened their kiss. It made her head spin.

And finally, she gave in.

Gave in to what she had known all along.

Ever since she was a seventeen-year-old girl who had the confidence to kiss her brother's best friend.

Her best friend.

It would always be him.

No matter what life or path she took, she would always be hopelessly in love with Charles Williams.

His mouth moved to her neck, pressing open mouthed kisses against her skin. "I missed you so much, Cartwright."

She tried to speak but words were unable to leave her mouth. Every part of her body trembled with feeling. She felt his palm start to slide down her side and her hips jerked up towards him.

"I missed you too," she managed to gasp. She nodded as if to solidify the fact before crying out sharply as his mouth began to torture her.

CHAPTER TWENTY-NINE

Lizzie woke slowly, her body clinging onto sleep like it was a safety raft as she forced her eyes open. A wall of heat was pressed up against her back, a strong lean arm thrown around her middle and a leg was looped through hers. She was entangled within somebody else.

Very slowly, she shifted her weight and rolled over to face him. His dark blonde hair had resumed its slightly wavy look in his sleep, his eyes were shut gently and the morning light was highlighting his strong features like he was made out of marble. He looked peaceful, younger, and she could smell his musky scent everywhere. She glanced down at their naked bodies and smiled. The night before had been...incredible. They had explored each other somehow with the knowledge that they had acquired of years of being together but at the same time as if it was all brand new. The colour rose in her cheeks and a giggle that was so unlike her escaped her lips.

"Should I be worried that you're looking down there and laughing?"

His sleepy voice broke through her thoughts and she snapped her head up so fast she smacked into his chin.

"Ow!"

"Fuck, I am so sorry!" She pushed herself up on her hands. "Should I go get some ice or frozen peas or something?" She began to try and disentangle her body from his but his legs closed around her calf and he grabbed her by the arm, pulling her back down onto him.

He was laughing, his torso shaking as he caught her against him.

"I'm sorry," he said, melting back into his grip.

"Sorry about offending me or sorry about the head slam?"

Lizzie blushed crimson again.

"I wasn't-that's not what-I promise-"

He watched her, letting her stumble over her words with an amused smile on his face. She shoved his shoulder playfully.

"You know that's not why I was laughing."

He smiled in response and rolled onto his back, pulling her easily along with him. She lay there happily, the rise and fall of his chest beneath her ear relaxing her. She tried to remember when she had last felt so content.

So why did you give it up?

The voice invaded her brain like an unwelcome wasp at a picnic. She closed her eyes tighter and curled her body more firmly against his. She didn't want to think about that right now. Not at the moment anyway. She wanted to bask in this happiness and the light-hearted feeling running through her entire body for just a little while longer.

"Coffee?"

"Yes, please, but," she tightened her hold on him, "just stay here for a little longer."

He stroked a hand down her hair and kissed the top of her head.

"I wasn't planning on leaving after coffee."

She smiled happily into his chest, the smell of him comforting her. She was enjoying his presence so much it almost hurt. She traced a finger over his stomach, enjoying the way he involuntarily sucked in as her hand skimmed particularly low.

"You can stay all day if you like," she whispered.

"I'd love that."

She turned her head up to look at him and his smile mirrored hers.

"And, um, you could stay longer?" She was blushing, she could feel it in her face but Charles's smile grew as his eyes skated over it.

He leaned forward and kissed her forehead.

"All weekend?"

"If you're sure?"

He stared at her for a second, something moving behind his blue eyes as he shook his head in amazement. "You really have no idea do you?"

He brushed a strand of her hair away from her face and she felt her breath catch at his expression. "To repeat what I said last night I really have missed you."

She shifted so she was leaning over him, her hair a wavy curtain to one side and a rush of lust fired through her as she noted her small movement had sparked the desire in his eyes. "I really missed you too."

"Lizzie!" a familiar voice called from the kitchen.

Charles's tensed beneath her, his arm locking around her protectively, and her own body turned rigid in his grip.

This could not be happening.

"Lizzie, I am borrowing the milk. Got company and need to make tea."

Shit. Shit. Shit.

Lizzie and Charles's eyes met. They were both wide awake now.

"That's fine," she called, trying to make her voice sound level and nonchalant, rolling off Charles and twisting to face the door. "There's a two pinter in the fridge."

"Great, I'll just pour some out-"

"Just take it. Don't worry about it," Lizzie said, her voice rising slightly desperately. Charles stroked her shoulder reassuringly but she could sense his own eyes were locked on the door too, waiting for what felt like the inevitable to happen.

They both lay tense and unmoving, not even daring to breathe in case he heard them. She could hear him moving around in the kitchen.

"Can I borrow the eggs too?"

"Yes!"

And that's when everything went wrong. The door swung open and Matt stuck his head around. "And a whisk would be- oh shit, sorry-" he ducked his head in embarrassment but then flicked it back up, even faster, his eyes murderous. "What the actual fuck-?"

"Matt, please calm down," Lizzie said desperately, clutching the duvet to her chest and quickly sitting up in bed. This was the wrong thing to do as his eyes clocked her bare arms. If it was possible his face got even darker.

She leaned forward. "Matt, please-"

"You absolute fucker-"

"Please try not to overreact," Charles said calmly, sitting up behind her. She appreciated him coming to her side but right now it was probably best if he stayed quiet.

"Get out of bed-," Matt jabbed his finger aggressively at Charles, "-and we can see just how much I can overreact."

Lizzie was pretty sure if Charles hadn't been on the furthest side of the bed from the door Matt would have launched himself at him. His body was shaking with anger, his hands in fists by his side and there was so much hatred in his eyes that Lizzie felt she could taste it on the air.

"Matt, please stop-"

He snapped his gaze to her. "You fucking promised me this wouldn't happen!" Lizzie flinched as he spat the words and she felt his disappointment hit her like a hammer to the chest. "Now get out of bed, put your bloody clothes back on and I'll meet you both in the kitchen." When they didn't make an immediate attempt to move he punched his hand into his palm. "Now!"

"Unless you want to see us naked then we can hardly do that with you in the room," Charles said darkly.

"Charles!" Lizzie hissed and turned her head to glare at him. Winding Matt up was not what they needed to be doing right now.

Matt turned and slammed the door behind him.

Lizzie jumped out of her bed, covering herself as best as she could and reaching for the pyjamas in her bedside drawer. Her head was ringing so loudly it was practically pulsing. This couldn't be happening. Why was this happening? Couldn't she have had one weekend with him? Just the one. She was only vaguely aware of Charles repeating her name when he suddenly grabbed her wrists and pulled her around to face him. She had managed to pull a blue oversized t-shirt over her head, it was the wrong way round but she didn't care, and only one of her legs was in her red flannel trousers she had got from Primark the Christmas before.

Before she could speak Charles leaned forward and kissed her, hard, pressing his lips against hers and despite the situation she felt a snatch of happiness spread through her as she couldn't help but kiss him back. When they parted, he rubbed his thumbs across the palms of her hands.

"Don't let your brother spoil this," he said quietly.

"He's so angry-"

"And we are adults, Lizzie. We aren't teenagers anymore. He has no right to be angry."

But he did. He had every right and as that realisation hit her, a much more terrifying feeling of dread entered her bloodstream.

"It's going to be okay," Charles said softly, misinterpreting her expression. But of course he was going to misinterpret it, he had no idea what she had done, what she had said to cover her lies, he had no idea why Matt was truly angry at him. "No matter what happens I'm still staying."

He couldn't promise that. Not if he found out what she had been hiding.

"Charles, maybe you should stay in here."

He raised an eyebrow at her.

"I think your brother will just come in and find me, don't you?"

As if hearing his cue there was a sudden loud banging on the door.

"HURRY UP!"

"Lizzie," Charles said reassuringly, he wasn't smiling but she could see in every corner of his face that he was still happy. It made her feel worse. Her stomach was churning and she genuinely thought she might be sick. "It's going to be fine." He walked away from her and began to pull on the rest of his clothes. Lizzie watched him helplessly, thinking she might as well absorb this moment because it was never going to happen again.

She was going to lose him. Every single part of her could feel it.

Why was she doing this to herself when she knew they couldn't be together? What kind of sadist was she?

"I'll go first," Charles said, walking up to the door but Lizzie managed to flit around him and beat him to it.

"No way, I'm not having him fly at you."

Matt was pacing up and down at the other end of the kitchen, his body rigid with anger, steam practically coming off him. He turned to glare at them, his eyes immediately locking onto Charles.

"Matt, please!" Lizzie said, slipping around the same side of the kitchen table as him as he began to make his way around it. She planted her hands on his chest. "Stop it!"

He took no notice of her.

"You have some nerve coming in here! You absolute tosser!" Matt yelled and pointed over her shoulder.

"Well, I would have happily stayed in bed."

Her brother surged forward and Lizzie slammed her feet into the floor to stop him toppling her over.

"Charles!" She snapped over her shoulder. "Not helping!"

"Move out of the fucking away!" Matt snarled, his eyes still angrily fixed onto Charles. Lizzie didn't move.

"Matt, please, just sit down-"

He pushed forward again and Lizzie stumbled back, having already reached the end of the table her back hit Charles's front. His hands came up to the backs of her arms protectively.

"Matt, stop shoving her," he growled.

"Seeing as she listens to you way more than she clearly does to me, why don't you ask her to get out of my way?"

"Stop!" Lizzie yelled.

Matt turned his green eyes down to her, the frown lines were darker around his eyes and the disgust in them reminded her of the way Craig had used to look at her. Hurt sliced through her chest.

"You're sleeping with him?"

"Matt," she said softly, reaching for his shoulders, trying her best to implore him to understand. "Please."

He jerked away from her touch.

"I hope this time you at least bothered to wear protection, he's probably riddled with diseases by now."

"That's enough," Charles snapped.

"Please," she whispered, shaking her head and trying to reach for him again. Beneath the disgust and hate she could see Matt's hurt, hidden in the backs of his eyes, in the rigid set of his shoulders and the thin line of his mouth.

"I can't believe you would do this to me," he said, staring at her. "I can't believe you would do this to yourself. After everything we've been through."

"She can make her own decisions."

"Not when it comes to you!" Matt yelled, looking up towards Charles and the sound shuddered around the room. He pointed aggressively at him. "Never when it comes to you. And it's all my fucking fault because if I hadn't introduced you into our lives this would never have happened!"

"No," Lizzie whispered, shaking her head. "You can't think like that."

"What is it that I am supposed to have done that was that bad, Matt?"

Lizzie's stomach dipped so hard she felt as if she was about to fall. Her eyes desperately looked up at her brother but he tore his gaze away from her, the hurt pushed back behind his barriers and anger once again coming to the forefront.

"Do you know how many times I nearly went to the newspapers?

Do you know how many times I nearly revealed what a fake you are?"

"What the hell are you talking about?"

"Matt," she grabbed his wrist, trying her hardest to get his attention but he pulled it away and in one swift movement he managed to push her behind him. "No-" she tried to move around him but he blocked her with an outstretched arm, trapping her in the little space there was between the worktop and the side of her kitchen table. He stepped closer to Charles.

"So, when you were in my little sister's bed just now, did you even stop to wonder where he was?"

Fear splintered into Lizzie's chest. "Matt, stop!"

"I have no idea what you're talking about." Charles's tone sounded bored but his eyes said he was everything but. Anger was shining from them.

Matt snorted in disgust. "You just presumed she'd get an abortion then? Like you asked her to? You just presumed Lizzie would do as you asked?"

Lizzie sucked in a sharp breath.

No.

She wanted to scream, she wanted to yell out some kind of denial or cover Matt's mouth but he'd said it. It was done now. The words were out there, floating in the air like bullets. She moved her gaze towards Charles. His arms were still folded across his chest but his shoulders had turned rigid. He tilted his head a fraction to the right, his Adam's apple dipping slowly.

Matt continued, not able to read Charles's movements like she could. "Didn't care to ask if she had bothered to give birth to your son? Didn't care to think where he could be? Just presumed she took the pills, like you demanded, and had gone about her life." He laughed coldly. "Sorry, you probably didn't even bother to find out that Leo was a he, did you? How can you sleep with someone after thinking you made them go through that against their will?"

"Matt, shut up," Lizzie gasped but her voice was merely a flicker in the air.

To the outside world it may have looked like Charles hadn't heard a thing Matt had said or that he simply didn't care, but Lizzie could see in the blue of his eyes a wall crumbling behind it and she felt as if someone had just stabbed her through the ribs. She looped her arm around her stomach, scared the pain might cause her to split open.

"You were my best friend," Matt continued, shaking his head. "My best fucking friend. I trusted you with her." He pointed behind him at Lizzie. "I trusted you. And then you got her pregnant and you scarpered. You absolute coward! Absolute bloody coward!" He yelled the last word straight into Charles's face but he didn't even flinch. "I always looked up to you. To your family! I wish I could have realised sooner just how ashamed you were of us. You couldn't bear to been seen getting a Cartwright pregnant. Couldn't have that, could you? Not quite in line with the Williams's reputation?"

"Matt, please stop," Lizzie said, her voice gaining strength as she pulled her eyes away from Charles to stare at the back of her brother's head.

"NO!" Matt shouted again. He took a step closer to the impassive Charles and shoved his shoulder. "You could at least look like you care. Thought you were meant to be an actor." He lowered his voice. "Did you ask her once about the baby before you snuck into her bed? Did you ask her once about what she had gone through? He was born sleeping by the way, if you wanted to know. He was d-" Matt couldn't say the word, instead he swallowed it back. "Your son. Leo was born sleeping. Do you have any idea how much we went through? How much pain Lizzie endured? On her own."

Matt's voice was catching and Lizzie knew he was crying. She could hear it in the thickness of his words and another part of her broke into fragments.

"Where the hell were you? Even afterwards, where were you? I was there! In the aftermath. Do you know how hard it is to be next to someone, holding them, trying to be this strong, supportive person when all they want, more than anything in the world, is your piece of shit of a best friend? She didn't want me, she needed you! Through the depression, through the long nights, through the constant night terrors, through the doctor's appointments. I was there, handling it on my own. Every two weeks I go to visit him, every December 7th I try and do something to celebrate his life even when I am not in the country. I am more of a father to that child than you are."

Charles took a deep breath, his eyes had glassed over and Lizzie could see the tremors in his hands as he lowered his arms to grip onto the worktop behind him. Everything seemed to still around them, the air ice cold and the moment painfully frozen.

"Lizzie," Charles said quietly, turning his head to look at her, his whole body eerily still and even though she knew he must be able to read it in her face, in her expression, in her tears, he still asked the question. "Is that true?" He paused, his glassy eyes scanning her face and there was a slight tremor to his lips. "Tell me it's not true."

"What do you mean, is that true?" Matt snapped angrily. Charles didn't so much as flinch, instead his eyes fixed solely on Lizzie's, his eyes reading her expression and she could see the pain coiled in them, ready to spring free the moment she opened her lips.

He knew. But he needed her to confirm it.

She closed her eyes, feeling more tears seep out from beneath her lashes and burn down her face.

"You broke up with me because you were pregnant?" His voice cracked.

Lizzie couldn't speak as sobs consumed her lungs and more and more tears streamed from her eyes. She gripped the table harder, her fingers digging into the wood painfully and splinters slicing into her skin.

Charles's blue eyes were pinning her to the spot and they shimmered as he breathed deeply. She slowly tilted her head back and forth once in a nod.

"I'm so sorry."

Matt turned to look at Lizzie, taking in her drooped posture and her tearful face. He slowly looked between the two of him, his anger frozen as if someone had pressed a pause button on his emotions.

"Was the idea of me being a father such a disappointment to you?" A combination of pure disgust and hatred began to build across Charles's face. She felt its heat as strongly as she felt the pain in her gut.

Matt looked back and forth between them both again and slowly, the redness in his face began to fade and he grew very, very pale.

"You didn't know," he said, his voice sounded heavy. He turned his head to look at Charles. "You didn't know," he repeated.

Charles fixed him with a look of pure anger.

"Of course, I didn't bloody know. How the hell could you think that of me?" He yelled, the sound striking Lizzie hard. She could feel his hurt like it was her own. She could feel how distraught he was and the way he wanted to run.

"Mate," Matt whispered, "I-I-"

"You thought I would leave Lizzie because she was pregnant? You thought I'd try and force her to have an abortion?"

"She said-"

"I don't care what she said, Matt! You were my best friend. Two weeks before we were…you and I were…" But he couldn't finish the sentence. He turned away from them both and heaved, pressing his hands against the worktop as if he couldn't quite hold himself up without support.

"Charles, I am so sorry. It wasn't like that," Lizzie whispered.

Matt turned to look at her as if just realising she was still in the room. The moment he clocked her, a shadow passed across his face and Lizzie felt the physical bond between them snag dangerously.

"I wish you had told me how little you thought of me before we slept together," Charles said coldly, still not looking at her. "I'll be civil at work but outside of it I never want to see you again." He pushed himself away from the counter and walked towards the front door.

"Charles, wait!"

He paused. "Why?" He fixed her with a steel cold gaze. "Why

should I?"

He walked out into the hallway and Lizzie found the strength from somewhere to follow him. Matt grabbed her arm.

"Leave him alone."

She yanked her arm away from him.

"Charles, please let me explain."

To her surprise, just outside of her front door she bumped into the back of him.

Charles didn't turn. His body was locked into place as he stared down the stairs.

Lizzie followed his gaze and more icy dread filled her body.

Lottie was stood there, two cups of coffee in her hand, her curly hair pinned back behind her, wearing a mixture of grunge with bright pink summer clothing.

"What are you doing here?" Charles asked, his voice soft.

"I…" Lottie flicked her gaze between all of them. "I was here to have brunch with Lizzie."

Lizzie felt her stomach drop. The silence following her statement was cutting and painful. Lizzie could feel it suffocating her. Charles turned his gaze around to look at her. "You knew where Lottie was? You knew where my little sister was this whole bloody time?"

"No, it's not like that!" Lizzie cried desperately.

"We only just bumped into each other, Charles."

"Long enough ago to be making brunch dates together," Charles snarled. Something broke behind the anger. "What did I do, Lizzie? What did I do that was so wrong?"

She reached out to him again, this time managing to wrap a hand around his forearm. He didn't move. "Nothing, honestly, this has nothing to do with you."

Charles laughed. It was cold and bitter and so unlike him. "I'm guessing that what's you thought when you found out you were pregnant too?"

Before she could respond he turned and walked down the stairs, sliding to the left to physically avoid having to touch Lottie in any way before slamming the front door.

Lottie winced.

"Hi Lottie," Matt said briskly. He shoved past Lizzie and followed Charles out the house. The door slammed loudly.

Lizzie couldn't breathe. Her lips were firmly pressed together and her chest was aching hard. Her back hit the wall and she slid down to the floor as sobs began to force themselves out of her.

What had she done?

What had she *actually* done?

She had thought it was for the best, she had thought she had done exactly what was best for Charles.

"Lizzie, look at me." Lottie was crouched beside her, her arm around her shoulders but Lizzie could barely make out she was there, let alone her features.

"I took Leo from him," she whispered, unable to stop the pain crashing through her. "He didn't even get to meet him. I thought I was doing the right thing but…" she covered her face. "I wanted to give him his life back, Lottie, I was trying not to be selfish." Her whole body was shaking, her feet tapping feverishly against the floor. Charles's face, Matt's expression, the hurt and pain written in both flashed behind her closed eyes.

What if…what if she'd made the wrong decision?

CHAPTER THIRTY

Charles had no idea where he was going. The pain running through his body was so intense it was all he could focus on. He couldn't even feel himself breathing, all he could feel was the ache in his chest that was threatening to split him open. He ducked his head and his footsteps grew faster and more off balance, like he was dragging his feet along after an accident. He didn't know how far he'd walked or for how long, but he could see a thick blur of trees up ahead and the sound of people in general was getting louder. It itched at his head. Before he knew what he was doing, he slammed a number into his phone and brought it up to his ear.

"Charles!" His mum's voice sounded so relieved it made him want to throw the phone across the road. He still hadn't had the guts to talk to her since the papers had exposed Jennifer's relationship. Not that it mattered now. He was pretty sure his mum had been keeping a much worse secret from him. "Kenneth, it's Charles!"

"Did you know?" He said, trying his hardest to keep the tremor out of his voice.

"Did I know what, Charles? About Jenni? No, of course not! I never thought she would-"

"Did you know about Lizzie?"

There was a short silence on the other end of the phone. He heard her take a shaky breath and the squeak of a chair as she sat down. "Know about Lizzie what?"

"That I had a son."

His mum didn't respond at first.

"Did you know?" He shouted.

"I...yes. Yes, I did."

"Were you there?"

She let out a long breath. "Yes," she said softly, her obvious concern pushing his anger to boiling point.

"On duty or…?"

"Charles, what's-?"

"Were you on duty or not?"

"…No. I saw her name on the board when I went in to see the Kimps and their twins. I knew he had to be yours."

"And you still didn't tell me."

"No."

Her admittance sent shards of fresh pain shooting through him.

"Charles, what's happened? Where are you?"

"Like you have any right to know!" He snapped and ended the call. He felt it vibrate a second later but he shoved it into his pocket.

Why hadn't Lizzie told him? Why had she lied to Matt?

Relationship aside, they had been best friends. Why hadn't she spoken to him? And what would have happened had his son lived? Would she have kept him a secret from him? Would she have denied him the right to know him?

Guilt crossed his chest for the millionth time. Despite everything he still hated the fact she had gone through that alone. He still hated himself for not being there. He had seen the pain and hurt in Matt's face, practically watched the flashbacks dance across his eyes as he had stood accusing him of the worst crime imaginable. Lizzie had gone through hell and he hadn't been there.

"I would have fucking been there!" He bit out, slamming his hand into the black railings on his left and barely noticing the hum of pain that shuddered up through his arm. He glanced at them, his blurred vision taking in the grass beyond.

Regent's Park.

He walked into it, hoping the greenery would do something to ease the pain that was now plaguing his entire body but if anything, it intensified with every step.

We used to come here together.

He shook his head.

We'd even sneak in at night.

"Shut up," he snarled, not knowing where the hell the inner voice was coming from or what it was talking about.

We stopped doing it. We should have made more time for ourselves.

He let out an anguished yell and a couple walking past jumped away from him. He reached for the collar of his blazer and turned it upwards, ducking his head as he continued to pace through Regent's Park. His phone continued to buzz in his pocket.

"Piss off," he snapped, taking it out of his pocket to glance at the screen.

It was Daniel.

He would know. By now Maria had probably rung him to try and get him to talk to Charles. Had Daniel known?

Charles lost his footing for a second, rolling on his ankle painfully before quickly straightening himself up. If Daniel had known...

Something dark twisted in his chest.

His pace was fast and soon he found himself on the North side of the park, near the water. It was still fairly early in the morning, the sun was only just brightening the sky and there was barely anyone around. In the water he could see the reflection of the bare branches overhead and it made him aware of just how cold it was.

A broken laugh escaped his mouth.

He had forgotten his coat.

A set of footsteps stopped just behind him and without turning he knew who it was. He had heard them from the moment he had walked into the park.

"You shouldn't be here."

"Mate, I am so sorry."

Charles turned to look at him, rage blistering out of him. "Sorry doesn't really cut it."

"I know." Matt took a step forward. "I bloody know that."

"Do you?" Charles snapped. "Do you have any idea what this feels like? I loved your sister. Two weeks before she broke up with me I asked for your permission to ask her to marry me!"

Matt winced. "I know."

"Two weeks! Did you really think in those two weeks I would have had such a change of heart I wouldn't even want to be with her anymore? Just because she was pregnant!" He could feel his face was wet. The wind was catching against it and making him even more aware of the cold.

"I was an idiot. She was my little sister, I had to believe her!"

Charles jabbed his thumb into his chest. "You should have trusted me! You should have known me! If it had been the other way around, I'd have known. I'd have known you weren't capable of that."

"She said it was to do with our background and Dad got into my head-"

"Not an excuse, Matt. Just because your father is a piece of shit doesn't mean you have to be one. I wanted to marry her! How the hell does that add up to not wanting to be associated with your family?"

Matt rubbed his hands through his hair and looked down at the ground. "I know."

"You're an idiot!" Charles snapped. "You know I still have the ring."

"What?"

"That is how much Lizzie meant to me, Matt. I couldn't return it. I'd never have given it to anyone else. It's still in my house! How could you think I could do that to her?"

Matt didn't reply, instead he looked just more torn apart.

"I wish you'd explained. Outside the church I wish you'd explained properly! When you were literally pummelling my face into the ground, why the hell didn't you say anything that would have actually let me put the dots together?" Charles shouted. He thought back to that night. Matt climbing over the graveyard walls, his face looking gaunt and lifeless. He understood now. He saw all the missing pieces of conversation. "I'm surprised you didn't kill me when I said it was Lizzie's fault."

"I nearly did."

Charles looked away. "I loved her so much and you... and she-" Grief and pain were threatening to stop him talking so he took a few deep breaths to steady himself.

Matt stepped forward, arms in front of him as if approaching a wounded animal. "Mate, I'm so sorry."

"Just get lost. We are done."

"But-"

He felt his phone buzz in his pocket again and he took it out to stare at the screen.

Mum

"My mum even knew." He held the screen up to Matt as if that would make his point. "My own mum." He stared at the screen, conflicting emotions balling up inside of him and stamping hard. It felt suffocating. The phone continued to ring and with an angry yell he chucked it into the lake. The surface rippled slightly before sucking it in, the green water hiding any evidence that it had been there.

With it went his anger. He felt his body sag and didn't snap as Matt approached him. He stared out onto the surface of the lake. Despite the fact there wasn't a fierce wind, small ripples were travelling across it, gaining speed. Something danced up his spine.

"Why did she do this, Matt? What did I do wrong?"

"I don't know."

"Why didn't she want a baby with me?" He looked away from the lake, blinking hard as he stared up into the sky and tried to push back the tears in his eyes. "Why didn't she want me to be a part of that? I just wish I..." he paused. The birds that had been tweeting in the trees around them suddenly became silent. The ripples on the lake froze and he felt something familiar wash through him. Matt was on the left of him but suddenly, he could feel a warmth on his right.

Say it, said a voice that wasn't his.

He balled his hands into fists by his sides. "I wish I knew what had been going through her head."

He heard laughter on the wind, followed by the sound of brakes and scream. Trepidation ran up his back.

"Bex?" Matt called, worry threaded through his voice.

And then, the world spun.

Both men stumbled as a million different images flooded back into their heads. Matt yelled out and gripped hold of the railing around the lake whilst Charles froze, his eyes wide and his heart racing, as everything began to slot back into place.

CHAPTER THIRTY-ONE

"What the hell were you thinking?"

Lizzie had opened the door to find her two best friends stood on the other side of it. She stared at them in disbelief. Seeing the two of them together was rare, seeing the two of them turn up somewhere together was even rarer, and seeing them both agreeing about something was simply not possible.

Lizzie turned to look at Lottie. She could see her on the sofa in the living room from the door. "Did you ring them?" Her voice was croaky. She had cried practically all of it away.

Lottie laughed. "I'm good at remembering things but remembering my sister-in-law's best friends' phone numbers, no, I'm not that good."

They'd spent the last forty-five minutes dissecting everything that happened. Once Lottie had managed to pull her in from the landing, reassuring Peggy from upstairs that Lizzie was okay, she had wrapped her in a blanket and fed her hot chocolate. Lizzie hadn't been able to stomach food yet. Every negative emotion had buried under her skin and eaten away at her. And no matter how many times she tried to tell herself this was for the best, that now Charles would no longer be interested in her and he could get on with his life for good, she still felt as if a part of her had been carved away.

She turned back to face them and frowned at Neil. Her eyes were red raw and even that small movement hurt. "Did you tell Bex?"

Bex looked affronted. "I'm sorry, did you tell Neil something before you told me?"

Neil smiled smugly. "Yeah, I wasn't actually going to mention that. Was going to save it up for a later date to use against Blondie here."

Bex made an irritated noise in her throat and pushed past Lizzie into the flat. Neil followed, ducking his head in silent laughter and catching Lizzie's eye fondly. Her heart felt heavy at the thought of their last conversation.

"Neil, I-"

"Don't worry about it," he said with a smile, leaning forward to kiss her on the forehead.

His kindness made her feel even worse.

"What are you two doing here?" She croaked.

"*What are you two doing here?*" Bex mimicked, throwing her a glare over her shoulder. She stopped for a second, running her eyes up and down Lizzie's frame. "What the hell are you wearing?"

Lizzie looked down at her clothes. She was still in the oversized t-shirt and Christmas pyjama trousers from before. "Pyjamas."

Bex's lips pressed so tightly together it made the lower part of her face paler than the rest. "You're making it very hard to still be angry at you when you're looking so pathetic."

Lizzie ran a hand across her forehead. "Why are you angry at me?"

"Hi Lottie," Neil said, with a wide grin, walking past Bex and into the living room. He took a place on the sofa directly next to her.

"Hey Neil," she answered. "Still never going to happen."

"I didn't say anything!"

"You didn't have to."

"Hang on, how do you two know each other?" Lizzie stopped in the doorway to the living room and stared at the two of them.

Bex flopped down onto the sofa, her expression angry. "Because, about thirty minutes ago in the middle of my Crossfit class I almost died on the ropes when suddenly the ghosts of Christmas past, present and future decided to explode in my head, all at the same time."

Neil laughed. "I was in bed. Thank, God, I was actually on my own."

"You really had to add that in, did you?" Bex snapped.

Neil laughed, leaning back against the sofa and turning his head to look at Lizzie. "So, what did you do?"

Lizzie looked between the two of them. "I'm still confused, what are you two talking about?"

"You remembered," Lottie said simply. She was staring at her phone. Her lip trembled slightly and her eyes appeared glassy. She held up it up towards Lizzie. "Five missed calls from Daniel, three from Mum, four from Dad, and one from Patricia. They've all remembered." A small smile crossed her lips. "And they are clearly better at remembering phone numbers than I am."

Lizzie swallowed, her gaze flicking back to her two best friends. Bex was glaring at her whilst Neil looked...well, like Neil. Smug and curious at the same time.

"You both remember?"

"Sorry, was that not obvious, Whiskers?"

"Yes, we remember. We remember bloody everything!"

"And how did you know it was me?" Lizzie's eyes slid towards Lottie but she was busy texting. "It might not have been. It might have been a coincidence."

"You're the only thing different in this lifetime. Doesn't take a genius to work it out," Bex snapped.

Neil wavered his hand to emphasise that he didn't quite agree. "See, I just thought, who is the most stupid, self-deprecating person I know who would chose to go back in time and actually make their life worse?" He tilted his head to the right and raised his eyebrows at her. "Even if this wasn't down to you, you are still the one who remembered and rewired everything."

"How do you know I remembered?"

"Because you've gone all self-sacrificing and changed your bloody life. And now you being so weird around Charles all the time makes sense." Neil shook his head at her but a wry smile still tugged at his lips.

Lottie looked up briefly. "I remembered too."

Neil let his eyes run up and down her. "Smart and gorgeous."

Bex rolled her eyes and Lottie laughed, shoving Neil playfully. "I've missed you."

His flirtatious grin slipped into a real one. "Likewise."

"But how?" Lizzie said, staring at them. "How do you remember?"

"No idea."

"Do you think the whole world knows?" Lottie said, her brow furrowing for a second. "Do you think everyone-"

"No," Neil said, shaking his head. "First thing I did was make a few calls. Talked to Lara. No one else seems to have had a life they didn't know about slam into their head."

Did Charles know?

Lizzie's stomach dipped. Did he remember?

As if the world had heard her question, a furious banging reverberated around the flat.

"Shit," she whispered, turning to stare at the door. Her feet stayed rooted to the spot as the banging continued.

"Go on," Bex said, furiously. "We're not going to answer it for you."

Lizzie couldn't. Her heart was in her mouth and her feet were failing to move at all. She curled her hand around the bottom of her t-shirt before pushing back the tears still wavering in her eyes.

She could do this.

She had done the right thing.

She rolled back her shoulders and jutted out her jaw, about to step forward when the knocking stopped. Instead, there was the sound of a key in the lock and the door swung open.

"Matt!" Lizzie cried out in alarm.

"Not really the time to tell me off about using my key, Lizzie," he barked, walking up to her angrily, his broad shoulders taking up most of the small space in the corridor and his anger radiating off him. "What the hell were you thinking?"

"I-I-I-" The words that had been so confidently set in her mind were getting stuck in her throat. Her eyes couldn't help but look past her brother to the corridor and landing behind.

"I don't think she was thinking," Neil added unhelpfully.

Matt's fury paused as he took in the fact there were three other people in the room.

"I was, actually," Lizzie said firmly, feeling some of herself coming back to her. She glanced again to the landing.

"Charles isn't here," Matt snapped, catching her. "You expect the guy to show up after you erased your life together? After you as good as divorced him?"

"I didn't divorce him!"

"No, you just deleted him instead." The anger coming off her brother's body was practically vibrating through the room.

"It was for his own good!" She bit out stubbornly.

"What the hell are you talking about?" He stepped forward, shoving her back into the living room and away from the door.

"Hey!" Bex snapped, suddenly at Lizzie's side. "You can be angry but you don't shove her! Lay another finger on her Matthew and I will floor you. As far as we know this isn't Lizzie's fault anyway."

Lizzie glanced at her. "That wasn't what you were saying five minutes ago."

"Shut up."

Matt shook his head. "Lizzie was the one who made up that Charles knew she was pregnant."

"What?" Bex turned her head to look at her.

"It's a long story," Lizzie mumbled. Bex would skin her alive if she found out.

"She was the one who derailed her old life and the only reason she would have done that was because she remembered the whole bloody time." Matt shook his head at her. "Why did you do this? I thought you loved him!"

"I did! Of course, I did!" She looked around at them all. "None of you actually get it, do you? I loved Charles more than anything!"

"Funny way of showing it," Matt said, his tone finally lowering to a normal volume but anger still threaded through each individual word.

"He's got a point," Neil interjected. His eyes flicked to the side for a fraction of a second, glancing at the way Matt had just come in. "But do explain, Whiskers, how, exactly, you changing time equals you loving Charles more than anything?" His voice rose a fraction louder.

Lizzie stared between them all. Lottie was the only one not looking at her with a baffled expression. She was also the only one who knew Lizzie's reasoning and instead she was looking at her with such a sympathetic expression on her face that Lizzie had to look away. Her chest tightened.

How were they all so blind?

Maybe it was the time thing. Maybe thirteen years had put rose-coloured glasses on them all and they couldn't remember.

"I loved Charles, you all knew that." She turned her gaze specifically to Matt. "You said you'd known all along." Her brother shifted on the spot and gave a slight shrug. "So, when you love someone, if you're holding them back, you have to let them go."

"Holding them back?" Bex said, crossing her arms across her chest.

"Oooh, you've caught the feminist's attention."

"I swear to God I'll kill you."

"How can you guys not see it?" Lizzie said, frustration seeping into her words. She went to tighten her ponytail but her fingers simply ran through loose strands of hair.

Charles still had her hair band. He'd taken it out the night before. God, that felt like years ago.

She turned to look at Lottie for help but she was now looking into the hallway, her eyes wide. Neil nudged her and gave her a pointed look.

"See what?" Matt said gruffly, bringing her attention back to him.

Lizzie almost laughed. "Just look at our lives. Charles is an actor, he's doing the job he always wanted to do, he's free to be with whoever he wants. It's what he always wanted. He didn't want to be a teacher. Not really. He was still applying to drama schools back when we were married! In his thirties! He knew it was still something he wanted to do. Something I hadn't let him do."

"You stopped him going to drama school?" Matt said, frowning. "I don't remember that."

Lizzie looked down at her hands. "Well, no, I didn't physically stop him but he was being Charles. He had to do the right thing. When Leo didn't...didn't make it." She swallowed and watched as Bex's hand reached across and closed around hers. "He gave up everything to look after me. He gave up his place at LAMDA. I held him back. I broke down." Lizzie shook her head. "And then, I just did it all over again when I couldn't actually have children. Charles wanted a baby and I couldn't give him one. He said it himself."

"Charles would never have said that," Matt said, coldly.

She sighed. "He did. And I overheard Patricia talking to him one night and when she asked if he ever regretted marrying me, he didn't answer." She looked around at all of them. "He didn't say anything."

"Hold up, I was there that night," Lottie said, frowning. "He might not have said anything Lizzie but I've never seen him more angry in my life. He didn't say anything because he physically couldn't."

Lizzie swallowed.

"You're such an idiot," Bex whispered gently.

Neil held up his hand. "Agreed. And did you actually talk to Charles about any of this? About overhearing it?"

"Well, no, but that's not important."

Neil guffawed, shaking his head. "Why am I not fucking surprised?"

"I still did the right thing. I made it easier for him."

Bex turned to face her, grabbing Lizzie's shoulders tightly. "Charles loved you! You absolute idiot!"

"I really don't think -"

"That's it. You nailed it on the head there. You didn't think. Charles loved you. He didn't give up anything for you."

"You don't understand!"

"Then explain better!"

"I have explained!"

"And it's a shit explanation," Neil offered from the sofa.

"Fine." Lizzie stepped away from Bex. She pointed between them all, her eyes flared and her mouth in a determined, fierce line. "So, imagine if you loved someone but they didn't want to have children and you did. They couldn't give you that part of your life that you wanted, what would you do?"

"It's totally not the same thing," Neil snapped, his eyes once again flicked towards the hallway. Something hardened along his jaw and he shook his head as if seeing something out there angered him.

"You were married!" Bex said exasperatedly.

"Only because of Leo. Charles only proposed because I was pregnant. He did the right thing but it meant he was stuck with me. Stuck with the woman who couldn't actually give him the thing he proposed for."

Silence filled the room. It was cold, awkward, running between all of them.

Lottie glanced at Lizzie and then back towards the corridor.

"What do you guys keep looking at?" Lizzie snapped.

The sound of the front door shutting quietly broke it.

Lizzie dropped her hand. "W-what?" She stepped around her brother to look to her right, through the doorway and into the empty hallway.

Lizzie turned to look back into the living room. It was Neil's turn to give her a sympathetic look, dropping his gaze to the floor and playing with his hands in his lap. Lottie looked crestfallen.

A sense of foreboding settled on her shoulders.

"That was Charles," Matt said softly. "He was behind me the whole time." He glanced at Bex and then back again at Lizzie. "I shoved you so you wouldn't see him come in. He wanted answers."

Charles had been there.

He had heard the whole thing… and he had chosen to leave.

"And he hid in the corridor like a bloody coward," Neil snapped.

"Neil, don't," Lizzie said, biting back tears. She looked between them all. "Well, that's settled then I guess. He agrees with me." She sniffed sharply, trying her hardest to smile. "It's for the best. Just like I thought. Just like he does. Clever man. Always has been."

Her mouth protested as she forced the corners of it even higher and shook her head at everyone's heartbroken expressions. God, she used to be so good at this. Shutting away her emotions, hiding how she felt. Recently, she felt as if someone had turned a tap on inside her and she hadn't figured out how to shut it off yet. Why was she so shit at boxing things away?

"Honestly, I'm happy. I fixed the problem. I solved it." She nodded, continually, trying her hardest to outwardly show she was fine. As they stood and watched her, she felt her knees begin to tremble. Fresh ugly sobs broke from her and within seconds her vision completely blurred.

Bex reached for her but Matt got there first, pulling her into his arms and squeezing her as hard as he could to his chest.

"It's going to be alright," he whispered firmly in her ear.

"I'm so sorry, Matt, for everything."

"It's forgotten."

She hadn't thought her body was capable of crying any more than it had that day but as three more sets of arms folded around her, she realised she had been mistaken.

CHAPTER THIRTY-TWO

The morning air smelt strongly of burnt wood and dying fireworks. The smell lingered in the air like fog. Sometimes it felt like November through to December was just a continual firework display. Lizzie could already see a few houses with Santa stickers in the windows and Christmas bunting around the railings leading up to their doors. Once upon a time she had been that person. She hadn't even waited for November. As soon as the children stopped knocking on doors for sweets on Halloween she would start decorating for Christmas. She and Charles would wait for December 1st to decorate the actual tree, however. It was their tradition no matter what day of the week it landed on.

Bex had stayed with her for the whole weekend but had to leave at around 2 a.m. to get to work that morning. She hadn't left her side, acting as a continual shadow, reminding her to eat and take a shower from time to time. Matt had left on Saturday night, stating he had something to do. There had been quite a comical moment midway through the afternoon when he realised he had left Zoey all on her own in his flat with no explanation.

Lizzie didn't think she had ever been so reluctant for a Monday. Dread crawled up inside her. The moment Bex had left her flat, Lizzie had simply tossed and turned until her own alarm had gone off. She felt almost weak with tiredness. It was why, despite the dark black sky above, she was walking to work, hopeful that the fresh air would calm her, or at least wake her up.

The corridors of Lightswitch Productions were empty. There was barely anyone around. It was nearing December and that was always a quiet time for the studios. Christmas specials were usually recorded in the summer and the soap opera Neil usually oversaw did extra recordings in early November so the cast and crew could get most of December off. It would just be the daytime television shows like *Jack and Jill* and *Elevenses* working up until the week before Christmas. Oh, and *Censorship*, of course.

She walked into the office and was surprised to see Neil already sat at his desk. There was a coffee and croissant placed on her desk and there looked to be stack of mugs on Neil's own.

"Neil?"

He turned his head and smiled, tiredness only just creeping around his eyes. "Thought you might want some company."

"What time did you get here?"

He yawned and stretched his arms above his head. "5.30. I couldn't be sure what time you would come in for."

She stared at him as he clicked his neck to the right.

"What?" He frowned ever so slightly at her expression.

She took six hurried steps forward and threw her arms around him from behind, squeezing him so hard he made a disgruntled sound in his throat.

"Alright, Whiskers, get off!"

She didn't, instead pressing her cheek against his and locking her arms even tighter around him. She only let go when he patted her arm gently and squeezed her hands.

"I love you," she said, kissing him on his temple before she went to sit at her desk.

"Yeah, yeah, yeah." But when she glanced at him, he was smiling. "You too." He lifted his coffee mug up towards her and she tapped it with her own. "So, you nervous?"

"Yep," she shook her head and straightened her posture. "But just got to face these things head on."

"That's the spirit." He yawned. "Tell you what, realising I've done all this before gives you some perspective on things."

"Yeah?"

"Yep."

Lizzie smiled into her coffee. "So, you told Lara you like her then?"

"Oh for fuck's sake," Neil groaned, rolling his eyes. "I take it all back. I don't actually like you at all."

Lizzie snorted with laughter, her shoulders shaking and Neil kicked out at her chair which sent her spinning backwards. She laughed, for a second the feeling pushing away at the cold numbness that had settled inside her as he continued to huff and puff dramatically at his desk, muttering under his breath about how annoying and idiotic she was. Behind it all though, there was definitely a smile there.

It was around nine o'clock that they were informed Charles wasn't coming into work.

Family problems.

Lizzie felt a simultaneous wave of relief as well as a new onset ache in her chest but it had to be pushed to the side as suddenly, she and Neil had their hands full, moving around schedules, ringing up crew members, contacting the supporting artist companies to try and move filming dates, and trying to stop more people coming in than already had. The work was like a drug, it blocked out her emotions.

By Friday, Charles still had not come in and it looked like the film would wrap early for Christmas. Lizzie felt completely responsible. On Friday afternoon she couldn't help but text Lottie.

Is he okay? X

He will be x

She didn't even notice November slip away as her mind only focused on Charles.

By the following Monday it was decided that the film was going to wrap for Christmas by mid-week, the day before Lizzie's only booked annual leave of December.

With everything going on she hadn't even realised how close it was getting.

She hadn't really spoken much to Matt since the weekend that *everything* had been exposed. Despite telling her he had forgiven her, he seemed to have been always busy whenever she tried to call on him. He had barely been in his flat all week and even Peggy had questioned where he was. Today, he was flying out to Hong Kong, which meant this year she would be heading to Tring on her own. It was fine, of course, she had done it many a time before, but her heart felt just a little bit more lost and vulnerable than usual.

When she got to Tring, she headed straight for her old home: she didn't want to risk bumping into any of the Williamses. The tenants had just moved out, going to their individual homes for Christmas and new people were going to be moving in at the end of January.

Her mum hadn't remembered anything. When she had called the previous week it was only to tell her to make sure the tenants hadn't left any milk in the fridge and to take pictures of the rooms for her.

Lizzie was grateful she had somewhere to stay but being back in her own home when it was empty of any kind warmth or familiarity made her feel weird. She felt like a ghost walking from room to room. She left some of the rooms closed, not wanting to disturb their peace with her solemn ramblings.

Everything still hurt. Especially when she was on her own. Her chest ached and her mind went back over and over what had happened. At night, her dreams had been filled with snippets from their night together, of his eyes looking down into hers, of his hands holding her - it was possibly the cruellest thing for her mind to conjure up.

The truth of the matter was that she missed him. Despite everything, she still missed Charles. Even just talking to him or being beside him. Even not seeing him at work had felt weird and not right somehow. He'd left his coat in her flat. When Bex hadn't been around – which had been very rare over the last two weeks – she'd found herself picking it up, holding the collar up to her nose and taking a deep sniff.

She had been right, she reminded herself for the millionth time. She had done the right thing and Charles agreed. She was right.

After lingering in the kitchen for a while, Lizzie went straight upstairs to her old room. It was late at night anyway and she couldn't really be bothered to eat. She hadn't been eating much the whole week. Everything tasted like paper. In her room, she fired a text off to Bex telling her she'd arrived before making the bed and climbing into it. Even her room smelled weird. It wasn't homely.

Her phone rang as she placed her head down against the pillow.

"Well?" Bex said, her voice sounded excited.

"Well, what?" Lizzie croaked, slipping down further under the covers.

There was a pause and Lizzie could have sworn she heard whispering in the background.

"You're in Tring, right?"

"Yeah. I'm in my room."

"You're in your room," Bex repeated slowly and loudly, as if talking to an idiot.

She could have sworn she heard someone's voice in the background.

"Bex, are you alright?"

"Did you go straight to your bedroom or did you go around the house?"

"I went in the kitchen I guess."

Bex swore softly. "Maybe you should go downstairs. Put some television on?"

Lizzie glanced at the clock. "I think I'm just going to go to sleep."

"Honestly, Lizzie, you can't just keep sleeping all the time. Go and watch some TV."

Lizzie frowned. "You literally told me last week that sleep and physical exercise would be the way to feel better, not watching every episode of *Gilmore Girls* like I wanted too."

Bex huffed. "Well, I've changed my mind."

"Look, I'm going to go. Night Bex."

"Lizzie, please don't go to bed."

"Fine, I won't," Lizzie said. "Happy?"

"Will you go downstairs?"

"Yep."

"Promise?"

"Course."

"Lizzie Cartwright-"

Lizzie hung up, turned over and closed her eyes. Thankfully, sleep came quickly.

CHAPTER THIRTY-THREE

She was awoken by someone prodding her in the back.

"Ow!" she snapped, spinning around to see no-one there. She rubbed the small of her back and groaned as she caught sight of the digital clock in the corner of the room. It was 3 a.m. She closed her eyes again only to feel another sharp prod to the spine. She spun over in the bed, the sheets getting caught up around her body but saw nothing. Running a hand over her tired face, she realised she'd been crying again. Her face felt dry with it.

A hot poker was placed between her shoulders. She practically yelped, standing up and almost tripping over her shoes. She stared at the bed.

Still there was nothing.

What was going on? She twisted her arm to rub the pain away from her back but it was already fading. A slight shimmer caught her eye by the mirror and she walked over.

There was a white polaroid on the dresser. The sight of it snatched the air from between her lips. The picture was the one the midwives had taken of Leo and her the morning of his birth. She picked it up and felt her heart pull inside her chest. He looked so small. Her face had been blotchy and swollen. She had been in so much physical pain but she hadn't felt any of it when holding Leo. She remembered not wanting him to be taken away, holding him tightly to her, begging him to open his eyes. He was wearing his giraffe onesie – it was too big for him so it hung off his feet.

Giraffes had always been their ongoing symbol of Leo.

She pressed the photograph to her chest and took a deep breath in.

She had refused a photo the first time. Instead, screaming at everyone to leave her alone. Charles had gotten a photo. He'd kept it in his wallet.

Leo had been wearing the same giraffe onesie.

God, she wished she still had that one.

A flicker of movement caught her eye but when she looked up she saw her own reflection staring back at her. She frowned, staring harder into the glass. She couldn't explain it but she felt...she felt as if she could see something standing just by her side. A shape that reached up above her head. She could feel them too. A warmth that was like no other and a smell she would recognise anywhere.

She turned in real life to her left but nothing was there.

"Course you were going to be tall," she whispered, wiping away a tear rolling down her cheek and feeling laughter blossom in her chest. *Obviously.*

Her breath hitched at the voice in her head and she reached forward just as a smash came from downstairs.

Lizzie dropped the polaroid down on the table, turning her head towards the door and feeling a stab of frustration.

Of all the days? Really? Some little prick was going to try and rob her house?

"There's nothing here to bloody take," she snapped.

She glanced at the mirror again. The weird distortion was still in the air right beside her. Her heart tugged dangerously. She didn't want to leave just yet.

There was another smash.

"I'm going to leave it, I'm going to stay here-"

Another smash and this time, she felt another sharp prod in her back. She jumped, glaring to her left accusatively.

Laughter tinkled in the air.

"Fine!" She hissed. She grabbed her dressing gown from her open suitcase and shoved it over her shoulders before creeping out onto the landing. When she got to the top of the stairs she could hear a low mumbling as if someone was talking to themselves. It was coming from the living room. She put her hand on the bannister and began to creep down the stairs. There was still a bucket of umbrellas left behind by the old tenants at the front door and she grabbed the longest one as she passed. It was hardly a scary weapon, but it would do. It was probably just some stupid teenager, she told herself. They had managed to smash three things already, it hardly sounded like they were an accomplished burglar. And what exactly was there to smash? The house should be empty other than the bare basics.

With a deep breath, she threw back her shoulders and slammed the living room door open. Shock jolted her fully awake as she saw a dark tall figure standing by a Christmas tree. Before he could react, she ran at him, her umbrella high above her head.

"GET OUT! GET OUT! GET OUT!" She yelled, slamming it over the head of the figure as hard as she could.

"Lizzie!" The umbrella was promptly ripped from her grip and she stumbled back, off balance as the voice practically winded her.

Hang on, *Christmas tree*?

"Charles!" She gasped, taking another step back as the silhouette rubbed their head.

"Of course, it's me!"

"What do you mean, of course!" She snapped. "There is no of course about it." She reached for the main light and flicked it on.

The room was filled with light and Lizzie stared at the sight in front of her. In the corner of the room was a Christmas tree, its branches bare but it was so big it looked like it was trying break out of the walls. Boxes were spread out around its feet, filled to the brim with ornaments of all different sorts and there were heaps of fairy lights stacked in the corner.

In the middle of it all was Charles, wearing a dark red jumper and jeans. For 3 in the morning he looked extremely well dressed.

"What are you doing here?"

He itched the back of his neck sheepishly. "I've been here all day."

"You were here when I came in?!"

"Yeah, must say that didn't go quite as I had planned. I kind of hoped you were going to come in." He smiled at her. "Hello, by the way."

A thousand and one emotions slammed through her and she reached behind her for the edge of the sofa, hoping it would make her feel steadier on her feet.

"Hi." Her voice sounded croaky. "How are you?"

"Honestly?"

She swallowed. "Yeah."

"Not great."

She stared at him, taking in his handsome face and broad shoulders. It had been nearly two weeks but seeing him again made her stomach tilt and her nerves pinch together.

"How are you?" He asked.

"Charles, what are you doing here?"

He lightly drummed his fingers against the side of his leg.

"Thought that was obvious."

Nothing in the world seemed obvious at this given moment in time. "No."

He tucked his hands into his front pockets as if he wasn't really sure what to do with them and rocked slightly on his feet.

"We used to always do the tree together so I got everything ready so we could do it when you came in. I spent the last week trying to find all the decorations we used to have."

Her eyes scanned the floor. He was right. There was the small Coca-Cola van, the Big Ben, a bunch of trinkets they had picked up when they had gone on their honeymoon and a dinosaur with a Christmas hat on that they had bought from the Natural History Museum.

"How...?"

"Matt helped." He smiled. "He's not in Hong Kong by the way, he only said that to get you off his back."

"You two are...?"

"Your brother can be very persistent when he wants to be."

Silence stretched between them. Neither seemed able to keep their eyes off each other. She wished she'd had some kind of a warning. She could only imagine what kind of a troll she looked like in comparison to him at this current moment in her old dressing gown, tear-stained face and messy hair. Charles took a step forward.

"Lizzie, did you really think the only reason I married you was because you were pregnant?"

The question startled her. Her body flinched.

"Yes."

"But you never said."

"I mentioned it once or twice. When you proposed you never actually said it wasn't for that reason. You almost avoided the question."

"You didn't think to ask me again?"

"I didn't want to remind you of the fact."

His eyes pinned her to the spot. "It never has been a fact." He had barely moved but Lizzie felt her skin prickle and her face flush. The air around them tightened. "I should have told you a long time ago, Cartwright, but two weeks before you told me you were pregnant, I sat in your kitchen and asked Matt for permission to ask you to marry me."

A cold stillness seeped into her chest.

No.

No. No. No.

He couldn't be serious.

"What?" She gasped.

"Well," he smiled and took another step forward, "I was hardly going to ask Craig was I?"

"You were always going to propose?" She was finding it hard to process his words or focus on anything but what he had said.

"Always. Yes. I just," he shook his head and then tilted his head partially at the Christmas Tree, "was waiting for a bloody romantic moment."

A whisper of laughter escaped her lips.

"Yeah, I know. Typical." He responded.

"But we were so young?"

"Actually, we were the exact same age as when my dad proposed to my mum."

A lump formed in her throat. "But you never said?"

"If I proposed and then told you that 'I was going to marry you anyway', would you have believed me?" He raised his eyebrows.

No. She would have thought he was just being nice. "I always thought it was out of doing the right thing. I always thought..." She gulped and felt a tear slip down her cheek. She hadn't even felt her eyes sting. "I thought it must have been something you...subconsciously regretted."

"Never. I've never, ever, regretted our marriage. Not once." He locked eyes with her. "Am I lying?"

"Charles, I-"

"Am I lying?" He said softly.

She stared at him, emotion building in her chest like a tornado. "No."

He stepped closer to her and lifted his hand to tilt her chin up towards him. Her skin tingled at his touch.

"You should have told me you'd overheard Patricia." He gently traced his thumb across her cheek. The tremors that ran along to her mouth were almost unbearable. "Cartwright, you've literally shown me the two worlds next to each other, the one where I am not with you and the one where I am. The one where I am an actor and the one where I am not. The one where I have money and the one where I don't. And every single time, Lizzie, I would choose you over everything else." His eyes met hers again. Vulnerable and honest. "Every single time. I'm sorry to say it, darling, but you didn't do the right thing."

Her stomach flipped at the term of endearment but stubbornness flared behind her eyes.

"But you gave up your dream to look after me!"

"To look after *my* wife who had just given birth to *my* son, and I'd do it again and again and again. You had just undergone one of the toughest experiences anyone has to bear and you were just nineteen. My dream changed. My dream was to look after you." Something shimmered behind his eyes. "When you gave birth to Leo, I was completely useless. I could do nothing. Absolutely nothing. You did it all on your own and you were absolutely incredible." His voice caught and he took a second to gather himself before continuing. "So, afterwards all I wanted to do was wrap you up and look after you. I never resented you for that. I never blamed you. I wanted to." He paused and then hesitantly whispered, "I still want to."

Her heart thumped so hard she could feel her ribs beginning to creak. "I can't let you do that." She pushed back the lump in her throat, trying her best not to get too caught up in the hope blossoming inside her. "It wasn't just the acting. What about a family? What about the fact I can't give you children?"

His grip on her became firmer. "My family is you." His words ricocheted through her, trying their best to hit every worry rooted inside of her. "I don't know where you got this idea from that you aren't enough but you are my family. If we can't have children, then we can't have children. I'd take you without them over everything else."

"Charles, I can't let you do that."

"You can."

"But it doesn't make sense."

"It does."

"It doesn't!"

His eyes ran across her face. "I'm in love with you, Lizzie."

She stilled, her breath catching in her throat, painfully. "You're...you're what?"

"I am in love with you. In this timeline and the last. When we were in your bedroom, however torturously long ago that was, I had to keep stopping myself from saying it." His eyes turned momentarily playful. "And trust me, that was really, really hard. I felt like a right idiot, not understanding how I could feel so strongly towards you after so little time. But I think…" He paused, running his eyes across her face. "I think it's because it's you, Lizzie. I loved you before we started dating last time so it doesn't seem so strange that I would still be in love with you after thirteen years apart."

She stared at him, her breathing faster and yet struggling to leave her lips.

He bent his head lower.

"I'm not letting you go, Lizzie. I want you. Only you. If you decide you want to have children then we can adopt, we can foster, we can do whatever you want but it's your call. You are my family." He brushed a strand of hair out of her face.

"And that's enough?"

"It is for me." For a moment a flicker of what looked like fear passed behind his eyes. "Is it for you?"

She felt his words begin to sink into her, bit by bit piercing through the walls she had built for years to protect herself. Charles was getting through. Again.

"You don't blame me?"

"No."

"You don't regret us?"

"Never."

A small smile spread out across her face.

"You broke into my house with a Christmas tree."

He laughed and rested his forehead against hers. "Yeah."

As if he could no longer bear to stay apart, his mouth dropped down onto hers. Her pulse kicked into overdrive as her lips exploded with feeling. She sagged against him, letting him take the lead, letting him coax her mouth open. Happiness and longing exploded inside her and she felt every nerve in her body suddenly spark to life as his kiss deepened. When they parted, he steadied her as she sank back onto her feet.

"You didn't decorate it?" She said, breathlessly, nodding behind him.

"I was waiting for you."

"What was all the smashing then?"

"No idea, it woke me up too. The ornaments started to randomly break."

Lizzie frowned. "What?"

"They just started to smash. I was terrified you were going to wake up. I had just got up to try and see if I had left them somewhere dangerous when someone smacked me round the head with an umbrella."

She laughed, her chest swelling.

Charles turned his head momentarily to look behind him. On the floor lay three broken ornaments. Lizzie felt her heart squeeze tightly as she caught sight of them.

"The giraffes?"

"Yeah," Charles whispered softly.

"I took Leo away from you this time." She shook her head. "Charles, I just wanted to protect you, I promise. I'm so sorry."

He took one of her hands and placed it on his chest. "As much as I think you're amazing, Lizzie, you've never had the power to take away our son. He's always here. In fact," he pulled his wallet out of his pocket and opened it up. "About three days ago, this appeared in my wallet again." It was the polaroid, creased, worn, but shining.

Emotion swelled up inside her as she took it from him, staring at the two people she loved more than anything in the world. She looked up at him. "Just in case it needed to be said, I am in love with you too, Charles Williams."

He brought his lips closer to hers.

"Thank, God, for that."

He kissed her harder this time. Heat, love, happiness soared through her body, making her chest rise and her legs sway. He caged her tighter into his body, his hands caressing her neck and waist. Her face was wet with tears she hadn't even realised she'd shed and her hands shook as she moved them to grip his hair, dropping his wallet in the process. Their kiss deepened. Charles hauled her up and she wrapped her legs instinctively around his waist, clinging to him.

"I love you so much," he whispered against her mouth. "I won't let you forget it this time."

"I won't," she whispered. "I promise."

EPILOGUE

Ringing woke Lizzie out of her sleep. She was lying on her front, her hair a mess around her and her arm thrown across a warm, solid body. She caught sight of Charles immediately, her eyes widening at the sight of his naked torso, his scruffy hair and his bright, blue eyes. He was fiddling with her phone and he winced as he saw her watching him.

"Sorry, I was trying to turn it to silent but I couldn't figure it out."

She reached across, a smile on her face as she took it from him and placed it on the bedside table.

"It's fine," she said sleepily, leaning over him and bringing her mouth down to his. He kissed her back, his hands moving to her waist before he expertly flipped them over so he was on top of her. She let out a laugh of surprise which was quickly swallowed up as his lips met hers again, hungrier this time, and she felt an alarming flare in her lower belly.

For Christ's sake, she had just woken up. How was her body reacting this way to him already?

Her phone rang again.

"Urgh," she said, turning her head and reaching over to flick the button on its side to silent.

Nothing happened.

Charles laughed and pressed a soft kiss to her neck. "Lizzie, when I said I couldn't figure out how to silence it, I didn't mean I hadn't tried to volume button."

She shoved him playfully and he grabbed her wrist, pinning it over her head.

"Think you can hold me down, Williams?"

He grinned in recognition, a small bark of laughter leaving his lips.

The phone went silent for a couple of seconds and Charles had just dipped his head down to kiss her again as it started ringing. Their eyes met.

"Why?" Lizzie said, pouting and Charles laughed as he rolled off her. Dramatically groaning, she lifted herself up onto her elbows and reached across for her mobile.

Neil

"Really?" She showed Charles the screen. "He wants a conversation right now?"

"Just answer it, Neil is more persistent than Matt."

The ringing stopped.

And then it started again.

"Neil, what the hell do you want?"

"Hold up, you answer when Neil calls but not me!" Bex snapped.

Lizzie sat up straighter, throwing Charles a confused look. "Bex, what are you doing on Neil's phone?"

"Told you I was special," Neil said, laughing in the background.

Lizzie's eyes nearly bulged out of her head.

"What are you two doing ringing me together, at-" She looked around hoping to spot a clock.

"10.30," Charles said.

"At 10.30 –" She paused and threw Charles a look, covering the phone briefly. "It's 10.30 in the morning?"

"Yep." He stretched his arms above his head. "We were up late."

Lizzie blushed and turned her head away quickly as she felt Charles's body vibrate with laughter next to her.

"At 10.30 in the morning?"

"We're eloping and thought you should know."

"Neil, shut up!" Bex barked and Lizzie heard another laugh in the background.

"Is that Matt?"

"Hey Lizzie, you're on loudspeaker by the way."

She pinched the bridge of her nose in confusion and lay back on her pillow. "What's going on? Why are all three of you together?"

"Please, for the love of God, just tell me you've gone to the bloody living room!" Bex snapped.

The living room.

A laugh escaped her lips and she turned on her side to look at Charles. He mirrored her and raised an eyebrow in question. Her heart did a little skip at the sight of his morning hair and slight stubble to his jaw. With her free hand she reached out and curled her fingers around his, giving his hand a slight squeeze.

"I may have gone to the living room."

Charles grinned at her, cottoning on.

"Hallelujah!" Bex yelled. "I've had to spend the night with these two, waiting for you to bloody call!"

"I'm telling everyone at work it was a threesome, just for your information – ow, ow, ow, ow, okay, I won't. I won't!" Neil yelled out. "Fuck's sake woman, get off me!"

She burst out laughing as she heard Neil yelp in pain and Bex's continual reel of swear words in the background.

"Lizzie?" It was Matt. Judging by the fact the fighting in the background had quietened, it sounded like he had turned the speaker phone off.

"Hey Matt, how was Hong Kong?"

He laughed. "Really sunny, went by in a whirlwind."

"I bet it did."

"Had to get you off my back somehow."

"Thanks Matt," Charles called.

"You're welcome!" Her brother called back, making Lizzie flinch away from the phone.

"He says you're welcome. And Matt, you're not on speaker. Please don't yell in my ear!"

"Matt, give me back the phone."

"Lizzie, I'm going to go before Bex does that ear twisty thing that she just did to Neil on me."

Lizzie stifled a laugh as she heard Bex growl. There was a slight shuffle as the phone was passed between them. "Violence is not the answer, Rebecca."

"It is when it comes to Neil Grayson," she huffed. "Anyway, I'm done with you. Can you put Charles on the phone?"

Lizzie shook her head, fighting back the laughter in her throat, and handed the phone over to Charles. He looked surprised but it took it from her.

"Hi Bex."

At first he simply listened, Lizzie could hear the murmur of Bex's voice on the other end and then his eyes creased with laughter. She loved it when they did that. Charles flicked his gaze to her and gave a flirtatious smile as he caught her staring.

"Yep," he said. "Ya-huh." He covered up the phone briefly and frowned at her. "Why are you so far away?"

"I'm right here!" Lizzie giggled but Charles swiftly reached out an arm and pulled her closer to him. She covered her mouth to stifle her laughter as she was partially dragged across the mattress.

"Bex," He turned his head away briefly and the smile on his lips faltered ever so slightly. "I'm not going to hurt her. I promise." Pause. "Yes. Yes, I know." He let go off her briefly to run his hand through his hair and pull at the ends. Lizzie squeezed his waist reassuringly but he looked distracted. "Yes. I agree. It was bad of me." He sighed. "I'll make it up to her. I promise." His eyes met hers and she saw the worrying niggle settle behind them.

I love you, she mouthed.

A smile broke out across his face and he turned away, trying not to grin too widely as a blush tinged his cheeks. "Is that the end of my bollocking?" A laugh passed his lips. "Yes, I'll tell her." He paused and it sounded like Bex was saying goodbye. "Oh, before you go, quick thing." A playful smile crossed his face. "Call him."

Lizzie frowned at him curiously.

"You know who I mean, call him." He sighed. "Yes I know, but you know what's he like." An angry burst erupted down the phone and Charles laughed. "Just do it, Bex. He won't think there's a chance in hell you're still interested." He paused. "I agree. Please call him. I'll see you soon, okay?" He put the phone down on the side. "Apparently, Neil's put an app on your phone so you can't silence his calls."

"Git!" Lizzie said, shaking her head but smiling as Charles looped an arm around her waist and rolled her under him again. "Who were you telling Bex to call?"

"Can't tell you yet."

"Charles!" She pushed against his chest. "Please!"

"I'll tell you soon, I promise. Just something I figured out." He rubbed his nose against hers. "I want to focus on our relationship for the foreseeable future, not anyone else's."

She grinned, happy with his response. "Okay. I think I can cope with that."

"And on that note, Bex gave me quite a hard time about leaving you in the flat when we all remembered."

Lizzie smiled. "Course she did."

"She had every right too. My head was all over the place. I'm sorry. I never agreed with what you were saying but I was just so…confused. And hurt. And scared that this was all my fault…which it was-"

She cut him off with a kiss. "Stop. It's forgotten. It was a really weird time for everyone." She shrugged. "And you came after me anyway."

He brushed her hair back. "I'll always come after you, Cartwright."

Downstairs, nearly everything was quiet. There was the slight hum from the boiler and the tick of a clock that could never be found but other than that, silence settled between the rooms. Inside the living room the Christmas tree stood up high, for the time being forgotten, with decorations fanned around it.

Three giraffe ornaments lay in pieces at its feet, the clean cuts sharp and distinct. Each ornament had a different name written in calligraphy across it.

Lizzie, Charles and Leo.

Laughter whispered through the air and slowly, too slow for the human eye, they began to piece themselves together.

The family of three was a whole again.

ACKNOWLEDGEMENTS

Wow, I can't actually believe I am writing an acknowledgments page! Well, firstly, thank you to you!! If you're reading this you have finished *Forget Me Not* and I really hope you liked it!! If you did, please let me know on Twitter or Instagram, you'd literally make my day. If you didn't…maybe don't tell me (I'm a sensitive soul!).

Thank you to any person who has shared their story of child loss publically or privately. I really hope I did a worthy job of portraying that loss and the emotions that come with it. I won't name the people I spoke to about their struggles conceiving or dealing with child loss, but thank you for trusting me. I used a lot of resources to try and make sure I could write Lizzie properly so thank you to; Tommy's, Happy Mum Happy Baby, Big Fat Negative, Ask Me His Name (by Elle Wright) and Dr Jocelyn Heins.

Thank you to my friends and family for the support they have given me. Words will never be able to describe how grateful I am for your love, kindness and encouragement. A few people deserve extra huge shout outs (and I am so scared I will miss someone so apologies in advance). Gemma Bicknell & Chloe Lewis – your support, love and kindness is indescribable. You've always gone above and beyond. The first two to read *Forget Me Not* and the ones who always made it top of your priorities. I can't thank you enough. Maxine Wright & Becky Dale – my Lost boys. You've been there for me for every step of the way, even when you've both been going through hell yourselves, especially these last two years, and I will never be able to repay you. Jessica Gottardo &

Rachel Marber – my girls. The ones always interested, always wanting to hear more, always being the ones who can make me smile when I am crying. I love you to pieces. Special mentions also go to Sarah Polley, Maeve Scarry, Cathi Collier, Jocelyn Heins, Annie Rooke, Jay Jullier, Dan Osborn, Dan Parry, Michael Molloy, Becca Molloy, Emily Smith, and Ruth Earley.

Family. Thank you for supporting me. Financially and in love. Special shout out to my little sister who has always been my writing confidante. Huge shout out to my parents for putting up with me being a hermit in my bedroom and letting me live with them. You taught me to work hard. Thanks to my wonderful Grandma and my Wigan, Leicester, Garstang family - love you all.

Thank you to my incredible editors. Cathi Collier, Gemma Bicknell and Katie Etoe – Katie, I can't actually apologise enough that you had to edit my novel when it was OVER 200k!!!! I am in awe of you and so grateful you took the time. You were the first person who wasn't a friend who told me you liked my story and the confidence boost that gave me…well, I can never thank you enough for.

Thank you to my WGGS diamonds – Sarah, Cathi, Jocelyn, Tasha, Mel, Kirsty, Emily. You've always had my back and I love you all to bloody pieces. Watford Grammar for life <3 You're the reason I am who I am today. My biggest protectors. I love you so much.

Thank you to my work family, Justin and Josh. You supported me from the get go without blinking. Never doubted me and let me talk about my writing as much as I needed to. And when I was down and upset you let me put on a tank and dive underwater for as long as I needed.

Thank you to my ((BOUNCE)) Army. From my fellow instructors who talk to me about my writing and constantly believe in me to my attendees. You guys literally make me smile on a rainy day and the amount of times I'd have faced rejections in the day and come to class, only to come out singing and dancing…is probably uncountable. You tell me constantly that my classes make you happy but MY GOD, you have no idea how much I've needed you over the past few years.

Thank you to Mrs Joyce for constantly encouraging my writing from when I was a shy and timid year 7 to debating literature in A-level classes. Other teachers who deserve a huge thank you for multitudes of reasons are Cyndy, Mrs Smith and Mr Fletcher.

Thank you to all my Hogwarts classmates. You know who you are. From this Hufflepuff to you, thanks for being amazing.

Thank you to romance writers who have inspired me (and made me fall in love with many fictional men). Samantha Young, Mandy Baggot, Sarah Morgan, Kathyrn Freeman, Tilly Tennant, Carrie Fletcher, Giovanna Fletcher, Lindsey Kelk, Ali Harris, to name but a few. These are the writers who I buy before I have even read the descriptions of their books. If you like mine, go and check out theirs as you will LOVE THEM.

Thank you to Halvir for my beautiful cover.

And once again, thank you to you. Thank you so much for stepping into my imagination and staying a while. I hope you love Lizzie and Charles as much as I do.

If you have been affected by any of the issues mentioned in this novel, please consider visiting tommys.org. Tommy's are the UK's leading baby charity and fund research into miscarriage, stillbirth, and premature birth, and provide pregnancy health information to parents. Please reach out.

ABOUT THE AUTHOR

Melissa Morgan is a scuba diver who spends most of her time underwater, looking after her favourite eels at the Ocean Conservation Trust. When she isn't underwater, she's either writing or on a trampoline as a ((BOUNCE)) Instructor.

At the age of six, she knew she wanted to be a writer and began writing stories about horses to read to her class mates. Spending most of her time with her head buried in a book, she loves falling for fictional characters and finding worlds she can escape too.

She is extremely lucky to have the best friends in the world and a supportive family. Oh, and the cutest two poodles you will ever meet – Saxon and Bonnie.

A Hufflepuff through and through, she'd love to hear from you.

Instagram @melissawritesthings

Twitter @melissaxmorgan

Printed in Poland
by Amazon Fulfillment
Poland Sp. z o.o., Wrocław